THE CORPS 2081

NON-FICTION BOOKS BY LARRY C. WHITE

Merchants of Death, The American Tobacco Industry

The New York Times, "Is there anything more to say on the subject? Unhappily there is, and Mr. White does it well in a book that is thoughtful, closely reasoned, full of curious details and mercifully free of moral posturing."

The Washington Post, "*Merchants of Death* is an indictment of the tobacco industry…its betrayal of American tobacco farmers, its manipulation of politicians and the press, its blatant campaign to market its noxious product…and its spurious attempt to connect the advertising of tobacco with rights assured by the First Amendment."

C. Everett Koop, M.D. former Surgeon-General of the United States, "*Merchants of Death,* because it tells the truth, is likely to be dangerous to the health of the tobacco industry"

Human Debris, The Injured Worker in America (as Lawrence White)

Studs Terkel, "What Upton Sinclair's *The Jungle* did early in the century, Larry White, in this explosive expose does today; it astonishes and infuriates."

Tom Wicker, former associate editor of the *New York Times,* "*Human Debris* explains with devastating effect the wastage of human lives that's commonplace in American industry, but almost unknown to the American public. A meticulously researched account of a national shame."

Jessica Mitford, "White's chilling account…calls attention to a disaster area in the American way of law."

THE CORPS 2081

Larry C. White

PUBLISHED BY ALCATRAZ PRESS

Alcatraz Press
180 Steuart Street #190782
San Francisco, California 94105
www.alcatrazpress.com

Copyright ©2013 by Lawrence White
All rights reserved

This is a work of fiction. Names, characters, places and incidents are either the product of the author's imagination or are used fictitiously, and any resemblance to actual persons, living, dead, or yet unborn is entirely coincidental.

Text design by Preston Thomas, www.prestonthomasdesign.com
Printed in the United States of America

The Library of Congress Control Number is 2012922354

ISBN 978-0-9886324-0-0

for Becky and Nathan, Sam and Jessica
and their children and grandchildren

Presentiment is that long shadow on the lawn
Indicative that suns go down;
The notice to the startled grass
That darkness is about to pass.
   Emily Dickinson

CHAPTER ONE

Both his mothers were dead—Jack woke into that fact each morning. It had been a week since their burial, and his new life was finally becoming real. As the next of kin, he himself had sewn their shrouds, rough linen cloth, no colors, and he'd been grateful to keep his hands busy with needful work.

Dozens of neighbors and friends made the ten-mile trip to the cemetery on a hillside above the ocean. The ceremony went on for a long time; it seemed like everyone who ever knew them wanted to talk about them, and they sang the familiar hymns, "Asleep in Gaia" and "Faith of Our Mothers." Jack didn't want it to end—they would truly be gone when it was over.

Why didn't they trust him enough to tell him what they were going to do? Margaret, his birth mother, told him everything on her mind, even when he was too young to know what she was talking about. The telling created a bond between them and an unspoken pact. He was sure she'd tell him anything important, and it was too late when he realized his mistake.

She often said that he and his half-brother, Gabe, would be better off without her, and he always assured her that he would take care of her, and that he didn't mind. Nothing could ease her pain except the medicine that would take her back to Mother Earth, to Gaia, but it never occurred to him that she'd actually take her life, or that Jean would join her and they would go together.

They had waited until Jack completed his schooling, that was obvious. He was now a competent carpenter, a sharp hunter, and a passable farmer. He knew which fish frequented the bay at what times of year and how to catch them. He had written a prize-winning essay on the recent history of his City, San Francisco, from 2020 to 2075, its time of transformation into independence, and had demonstrated that he knew the scientific method and the basics of biology and chemistry. He had a good understanding of human anatomy and knew the important medicinal herbs and where they grew. He wasn't a great soccer player, but he enjoyed it and was a welcome team member.

His hobby was geography, and he could describe in great detail the deserts and floodplains that covered most of North America. He didn't know much about the rest of the world that had changed so profoundly since his grandparents' time, no one did anymore, but it was probably similar.

Margaret had quizzed him about all of his accomplishments in the weeks before she died. She was making sure, he now realized, that he could take care of himself and Gabe.

Jack tried to keep his morning routine the same, though they were gone. He struggled out of bed, opened the window, and stuck his head out, as he'd done since he was a small child. The low, gray sky gave him some comfort; he inhaled the clean air off the great western ocean. He heard the sounds of the street—the low hum of the occasional car, the clip clop of horses, and the almost inaudible whoosh of bicycles. Margaret and Jean were gone, but the world went on, oblivious and solid, infuriating and reassuring.

Jack went into the bathroom off the long hallway that ran the length of the apartment. First thing, he always splashed cold water on his face. But this morning nothing came out of the tap. There had been talk for a while—the City of San Francisco would no longer be supplying water; that was something best left to private enterprise. That's what it said on the neighborhood Notice Rack. But Jack didn't know what that meant; it was an abstraction. He didn't expect that the taps would be dry.

He dressed quickly and went outside. Right down the block from his building, Jack saw a large, silver truck with a corporate logo on it. Nestle Waters, it said, and there was already a line forming around it. Next to the water truck was a shed where the company was selling metal and earthenware water jars along with other paraphernalia, like a special backpack that had hooks for the water jars and a selection of small shopping carts made of bamboo. The jugs and backpacks were in a variety of bright colors.

A friendly crew of attractive young people in company uniforms handed out leaflets and instructional booklets. Jack could see immediately that they weren't local. No one he knew had such perfect teeth and shiny hair. He went up to one particularly perky girl and asked her what this was all about.

"This is the first day of our new service and we want to help you with the changes!"

"Well, what are the changes?" he asked.

"First, you're not going to have to worry about getting water out of those old pipes anymore!" she said. "It's guaranteed clean fresh water and we'll be here for you on Mondays, Wednesdays, and Fridays, six to nine a.m. and four to nine p.m. No problems!"

"Hey, what about the people who can't carry it up the stairs?"

"Not a problem. We'll give them a list of people who they can hire to help them."

"What is this going to cost?"

"Here's the price sheet." She handed him a slim booklet. "And you know, there's no limit on this—you can buy as much water as you want."

Jack looked at it. They were selling water at twenty-five cents per liter. No more showers, was his first thought; a lot of people are going to be smelling really bad. He glanced at the list of water carriers, but there was no price attached to their services, just an asterisk with a note saying their hourly fees were negotiable. He bought two large containers and a backpack and hauled the water up the stairs. He was surprised by how heavy it was.

Later in the day, he was on his way home, just crossing Guerrero Street, when he first heard the yelling. He started to run toward the sounds, and when he turned the corner he saw a large crowd of his neighbors surrounding the water truck and pushing away the water company employees. He laughed out loud when he realized that the principal instigator was Angela, the eighty-five-year-old former opera singer who lived downstairs from him. She was at the truck's tap, operating it as if she knew what she was doing. People were filling up their jugs and walking away without paying. The driver was sitting in the truck's cab looking bored but the perky woman Jack had talked to earlier was yelling at the top of her voice, "Stop it, you people! This is private property you're taking. You better stop it and back off!"

"Or what, you corporate whore?" yelled a man with a yellow beard.

"I've called the police—you'll see!" she screamed.

"Why don't you call the army and the air force too?" shouted a teenage boy with long, black hair. A few others took up the call, "Yeah, call the military. Bring in the helicopters!" They all laughed.

Then people began to close around the water company flack, yelling and waving their fists, and the almost festive mood suddenly turned angry. Jack saw the frightened look on the young woman's face, and he stepped in. "Hey, leave her alone. She didn't make this happen, she's just someone who needed a job."

"She's another one of those Helpers, fuck her!" someone yelled.

"So what if she is? They're not citizens like us. They have to do what the Owners tell them to do," Jack said.

The angry people surrounding the young woman lost interest; they didn't want to hear a debate, and the crowd melted away. Jack walked away from her too. Like other city dwellers, he had a visceral disgust of Helpers, but he didn't like being part of a threatening mob. He could feel her fear and was sorry to have been partly the cause of it. But he didn't want her to thank him; he wouldn't know how to respond honestly.

No peace-keeper came, and the truck was drained. It drove away, and the few people remaining cheered.

That evening, the neighborhood council met in an emergency session in the elementary school two blocks away from Jack's apartment. Jean had always attended for them—just about every household sent someone—but now Jack had to go. He was over twenty-one now, by a year, so he could be a voting member. It took him a while to get into the meeting room—it seemed like every one of his neighbors wanted to hug him and say how sorry they were to hear about his loss. And he had many people to thank for all the food that now filled his kitchen.

The meeting went on forever, Jack thought, as people complained and discussed the alternatives to water privatization. At the end they came to a consensus that the council would send representatives to the Board of Supervisors' next meeting and demand that the City resume supplying water. They would also work with all the other neighborhood councils to try and defeat the incumbent mayor in the upcoming election. In the short term, they would tap the emergency wells and ration that water. Each household would get twenty gallons per day per person free of charge. There would be no buying and selling of water in the neighborhood.

The next morning Jack was prepared, with plenty of water in the apartment. He and Gabe were struggling to regain the feel of a normal life. After breakfast, Jack left the apartment to go to his girlfriend Kristin's place, but when he got to Valencia Street, only a short block away, he couldn't cross. The street was filled—columns of men, women, and children marching slowly, surrounded by men on horseback with whips. A couple of thousand people. Jack stood on the curb, shocked. What the fuck is this?

His neighbors were asking each other the same question, but there were no answers. No one knew who they were or where they were going.

The horsemen were obviously Owners from MarinHaven, and they seemed to be having a ball. Some were dressed like cowboys; others wore tight, black uniforms with silver lightning bolts on their sleeves. One cowboy pulled out a gold flask and drank from it. They laughed and called to each other. The people they were herding begged for food and water, and, like many others, Jack ran back to his apartment and grabbed bread, apples, and bottles of milk, and put them into the outstretched hands. The horsemen studiously ignored the bystanders and didn't interfere.

Then the city people started to make a noise—just a low murmur at first, which turned into a loud booing. They began to follow the procession and curse at the horsemen. One of the Owners brandished his whip and whizzed it above the head of a few of the city people. Several people threw bottles at the horseman, but they missed and the bottles crashed onto the pavement. The crowd of onlookers surged forward and the Owners turned their horses away from the prisoners and faced outward. The procession stopped altogether, and one of the Owners took out a portable telephone—most city people had heard about them but never seen one—and made a call.

Within a few minutes, city volunteer peace-keepers arrived, twenty of them, all neighbors of people in the crowd, and they moved among the people explaining that the City had given permission for this action, and that it was best to just let it pass through. No one liked it, but there was no point in a confrontation—it would just make things harder for the captives. There was a lot of muttering, but the city people stood back and the Owners marched the prisoners away.

That night, Jack and five of his friends rode their bikes down to the ocean together, as they always did, because you just didn't ride alone out there. The last mile was on a path through high sand dunes, and there was no perspective. It was kind of like Outside, although actually within the borders of San Francisco.

They stood around a bonfire on the parapet above the surf; waves broke right onto the retaining wall. There were piles of driftwood on the wide stretch of cracked asphalt, and no one to bother them. On this moonless night all Jack could see was the fire leaping into the darkness and the bright faces of his friends. They talked about what they had seen that day.

"They had to be criminals. Why else would they be prisoners?" Kristin said. She and Jack had been together for almost six months.

"Hey, they were families with kids, some of them were carrying babies," Jack said.

"Then where were they going?" She rarely agreed with him about anything.

"They're not criminals and they're not going to jail. I think the Owners wanted to impress us." Jack threw another log on the bonfire.

"Impress us? I think not; they don't give a shit about us," Seth said with certainty. His father was a City Supervisor, and he thought he had the inside track on everything political.

"Maybe you're right, but why did they bring those poor people right here to the City?" Jack asked.

"I don't know why we allow those bastards here anyway; they don't allow us in their Havens. We should have spooked their fucking horses," Gabe said, jumping around crazily and waving his arms. They all laughed.

"Yeah, like we're going to start a fight with them. There's a reason they're called Owners," Seth said.

"But they don't own anything here, right? Wasn't that the deal?" Jack asked.

"Yeah, sure. They don't own anything in the City except the mayor and they got him cheap," Seth said and spit into the fire.

Jack dragged another piece of driftwood over and threw it on the huge blaze. It burst into flames in seconds.

He once asked Margaret how they could build a wall with the surf pounding right on it. She told him that when it was first built the surf broke a hundred yards away to the west. Then the ocean rose and swallowed the beach.

"What's a beach?" Jack asked her, and she showed him some pictures. It looked odd to him, sand going right down to the ocean. He was more impressed with the pictures of a park with large cypress trees and flowering bushes.

They kept the fire alive for hours and talked until the sky turned light and then they rode back home. Later that morning Jack found the note, which one of his mothers, it must have been Margaret, had carefully placed beneath his clean underwear, where he was sure to find it. In the same envelope was a wad of money. His mothers had left him about fourteen thousand dollars, not San Francisco currency but real ChaseAmericanWells banknotes. Jack was shocked by the amount—he had no idea they had that much. They left Gabe seven thousand because, they said in the note, his father was nearby. There was an address on the note; it was someone in a place called Maine. Margaret had written under the address, "This is your father and here is where he lives."

That night when Gabe came home they lit a candle. There was enough power for lights, but energy conservation was second nature to them and, anyway, Gabe's boyfriend Eric was a candle maker and they got them for a good price. Jack brought out some of their mothers' best wine, and they sat at the kitchen table.

"Gaia is trying to tell us something," Jack said, attempting to put some humor in his voice.

"Yeah, like what?" Gabe asked.

"Like maybe it's time to get the hell out of here, at least for a while."

"Why? Where would you go?" Gabe got up and walked to the cabinet where he kept his little wooden horses. He picked up his favorite Appaloosa and brought it back to the table. He had painted it himself, carefully drawing in vertical stripes on the tiny hooves.

"Hey, buddy," Jack said, "I'm not going anywhere without you. You're my only family now."

"And you're my only family too."

"But you do have a father and sisters."

"Yeah, and I have a step-mother. She's got my father and sisters, not me."

Jack laughed. "I guess you got that right. Why does he put up with it?"

"I don't know. There's something about you straight guys and women. You let them run you."

"Not me," Jack said, "you don't see Kristin telling me what to do."

"Yeah, and you two are fighting all the time." Gabe got up again went into the pantry and took out another candle. He put it in a brass candlestick, lit it from the one that was burning between them, and sat down.

"This is a two-candle conversation. Jack, why did they kill themselves?"

"Hey, little brother, that's not for nighttime—we should only talk about it in the morning."

"I'm sick of people killing themselves; it's disgusting. And who wants that anyway? The Owners, they want us dead. Hey, that's the reason to live—cause they want us to die." Gabe's foot was shaking as it always did when he was agitated.

"The Owners have nothing to do with it. They have their realm; we have ours. They live by their rules; we live by ours." Jack hoped that was true.

"Yeah, that's what they taught us, that's what they say, but you saw what they were doing to those people on Valencia Street. That could be us someday."

"How could it be? We're citizens of a free City. The Owners can't do anything to us. Don't worry, Gabe, I'll never let them get you!" They both laughed.

Jack got up and rummaged around his room until he found his little stash of ganja. They carried the candles into the living room and sat back into the deep sofa. Their apartment building dated from a year after the 1906 earthquake, and it had survived the 2031 earthquake intact. It was what they used to call "Victorian," with sixteen-foot ceilings and a collection of rooms off a long hallway. Bay windows ten-feet tall let in the gray, foggy light. Gabe's other family lived in a similar place, but they had the whole house—about two miles away, on Steiner Street.

The boys were silent for a while as they smoked and looked at the candles. Finally, Jack said, "Let's talk about something fun. What's the opposite of killing yourself?"

"Sex, bro, sex and more sex."

"Hey, that can't be the opposite because once it's over you're back to real life."

"Then you just do it again," Gabe said.

"You really are a teenager."

"For one more year anyway, and I'm going to make the most of it," Gabe said. "Hey, you're only three years ahead of me."

"Yeah, but I was never like you. Anyway, girls don't let you sleep around like that."

"Jack, what are we going to do now?"

"Something inside me is telling me that we need to go, to leave here, but I don't know why. It's a really strong feeling."

"But where? Where is there to go to?"

"There's my father in Maine. Margaret left me his address for a reason," Jack said. "How about this? You go play with Eric and whoever and let me alone for a few days and then we'll talk."

"Are you going into one of your trances again?" Gabe asked, "'Cause that freaks me out. I can't talk to you and I don't know what's happening."

"I don't know, maybe. I've got to go deep. Don't worry, it's good for both of us."

"This is all too damn serious. Let's play some music," Gabe said.

Jack picked up his guitar. Gabe brought out his harmonica, and Jack began to sing,

> *I'm just a poor wayfarin' stranger*
> *I'm traveling through this world of woe*
> *Yet there's no sickness, toil nor danger*
> *In that bright land to which I go .*
> *I'm going there to see my father*
> *I'm going there no more to roam*
> *I'm only going over Jordan*
> *I'm only going over home.*

Gabe joined in and they sang together, boisterously,

> *I know dark clouds will gather 'round me*
> *I know my way is rough and steep*
> *Yet golden fields lie just before me*
> *Where Her redeemed shall ever sleep*
> *I'm going there to see my father*
> *She said he'd meet me when I come*
> *I'm only going over Jordan*
> *I'm only going over home.*

The next morning Jack walked over to what was still called the main library, although there were no others, and signed up to use a computer. The librarians knew him well; he had spent a good part of his life there, graduating from reading books about animals to sports, then to natural science. It was the only public place in the City that still had books, and he loved to touch them and open the hard covers.

Maxine, one of his favorite librarians, whispered to him, "There's a no-show right now—take computer ten and you can have it for half an hour." That was lucky; every other time he'd wanted to use a computer he had to wait for days.

He showed the computer the address in Margaret's letter and a map popped up, along with lots of pictures. It was very green—that was Jack's first reaction. They must have a shitload of water there. And not many people either. The houses were few and very old; each one seemed buried deep in the forest. As he looked at the pictures, he began to feel a strange sensation along the back and then the top of his head. His hair was tingling, beginning to rise. He knew this land; he knew those houses, from the inside, which was impossible. He clamped down on himself as he had often done before *this is not happening* and ran his hand over his head. He hated it when he saw and heard and felt things beyond his five senses. When it happened, he felt powerless—he didn't know how to use it or let it go.

Then he called up a map of the area showing the Havens. Sure enough, there was one just north of his father's place. That was both bad and good. Like most of the City people, Jack disliked the Owners, but he also knew their Havens had been chosen because of favorable weather and proximity to fresh water. No deserts or floodplains there.

Jack used ten of his minutes to check the news. There was a lot of chatter about the water being turned off. But Jack had been brought up to distrust anything he read on the Net, so it was always a puzzle to read the news. Counter-knowledge had become such a science that it was virtually impossible to differentiate it from knowledge. Jack had been trained to pay attention to what he actually saw and heard: "everyone a reporter," was the saying.

Still, he was able to piece together some of what happened. The city had leased its rights to the Hetch Hetchy water from the Sierras in exchange for a lot of money. Mayor Adams had given the exclusive rights to sell water to the Nestle Water Company, which would also pay a user fee to the City. The mayor declared that it was the best deal the City could have made. It wasn't what he wanted, he said, but the alternatives were worse.

Just then Maxine was at his side: "Jack, I'm sorry but it's time for you to sign out. Somebody's waiting for the computer." Jack didn't have time to read what those alternatives were.

He wasn't in a hurry to get back home. As long as he was walking he didn't have to think about his future; he could just look and feel and listen. He turned up Market Street and watched a horse-drawn trolley make its way slowly west. Some people were on horseback. Manure pickers combed the streets every few hours to harvest the valuable fertilizer. Many people rode bamboo-frame bicycles.

The houses and apartment buildings were powered any which way. Some had a roof covered in solar panels, others had small windmills, and a few had both. The excess power they generated went into the City grid to join with other energy sources—burning waste, wind, tide motion capture, and solar. The result was a decent minimum of power for everyone, but not the wild excess of power of the fossil fuel era.

Kristin was waiting for him at his apartment. Jack wasn't in the mood to see her. He wanted to be alone, but he could see she was upset. They went into the living room and sat down on the sofa. She huddled next to him, searching for reassurance. Jack was a head taller than her, but he was spare, muscle and bone, while she was soft and fleshy and seemed to take up more space.

"What do you think about us taking over the water truck?" she asked.

"I kind of like it; it's good to show them that we can't be pushed around," he said. "And there's really nothing they can do about it. This water thing is really unpopular."

"But what can we do if they don't send the trucks?" She picked at her hair nervously. It was a habit that was starting to make Jack cringe.

"We've got water; we're just not using it. There's a huge spring on Lone Mountain and there's plenty of water on the Peninsula. This is really a scam."

"Jack, I'm scared. The Owners run just about everything outside us and we don't know anything about them. They have these Great Companies, and they want to do business here, and we don't let them. But we let the water company in and now this. Are they going to be mad at us?"

He put his arms around her and said, "It doesn't matter what they think of us. They're holed up in their Havens and we've got our community. We don't have to have anything to do with them."

"I'm not really scared as long as you're with me, Jack," she said, and she put her hand on his thigh and moved it up toward his crotch. Her touch lit him up, and he put his face between her breasts. In a moment they were struggling to take their clothes off.

After, they lay together not talking for a few moments. Jack heard the warbling of a finch outside and the general hum of the City. Margaret is gone. Jean is gone. I'll never ever see them again.

"Look, Kristin, I don't know what I'm going to do now. I've even thought of leaving the City for a while."

She got up, put her clothes on, and went to the hall closet. She grabbed a broom and went back to the living room and started to sweep the floor.

"Don't do that," Jack said. He didn't like her acting like she was at home. She ignored him, finished sweeping, and put the broom away.

"What do you mean about leaving? That makes no sense. People come here; they don't leave here. Hey, why don't you just join the Corps?" Her voice was brittle.

Jack was silent for a moment, then he said blandly, "Why would I do that? Anyway, they don't want our kind."

"How do you know? What do you know about the Corps, anyway?"

"They go all over the world, that's all I know," Jack said. "And no one else does, that's for sure. Hey, I'm not going for good, just for a while, to see what's out there."

"Jack, I need you. Don't leave me," she said, and she went to him and put her arms around his neck.

He pulled away and said, "I don't know. Let's talk later."

She retreated. "Alright; I've got to go to work." She walked over to the hall closet and took out her woolen coat, the light blue one that had cost her a month's salary. Jack felt lost and relieved when he heard the door slam shut.

He went over to the bookcase and pulled out a large atlas and a small paperback book with the old MultiCorps logo on it. Then he telephoned the library and booked an hour on the computer for the following week. Not everyone had a phone anymore, but Jack's mothers had insisted on it, and he was glad they had. He had heard that people used to have phones they carried around with them, but he found that hard to imagine. How would you keep them powered? Batteries were only for the rich.

He couldn't really explain to Kristin why he had to leave. How could she understand when he understood so little himself? His mothers' absence was a flame and he was the moth that couldn't stop flying toward it. He was attuned to his mothers somehow and he couldn't stop trying to connect to them, though his rational mind told him emphatically it was impossible. Every room, every chair cried to him. The sorrow and frustration were unbearable.

And what would he do if he didn't leave? If he stayed in the City he'd have to work at some point. He could farm, of course. There was land on the Peninsula, now once again within the City borders, and the City was still providing water for farming, although how long that would last was anyone's guess. Or he could become a carpenter like Gabe's father. There was always work keeping the old wooden buildings habitable. No, maybe someday, but not yet. Now he had to leave—he would suffocate if he didn't go.

CHAPTER TWO

Nils Rakovic sat down at his desk and began putting the few papers he hadn't already packed into his briefcase. He was a tall man, with a thick chest, heavy shoulders, and a shock of strawberry-blonde hair. The white uniform, regulation for Corps officers in the tropics, suited him, and he drew admiring glances from most women and not a few men. He was thirty-eight but looked younger. Nils was a psychologist who specialized in the effect of climate on Guests—the people who toiled in the Plantations.

He had been looking forward to this day for a long time, his last day on MobilePlantation. By tomorrow he would be home in San Francisco, where he could relax for a few weeks at least. Then he would find out about his next assignment, which he'd been promised would be no more than a two-hour sonic trip.

Finally, it was time. He brushed his bracelet with his left thumb, and after the moment it took for her to acknowledge the call, Philippa appeared in front of him so clearly that he felt that he could touch her. He knew she was seeing him in the round too. Sometimes he resented these holographic images—they were teasers, they mocked his need to feel her arms around him. How shocked her neighbors would have been to see his image—she was probably the only one in the City with a holographic computer—and he was the only Corps officer who was also a citizen.

"Nils, I'm so glad to see you," she said.

"Me too, honey. I wanted to call yesterday but I was out in the field all day, and by the time I got back to my quarters it was too late."

"It's fine. I've been busy hauling water from those stupid trucks."

"Oh, they started that already. Damn, I was hoping the deal would fall through."

"No, it's happened. The Nestle trucks are here every other day. I heard there was a riot about it down in the Mission."

"Yeah, well I can see why people would be pissed. This is the first time one of the Great Companies got into San Francisco. I wonder what it means."

"The first and probably the last because everyone here is really angry," she said.

"Well, the Owners are angry too—they hate being kept out of the City."

Philippa threw her head back and laughed. "Well, isn't that too bad? They have to content themselves with the whole rest of the world."

"Seriously, honey, are things in the City getting hard for you?"

"Nils, stop worrying about me. I'm fine. Anyway, we've chosen our community. This suits us. It's really the only place I feel comfortable anymore."

"But is it safe, in the long run?" he asked.

"Is anything really safe anymore?"

"The Havens are as safe as anything can be, I guess."

"You know that's impossible for me, Nils. Why even bring it up?"

"I'm sorry, honey, of course you're right. When I'm gone from home I kind of lose focus. I see so many terrible things out here."

"Now I'm sorry, sweetheart. I didn't mean to sound so sharp. Just come home and we'll both feel better. When will I be able to actually touch you?"

"Tomorrow night, pretty girl. See you then!"

After they said goodbye, Nils had that familiar feeling of disconnect with his surroundings; she was more real than what was actually around him. He cherished that feeling; Philippa was his home.

Nils walked down the long corridor to the commanding officer's suite. There were windows on both sides of the entire length of the hallway. Outside it was sunny and the palm trees were swaying gently in the breeze. But the heat was intense—the tropical climate zone had marched north and captured Alabama.

He knocked on a door, then went right in and snapped a salute. Nils enjoyed the military rituals, and his superiors rarely caught the irony he insinuated in them.

"Reporting for dismissal, sir," he said to the man sitting behind the large, teak desk.

"Sit down, Rakovic," said his superior, Colonel Lorenzo Wilson, a grizzled man with the sardonic air of someone who often found himself in places he hated. "I've got some news for you. You are to report to HQ in Denver tomorrow."

Nils showed no expression but he was bitterly disappointed. "I thought I was to go to MarinHaven tomorrow. They're expecting me: I'm scheduled to give a lecture."

"That crowd will just have to wait. You're to take the next sonic. It leaves in four hours."

"I'm ready to go. What is this about?"

"I don't know. Officially, that is. So officially, you go to Denver knowing nothing. In point of fact, I don't actually know much. Just this—there's a new project regarding human bioclimatology that seems to be considered ultra-high priority. They want to talk to you about it."

"I wonder why me. My time has been booked for the next two years at least."

"We all know how important you are, Major." Wilson got up and walked over to the window—banana trees marched over the hills into the far horizon. "I have to admit this is unusual; it's coming from a division of the Corps I don't know much about. Well, nothing we can do about it. Pick up your orders from Jeanie."

As Nils closed Wilson's door, the secretary came up to him with a sealed envelope.

"Here you are, Major, and good luck."

A few minutes later, Nils got into the passenger seat of a car driven by a young Corps sergeant. The large, iron Plantation gates swung open, and they headed down the smooth, black road to the airport. Nils was happy to leave, as always. The Plantations were all depressing, although this one was not as bad as some he had seen. The locals were docile and relatively easy to study. Even though the work was hard and unrelenting, the Plantation Guests were happy just to be there. They were fed, they had all the clean water they could drink and they knew they wouldn't be killed by bandits, swept away in a flood, or starved to death. The gates were there to keep people out—only the fittest were allowed to become Guests.

Later, after calling home and telling Philippa the bad news, Nils boarded the supersonic jet transport that was to take him to Denver. He settled into a comfortable seat, looking forward to an hour of quiet. Most of the passengers were somewhere else in their vision glasses. A few people had the new holo helmet, which permitted the user to experience complete holographic projections without disturbing the person in the next seat. Nils had seen an ad for it on the Net. It was great for trains but wasn't that useful for air travel because you could only watch recorded videos; you couldn't communicate in the air. Once there had been communications satellites orbiting the earth, but with no governments to sustain them, they had all eventually fallen out of the sky and were never replaced.

The sonic's interior was luxurious; all flying was now what they used to call first class because only first-class people flew. You had to be on the Data Base to get a plane ticket, and that meant only Owners and Corps officers and a few privileged others could fly. Almost every time he got on a sonic, Nils tried to remind himself of his good luck, and he made a silent vow not to forget where he came from. He settled into his seat, adjusted the head rest, and fell into a deep sleep that lasted a full ten minutes.

Rising into consciousness, he looked around him. The seat next to him was occupied by a woman perhaps in her late twenties. She had short blonde hair and was casually dressed, obviously a Corps officer on leave. She was altogether unremarkable except that she seemed to have no interest in talking to Nils. That was unusual.

Nils tuned her out and took out the book he was reading, *Crossing to Safety* by Wallace Stegner. His books often earned him curious looks. Some people thought it was an affectation to read a paper book, even perhaps a bit shocking. All that paper for just one book! As an officer he was entitled to the best reader available, but he didn't like them. Nils had happily adopted city ways. He knew what it was like to live with unreliable power, and he liked the idea that the words on these pages were unalterable. And that no one could track what he was reading.

The plane's cabin was very quiet, and he was just a little startled when his neighbor began to talk to him. Her voice was surprisingly pleasant, not the twang he had imagined.

"I like books too, " she said,

"Oh? What kind of books?"

"Oh, you know, statistical reports, official biographies of Great Companies' CEO's, that kind of thing," she said with a smile, "What about you?"

"Me? Oh, I only read books about management theory," he said, falling easily into her bantering tone.

"I love management theory. In fact, I love all kinds of theories."

"How about accounting theory? Do you love that too?"

"Sure. I love accounting. It's just numbers I hate," she said and they both laughed.

Her name was Rayna Caskey. She was a lieutenant in the Corps, and they had a few people in common. Nils was a bit chagrined to have his precious reading time taken away, but he enjoyed talking to her. She confessed that she liked Stegner as well but spent too much of her time reading Trollope and Dickens. They agreed that it was comforting to read about the Victorian world and its stable society. The seasons then were as reliable as the rising and setting of the sun.

Before they landed they exchanged addresses, and Nils invited her to San Francisco to have dinner with him and Philippa.

When he got off the plane, Nils was met by a sergeant who seemed to know him. The man escorted him to a car, and they drove west into the mountains. Within a few hours, Nils was standing in a plush office a mile underground. It was a little disorienting because two sides of the room appeared to open onto the kind of jungle that had surrounded the Plantation he had just left. A door opened in one of the visible walls, and a young officer came in and introduced himself. "Major Rakovic, we'd like you to sign a confidentiality agreement before the meeting starts."

This was a first for Nils, but he couldn't think of any reason not to sign. The officer left and Nils was alone, looking at the jungle, feeling like he could enter into it, although he knew if he tried he would bump his head against a wall.

Soon, four men wearing Corps uniforms emerged out of the trees. The one who was clearly senior, a major, laughed at Nils's expression.

"Do you like our holography?" he said, "This is state of the art."

They sat down and invited Nils to sit at the head of the table. "We have an exciting new project and we want to get your input on it," Major Bryson said.

"Yes, and we thought that you'd be interested; this is right down your alley," a younger officer said.

"Well, I'm flattered, that's for sure. But I kind of doubt I'll be able to help you. I have a lot of responsibilities at the university, and then I'm going to be sent to another Plantation, probably in old Costa Rica."

"Oh, don't worry about that. We have higher priority. Your department's already been notified that you've been transferred to a Special Project."

Bryson registered Nils's dismay and added, "Not permanently, of course. After implementation you'll have a choice."

"I've been transferred? No one told me that."

"Don't worry, this is close to home. We're not sending you to Mongolia."

The meeting lasted an hour and Nils came away from it with more questions than answers. They had booked him on a sonic bound for MarinHaven the next morning, so he had a night to kill, and he called Rayna and asked her to have dinner with him at the officers' club.

"Thanks, Major, but I'm busy tonight," she said, her voice a little frosty. Nils was surprised—she had been so friendly only a few hours ago. Had he said something wrong?

He couldn't wait to be home, and he almost gasped with relief when he let himself into their house. "My darling, come here." Philippa opened her arms and Nils bent down to meet her. His homecoming was a ritual that had evolved over the years of his comings and goings. He came in and they put their arms around each other. Then they drew back and looked into each other's eyes. Then they kissed. So far it was just sweet and affectionate, almost like brother and sister. Perhaps that was the spice they needed, because that innocent moment was usually followed by a storm of lust, and they never made it all the way to the bedroom.

Later, they sat together on the sofa, naked, covered to their necks by a thick cashmere blanket, looking out the north-facing window, his arm around her narrow shoulders. Sometimes she seemed so fragile, a delicate child he wanted to protect with his life. But he knew how utterly wrong that was; she was a steel rod, not a slender reed, but that's how he felt and she let him feel that way. The moon was bright, and it made a silver ribbon on the black water of the bay. Although they were off the grid now and safe from its vagaries, they often kept the lights off, and it made the view more immediate.

"Phil, I have to tell you something," he said and began to describe the meeting. "They made me sign a confidentiality agreement. I'm not supposed to discuss this even with you, so you better not share it with anyone else. Absolute. Swear?"

"Cross my heart and hope to die."

"I hope not." He was certain of her discretion. She knew how to keep a secret, and this wasn't the first one he had shared with her.

"They want me to work on a project, to set up a Plantation in the Central Valley."

"What? I thought the Valley wasn't habitable."

"Well, I guess someone thinks it is."

"Why in hell do they call it a Plantation anyway? So la-de-da. Some of them are nothing but factories anyway."

"For the same reason they call the workers Guests. Or me a Helper, for that matter."

"Stop it, now we're citizens of San Francisco, that's all, and that's all I want to be," she said.

"I know you're right, but I keep worrying about you. The City seems so vulnerable, and you wouldn't be here if it wasn't for me."

"You wouldn't be here if it wasn't for me!" she said. "Look, I do not want to be in a Haven. I despise those people."

"There are the Villas there too—my people," he said.

"You know how awkward it would be for me in the Villas, Nils."

He sighed and pulled her close, and they sat quietly for a few minutes. They talked for a while about small things and then went to bed.

The next day Nils took a taxi down to the Montgomery Street ferry dock. He walked off the ferry in Berkeley and went over to an adjacent dock. There he showed his Corps passport and was waved on to the small, white yacht that took the privileged to MarinHaven. There were few passengers. He disembarked at San Quentin and went through the border control quickly; the retinal scan was fast and certain.

He picked up a car in the parking garage near the dock and headed west and north. The conference center was in the rolling green hills about an hour's drive from the ferry dock. In the City there was only water for the necessities, but in the Havens water flowed freely. The Owners loved their broad lawns and golf courses.

CHAPTER THREE

Perhaps twenty-five people were assembled when Nils walked into the windowless meeting room. Once again he noted how distinctive the Owners had begun to look—as a group they were taller than the other castes, their skin was clear and unwrinkled, and their hair thicker and shinier. There were few marriages between Owners and Helpers these days and none between Owners and city dwellers. The trend was toward caste exclusivity, although intermarriage, while rare, was still possible. Nils sensed that the Owners he met all knew that his parents were Helpers and that he had grown up in the Villas. But now he was an officer of the Corps and technically not part of any caste.

Nils was introduced by a woman named Georgina Hopkins, who seemed to know everyone in the room. After greeting her fellow Owners, she said, "Our speaker today is Nils Rakovic, who is a major in the Corps, and also a professor at the Corps University in Berkeley." There was some laughter from the audience. It was still called the University of California, but the Owners knew that it was actually now a division of the Corps. "Major Rakovic studies the effect of climate on Plantation Guests and he's going to tell us about the exotic world they inhabit. It's an exciting topic and we're lucky to have him here. Also, I want to remind you that our next speaker, in two weeks, will be Justin Roking, the famous jeweler, who will talk to us about silver. His talk is entitled "Turning the Glut of Silver into Decorating Gold." Now please join me in welcoming Major Nils Rakovic to our forum."

There was some polite applause and then Nils began. The lecture was called "Adaptation to Plantation Life: the Guests' Perspective." He knew the audience was there to see his pictures and videos of exotic people in strange places, and he kept his comments as brief as possible. They had asked him to bring a holo, but Nils declined—that crossed the line into entertainment.

After he finished the lecture—to polite applause and no questions—Nils went to lunch with a small group of influential Owners. The restaurant was embedded deep into a hillside. The theme that day was "tropical resort" and it appeared that they were on a terrace overlooking the Caribbean on a sunny day. The tables seemed to be shaded from the "blazing sun" by a brightly colored awning.

He thought it interesting—something worth studying and writing about, if he ever had the time—that the more the Owners gathered the world's resources into their own hands, for their own benefit, the more they turned away from the natural world into their own simulations, environments they could control. It was the city dwellers who appreciated nature and who were learning to live within its constraints. They had incorporated nature into their religions and Gaia was now present at altars throughout San Francisco, along with the Buddha, Christ, and the Torah.

Nils was seated at a table with three Owners, but the conversation was dominated by one of them, a large man who looked to be about forty. His hair was yellowish and his face pale. Many Owners projected an almost languid air, but this man's intensity couldn't be concealed.

"Nils, I wonder why you're so interested in the psychology of the Guests," said Hugh Rowan.

"These are people who live in extreme situations. Of course I wonder about how they think and behave," Nils replied.

"But aren't they a perishable commodity? Eventually they'll be gone and the world has to move on, after all." Rowan raised his glass, showing perfectly manicured fingernails, smooth white skin, and a gold ring with a large diamond.

"I don't think I would call them a commodity, Hugh, they are human beings after all. And we don't know if they will be gone, as you say. They may learn on their own to adapt to the climate changes." Nils did his best to keep the annoyance out of his voice. It would be stupid to offend Rowan, but it would be craven to agree with him.

"Oh, I doubt that they'll be able to adapt. They don't have technology, for one thing," Rowan said.

And who keeps it from them? Nils thought. "No, they don't. But we just don't know what they will do. A lot will depend on the social structures they set up on their own."

"Well, Nils, the question I have is why should we be concerned about them at all, assuming, of course, that we can automate the Plantations?" Rowan looked around the table and motioned to the waiter who was standing behind him to bring more wine.

"Full automation, I can tell you, is a long way in the future," Nils said.

"The solution, of course, is robotics. Why doesn't the Corps do more to replace the Guests with robots? I have to say I'm pretty frustrated with the Corps. Nothing ever seems to happen in Denver," Rowan said.

"Robots would be more expensive in the long run. And we did make agreements that we would help as many Outsiders as we could. The Plantations give them work and safety, at least for a while."

"The Corps made the agreements, Nils. The Great Companies didn't. And the governments you made those agreements with don't exist anymore," Rowan replied.

"Perhaps if more Owners were active in the Corps it would be more to your liking," Nils ventured. He took his first sip of the fruity Pinot Noir that had sat unnoticed in front of him throughout lunch.

Rowan gave him a quick, sharp look, "Well, yes, certainly. If I were twenty, I'd join. But our young people have a lot of other responsibilities."

"Sure, we all have to make choices," Nils said. He was tired of this conversation. Then he noticed that it now looked like a tropical night, and in the distance he could see the moon rising over the sea.

"But getting back to what you know about, Nils, I have a question. Assuming their conditions change, how long does it take for people to adapt to being Guests?"

"Well, there are a number of stages, depending on where they come from and their original culture. One thing we do know—rural people, farmers and peasants, find it easier than city dwellers."

"Well, yes, of course, because city dwellers have coddled themselves and they hate having to actually work. You know, I'm tired of all this pretending; we don't need all these people; the world doesn't need them and we have to face that. They're not our problem." He stood up and nodded to the other Owners; he ignored Nils and walked away.

Hugh Rowan was proud of his family. There were other Owners as rich as he but few who could boast that their family had been prominent for two centuries. The Rowans had been in railroads and oil long before they were in holography and nanotechnology. He liked to think of himself as progressive and future-oriented. You couldn't rest on your laurels, certainly not these days. But then he didn't come from people who lived on the interest of their interest. His was a family of doers, explorers of business and finance. The urge to dominate was hard-wired in the Rowans and even more in the Smyths, his mother's family. These two strains joined together had produced lions, Hugh thought. He was a tall, muscular man, not handsome, but frighteningly robust. Born to command is how he had always thought about himself.

Hugh had a wife and two mistresses. Sylvia bored him, as did his three children. The boy was especially annoying, constantly demanding attention. Georgia, in Denver, and Melinda, in Maine, were both excellent hostesses and skilled erotic companions. At home in MarinHaven, his personal assistant was a young woman who understood his needs and was most eager to satisfy them. He didn't enjoy the company of men.

With all of his success and prominence, Hugh Rowan was a frustrated man. His people had thrived on growth and expansion, but the world was now shrinking and there was nothing anyone, however strong, could do about that.

There was very little trade with Asia now. China had fractured into autonomous provinces dominated by warlords. India was crippled by famines whenever the monsoons failed, now more often than not. Whole populations of coastal and island countries were migrating away from the rising ocean. Europe was a disaster zone, its cities uninhabitable in the scorching summers and its best farmland flooded by frequent torrential rains.

Global warming seized the earth just as fossil fuels became scarce and expensive. The confluence of all these events had wiped out the global economy with the ease of a teacher erasing a blackboard.

Although the current Rowans were confined to North America, they and their kind had done the best they could under the circumstances. Hugh's great-grandfather was a visionary who saw that the old government, still mired in notions of democracy, would try to spread the pain of the coming climate catastrophe among all classes and thus threaten his family's way of life.

So Joshua Harrington Rowan and his powerful friends systematically weakened and then dismantled the United States and its constituent states and replaced it with a patchwork of semi-autonomous Havens. At the same time, the old discredited formula of "all men are created equal" was supplanted by a new caste system where each man would have a place inherited from his father. Except for the out-castes—the majority of the world—who had no future anyway.

The Owners had concluded that the post–climate change earth could sustain only a small fraction of the human population that had existed before. Since most people couldn't be saved, there was no point in wasting valuable resources on them. It was only logical that the Owners should take as much of the earth's resources for themselves as possible—water, arable land in temperate climates, vital minerals. The Havens were lifeboats for the richest few.

As with resources, so with technology: The Owners had agreed among themselves that all new technology would be reserved for their benefit alone.

Hugh wasn't complacent (that wasn't in his nature), but he profoundly agreed with the order of things—it all felt right, proper. The rigid class system of the late twenty-first century was as natural to him as the sun rising in the east.

But there were irritants in this new world, chief among them old San Francisco, which stubbornly resisted the Owners. When he was a child and a young adult, Hugh would travel across the bay, first with his mother and sister and then with friends. It was exciting, walking among crowds, not knowing what would happen next. But the City's excellence was all in its potential—what it could be if it were properly organized. For now, it was just a jumble of people all mixed together, crudely lacking in any appreciation of hierarchy. It had always been jarring, being treated by people in the City as if he were just like anyone else, like one of them. But as he got older it became intolerable.

An idea came to him one day when a few of his friends were talking about how useless the Corps was and why couldn't they take some action on their own? Hugh told them that he had heard a group of Outsiders were being shipped to a Plantation, and wouldn't it be great to actually do part of it themselves?

He suggested marching them right through San Francisco—teach the troits a lesson. It took a lot of organization, how to transport the horses, where to get all the boats to take the Guests across the bay, and on and on. And then there were the politics. Convincing the mayor wasn't hard—Adams was deeply flattered to be invited for a dinner in the Haven, and he readily accepted a few presents. Hugh and his friends had a hearty laugh after the mayor left his estate—it had cost them next to nothing to get his acquiescence—and the man had acted so grateful! Hilarious.

The Corps bureaucracy was a lot harder to deal with. No one involved in Guest transportation would say "no" to Hugh, but it seemed impossible for weeks to find out who would say "yes." And then when Hugh did identify that officer, he found him hard to pin down. Hugh and his friends didn't want to be responsible for the entire transport, they just wanted to take them through San Francisco. That was a big fight in itself. The Corps had a policy of avoiding the City completely.

It was all worth the effort, in the beginning at least. It made you feel like a man, sitting up on that horse, bullwhip in hand, as the huddled Outsiders cowered and groveled. This is the way things should be, Hugh exulted. But then the crowd of troits interfered and Hugh had to call the local security. It was one of the most frustrating moments of his life.

Why should we, the great ones of the earth, have to call the troglodytes' police? This is so wrong, Hugh felt, it's contrary to reason and nature. But there it was and, for that moment, there was nothing he could do but taste the bitterness. Sure, the rest of it had gone smoothly and the Outsiders were delivered to a Corps barge at China Basin, but all the fun went out of it, and by the time Hugh got home to the Haven he was in a foul mood.

CHAPTER FOUR

The sun climbed over the Oakland hills, and its rays flashed across the bay and enlightened Twin Peaks. At that moment, Jack's uncertainty evaporated. He had hiked up the day before and spent the night huddled over a fire, in the lee of a twisted mass of rusted metal girders that had once been a television tower. All night he had meditated in the darkness and slept and then meditated again.

Morning was glorious. The sun still rose and set to a fixed schedule and the stars moved in their appointed patterns and didn't care about the rapid transformation of earth's surface. These thoughts comforted Jack, although he knew the facts were no help. The hash of thoughts and feelings of yesterday had settled and clarified and what was left was no longer insurmountable. Suddenly he was very hungry.

He walked down the hill, heading northeast to the house on Steiner Street. Gabe's step-mother Thalia answered the door. She and Margaret had once been best friends—until Margaret's husband Jonah left her for the younger woman only a few months after Gabe was born. Jack rarely saw Thalia while his mother was alive, but he now found himself wanting to make contact. Although sometimes she seemed a little wary of him, she always made him feel welcome at her house.

She was usually up at dawn, and by now she'd have collected eggs from the chickens they kept in the backyard. Jack loved fresh eggs. She had just taken her bread out of the oven and the whole house was fragrant with it.

"I suppose you want to stay for breakfast," she said.

"Sure, Thalia, thanks, I'd love to. Is Gabe here?"

"He's in the spare room. You can wake him up."

By the time Jack came downstairs with Gabe the rest of the family was gathered at the kitchen table—Thalia, Gabe's father Jonah, and his half-sisters Becky and Jessica. Now Jack felt no obligation to stay away, and he liked the family atmosphere. The girls adored him.

The talk turned to Jack's future: "I'd like to go to Maine," Jack told them.

"What would you do there, Jack?" asked Jonah.

"Find my father, and then I don't know," Jack replied.

"Have some more bread," Becky said, passing the basket to him.

"Have some salt," Jessica said quickly. She was ten and worked hard to get attention.

"I don't know anyone who's traveled across country in the past twenty years," said Jonah. "Have you figured out how you'd do it?"

"I did some research. Some people say it's possible to go by road, but it's pretty dangerous and there are some long detours in places where the bridges have fallen. But I'd have to find someone with a car. I don't even know if there are enough charging stations on the way. I don't think you could make it just on solar."

"Wow, that would be some trip," said Gabe, "a lot of desert."

"Yeah, pretty much from east of the Sierras all the way to Ohio," Jack said.

"Well, it's not the desert that scares me, it's the tornadoes," said Becky.

"And the floods," added Jessica.

"How can there be floods in the desert?" asked Becky.

"Well, there are in these deserts. Once in a while the rain comes down in buckets but it just runs off and then nothing's left," Jack said.

"We like it when it rains, don't we?" Becky asked her father. "You always say that."

"Sure, sweetie, but it's different here," Jonah said. "We've been lucky because our weather is fairly stable, but we don't know if it will last. Depends on the ocean currents. You know, Jack, people used to travel across country all the time. Sometimes just for curiosity, for fun. My father flew in a plane across country once. There was a time when anyone could fly."

"You mean a sonic, Daddy?" Becky said.

"No, sweetie. Planes in those days were sub-sonic. But there were a lot more of them."

The girls looked at him with a mixture of wonder and skepticism. They weren't sure if he was kidding or not. He loved to make up stories for them.

"I wonder what things are like on the East Coast," Gabe said.

"And another thing," Jonah said, "there used to be newspapers that reported on all kind of things, weather included. Thalia, do you remember the *New York Times?*" he asked.

"Oh, yes. Mother used to read it on her computer every day," she replied, "It had new stories every day about all kinds of things that were happening everywhere in the world."

"That would be handy," Jack said.

"Did grandma have her own computer?" Becky asked.

"Yes, and her own connection to the Net. She knew what was going on all right," Thalia said. There was pride in her voice.

After breakfast, Jack went out to the yard to help Gabe feed the pig and the two goats. When they finished, Gabe said, "When do we leave?"

"We have to find out how to get there first," Jack said.

Jack's session at the library's computer the next day wasn't that helpful. Travel information for crossing what was still called, inaccurately, the United States was mostly about the old days. The recent information was discouraging. It seemed that no one made the trip from coast to coast anymore. No one who couldn't fly—the vast majority of the continent's inhabitants. There were a few references to trains run by the Corps, but no information about where they went or who could travel on them.

There has to be a way to go, Jack told himself. People used to make the trip routinely; there must be some way to do it still.

From the library he biked over to Kristin's house on Bartlett Street and left a note for her. An hour later she knocked on his door. They went into the kitchen and sat down at an ancient wooden table by a window. Jack took her hand and said, "I think I am going to go. I've got to get out for a while. And find what's left of my family."

"Hey, whoever they are, they belong somewhere else, somewhere different from where you belong," she said.

"Yeah, but I want to know them—like I want to get to know myself, where I come from," he said.

"You come from here, from right here. Not there," she said.

"I know. But don't you want sometimes to find out about the bigger world—what's going on outside our little City?"

She shuddered. "No, of course not. You know what's going on. The earth is fucked up, people are dying everywhere. I don't want to know about it!"

"We hear about it, but we don't know for sure what's happening. That's the point, Kristin! I want to see for myself what this world is like."

"Listen, Jack, why are you running away? It won't bring your mothers back. You should stay here and face your problems. What is it with you?"

"I need to go, that's all. I don't know why but something is telling me that I have to get out into the world. Do you ever have voices in your head, telling you to do things?"

"Jack, now you're starting to sound really crazy," she turned away from him.

He rocked his chair on its back legs and laughed. "Yeah, I know how it sounds. Bad. But all I'm trying to say is that I can't just stay here anymore, at least not right now. Too much has happened that I don't understand."

"And what about us, Jack?"

He went to her and put his arms around her.

"Kristin, I care about you a lot, but this is something else. My mothers, the water, those people being herded like cattle, it adds up to something, what, I don't know. I can't just stay here and pretend that things are the same. I hear voices all the time, almost like other people thinking. I don't know what to do."

"Is this what you wanted me to come over for?"

"Yeah, I guess. I had to tell you what I was thinking."

She stood up and walked to the sink, picked up a wine glass that had been washed, and held it up to the light. Then she washed it again. "I think it's time for you to grow up," she said, frowning, "get a job like everyone else and make a living. Don't worry about what you can't control. That's what my mother always says."

"That's not the way you operate," Jack said. "You're worried all the time."

"No, I'm not. You want me to be crazy like you, don't you? Well, I'm not going to be." Her voice was sharp, almost a shout.

"Hey, calm down, I'm not trying to upset you."

"Upset? I'm not upset. You're the one that's upset. You're crazy. I should have known it earlier."

She stalked out of the room toward the front door, and Jack followed her. At the door Jack grabbed her shoulder. "Don't leave like this!" he said.

She turned around and opened her arms. "Jack, there's so much for you here. Everyone loves you and you're never going to have a problem making a living."

Jack stepped back. "Thanks, I know this is my home and it always will be. But I can't stay right now, it's unbearable. I have a father somewhere and I need to find him."

"Yeah, and what about me, you're just dropping me?"

"I don't know, Kristin, I don't know what I'm doing. I just have to go."

"Oh, Jack, listen. We have something special, don't just throw it away. I can help you get through this, let me help. Come to my house and live with us for a while. My parents love you and they'll be happy to have you there. You won't have all the reminders of your mothers."

"I can't leave Gabe, you know that."

"Gabe's got another family. Why can't he go to them?"

"You know he's not happy there."

"But what about me, Jack?"

Jack tried to pull her into a hug but she pushed away from him. Her face was flushed. "Doesn't my happiness count, Jack? What do I have to do to get through to you?"

"This isn't about you, Kristin. This has nothing to do with you. I don't know what else to say."

"So you're saying it's none of my business?"

"No, I didn't say that!" Jack suddenly felt a jolt of anger. Kristin's face looked distorted, out of focus.

"Listen, I don't need you," her voice rose an octave and she ended in a shout. "If that's the way it's going to be you can just let go of me, and don't leave me any notes until you've decided to grow up."

Jack watched her walk down the stairs quickly, not looking back. *Thank you,* he finally said to her, silently. *You've made this decision much easier.*

He had to be outside, but when he got to the street he couldn't go a block without having to stop and chat with someone, and he needed to clear his mind. So he went down to Mission Creek and rented a kayak. It was a bright November day, sunny, sparkling. He slid out from the dock and headed away from the old Bay Bridge, which was still standing, although now a danger because of decades of neglect.

A few years earlier he had walked across it in the day time, watching out for the huge holes in the deck. He could see through to the water two hundred feet below. But then a section of the western span had fallen into the bay and the towers were now leaning crazily toward each other. The thick cables that used to hold the towers in place had unraveled, and long metal strands hung down into the water. When the wind was high, the metal ropes flailed like giant whips.

He got into the water just at the height of the flood tide, and he paddled across to the East Bay without much effort. There were times when the current was a river in flood and he wasn't strong enough to make it across, so he always checked the tide tables before he made the trip. He was careful to stay clear of the ruined bridge to the north.

When he got to the Oakland estuary he pulled his kayak up to the dock and locked it. Huge ships used to come here—he had seen pictures of them. It took a long time for large-scale shipping to die—when oil became impossibly expensive, sailing ships made a comeback. But then the weather became too unpredictable. Typhoons the size of a continent occurred often and thirty-meter or even larger waves in the open ocean were now common. The death blow to shipping was delivered by the AmerAsian Insurance Company, the last marine insurer. The risks were too high and it stopped insuring ships. It was that simple—no insurance, no shipping.

He hadn't been to this side of the bay for a long time, and he was glad he'd made the trip. This was much more of an adventure than taking the ferry to Berkeley and the tram to the campus. Everything there was manicured; it had a sinister patina of wealth, and people said it was only a matter of time until the Owners took it over and made it part of the Haven.

Oakland was a world apart, more farmland than city. When he was younger, Jack and his friends would come over here and work on people's farms for a few extra dollars and the fun of it. During the summer there was plenty of work. And he could bring things back to his mothers, strawberries, corn, hops to make beer, and later tomatoes and squash. Apples. Once in a while he helped load hay on the scow-schooners that were the trucks of the water. There was always work transporting hay—the City's horses never got too much of it, but Jack liked the farm work more.

He decided to find his favorite farm, on West Street. You could tell that there were once many houses here, their foundations faint outlines in the ground, but most of them were now gone, probably because of the last great earthquake. And there were a lot fewer people now than there used to be. The bay had risen and flooded all of the low-lying land. Salt water had intruded into the seasonal streams that used to flow under West Oakland, and now the area was a large marsh.

West Street was still familiar, a quiet country lane where you heard bird song more often than human voices. Jack was looking for the Wards' place, where he had spent many days planting and harvesting. That had been a long time ago, when he was fourteen. Emily and John Ward had a son Jack's age, and the boys enjoyed playing together after the farm work was done. What happened to him, Jack wondered.

Soon he found the old Victorian farm house, not large but well kept up, painted a buttery yellow with blue shutters. Jack knocked on the door.

"Hello, may I help you?," asked a rather broad woman wearing an apron with yellow roses all over it.

"Hi, Emily, it's Jack."

"Oh, my goodness, you've grown!" she pulled him into the house.

He immediately was overcome by the pleasant smells he remembered from those years. But the house had shrunk, and he was sure that Emily used to be a foot taller.

"Come on into the kitchen and I'll get you some cookies and milk," she said. "We have a cow now and I make some money selling the milk, but we have plenty for ourselves! And how are your mothers?"

When Jack told her she didn't say a word. She just went over to him and put her arms around him, hugging him tight for a minute.

"Where is Sam?" Jack asked, pulling away.

"Oh, you haven't heard?" she asked. "He joined the Corps."

Jack felt his heart skip a beat. "What, how did he do that? I thought the Corps was only for Owners and Helpers."

"No, turns out that's a myth. They're not restricted. It's just that the Corps is hard to find for us."

"What do you mean?" he asked.

"Well, Sam explained it to me," she said. "The Corps recruits in the Villas, where the Helpers live. You know, that's in the Haven, but they'll take anyone, including city dwellers, but we have to get to them."

"How can we do that? We're not allowed into the Havens, everyone knows that," Jack said.

"Well, Sam told me the Corps accepts anyone at its headquarters," she said.

"And where is that?"

"Denver."

"You mean Sam went to Denver?" Jack asked, incredulous.

"Yes, he did," she said.

"Well, how did he do that?"

"He took the train," she said.

Jack looked at her in disbelief. "How did he do *that?*"

Emily laughed at his expression. "Why, he had to get to Sacramento first."

"Emily, will you tell me all about it?" Jack asked. "I want to go on the train too."

They sat for half an hour while Jack questioned her closely. He tried very hard not to get frustrated or annoyed when she became vague and wouldn't try to remember the details that were so important to him.

Just as he was about to leave, her husband arrived and insisted that Jack stay for a few minutes more. He questioned Jack about what was going on in San Francisco.

"What was the reaction to the water trucks?" John asked. Jack told him about the near riot, and the older man chuckled. "Well, good for them. There's plenty of water in San Francisco, if they'd use it. But you got to have leaders who'll fight for you. We still have our running water here."

"How did you keep it?" Jack asked.

"If your mayor had pushed back hard you'd still have running water. That's the fact. This is a small city, and it's pretty hard for the mayor to have lunch with someone without everyone knowing what kind of pie they had for desert. The Great Companies just weren't able to buy us off, that's all."

"Say, John, have you heard from Sam since he joined the Corps?" Jack asked. The older man's expression changed instantly, like he had been slapped in the face. "No, he knows how I feel about the Corps. I love my son, but I don't approve of what he did."

"Why do you say that? I don't know anything about the Corps except that they can go anywhere in the world they want."

"True, but what do they do when they get there? I'll tell you what they do. Whatever the Owners want them to do, that's what," he said.

"But I thought the Corps didn't have any caste. Or maybe they were their own caste."

"Look, Jack, I'd like to talk some more, but I have a shitload of stuff to do right now. I'm sorry to break this off, but I'm not kidding; I have a lot to do. Take it from me: the Corps might look good to a young guy like you, but there's no future there for a city dweller. All I can hope for is that Sam will serve out his enlistment and come back home."

Jack's paddle back across the bay was hard. The tide was turning but he enjoyed the struggle—his back and shoulders tight as he pulled against the water. The delicate balance of the tiny craft, not still for an instant, dancing with the waves.

Later that evening Jack and Gabe walked together to Steiner Street and talked about what Jack had learned.

"There's a train. The Corps operates its own train and it goes all the way to Denver and maybe farther," Jack said.

"Let's go, then. How do we do it?" Gabe said.

"It's not that easy. I'm not sure what you have to do to get a ticket. I think the nearest place we can get on is Sacramento," Jack said.

"Okay. We'll go to Sacramento. Where is it anyway?" Gabe asked. "I guess we better tell my Dad tonight."

Dinner was over by the time they got to the house, but Thalia gave them plates of leftovers, corn fritters and chard, and they talked while Jonah did the dishes and Thalia put away the plates. Jack had been thinking about how he was going to tell them of their plans, how to frame it to provoke the least resistance, when Gabe blurted out,

"Guess what? Me and Jack are going to Maine. His father lives there. First we go to Denver. Isn't that great?"

Jonah turned around and his face was red. "You're only nineteen, Gabe. You're not talking about a camping trip on the peninsula. You have no idea what you're doing. No, you're not going."

Gabe looked at Jack, who looked down at the table. Gabe said, "We can take care of ourselves. What is there to worry about anyway? We'll watch the weather all the time, and if we have to stop until it clears up, we will."

"You have no idea what you're talking about. Jack, do you want to take this responsibility for your brother?" Jonah asked.

"I think there's a way to do it. We'll take the Corps train, that's probably safe."

"So you'll put yourselves at the mercy of the Corps? Do you have the slightest idea of who they are and what they do?" Jonah's voice was low and even, but Jack felt it cutting into him.

"What I was thinking is that we'd sort of feel our way through this. If something doesn't seem right, we won't do it." Jack looked directly into Jonah's eyes. There was fear in the older man's eyes, but also hesitation.

"Jack, do you know what's Outside?" Jonah asked.

"No, I don't. But that's one of the reasons to go. Some of us have to see what the rest of the world is like."

"Oh, we have a good idea. Have you ever seen a tornado that's a mile wide? Do you know what it can do? How about a thousand starving people on a rampage? Ever seen that? Been buried in a blizzard where it snows all day and night for a week?"

"I know it's safer and smarter to stay home," Jack said, "but, Jonah, aren't there times when you have to do something crazy, just to get out of where you are?"

"Look, Jack, I can't stop you from doing this, you're not my son. But why does Gabe have to go too?"

"Because it's my time to see the world too. I may not get this chance again," Gabe said.

"No, you're not going, and that's final," Jonah said.

"Listen, Dad, I'm old enough to make my own decisions," Gabe said. "It's not like you really want me to live here with you all. My home was with Margaret and Jack and now it's just Jack. I want to go!"

The room was silent for a moment. Jonah turned away from the boys and looked out the window. Thalia put down her dishtowel and said firmly, "Let the boy go if he wants to, Jonah. You can't stop him anyway."

Jonah looked at Thalia and then at Gabe and Jack. "No. If he goes it's against my wishes. Is that what you want, Gabe?"

"I'm sorry, Dad, but I have to go. I'm not letting Jack go alone."

For the next two days, the boys talked about what they were going to do. Jack said, "You shouldn't go just for me. I'm looking for my father, but you've got one."

"Oh, come on, Jack. You know that's not the only reason you're going."

"Well, yeah, I have to get away from here for a while. Too many memories, I can't breathe."

"So what's there here for me if you go and I stay? I'm not going to live on Steiner Street with Jonah and Thalia. I miss our mothers just as much as you do. I want to see what's out there in the world too. Jonah'll get over it and Thalia couldn't care less if I never come back."

"Hey, that's harsh."

"But you know I'm right," Gabe said.

Two days later Gabe came into Jack's room at five a.m. and woke him up. "It's time to go, bro."

Jack quickly got dressed; he could smell the coffee brewing; it was still dark outside. He walked into the kitchen; Gabe was frying eggs and toasting bread. "Jonah set us up pretty well, bro! We've got lots of good stuff to take with us, dried food to last for weeks. You're bringing the money, right?"

They walked down to the pier at Montgomery Street. It always struck Jack as funny that there were dead skyscrapers sticking out of the water east of where he stood. Why did they ever build them there, he wondered. Did they think they could master the ocean? But there was so much that was done in the old days that made no sense. If you added it all up it was total madness.

The ferry to Berkeley was pretty full. A few students, but mainly people going to work at the university, janitors, repairmen, and even a few professors who lived in the City because they couldn't afford Berkeley. As they pulled away from the San Francisco dock, Jack was overcome with a feeling of the moment. I want to remember this. Today is November 11, 2081, and this is the first day of my new life. The crossing was fast. They had paid the extra to go on the motor ferry instead of the much cheaper sail boat, and as they glided into the dock, the sky became just light enough to see that there were storm clouds coming in from the west.

Jack and Gabe were the only disembarking passengers who didn't jump on the tram that went directly to the university. They walked on the deserted highway, bound north for the Carquinez straits. Figuring an easy four miles an hour, they'd be at the straits by nightfall. They'd camp there and find a way across in the morning. Jack had no idea what to expect once they passed the Berkeley border.

The storm came on them a few minutes after they got off the ferry. They sheltered under a ruined freeway underpass; it made a dry cave facing east, away from the wind, which howled around them. Rain smashed into the concrete, nearly horizontal. Then a crackling, almost rhythmic sound—thousands of sharp taps. The ground was quickly covered in balls of hail big enough to kill. The storm passed, moving quickly eastward over the Berkeley hills.

They walked for a few miles on the old roadbed, dodging the holes in the pavement. There were too many fallen bridges to clamber over so they decided to walk on the eastern side of the old freeway. It was a good choice because in some places, where the road was close to the bay, the rising water filled up the freeway trench, now a stagnant canal, and in other places the elevated road had collapsed. The neighborhoods they passed through were empty of people, the houses and apartment buildings moldering into the ground.

"Where did they all go?" Gabe asked.

"I think the better-off ones moved to the City or to Oakland. No one knows exactly where the rest of them went. But they had to go. Everything was shut off, first the gas and the power and then the water and there was no community here to keep things going."

They walked on for several hours in silence. The air had cleared; there were no clouds. It was warm in the sun, and they took their shirts off and put them in their backpacks. They were used to sudden changes in temperature and prepared for them. They knew that after sunset they would need down jackets. Both of them had spent many months camping in the Santa Cruz Mountains and one time had done an expedition with some others into the wilderness of Big Sur. That had taken all of one summer and a part of the fall. They went to a place called Crystal Mountain, which was entirely covered in quartz. It sparkled in the sunshine like snow. Like most of the City's children, they had learned to hunt and fish and were confident in the wild.

"Hey, Jack, so what do we do when we get to the straits?" Gabe asked.

"We find the ferry to the other side and then we go to Sacramento," Jack said.

"Okay, so we find the train. What do we do then? How can we get on it?" Gabe asked.

"I don't know. We'll figure that out when we get there." Jack felt very confident, now that they had started—he had no idea why.

"What do you think about the Corps?" Gabe asked.

"I don't know. We just don't know much about it. But it seems like the only really organized thing in this fucked-up world," Jack said.

"My Dad doesn't like it. He says it just works for the Owners," Gabe said.

"Well, John doesn't like it either and he's a smart guy. Did I tell you his son Sam joined the Corps?" Jack said.

"Really? Wow, that's hard to believe. I don't know anyone who did that," Gabe said.

They had kept the bay within sight on their left most of the way, and now they could see the sun setting behind the City, beyond the shore where they had their bonfires. Jack felt suddenly far from home. He shivered and was briefly ashamed of himself. He turned to Gabe. "Let's camp around here and we'll try to cross tomorrow."

CHAPTER FIVE

Nils sat by himself for a moment after Rowan left, struggling to control his anger, and let go of the humiliation he felt. He tried to focus on the wine: This is lovely, so earthy and rich. Then, just as he was about to get up, a woman sat down across from him.

"I enjoyed your lecture, Major. Linda Crowley," she said and offered her hand. She was blonde and wore a tailored suit of lavender silk. Her hair was pulled back from a face that needed no embellishment. She looked at him with frank eyes, a look he didn't associate with Owners. Not true to caste, he registered automatically.

"And what is your interest in the Guests, Ms. Crowley?"

"I'm an actress, Major. I'm interested in extreme experiences and we don't get that much in the Havens anymore."

Nils mentally kicked himself. She was a movie star; anyone would have recognized her.

"Yes, of course I know who you are."

She smiled at him. "Tell me what it's like to be down there, to actually be among those people. What kind of clothes do the women wear? Do they smell? Are they affectionate with each other? I have a million questions. I wish I could go to one of the Plantations, but the Corps is so strict."

"The Guests are required to take showers twice a day and they wear a kind of simple unisex uniform." Maybe she was a typical Owner tourist after all.

"Oh, but Major, I want to get a real feel for those places."

Oh, no you don't, he thought, and the image of a dozen no-longer useful Guests being driven out, screaming and begging, their children running after the truck and being beaten back, flashed in his mind. "There are some video books about them, if you're interested."

"Well, yes, of course. For some reason I thought you might be able to help me. Can I come and talk to you when you have more time?" she asked.

He couldn't figure out how to decline, and he wasn't sure he wanted to anyway. "Sure, of course. I'll be on leave for a week. Here's my number." He touched his Corps bracelet and she looked at the address floating in the air in front of her, and her eyes widened slightly.

"You live in the City? How adventurous." That might have been ironic, but he couldn't tell.

"Yes, my wife and I are citizens and we like it there," he said.

"I go there as often as I can. It's so much more alive than the Haven. And just between us, it's a relief to go somewhere I'm not known. I know it's shocking they don't have movies there but I'm sure that's just because they can't afford them. Well, maybe one day…."

She seemed sincere, and Nils couldn't think of anything to say for a moment. The last thing he expected at this Owners' gathering was to encounter a free spirit. Then she said, "Major, I don't usually ask strangers for a favor, but I'm going to do it this one time. Can you help me visit a Plantation? I would be very grateful." She smiled again, and he was dazzled. He knew it was a smile she could turn on and off at will, but it moved him, and he wanted to see it again.

"Well, Ms. Crowley, I've never seen a tourist at a Plantation. Only the Guests and the Corps. There aren't even any visitors' quarters. Maybe if you joined the Corps you could go," he joked.

She suddenly got a serious look on her face. "That's it. I'll talk to General Couseau! Why not? It wouldn't have to be for very long."

Nils laughed out loud; he couldn't help himself. "My God. You're serious. Well, if you can reach the Commandant of the Corps to make a personal request, all power to you!"

They both stood up and were quickly joined by a tall man with silver hair and a deep tan. Like the other Owners, he was fond of jewelry—almost every finger had a ring with precious stones on it, and he wore a gold necklace and a diamond-studded bracelet. He was old enough to be Linda's father.

"Major, this is my husband, Ronnie Simpson," she said.

Nils knew him by reputation. He was one of the richest of all the Owners—he had large blocks of stock in all of the seven Great Companies, the monopolies that controlled the entire economy.

Simpson was known to be different from most of his peers, something of a freethinker and a Bohemian. Nils looked forward to telling Philippa about meeting him.

"Congratulations, Major, on a very interesting speech. I never thought about how much you need to understand the psychology of the Guests to run a Plantation. Human motivations are at the bottom of everything, aren't they? Even with Guests, we have to understand what makes them tick."

"Ronnie, I was telling the major how much I want to visit a Plantation. What if I joined the Corps?"

Simpson laughed heartily. "I don't think you'd pass basic training, darling. There are some video books about the Plantations. Why don't you just look at those?"

"Darling, I'm serious. It could be a special assignment kind of thing. You could fix it up for me. I'm sure that nice Felix Couseau could do it."

"He's a busy man, darling. Do you really want to bother him for something like this?"

"I think it's important, even if you don't. I need to get into a Plantation, one way or another. Alright, I'll tell you," she looked around and dropped her voice slightly. "We're doing a movie about a Plantation and I'm starring in it! I need to know what it's about, to get under the skin."

"Darling, why don't you look at the books, talk to this man, read his papers, talk to people who've been to one? Just use your imagination!"

"Ronnie, you are so literal! You're not an artist. We need to feel it, to touch it, or it isn't real." She put her arm around her husband's neck and pulled him toward her. He tried to pull away but she wouldn't let him.

Nils felt awkward as they argued lightly with each other. Was this a scene for his benefit—some couples needed witnesses to their fights—or were they actually as oblivious to his presence as they seemed?

"Major, I'm sorry to get you involved in our squabbles. It was a pleasure meeting you." Simpson shook hands with Nils, and they left.

Nils was surprised and pleased at Simpson's manner. Few Owners were so polite to their inferiors.

It took him almost four hours to get back home. He just missed a ferry leaving MarinHaven for Berkeley and had to wait an hour for the next one. Then he had to wait for the Berkeley to San Francisco ferry. Luckily, when he got to the City there happened to be some taxis waiting at the dock. It was nighttime when Nils got back to his house on Jackson Street, at the top of Pacific Heights. He let himself in and went upstairs, calling to Philippa before he entered their bedroom so she wouldn't be startled. His wife was sitting in the bed they had made for them (it looked like a large sleigh), reading a book. She looked up, her long, dark hair loose around her shoulders, and stretched out her arms for him.

Nils was even busier at home than at work. He wanted to pack in as much connection as he could; he was stocking up on love for the lonely times ahead, away on duty. He and Philippa cooked meals together for friends and, on the best nights, for just the two of them. He walked up and down the City's hills, stopping in cafes and shops. The demise of the global economy had proven a boon to small craftsmen, local farmers, and entrepreneurs of all kinds. There were now people who tanned leather and made shoes, weavers, dressmakers, blacksmiths, and every other trade to make whatever was needed by the City's citizens.

Sometimes he wished that he was truly one of them, a real city dweller. He was tired of concealing himself. What would our neighbors do, he thought, if they knew I was an officer of the Corps? Maybe we've been mistaken in keeping ourselves so mysterious. Philippa and he had talked about this many times. She was tired of the deception too, but she was sure that they would be shunned if people knew that he was not just a professor.

One day Nils and Philippa were walking down Union Street, and they decided to have lunch out at a restaurant for a change. First they stopped at one of their favorite places, a store that sold antiques. The shop window was always filled with old photographs, which were changed often. Sometimes there were pictures of people who had owned the store in the past or lived in the neighborhood.

Other times there were pictures of San Francisco as it had been in the early twenty-first century or the mid-nineteenth century. Inside were playbills from forgotten shows, lamps that used bulbs that hadn't been made in sixty years, and tables made of wood imported from countries that no longer existed.

Right after they entered, Nils saw someone familiar standing among the chinaware and cutlery. For a second he couldn't place her: a short, neat woman wearing yellow cotton pants and a green sweater and looking very young. She smiled and made her way to them through the old chairs and tables.

"I'm Rayna, do you remember me?"

Nils laughed and said, "You sure look different. You're the accountant, right?"

She laughed and said, "Yes, very funny. But you do remember?"

"Sure I do. This is my wife." He introduced them.

Rayna said, "I'm so glad to meet you. Oh, my God, I love your hair! Where do get it done? You don't have to tell me. Right now, anyway."

In a few minutes the three of them were having lunch together. Philippa said, "Where in the City do you live? Funny I've never seen you."

"Well, actually I live in MarinVillas. But I take the ferry over here as often as I can." Nils could see Philippa thinking, Oh, she's a Helper. Before his wife could react, Rayna went on, "Yeah, I love coming over here. It's a real blast from the past for me. My mother was born here, on Scott Street, and we used to come over to visit my grandparents. They're all gone now."

"Rayna and I met on the sonic to Denver," Nils said, and then turning to Rayna, said, "You look really different. For a minute I thought I didn't know you."

"You only saw me in uniform, you know."

Nils said to Philippa, "I told you about her, didn't I?"

"Well yes, now I'm putting it all together. I understand you're in the same line of work."

"Well, kind of. Same employer, anyway. I'm not a specialist like your husband."

A waiter appeared and they ordered. Everything on the menu was grown or raised within thirty miles of the City, except the wine, which was from the Anderson Valley—deep in MarinHaven. Wine was the only product sold by the Owners. They brought in Guests as needed from one of the Mexican Plantations to do the heavy work. The vintners and wine brokers were Helpers from the Villas. Many city dwellers refused to drink the Owners' wine but Nils saw no reason not to. Outsiders were growing grapes around Carmel, but Nils thought the wine from there wasn't as good.

"I'm glad we ran into you today," Philippa said when the dessert, an apple cobbler, was put in front of them.

"Yeah, it's been fun," Nils said.

"Thank you so much," said Rayna. "I've really enjoyed it too."

"But one thing," Nils said, "when I talked to you last on the phone you sounded almost angry. I thought you were brushing me off."

Rayna laughed. "Oh, I had just gotten some clothes back from the cleaners and there was a big splotch on one of my skirts. Sorry if I was short with you."

Later Nils and Philippa walked up Scott Street.

"Now that was very strange," he said.

"What are you talking about?"

"There are no cleaners at HQ in Denver. That's where we were when I called her."

"Why would she tell you something you knew was a lie?" Philippa asked. Nils didn't answer, and they puffed slowly up the steep hill.

They arrived at their house, and Nils felt the pleasure of flat ground after a climb—his leg muscles relaxed and his breath began to come without effort. They went into the living room and sat down on the rose damask-covered sofa. Philippa wanted to talk more. "There was something a little off about her," she said. "Do you know what I mean?"

"Helpers sometimes feel a little self-conscious around people they can't quite peg."

"I didn't get that. She was curious," she said.

"What's wrong with that?"

"Was it accidental that we ran into her?" Philippa asked.

"Well, we went into that store on a whim," Nils said.

"But we've been there before, often."

"What are you trying to say?" Nils asked.

"I don't know. It just doesn't feel quite right."

"I'm not doing anything important enough to be under surveillance. I hope I never do! So what's the big deal?"

The next few days were tense. They talked about his new assignment for hours but they couldn't come to any plausible conclusion about it. Philippa thought it a promotion but Nils wasn't sure about that.

"Why else would they transfer you from your regular work? There aren't many psychologists who are experts in bioclimatology and you're the best."

"Yes, but maybe I wasn't giving them the answers that they wanted. You know I'm notorious for pushing mitigation," he said.

"Oh, you mean like the air con dormitories you wanted for the Guests?" she asked.

"That's minor. Those papers I published that demonstrate that the death rate among Guests in some of the Plantations has actually been increasing. They don't like that, I'm sure."

"But who doesn't like that? Is it the Owners or the Corps brass?" she asked.

"Probably the brass. For the Owners that's a detail," he said.

"You'd think that the Corps would want the most efficiency in the Plantations."

"They do, but the Owners don't care that much. They think there's an unlimited labor pool Outside, so they argue that it's a waste of money to try to lower the death rate of the Guests. There are too many humans on the earth anyway, but they can't put that in writing, at least not yet."

"God, is this what we've come to? It's easy for the Owners to say that. They don't have to actually see what's going on," she said.

"Hey, let's not talk about it right now. I'm on leave and I want to enjoy it."

"Yes, yes, yes. Forget it. All's for the best in this best of all possible worlds." The phrase always made them laugh and put their worries in some kind of perspective.

Nils departed one quiet morning. They said goodbye at the house, and he took a taxi to the ferry. When he got to MarinHaven, he changed into his uniform and boarded the flight to Denver. His orders were to check into a hotel there and wait for instructions. It took three long days before the packet came. He was to stay "until further orders."

The first week was spent in the usual organizing meetings. Nils had worked on setting up a new Plantation several times before and he knew the drill. Many different specialties were required, and the hardest part at first was planning the sequencing, followed by the coordination of tasks. Getting structural engineers to pay attention to psychologists and everyone to listen to the bioclimatologists was difficult, at best. It all seemed fairly routine except that this time there was an officer from Corps Internal Security present at all of the meetings. Usually they got involved just at the end—they were called in and briefed mostly as a matter of courtesy.

Nils was surprised at the location of the new Plantation. It was to include most of the San Joaquin Valley in California, which had been considered in recent times too hot to support human life. There must be some cost-effective way of mitigating. He knew the valley had been the main source of food for what was once a very large population, but since the collapse of the California Water Project and the increase in temperatures, it had been largely abandoned. Some of it had reverted to marshland, some of it to desert. It was not his job to figure out how to make it productive again—there were other specialists for that.

One day he walked into a room to join a meeting about weather, and there sitting at the table was Rayna. She was wearing the black uniform of Internal Security. Nils couldn't stop himself from doing a double take. She saw it and laughed.

"Gotchya, Nils! It's time for us to meet."

"Hey, you pop up in the strangest places! Are we working together now?" he asked.

"I hope so," she said. She got up and closed the door.

"What—it's just you and me at this meeting?" he asked.

"That's right. And no one knows it."

Nils sat down. "What's this all about?"

"Let's just put it this way. This is the biggest operation you've ever worked on and it is the biggest opportunity you've ever had. If you want to look at it from that perspective."

"I know it's big, I don't need you to tell me," he said.

She looked at him speculatively. "If I tell you something, will you promise not to talk to anyone else about it?" she asked.

He blew up, "What the hell are you talking about? What kind of garbage is that? Do you think I'm an idiot?"

"Okay, Okay. Calm down. I know you signed a confidentiality agreement."

"Yes, and you're going to tell me what you want to tell me, so stop the games or I'll walk out that door."

"I didn't know that you had a temper like that," she said. "I like it."

He laughed, in spite of himself. "Oh, stop it. You're trying to manipulate me for some reason and I don't know why."

"What I'm going to tell you is true. You can do all the digging you want; you will find out that I'm telling you the truth," she said. "Who do you think is going to inhabit the new Plantation?"

"Who? There are people all over the west, Outsiders, who will beg to be allowed to come into a protected place. Filling up a Plantation has never been a problem. There are always more than we can accommodate."

"You were not supposed to know this yet and I'm risking a lot by telling you," she said.

He suddenly noticed how quiet it was in the room. No whirring, no ticking. Silence.

"Nils, the Plantation is being set up to take the population of San Francisco."

CHAPTER SIX

Crossing the Carquinez Straits was easy. One of the two old bridges was still standing and they walked across it. Getting off on the north side was a little tricky—the roadway connecting it to the land had collapsed, but Jack and Gabe clambered down and waded to the other side.

From the bridge they could see a settlement of some kind on the north side of the straits. The streets were dirt, turned to mud in many places, and lined with huts made from the debris of houses that had once stood here. Crude boats littered the shore. Everything smelled of fish.

An old man was sitting in front of his shack mending a net. The boys went to him.

"Hi, I'm Jack and this is my brother Gabe. We're from the City and we're traveling through. Do you know where the train is?"

"The City? I know it's still there. Once in a while I climb up that hill there and look at it. Night's the best. You can see lights there sometimes. Not like the old times, course. The whole damn thing was lit up. But still they got lights you can see clear across the bay."

"Yeah, that's right. But we're wondering about the train. Where is it; how can we find it?"

"Young people here, they think there's magic in the City and that's why there's lights. Damn fools. They never saw no 'lectric lights. I tell 'em but they don't believe me. They think City's fulla demons, eat 'em up if they step foot on the other side o' the straits. They think train's magic too." The man went back to his net and was quiet for a moment.

Jack and Gabe waited, and then they saw people creeping out of the huts and coming toward them. In a moment a small crowd surrounded them. The people were wearing rags, and they smelled foul. Hands started to reach out and touch them. There was a low murmuring coming from them and a smacking sound.

The old man clapped his hands and yelled sharply, "Go back—these are Visitors you dare not touch!" The people retreated and the old man said to them, "Don't know why you want the train. There's nowhere to go no more. Don't know where the train goes anyway. You boys go back to the City—you be safe there."

"Thank you, sir," Jack said, "but we have to go on."

After they had taken a few steps they heard a muttering behind them. They turned back just in time to hear the old man say, "It's north 'bout five miles, just beyond the crest of those hills." He pointed with his elbow.

Soon they were standing on a hillside looking down on the tracks. Suddenly Jack yelled, "Here comes one!" The train was not long, maybe eight cars, and it was going very fast. It flashed out of the west, rushed past them, and whooshed around a hill in a few seconds. "I'm glad we saw it together," Gabe said, "or I wouldn't be sure I really saw it."

"Yeah, it was so fast. I wonder how long it takes to get to Denver," Jack said.

"Hey, what do we do when we get to Denver? How do we go on from there?"

"Don't know. We'll figure it out when we get there."

Gabe took a deep breath. "Feels good out here. I can smell the grass. What I'm wondering is how the hell we get on that train."

"We go east, to Sacramento—that's where Sam got on," Jack said.

They couldn't find a road, but the hills and valleys were covered mostly by knee-high grass that was easy to pass through. Then they climbed a hill to get a better view of where they were going, and they both saw it at the same time. Directly ahead of them was what looked like a gigantic lake dotted with islands, hundreds of them.

"Where did the train go?" Gabe gasped.

"There. Can you see the bridges?" Jack pointed to the trestles that shot through the islands like a single thread through a patchwork quilt.

"So what do we do? Looks like if we try to go around it will take us weeks," Gabe said.

"Oh no. We're going right through. Just like the train."

They descended the steep hill and pushed their way through the grass. It seemed odd that there were no animals, no cows or sheep, but there were no people either. For a moment Jack felt the weirdness of being Outside.

"That old man in the shack. He must have seen a lot in his lifetime," Gabe said.

"Yeah, and look at the village now. They don't have any power at all. Not even electric lights. I bet the kids don't even know how to read."

"I guess they know how to fish though," Gabe said.

They came down to the water about five hundred feet south of the train trestle. They had never seen anything like it before—it wasn't like an ordinary bridge—and when they got to it they were dismayed to see that there was no walkway of any kind.

"We'll have to walk between the tracks," Jack said.

"What if a train comes?"

"We're cooked, I guess."

"Why does that not comfort me?" Gabe said with a laugh. "No, seriously, what do we do?"

"Before we start, we put our ears down on the track. That way you can hear a train coming from miles away," Jack said.

"Sure. Okay. Yeah, I believe that. But what if it comes faster than we know?"

"I have an idea. We'll wait here and listen for the train and we'll time it from when we hear it on the track to when it passes by us," Jack said.

"Good thing I have my watch," Gabe said. His uncle was a watchmaker who could repair the very old mechanical watches that were much in demand in the City. He had given Gabe a Bulova that was more than a hundred and forty years old but still ran perfectly. Battery-powered watches were useless now; there were no batteries sold in the City.

They waited for hours, watching the seagulls soaring idly and the pelicans, flying in formation, as many as fifty in a flock. Once in a while a pelican would dive nose first into the water and disappear for a few minutes. The sun sank slowly behind the hills to the west and the air turned chilly. Still there was no sound of a train.

"Damn, we could have been across a long time ago," Gabe said.

"You were the one who was scared," Jack said.

Jack put his ear down to the track and jumped up, "It's coming!" They climbed down into a thicket of bushes and waited. Soon the train was upon them. It thundered by, a blur, gone in an instant.

"Three minutes from the time you heard it," Gabe said.

"Yikes. Scratch that idea. Let's go right now. There isn't going to be one for a while."

"How do you know that?" Gabe said.

"I don't. I'm guessing."

"Okay, let's go anyway. Maybe you're right."

They clambered up to the trestle and walked across as quickly as they could, trying not to look down between the ties.

They made their way for several days through the strange archipelago, crossing dozens of trestles and encountering no one. They ate twice a day, in the morning and evening, mixing the dried meat and vegetables they carried in their backpacks with water from streams they came upon. They were careful to boil it first. There was plenty of kindling to start fires and dead wood to keep them going. One day they came upon an apple orchard. There were still some red apples on the branches. At night they stretched out their sleeping bags under whatever shelter they could find—any simple protection from the sky. They wouldn't sleep inside the abandoned, moldy buildings.

One day they discovered that they had made it to the other side of what they finally realized was the great Delta.

"Now I understand where we are," Jack said. "All we have to do is follow the river and we'll get to Sacramento. Emily said the train stops there."

"Following the river sounds like a lot of wasted time. What if the river meanders all over?" Gabe asked.

"Oh, I guess you're right. As long as we keep the river on our left, it will take us there."

They walked on, sometimes talking incessantly, then falling into long silences. They had lived their whole lives on the shores of the ocean and now they were going away from it, deeper and deeper inland. The sense of earth in all directions, hard and unchanging, was alien to them. Jack was elated by the strangeness and a little frightened.

The hills had given way to flatness. In the far distance they could make out a line of white crests thrusting above the horizon. Finally, they came to a road. It was paved with some kind of black substance they had never seen and was surprisingly smooth. They walked along it for an hour and were talking when a silent car pulled up to them, the only car on the road, as far as they could tell.

"Hello, boys, do you need a ride?" The driver was a middle-aged woman wearing a uniform of some kind.

Jack and Gabe looked at each other and smiled broadly. Riding in a car was an adventure in itself—they had been inside one only a few times before in their lives.

"Sure, thanks," Jack said. He got into the front seat and Gabe climbed in the back. The seats were covered in dark brown leather and the floor was carpeted in something that might have been wool. Comfortable.

"Don't often see people out here," she said. "My name is Gladys."

"Hi, I'm Jack and this is Gabe."

Gladys looked at Jack and he felt suddenly naked, as if she was looking right into him. She quickly turned back to the wheel and said casually, "You might be wondering what I'm doing out here. I'm here to Translate," she said.

Jack and Gabe looked at each other.

"Yes, my job is to translate the word of God so folks can understand it. That's why we're called the Translation Army."

"You must be a mighty army," Gabe said, "if you can afford a car like this."

"Oh, this belongs to my husband. He's not exactly a believer, but he lets me take it on TA business. I'm coming from a funeral down in Stockton, one of our members. I gave the eulogy. God's blessings to our dear departed and to our Army, may it translate the Word to all who don't understand it. Sad case. A young woman who just didn't make it. Stockton is officially Outside now, and it's getting harder and harder to survive there."

"By the way, where are you going?" Jack asked. He had been so taken by the novelty of getting into a car that he had forgotten to ask.

"Why, Sacramento, of course. The road doesn't go anyplace else. Where are you boys from, you don't look familiar," she said.

"We're from the City," Gabe said.

"Oh, my. That's a long way. I was there once when I was a little girl. My mother took me to the opera. We took the train to Vallejo and a ferry from there. There was an electric bus took us to the opera house. I remember it like yesterday. No ferry there anymore, I know. Actually, no town there anymore, it was abandoned twenty years ago."

"Yeah, and we don't have electric trams anymore," Jack said. "Now they're pulled by horses."

"Well, what are you boys going to Sacramento for?" she asked. "You'll have to state the reason once we get there. But I guess if you can prove you're from San Francisco it's okay anyway. We're not letting in Outsiders anymore. I think it's a shame, but I guess you have to draw the line. To tell the truth, my husband doesn't like me to go Outside. He says it's dangerous and we can't be responsible for everyone in the world. I think we're just lucky to be living in a real Community. What if we had been living in Stockton? It's not like those people are dangerous. Why, they're no different than you and me. It's just that they couldn't figure out how to help each other."

Finally they got to the gates of Sacramento. There were barbwire fences running both north and south and a dozen or so armed guards at the gate. Jack and Gabe had to get out of the car and go into a small shed for questioning.

"I'll wait here for you," Gladys said. She seemed to know most of the guards and they joked with her.

"What are we going to say?" Gabe asked Jack as they got out of the car.

"I don't know. What do you think?"

"Just tell them that you're here to find a wife and I'm looking for a husband."

"Very funny. Let me do this."

A uniformed man looked intently at Jack and Gabe. "What is your purpose in coming to Sacramento?"

Jack had decided there was no reason to conceal the truth. "We want to get on the train. We think it stops here."

"Of course it stops here. So you want to join the Corps." It wasn't a question.

"No, we just want to get on the train."

The guard looked at Jack as if for the first time and said, "Where do you think you're going?"

"Well, first to Denver."

"Yeah, well where else can you go on the train? What are you going to do in Denver?"

"From there we'll figure out how to get to Maine. That's where my father is."

"Where are you staying in Sacramento?"

Jack and Gabe looked at each other. "We don't know yet."

"Alright," the man said, "I'm not letting you enter. You'll have to go back to where you came from." He stood up and motioned for them to leave the shed.

Jack's mind was a blank until he saw Gladys. Somehow he knew what was about to happen. She would walk over to the man in charge of the border crossing and talk to him. He would come to Jack and say, "You boys are going to join the Corps, right?" and then Jack would say, "Yes, sir." At that point they would get into the car and it would drive through the checkpoint. The next few minutes unraveled exactly as he thought.

Soon they were driving along a pleasant street lined with tall elm trees. In the near distance was a pale gold dome, the old state capitol. The houses looked old but well kept. Most had vegetable gardens around them, some elaborate, bordered by flowers. Gladys said, "I've got to go to the church right away and give them the list of people I've seen who need help. You boys come with me."

"We'd like to, but we really want to get on that train," Jack said.

"Don't worry, there's one every day and today's train is gone anyway," she said. "Anyway, we're there already." She pulled up in front of a white church, very plain, and said, "You can wait here. I'll be finished in a few minutes."

They were in downtown Sacramento. There were a few tall old

buildings, obviously abandoned. Most of the structures were two or at most three stories. There were fewer bicycles than in San Francisco and more horses, which Jack thought odd, since the land was so flat. There were some cars and as many horse-drawn buggies. The boys were astonished to see an electric tram slide by on tracks they hadn't noticed.

As Gladys was emerging from the church, Jack and Gabe were standing next to the car, and they heard a booming voice behind them: "Gladys, my little flower, come out from your sanctuary." This came from a heavy man on a massive black horse. There were a few riders behind him.

"I will if you repent, you old horse thief!" she called out merrily.

He got down off his horse and they hugged. "You should meet my new friends. This here's Jack and that one's Gabe," she said. "They're from San Francisco. Boys, meet the governor of California, the honorable Reynaldo Cruz."

At the end of the day Jack and Gabe found themselves sharing a room in the governor's mansion. "I think I can wait a few days for the train," Gabe said, "I just want to sleep in a bed and maybe we'll get some real meals."

"I want to get on that train," Jack said. "Let's see what's going on here."

Later they were directed to a dining room. They joined a small group: two older men and three women. They barely looked up when Jack and Gabe came in and no one said anything. Food was brought in by large women wearing aprons: a big tureen of thick potato and leek soup; a platter of roast beef already sliced into thick pieces; dishes of turnips and carrots; mashed potatoes; hot rolls and fresh butter. The room was warm and steamy and everything smelled delicious.

Jack and Gabe ate quietly. They wanted to exclaim about the beef. It was a rare luxury in the City. When it was served they would get a few tiny pieces, just for the taste, the way they ate chocolate. Never had they imagined large pieces of meat for each person. It seemed wildly extravagant. But they didn't speak; they couldn't figure out how to break the silence that blanketed the table.

That night as they climbed into their beds, Gabe said, "This is really nice. I could get used to it."

"Well, don't, because it's not going to last," Jack said, "and I wonder who those people were. Not a very friendly bunch."

"Yeah, they didn't talk to us, but they didn't talk to each other either," Gabe said.

The next morning, early, Jack opened his eyes and saw their door knob turn. A small, bald man came in and said in a loud voice, "Wake up, boys, the governor wants to see you."

They scrambled to get dressed and were led down to a large room that was lined with bookshelves. Hundreds and hundreds of books—a dazzling display of wealth.

Cruz invited them to sit down. A woman carried in a large tray with coffee and cream and sugar and toast and butter. When she left, it was just Jack and Gabe and the governor. Cruz asked them some questions about their journey, and he laughed heartily when they described walking across the train trestles, but he seemed most interested in hearing about San Francisco. He questioned Jack closely about the near riot at the water truck. And he asked about their plans.

"Yes, you can get on the train here and go to Denver, I can arrange it. But what are you going to do when you get there? It's a Corps town, you know."

"We're going to Maine, to find my father," Jack said.

"Maine. You know there's a lot of weather between here and there. The people aren't what you're used to. Do you know what Outsiders are? I don't think you have any idea how dangerous the trip could be unless you've got somebody protecting you. Are you going to stay there?" Cruz asked.

"No," Jack said. "I need to find my father but the City's home; we belong there and we'll go back. If we can get to Maine, we should be able to figure out how to get home."

Cruz had honed in on the conversation but now he seemed to become distracted, thinking about something else. He looked out the window. The room was quiet for a few moments. Jack was slightly alarmed, although he had no idea why. Cruz turned toward them, once again engaged.

"What do you boys know about the Owners?" he asked.

Jack told him about the incident on Valencia Street, the families being herded through the streets. He didn't attempt to keep the anger out of his voice. Gabe nodded, his face drawn.

"We don't know who those people were or where they were going," Jack said.

"I can tell you that. They were once residents of a town called Gilroy, which is now Outside. They sold themselves to the Owners, who were taking them to MarinHaven for air transport to a Plantation in Mexico."

"So you knew about that?" Jack asked. "Why didn't you stop it!"

Cruz looked at Jack. "Those people were starving and they decided to go for the safety of a Plantation. It was their decision. The Owners gave them an opportunity to survive and they took it."

Jack stood up and said, "Thanks for your hospitality, Governor, we have to go now."

"Sit down," Cruz said, "we're not finished yet."

CHAPTER SEVEN

Nils was drifting—it was bright morning, lilacs arched over the bed, Philippa asleep, her slender body spooned next to him. He was hard but he didn't want to wake her. Then he was in a high tunnel, no, that was wrong, it was an iron space into which many tunnels debouched. If he was hyper-vigilant he could avoid the cars and trains that were coming at him from all sides. He used to know the way out but now he couldn't remember, he couldn't remember.

He woke up and looked around him at the room he had slept in forever—for two months now. It was all gray and beige and on the walls were watercolors of the mountains that he could see out the window. Now, it was time to shower, shave, put on his uniform, and drink some coffee. Then he would go to an office, make some phone calls, attend meetings. Plan the apocalypse.

It's going to be alright, he told himself. They won't really go through with this. It's just too big, too complicated. They'll realize they bit off more than they can chew. At some point someone will tell them that the whole idea is crazy. Why do the Owners need San Francisco, anyway? They already have the choicest lands. It's not worth the money and energy needed to do it.

All this he told Rayna, one day at lunch in the officers' cafeteria.

"There are some people in the Corps who want it," she said, between bites of her sandwich. "They think they'd be able to move the headquarters there. There aren't a lot of places outside the Havens where you don't have to live underground at least part of the year."

"But would we really want the headquarters to be in an Owners' city? Right under their thumb?" He ate the last morsel of his banana cream pie, a treat he rarely indulged in.

She gave him a look he couldn't interpret and laughed lightly. "Oh, there are great plans for the City."

She went on to explain what was being prepared for San Francisco. The Owners wanted a completely new city, so all the old Victorian houses would be demolished along with almost everything built before 2080. Instead of small houses and apartment buildings, there would be great estates on the hilltops, palaces surrounded by dependent buildings. The small shops selling homespun goods made locally would be razed and there would be one huge mall that would sell only products manufactured by the Great Companies.

Only Owners and senior Corps officers would live in the City. Helpers would commute from MarinVillas for day jobs. Either Protrero Hill or Bernal Heights would be reserved for Corps officers and their families, who would be free to go almost anywhere in the City. Nils could commute to his work on the new San Joaquin Plantation, and he would no longer have to conceal his true identity.

"The Owners will finally have their own capital," Rayna said, "which will be called New Frisco."

"Do you buy that bullshit? How could you? And why choose me for this? I'm the Corps bleeding heart, everyone knows that." He asked Rayna, "Why did they select me for this project?"

"You probably know that better than anyone."

Nils felt a flash of anger and said, "I guess I'm the dumb one then, because I have no idea what you're talking about."

She picked up her glass and took a sip of her dark beer. "Oh, well, it's probably because you know the city people better than any other Corps psychologist who is available. This could be a lucky career move, you know."

"The fact that this is, uh, different than anything we've done before…what do you think of that?"

"What do you think of it?" she asked. "Some people here are saying what's the point in questioning what we're told to do? We'll have to do it anyway. And maybe it'll ultimately be to our advantage."

"Is that right?" he asked. "I've got a busy day, so if you don't have anything else to tell me, I'm going back to my office."

"Nils, you've got a meeting with your bosses in an hour."

"What? No one told me about it."

"I'm telling you about it. The chief wants to meet with you."

They left together and Rayna took him to one of the Internal Security meeting rooms. The empty room was not large, and it had a square table in the middle big enough to seat perhaps ten people. There were no wall images and it felt claustrophobic. She sat next to him and they waited. She flipped a switch on the table and the walls began to vibrate softly.

"Where do you want to be?" she asked.

"Home. San Francisco," he said.

"I can't get it that specific. Generic—tropics, arctic, mountain top, that kind of thing."

"Okay. Let's be on a ship in the middle of the ocean." She waved a small arc and described a square with her left hand and the walls dissolved as if they were being washed away to reveal the scene outside, the ocean on two sides. They were on the deck of a large ocean liner of a hundred and fifty years ago. Behind the railing was only sky. Then the "ship" rolled and behind the rail was only ocean. Up to sky again. Then down to ocean. He could almost feel the ship pitching, down in front, then up again. "You're sure you want this, Nils? I think I might get seasick," Rayna said.

"Ok," Nils laughed, "just do the tropics."

Nils relaxed a little, pretending to himself that he was somewhere else, back in college, waiting for a class to begin, in an airport waiting room, on his way home. An hour later, the others arrived. Nils was introduced to the chief of Internal Security of the Corps, Colonel Douglas Hastings, and two captains.

Hastings told one captain to run the meeting. "What's on the agenda today?" Hastings asked. An aide read from a paper, "Preparation for Project Moses. The purpose of this meeting is to interview Major Radovic about the psychological challenges of phase one."

"Oh, that's right. Now I remember—you're the one who lives in San Francisco, aren't you? That's convenient. Here's the problem, Radovic. How do we get those people to move voluntarily to the new Plantation?"

"My name is Rakovic, Colonel. I don't have a magic bullet for you. My past work has been done in situations where people from the Outside have been most eager to get into a Plantation. Even for them, it's a hard adjustment. I don't see what we can do to convince citizens of a viable city to leave."

"Obviously, Major," Hastings said, "it will take preparation. Let's assume that the City is no longer viable, what then?" Nils suddenly realized that his collar was chafing his neck. It was too tight, but he didn't want to loosen it. He remembered that he should get his dress-black shoes repaired by Jerry McCarty down on Chestnut Street. Jerry's mother had just celebrated her ninetieth birthday and was doing poorly. Her neighbors made sure she was well taken care of when Jerry was at work.

Nils took a breath and tried his best to be calm. "There are many examples of depopulation of non-viable cities. Miami is the classic example. Of course, that was extreme, but there are a lot of others,

New York, Atlanta, Dallas-Fort Worth, Houston, St. Louis, Kansas City, and the list goes on and on. And that's just North America. But those were places where the combination of floods, drought, and extreme weather—and the lack of local resilience—made the landscape impossible for humans. In most of those places, the population scattered, and we're not sure what happened to them. Most of them died, probably. San Francisco is one of the four or five thriving cities left."

"What do you mean by 'resilience,' Major?" one of the captains asked.

"That's the ability of a community to take care of its basic needs."

"That's ridiculous," Hastings said. "The Great Companies are there to take care of people's needs. What has that got to do with the viability of a city? Okay, since you're having a hard time understanding, let me try it another way. Let's just assume for a minute that the City's entire population has been moved to the new Plantation in the Central Valley. What do we do to keep them relatively docile?"

Nils hesitated for a moment. He was flushed with anger, but he had to be tactful. "I'm not sure it will be possible to keep them there. I think many of them will drift back to the City. After all, it isn't that far away."

"Oh no, Major," Hastings said, "you don't understand. There will be no leaving this Plantation. Once put there, the Guests will stay. The electrified fences are already being constructed. Luckily, there's lots of solar in the Valley." The officers chuckled.

"This is a different model than what you've been used to, but times change. We are hoping that this new Plantation will provide just about everything needed in the expanded MarinHaven, so these people will continue to have social utility and we will need to make sure they stay put."

"But the Plantations are places for workers. The population of San Francisco is made up of children and old people and disabled people, too. Not everyone can work," Nils said.

"We're taking that into account."

"May I ask what the plans are for the non-workers? That will have a lot to do with my work."

"Nothing is specific yet. But, as I just said, they should be useful."

"I'm sure you'll understand that I would like to consult with my colleagues and report to my supervisor, the Chief of Behavioral Sciences of the Corps, before I go any farther with this," Nils said.

"I don't think you understand, Major. You have been transferred to Internal Security. You may not discuss this project with anyone outside your new chain of command. That means anyone not in this room. You will draw up a plan to convince the troits to cooperate with—or at least not resist—their move to the Plantation and also a plan to make their transition understandable to themselves." The colonel got up and everyone in the room rose to their feet. "Oh, and include a section on the non-working population, explain where they went. You'll have to make that up—maybe we'll get some ideas from you. Have it on my desk in two weeks." He walked out the door with his entourage.

Nils sat down and looked at Rayna, although he didn't really see her. His eyes refused to focus and his mind was adrift. Hastings used that demeaning word "troit" to refer to citizens of San Francisco.

I wish I was in bed on Jackson Street, watching Philippa at her dressing table, brushing her hair and complaining about the latest symphony benefit. Then he noticed Rayna and felt a sudden surge of lust for her. Where did that come from? Fear, yes, fear. Is this really happening?

"Nils, Nils?" Rayna said softly. "I was told that you can go back home and write your report from there. You can catch the next sonic, if you like."

He went back to his room and threw together his things and took the shuttle to the airport. He went to the gate and flashed his badge. He knew there would be a seat for him on the plane; there were always lots of empty seats. He wasn't surprised to see Rayna walking down the aisle. She sat down next to him.

"How much of this did you know?" he asked.

"Pretty much all of it. There is more."

"What more?"

"I'm not supposed to tell you. I don't think you want to know," she said.

"Were you supposed to tell me that there was more?"

"No."

"Are you on board with this plan?"

"What do you mean?" she asked.

"I mean do you think the Corps should be doing this?"

She paused for a few moments and Nils waited patiently.

"I wouldn't attempt to answer that. It's above my pay grade," she said.

"Why are you the one to shadow me, and why was I chosen for this job?"

"Nils, try to be patient. I know it's hard right now, but just hold on. Take one step at a time and we'll see what happens."

"Why have you told me things that you weren't supposed to tell me?" Nils asked.

She turned toward him with a faintly mischievous smile that he found infuriating. "Is this just a game for you?" he asked.

"No. I can assure you that this is deadly serious."

As they were landing at Ellison Airport in MarinHaven, Rayna turned to Nils and said softly, "I'm coming to talk to you in a few days." She had spoken very softly and he wasn't even sure he had heard her right.

When he finally got home it was night and the lights were on in the Jackson Street house. What a stupid arrangement, he thought, having to take a ferry to Berkeley and then another one to the City. Why couldn't there be direct transport to the City? Oh, yes, there will be soon. But it won't be San Francisco anymore. It will be a rich man's theme park. No, it can't happen.

A lot had changed in the two months that he was gone, Philippa told him. "The water shut off was the last straw, I guess."

"Phil, let's just go to bed," he said. "We'll have plenty of time to talk later."

The two months apart melted away when they touched and they found each other easily, quickly. Nils had a few blessed moments for which he was deeply grateful. He slept deeply and had no dreams. In the morning, sitting in the study, a white-plastered room lined with bookshelves, he said, "Honey, we have to talk."

Philippa poured coffee into two ceramic mugs she had made

herself. They were glazed sky blue on the outside and white inside. She wouldn't drink from a mug that was dark inside.

"I don't know how much you heard in Denver," she said, "but people here are getting pretty fed up. They want the water turned back on, and they're after the mayor and the Board of Supervisors. I think it's great. Finally we're getting some backbone. Thank goodness we have an election coming up," she said. "And we've got a great candidate for mayor. You know John Johnston, don't you? He's tough and he hates the Owners."

"Honey, I have to tell you something," he said.

After he was finished, Philippa stared into the fireplace. It was a luxury to have logs hauled up to their house, but they would have given up a lot of other luxuries before they'd give up this one.

"This doesn't really surprise me. I always kind of thought in the back of my mind they'd come after us someday."

"You absolutely can't let anyone know I told you about this, you know that?" Nils said.

"Don't condescend, Nils. I understand the risk you're running. Still, we've got to find a way of spreading the alarm. And what about Rayna—is she going along with all this?"

"She says that we have to follow orders. But then she tells me things and gives me hints that make me wonder where she's really at. I think she said she'd come and see us soon, but I'm not sure. I don't know why, either." Nils got up and started to pace around the room. "Maybe we should have moved to the Villas a long time ago. It's limited, but at least it's safe."

"Sure, we could escape, but think of our friends, our community. How could we live with ourselves knowing what is going to happen to them?" she asked.

"We don't know, not for sure. I still can't believe it will happen."

"Listen, whatever we do, if the Owners take over the City, it's back to square one for us. It'll be like in the Havens. I know the Owners. I know what they're capable of."

"I just don't understand this. Why are they doing it? They already have more land than they know what to do with."

"Nils, try to look deeper. What is it about? I'll tell you—this isn't just an attack on our City, it's an attack on our whole way of life. In this terrible world there are two paths to the future. Either the rich take everything for themselves or ordinary people work together and we help each other. San Francisco is a community, and that's what those fuckers want to destroy."

"Phil, what can we do? What can I do? I'm right in the belly of the beast!"

"Nils, take it day by day. At the very least you can pass on information to me. We're in this together, sweetheart. I made my choice when I married you, and I've never for one minute regretted it. We'll find a way to fight. The Owners will not have our City."

The next few days were hell. Nils tried to write his report. He gave it the title, "Psychological Assessment of San Francisco's Residents: Toward a Persuasive Model," trying to be as bland and neutral as possible. He questioned himself for writing "residents" instead of "citizens," but he knew that the latter word raised hackles among the Owners. Who knew who would read his report?

One day there was a knock at the door. Nils opened it and there was Rayna, wearing her Corps uniform. He let her in quickly. "Why are you wearing that here?" he asked.

"Didn't you hear? The City has relaxed its rules and we can wear our uniforms in public now."

"No, I haven't heard. But you must have gotten a lot of dirty looks on the street."

"I haven't been on the street. I took a taxi directly here from the ferry."

"I can't believe you came to my house in broad daylight wearing the uniform! Who knows who saw you?"

"It's getting very late for all those niceties, Nils. Please get Philippa. I need to talk to both of you."

Philippa greeted Rayna frostily and Nils led them into the bright living room, and they sat down around a large coffee table.

Rayna started, "I know that Nils has told you everything," she said to Philippa, "and I'm sure you're upset. That's natural."

Philippa interrupted her, "Why are you here? Have you just come to tell us what we already know?"

"That wouldn't make sense. No, I'm here to tell you that nothing is inevitable. And that Nils could make a big difference in what happens, for reasons I can't explain."

Nils felt anger rising, "Again you're talking in riddles. Damn it, I want to know what is going on!"

"I can't tell you yet. I hope that I will be able to at some point. Keep what I just said in mind. There is more."

Philippa got up and moved to the kitchen. "What do you want to drink, Rayna? And Nils, what do you want?"

"Do you have any beer?" Rayna asked, "Something amber?" Nils asked for red wine. Philippa brought the bottles in and put them down on the table. There was a moment of quiet as she poured the wine and beer. Rayna looked around the room, frankly curious.

"What a beautiful view you've got. You can see right into MarinHaven. Look, there's the Bush Tower just in front of Mt. Tam. I never understood why they put a forty-story building right there, just where it blocks the view, until I was in one of the apartments. They have the view, from inside. You have to hand it to the Owners; they know how to maximize the value of an asset."

"Rayna, I don't think I can bear small talk at this point," Philippa said.

"Oh, sure. Sorry if I'm rambling. It's been a while since I've been in someone's house here in the City, since my grandma died, and it makes me go all mushy."

"Please, please get to the point," Nils said, "and tell us what you came here to tell us."

"The fact that I'm here at all should tell you something. That we're talking freely—that should tell you something. You know, the Corps is not a monolithic structure. It has lots of cracks and fissures. Currents and cross currents."

"Stop it! How dare you play with us," Philippa said.

Rayna replied, "I'm sorry. I don't mean to do that. I'm going to tell you what I know."

CHAPTER EIGHT

"Why should we leave Sacramento right now?" Gabe asked. "The governor told us we could stay here as long as we want. It could be fun."

"What are we going to do here?"

"Eat," Gabe said with a laugh.

"Yeah, right. Listen, we have to go to Denver first and then figure out how to keep going. That could take time. We have to get to the East Coast before summer starts," Jack said.

"Hey, don't stress. I'm with you, bro. I want to go too."

They were riding horses down D Street toward the old town. The governor had lent them two mares from his stable, one gray and one black, and told them to take a look around town. Like most San Franciscans, they had learned how to ride as children—it was a skill as essential as riding a bicycle. Gabe loved horses and was a natural rider. Jack merely tolerated them.

"Let's go to the train station. Maybe we'll be able to see a train stop," Jack said. They rode over to a young woman on a bicycle who had stopped for cross traffic. She looked at them and said, "What are you boys doing on the governor's horses?"

"How did you know?" Jack asked.

"I know them all. I ride them too. He's my uncle," she said. "You know these ladies like to walk. You're not going to get them to canter."

"Doesn't matter," Jack said, "we're not going to be here very long. We're trying to find the train station. We're going east."

"You're going up to the mountains? Why—is there construction work up there?"

"No, we're going to the East Coast, to Maine," Jack said.

"That's impossible. The only way to get there is to fly, and you boys don't look like the flying kind."

"How do you know it's impossible?" Jack asked.

"Everybody knows it."

"We're going to Denver," Gabe said. "Does everybody think we can't do that?" Jack smiled.

"Denver. So you're going to join the Corps."

"Why does everyone say that?"

"Why else would you go there? You can tell me; I won't say you're traitors. If you ask me, it's a pretty smart thing to do. It's a lot more interesting than hanging around this place. I'm Harmony Cruz, by the way. The train station is over there. Only a few blocks." She pointed north.

They dismounted and led their horses along with her for a while, and then she turned to them and said, "Come over to my house after dinner. The folks'll like to hear about the City and how you got here. Here's the address. Nine o'clock." She looked in her leather backpack and pulled out a small engraved card.

"How did you know we're from San Francisco?" Jack asked.

"Your arrival was big news around here. Sacramento's a quiet town." She got back on her bike and rode away without another word.

"I hate to say it, but she was very cute," Jack said.

"Yeah. Your type, small and dark, right?"

"But I wouldn't want to get too close to her, you know what I mean?"

"Eat you alive kind of thing?" Gabe said.

"Pretty much."

"Well then maybe we should join the Corps," Gabe said.

"Very funny."

That night they knocked on the door of a very large Victorian house set back from the street and framed by live oak trees. Harmony led them to a room that was heavy with furniture: sofas and loveseats, tables of inlaid wood, and chairs with ball feet gripped by claws. The walls were orange and magenta and covered with paintings of men and women of the nineteenth and twentieth centuries. There was a large fireplace and a roaring fire.

A tall man with a shock of gray hair held his hand out to the boys. "I'm Greg Cruz, Harmony's told me about you. Welcome. I'm sorry my wife can't be here tonight. Would you like a drink?"

They sat down in front of the fire with their drinks and Cruz started to talk. Jack was surprised by his voice; it was a youthful tenor. He looked and sounded very different from his brother, the governor. He asked Jack and Gabe detailed questions about their trip to Sacramento and also about their lives in San Francisco. They told him what they ate for breakfast and what animals Gabe's father had. He wanted to know what people thought about the mayor.

Cruz fell silent for a moment and then said, "I know my brother told you that something is going on in the Central Valley. The Corps is building something. We need to find out what it is, what its purpose is. It's very large, more than a hundred square miles. We have an offer for you. If you agree to help us, we'll make sure you get to Denver by train and from there to Maine. And back, if you want."

"You can do that?" asked Jack.

"We'll have to get you on the Data Base so you can fly, and, yes, we will do that when we get the information."

"What do you want us to do?"

"Find out what this project is for. Who's in charge. Why there, why now."

"How are we supposed to do that?"

"That's up to you. Denver's a wide open town. If you go to the right places, you meet the right people. No one's going to suspect you of trying to get information."

"How do we know what the right places are?"

"Just keep your eyes and ears open; you'll find them—or they'll find you."

"Why don't you or your brother just go and ask the Corps directly?"

"We have asked them. They told us it was to be a training facility. We don't believe that."

"Maybe it's true. Why would the Corps lie to you?"

"What do you know about the Corps?" Cruz replied.

"Not much. Except that they can travel anywhere."

"Yes, but they do a lot more than that. They supply most of the Havens with food and they protect the Owners."

"Protect them? From what?" Jack asked.

"From you; from us; from what is left of the United States of America and the state of California—from Outside. The Corps started out as a private security firm that grew and grew until it became an army. Did you know that we once had an army? Yes, and a navy, and air force. They really existed. Until there was no money left to keep them going. My grandfather was a colonel in the U.S. Army; he was one of the last to graduate from the real West Point."

"West Point. I think I've heard the name," Jack said. "What is it?"

"It used to be a military academy but now it belongs to the Corps, and that's where they train their officers."

"Mr. Cruz, how do you know about all this?" Jack asked.

"Well, Jack, we do business with the Owners. We go to MarinHaven all the time."

Jack looked into the fire. He was feeling overwhelmed and confused. Was this real information or stories made up for some purpose he couldn't fathom? Cruz seemed sincere, but little warning bells were going off in Jack's mind. None of it could be verified, *everyone a reporter,* but then somehow it all did make a kind of sense.

"How long would we have to stay in Denver?" Jack asked.

"We hope until you get the information. We can't keep you there if you decide to try to move on before you find out, but we won't be able to help you if we don't get anything from you."

"We've got to get across before the heat starts," Jack said.

"Yes, of course. And we want the information as soon as possible."

"Can we think about it for a few days?" Jack asked.

"We need your answer by tomorrow."

"What if we say no?"

"That's up to you. We'll part friends. But you'll be on your own."

"We've been on our own ever since we left home," Jack said.

"Lucky for you you've been in friendly territory," Cruz said.

An hour later, Jack and Gabe were walking back to the governor's house, happy to be outdoors and not in a hurry. "All I want to do is go see my father," Jack said.

"The father who did nothing for you your whole life."

"Yeah, well, he's still my only family besides you. I need to see him."

"I sure like the idea of flying. That would be something to tell the folks back home!"

They laughed and for a moment felt homesick. Back in their room at the governor's house they found themselves still confused and uncertain about what to do.

"Let's pray," Gabe said.

"Why not, can't hurt," Jack replied.

They sat in the lotus position facing west, put their hands together, and prayed as they had been taught as children: "Dear Mother, please grant me wisdom and compassion and guide me to heal the earth. Keep me through the storm to awaken in the light. Lead me to speak the truth."

And then Jack added, "Please, dear Mother, help us decide what to do."

"Amen," Gabe said.

The next morning Gabe woke Jack up and said, "Hey, bro, can we talk about this thing?"

Jack was instantly alert. "Sure, Gabe. We don't have to do it, you know. We can get on the train and go to Denver and take our chances from there. Maybe that makes a lot more sense anyway."

"No, that's not what I was thinking. I think we should try to find out what the gov wants. I think it'll be fun. Maybe we'll meet some interesting guys from the Corps."

Jack laughed. "What a one track mind you've got! The whole thing seems kind of crazy to me and it's like a diversion for us."

"No, I think we'll learn a lot if we stay in Denver for a little while. It's a big world out there and we don't know anything about it."

"Look, how about this—we can agree for now and when we get to Denver, we'll decide what we're really going to do. That way we at least get some help getting on the train. As long as we leave Denver well before summer, I don't mind checking it out. Give me a few minutes to think."

Half an hour later they were summoned to talk to the governor, who said, "My brother told me about the conversation last night. Have you made a decision yet?"

"Yes, we have," said Jack.

"Well, what's it to be?"

"We want to do it. Yes. We're on." Jack said. He looked over at Gabe, who nodded.

The governor smiled broadly and then called for his assistant, a tall woman with long, brown hair. "Joyce, clear my calendar for today. Call my brother and tell him to get over here right away. Tell Rafael we need him here now." He turned to the boys. "We're going to prepare you for this trip and it will take a while. Go pack your things and come back here as soon as you can. We can get you on the seven p.m. train, I think."

An hour later they were all gathered in the governor's study. Greg Cruz began with a geography lesson. He talked about the great Central Valley and how it used to be the breadbasket of the world. The soil was good, the growing season year round, endless sunshine, and although water had to be brought in, it wasn't far away, in the Sierra Nevada Mountains. There was once a huge water project, a series of reservoirs and canals, that allowed the whole valley to be irrigated, but when everyone stopped paying taxes, the water project fell apart and farming became impossible there. The Sierra water began to flow again, in the forties, but then it was redirected to MarinHaven.

There was still enough water left in the mountains to irrigate at least part of the Valley but there was no longer any reason for large-scale production. Food grown in the Valley used to go all over the country, but that was not possible anymore—the highway system had decayed into uselessness as the federal government withered. The Corps had its system of trains, which went everywhere in North America, but it was only for the Great Companies and Corps business.

"How big is the Corps? We never saw it in the City," Gabe asked.

"Their policy is to stay out of sight of the city dwellers—you won't see the Corps here in Sacramento either. They're here but they never wear their uniforms in a community. Don't know how many people are in the Corps, but it has to be a lot, my guess is at least a few hundred thousand. The Corps is the only really organized force Outside; they run thousands of farms and factories that they call Plantations."

"Greg, let's get to the point now," the governor said.

"Sure. You are going to Denver, where the Corps has its headquarters. It's officially a community like San Francisco, but unofficially it's totally dominated by the Corps."

"The Corps chose Denver because of its elevation; it doesn't have the killer heat waves that made the continental interior a living hell. Also, there's a kind of underground city not too far away that had been carved into the Rocky Mountains by the old government. The Corps uses that for some of its operations.

'There's no love lost between the locals and the Corps. Okay, fact is they hate each other. Everyone will assume that you've gone there to join the Corps, so that's the side they'll think you're on. They'll also assume that you're Outsiders. Not many people from communities join the Corps, obviously. Let them think that—do not tell anyone who you are and where you're from. That's really important, boys, so don't forget it."

The governor said, "Sure, let them think you're intending to join the Corps, it'll be a lot easier if they can stereotype you. Just don't actually do it, because if you join the Corps, you belong to them. Don't think you can walk away from the Corps. They pursue deserters, even in the cities."

Gabe was sitting near a wall of bookshelves. Jack saw him turn away from the conversation and start looking at the titles. Jack felt a stab of anger for a moment. He was always the older brother, the one who ultimately made the decisions—alright, but at least Gabe could pay attention to what was going on.

"What if we can't find out anything about what they're doing in the Valley?" Jack asked.

"Our deal is for information. If you don't have any, you're on your own from that point. But if you do give us useful information, we'll make sure you get on the Data Base and on a sonic to Maine. And one back to MarinHaven whenever you want to go."

"Data Base—what's that?" Gabe asked, turning around. He had been listening after all.

"The only people that matter now—outside of communities like your little City—are people on the Data Base. All the Owners and everyone in the Corps. There are a few others on the Data Base, usually officials from the old governments and some of their relatives. Oh, yeah, there are some rich Outsiders on it too," Cruz said.

"Hey, the planes land in the Havens. We can't go there," Jack said.

"Part of the ticket is a short-term visa for the Havens. Every airport has ground transportation to the border."

"Okay, let's say we get some information. How do we tell you?"

"I'm going to give you a phone, the kind Owners have. A few of us have them too," the governor said. "When you have something to tell us, call this number and ask for Uncle Ray. Tell them exactly where you are. Whoever answers will say that he's not there but will call back. He won't call back. Someone will come to you and will tell you that we sent him. You should tell him what you have learned. He will help you the rest of the way."

A few hours later they were on a train that was traveling so fast that outside was just a blur. Inside was comfortable but sterile, everything made by machines, no seams, nothing touched by a human hand, a world Jack found slightly frightening. It was a shock to see people wearing the Corps uniform. Few people were talking; most of them had on dark glasses and seemed preoccupied; a few were wearing some kind of light helmet that covered their eyes and mouth. Many of them were gesturing or moving their hands. They looked like sleepwalkers. Jack felt like he and Gabe were the only ones actually present. He was a little disappointed but also relieved. No one paid any attention to them, and they didn't have to answer any questions.

Gabe said, "Let's walk around. There must be something else to see."

"Alright. But remember we're Outsiders."

They got up and walked down the aisle going toward the front of the train. They passed through a car with rows of seats all facing forward, then they went through a car that had a narrow corridor with windows on one side and doors on the other side. When they opened the doors to the next car they were pleasantly surprised. People were sitting at tables and chairs and talking to each other. Not all of them were in uniform.

They sat down at an open table by a window, and immediately a squat robot holding a tray glided up to them. "What will you have, gentlemen?" the robot said in a pleasant, high voice, cocking its head in a questioning posture. They asked for coffee and were amazed as two cups appeared out of the tray while the robot poured the hot steaming liquid directly from two fingers of its free hand. "Cream and sugar, gentlemen?" the robot asked. Jack and Gabe broke into nervous laughter; they couldn't help themselves, it was all so strange. Gabe said, "Do you see those two girls over there? They're watching us."

Two young women were sitting at a corner table drinking something green in tall glasses. They were wearing smooth, cotton dresses, one iridescent green, the other pink, and shoes in blue and yellow. One of them got up and walked over and introduced herself. In a few minutes they were all sitting together.

"What are you going to do when you get to Denver?" Cecilia, the tall blonde, asked.

"Look around. Figure out what comes next, I guess," Jack said.

"I bet I know what you're going to do!" she said. "You're going to join the Corps. I know it."

"You don't know it. There are other things they can do, I'm sure. They don't have to join the Corps," said Alfreda, a short, dark-haired girl.

"What's wrong with joining the Corps?" Jack asked.

"It all depends on where they send you. Mostly it's to a Plantation, and some of them are horrible. That's what I've heard, anyway," Alfreda said.

"What are these Plantations?" Jack asked.

The girls looked at each other and then Cecilia said, "Where are you boys from, anyway?"

"Carmel Valley," Jack said quickly, "our families farm there. We sell to the City when we can."

"Oh, so you're Outsiders. How exciting! What's it like there?"

Gabe said, "It's so horrible, you wouldn't believe it. The crocodiles eat little babies but the worst is the dinosaurs."

Jack laughed and the girls looked puzzled.

"I don't believe that. But, really, is it dangerous?" Alfreda asked.

"What's it like where you live?" Jack asked.

"We live in MarinHaven. It's haven on earth," she said, and both girls giggled. "Seriously, it's nice. You should come and visit some time."

"Very funny. You know we can't go there," Jack said.

"You can get a day pass if you get a personal invitation," Cecilia said. "We've had Outsiders before."

"Hey, we're going in the opposite direction," Gabe said. "And what are you two doing in Denver?"

"We're visiting Cecilia's fiancé. Usually we fly but we thought it would be fun to take the train this time," Alfreda said.

"Have you ever been to the East Coast?" Jack asked.

"Sure, we have family in MaineHaven. We go there every summer. It's hot but the ocean is the perfect temperature to swim in, and of course everything is air conditioned," Cecilia said.

Jack didn't know what she meant by "air conditioned" but he let it pass. "My father lives near there," Jack said.

"You mean Outside?" she asked.

"He's not an Owner, so where else would he live?" Jack said.

"I'm sorry. Of course. That's fine. Yes, nothing wrong with being an Outsider," Cecilia said.

"You sure?" Gabe asked.

There was an uncomfortable silence for a moment and then Jack said, "What is there to do in Denver?"

"One thing is they have movie theaters there, and they're a lot of fun. At home everyone has their own screening room, but it's not the same as watching in a big place with a lot of strangers."

"Can anyone go?" he asked.

"Sure. The movie theatres belong to the Corps. They put them on mainly for the city dwellers, but everyone goes. That's why it's so much fun," Alfreda said.

The robot came up to them and offered more drinks and said, "Last call, ladies and gentlemen. We're closing for the night, and we'll be arriving in Denver first thing in the morning."

CHAPTER NINE

The sun was falling behind the Golden Gate Bridge, and the living room had become dim. Nils suddenly realized that he had not moved a muscle for a long time. Rayna was doing most of the talking.

"There are people at the highest levels of the Corps who are against the Owners attacking San Francisco; they think it's a misuse of the Corps."

"But then why is it happening?" Nils asked.

"Because there are others in the Corps who want to please the Owners; they think that when San Francisco is taken, they'll become Owners themselves."

"I know that's a delusion—no one 'becomes' an Owner these days, you have to be born into it," Nils said. "But that's what everyone wants, isn't it?"

"Not everyone," Philippa said.

"Yeah, well us ordinary mortals aren't familiar with how the Owners work," Rayna said. "Listen, I'll try to be as clear as I can. Colonel Hastings and the Internal Security Branch are supposed to report to the Central Corps Command. Internal Security proposed the take-over of San Francisco and were told to drop the plan. Colonel Hastings ignored his orders and went ahead with it anyway. Hastings is taking his orders from an Owner, someone so powerful that the Corps command can't overrule him directly."

"What Owner, who is it?" Philippa asked, her voice sharp.

"I think you know the answer to that," Rayna said.

"Why don't you just tell me?" Philippa snapped back.

There was silence in the room for a moment. Nils looked from one woman to the other, feeling very stupid.

"How do you know all this?" he asked.

"I can't tell you that. But I can assure you that what I'm saying is true."

"Why are you telling me this now?"

"I think you know the answer to that," Rayna said to him.

Nils groaned, "No I don't! What the hell do you want from me? And why didn't you tell me this before?"

"You weren't ready to know," Rayna said. She put down her glass and stood up. "Look, now you know the backstory, and I hope that will help you."

"Rayna, what should I be doing?"

"If your report is incomplete, you'll have to take more time with it. You know, time is a good thing. The more time it takes to understand this project, the better. It takes some creativity on your part, but you've got the reputation as a kind of perfectionist anyway. Don't fight it. Make sure every detail is nailed down, even if it drags on and on."

"Are you telling me that the Corps is not going to invade San Francisco if I don't finish my report?"

"I can't say that, but I can say that your report is necessary to the process. No one knows how all this will play out at this point."

Philippa turned the lights on bright. "How do we know we can trust you?" she asked. "I don't think you're telling us everything you know." She and Nils stood up and faced Rayna.

"It doesn't matter what I know," Rayna said. "I'm on your side, and all I'm telling you is that Nils just has to seem like he's doing his job, and you both should keep your eyes and ears open. A moment may come when you have to do something. I may come back and talk to you again. Or I may not. Maybe someone else will come to you. Maybe no one."

"Who *are* you?" Philippa's voice was sharp.

"A friend. That I can tell you," Rayna said.

"Are we being watched?"

"I doubt it. They're moving too fast to take care of those details."

"I think we've got to warn people here," Philippa said.

"Warn them of what?" Rayna asked.

Nils felt a sudden chill and realized it had gotten cold in the house. He looked at Philippa; he noticed for the first time that she was beginning to get tiny wrinkles around her eyes, her pale Northern-European skin. They were all silent for a moment.

Then Philippa said between clenched teeth, "Goddamit. What are you doing? Do you think we're fools? 'Warn them of what.' That they are all going to be shipped off to hell. That evil people are plotting to conquer their City. That's all."

Rayna's expression changed suddenly. Before she had been almost flippant but now she looked more serious than Nils had ever seen her. "You are such an alarmist!" she said. "Don't forget—all's for the best in this best of all possible worlds."

Nils said, "I think it's time for you to go."

"Oh, yes, I have to go. I'm getting my hair done. At your salon, Phil."

Later Nils and Philippa went for a walk, down the hill to Union Street, then west into the forest of the old Presidio. It was a mild evening, dry and cool. The smell of Eucalyptus was strong.

"What do we know about her? For sure." Nils asked.

"She's watching us. We know that for sure."

"What do we do, for Gods sake?"

"Don't panic. That's number one. You take your time writing your report. We do have to warn someone. I'm just not sure who. That's what we have to figure out," Philippa said.

"But what do I say in my report?"

"I don't know! Make the whole operation look terribly hard. Logically, we should warn the mayor, but I don't trust this one. We'll see who's there after the election."

"I think I have to talk to my people in the Corps." Nils felt slightly relieved as he said this.

"Didn't you say you were forbidden to talk to anyone else in the Corps?"

"Yeah, but if what Rayna says is right, there is some wiggle room for me. Maybe they will know how to undermine Hastings and whoever that Owner is."

Nils flew to Denver the following evening. He checked into a modest hotel downtown, trying to ignore the curious looks that followed him as he walked through the lobby. Corps officers rarely frequented this part of town. As soon as he got into his room he changed out of his uniform and put on cotton jeans and a green flannel shirt. It felt odd to be out of uniform in Denver; this was a first for him. He associated the freedom of civilian clothes with home. This was an adventure, and it had been a long time.

The first thing he had to do was get another phone. He couldn't risk calling his colleagues on his own mobile. He went to a nearby pawnshop, showed his Corps ID and bought one. It was cheaper than he expected and was guaranteed to work. He planned to throw it away when he was finished. He took it back to his room and made three calls. Then he wiped it carefully and put a tissue around it. Then he changed his mind.

Wouldn't throwing it away prove some kind of guilt—that he knew he was doing something wrong? Let's go back to what Philippa said, "What do we know for sure?" That there are cross currents in the Corps. Certainly. Why do they call it Project Moses? Oh, yes, it has something to do with the Promised Land, it's a sardonic joke.

The Corps was supposed to protect the Owners and the Havens. But that was at the beginning, when the Corps was just a private security force. Now it's much bigger and more independent. The Corps has its own agenda and it doesn't have to be the same as the Owners'. Internal Security was never that powerful. Transportation and management of the Plantations is where the action is. How is it that the tail is now wagging the dog? Why is Rayna, if that is her name, following us? What is she trying to get me to do? For some reason I'm important, he thought, and she wants me to be confused. Why?

Tomorrow he would meet with his old boss. Maybe he'd get some clarification. Why and how did he get transferred to Internal Security? How could he get back to Behavioral Sciences? And how to survive tonight—there wasn't even a video in his room.

Jack and Gabe were excited; they had never stayed in a hotel before.

"This is amazing," Gabe said. "Look, we have our own bathroom."

"Yeah, and we have dates for tonight," Jack said.

"I'm really thrilled," Gabe said.

"I can tell. Don't do cartwheels; you'll break a window."

"They're spoiled brats. They're Owners, for god's sake!"

"C'mon, face it. You just don't like girls," Jack said.

"Duh. But even if I did, I wouldn't like them."

"Hey, we're just going to the movies with them, that's all."

"I know you, bro, you're a horn dog. You've got designs."

"So what are we going to do with the other one, later?" Jack asked.

"You can have both of them. Wouldn't be the first time, either."

Jack couldn't wait to get outside and take a look at this new City. It had been a short walk from the train station to the hotel, and there hadn't been much to see. Small garden plots between run-down brick buildings. They hurried out of the hotel and headed toward the middle of the city. Jack's senses were alive, awake. Everything was new and different, the air was thin and dry, and there were no horses and only a few bikes. And there were a lot of cars, gliding by quietly. Men and women wearing the Corps uniform mingled with others, and no one seemed to pay attention to them. There were beggars everywhere and small stands lining the streets selling food—fried potatoes, buffalo stew, boiled cabbage.

"Hey, look at that," Gabe said, pointing to a crowd of people surrounding what appeared to be a small stage. They were in high spirits, laughing and yelling cat calls. Opposite them was a group of nearly naked people, shivering, silent, and chained together.

"What the hell," Jack said, "What is that?" They saw a woman who was probably about eighty wearing a worn leather coat and a silk scarf around her neck. She was carrying a sign that said SHAME. They went to her and Jack said, "Ma'am, can you tell us what this is?"

"Where are you from?" she asked. "So you've never seen a slave auction before? They have them here almost every week now. Those poor people, they were dying Outside, and they went to a shelter and before they knew it, they had been branded and sold to a wholesaler, who brought them here. They didn't do things like this in my day. We had a constitution."

Jack said, "Is this the Corps?"

"Oh, no. This is a city market. The Corps doesn't need to buy; there are plenty of Outsiders who will go to their Plantations."

"Hey, let's go," Gabe said, "this is disgusting."

"I bet you boys are planning to join the Corps. Why don't you come to my house for a cup of tea first and we can talk about it?"

They walked away with her down a street lined with ramshackle huts. The street was wide and filled with holes, many of which were full of water from the last rain. Then they turned down a side street. Soon they were walking under tall catalpa trees. Jack was fascinated by the red brick houses. Brick buildings, rare anyway, had been outlawed in San Francisco after the last great quake, and any remaining ones had been pulled down. They turned into a house that was small and plain, but comfortable. She led them into the kitchen.

"My name is Dorothy Haines. And what are your names?"

Jack remembered the governor's admonition but he couldn't lie to this old lady. He said, "I'm Jack and this is my brother Gabe."

"Well, pleased to meet you. Why don't you tell me why you want to join the Corps? I've heard just about everything and maybe you can learn something from me."

He had to draw the line somewhere. Maybe it wasn't quite as dishonest if they weren't lying directly, just letting her keep her preconceptions about them.

"We want to see the world," Jack said, truthfully.

"And what about you, Gabe?" Dorothy asked.

"Same thing. And we get to wear the uniform. And maybe one day we can become Owners," Gabe said. Jack shot him an irritated look.

The woman started explaining to them in great detail the history and structure of the Corps but Jack had a hard time paying attention to what she was saying. As he looked at her, a form organized itself in her shadow—a man in uniform. The man was her son and he was dead. She never stopped thinking about him.

Jack blurted out, "How was he killed?"

The woman stopped talking and put her hand over her mouth. She moved away from Jack, as far as she could, and said in a strangled voice, "You have no right! I won't have your kind in my house! I'm going to have to ask you to leave now."

As the boys walked away, Gabe said, "Jack, what the hell was that about? Did you see something?"

"Her son was an officer and was killed somehow and she hates the Corps."

"But how did you know that? Why did she get so mad at us?"

"At me. Because I saw him."

"What did she mean by 'your kind?'"

"Hell if I know," Jack said, "but whoever we are, she doesn't like us!"

It was too late to see anyone that night, so Nils decided to do some exploring. He'd been to Denver many times before, but he was always on official business and anxious to be somewhere else. He'd never walked around and mingled with the locals. Surprising, he thought, how dreary it looks. You'd think there would be some kind of civic pride; it was a kind of capital, after all. But there were shacks everywhere, some leaning up against more substantial buildings, streets full of holes, and no attempts at beauty or distinction.

The people too were unattractive. Most seemed to be wearing the cheap clothes made on Plantations, and they didn't seem to care how they looked. He made his way to the slave market, which was one of the more interesting sights of Denver. He'd heard about it, of course, but never seen it. Most people in the Corps found the idea of slavery distasteful; a slave market was beneath their notice. Nils was curious.

The slaves were quite a mixed lot. Nils had studied history and he knew that once, in the United States, only people of African origin had been slaves. But racial distinctions had been blurred by intermarriage and now anyone could be a slave. He noticed a young man with blonde hair looking around wildly, pulling at the metal collar around his neck. A girl with light-brown skin could not have been more than sixteen and seemed to be communing with another world; she was absent from this one for sure.

The Denver slave market was a pilot project. The earth, stressed by climate change, couldn't sustain "excess" human beings, and some distinguished economists had argued that their chances of survival would be maximized if they had some economic value. There had been a time when these people were valuable as consumers, but that was long passed. Now, the most efficient way to deal with them was to make them a commodity and let the free market assign them a value. Otherwise, they would be worth nothing. The Archbishop of Denver preached a moving sermon on the merciful nature of slavery and the duty of believers who could afford it to buy and maintain slaves. The Church set the example—it was the largest slave owner of all.

The Owners were following the experiment with great interest, some of them hoping to extend slavery throughout North and South America. But most Corps officers were opposed to it—they feared that the Owners would want the Plantations worked by slaves instead of local free labor. That would complicate the Corps' job immeasurably.

Nils walked away quickly. After a few blocks, he found himself on a street that was teeming with people. Denver was an open City and it was full of Outsiders. There were bars on every corner. Nils went into one at random and sat down on a bar stool.

The bartender came up to him and said, "What are you doing here, scum bag?"

Nils froze for a moment. "What did you say to me?"

"I said, what would you like sir?"

"Is that right? I thought I heard something else."

The bartender didn't reply and just looked at him with a neutral expression.

Nils walked out and kept walking. What was that about? Did he reek somehow of the Corps? Or did the bartender mistake him for an Outsider?

He decided to go up-market, to a bar he knew.

CHAPTER TEN

Jack was confused by Denver. At home, he knew who people were—once in a while he'd see someone who didn't belong, but that was rare. Here there was a strange mixture. Owners mingled with Outsiders, Corps officers with city dwellers. The slave auction shook Jack's sense of reality. What kind of world was this?

They were back in their hotel room. Gabe came out of the bathroom, sat down on his bed, and said, "Hey, bro, what's wrong? You look like you just saw a ghost."

"Aren't you feeling it? This is a really fucked up place."

"Hey, the world is fucked up. We knew that."

"Yeah, that's what they always told us, but we didn't actually see it. I'm a little scared," Jack said.

"Don't say that! It makes me scared."

"I didn't say I was paralyzed. I'm just wondering what we are up against," Jack said.

"I don't know. But I know where we're from and where we belong. And it's a good place," Gabe said.

"Yeah, we don't have slave auctions! That's the most disgusting thing I've ever seen. Hey, do you think we can trust the governor?"

"I don't know. Do we have any choice?" Gabe asked.

"We could try to get to Maine on our own and forget about what he wants us to do."

"Is that what you wanna do?" Gabe asked.

"In a way, yeah. I wish we could get out of this place right away, but if we leave we're totally on our own. We're not even sure if we can take a train all the way to Maine."

"I think we should stay here and try to get the governor's info. I want to fly on a sonic!"

Jack laughed. "Alright, we'll give it a try, but I can't figure out how we could possibly get the information he wants."

"We don't have to do it tonight. Let's just have fun. We're going to the movies." Gabe capered around the room waving his arms.

It wasn't hard to find the movie theatre. Everyone seemed to know where it was. Alfreda and Cecilia were waiting for them. They were both dressed in jumpsuits made of some material that fit them like second skins. The colors kept changing, seemingly at random. One minute Alfreda was lime green and Cecilia was cornflower blue and the next they were reversed. Gabe said, "Are your outfits coordinated?" The girls laughed, "Of course, it's fun this way."

Jack said, "Can you stop it? It's very irritating."

"All right, if that's what you want," Cecilia said, and she brushed her hand down a seam. The suit turned a neutral gray and stayed that way.

"I didn't mean you had to be gray, I just wanted to stop it from changing," Jack said.

"You sure are hard to please," Alfreda said.

"Alright. Just do what you want," he said.

"Hey, let's go in now," Gabe said.

They walked into a large, nondescript room with black walls and ceiling and sat down in comfortable upholstered chairs. Jack was disappointed. Except for the seats this wasn't much better than the movie house back home on Folsom Street. He used to go there often with his mothers to see old films; there weren't any new ones. Here there wasn't even a screen.

The lights went down and the walls and ceiling dissolved. Jack and Gabe gasped and the girls laughed at them. They were no longer in a room; they were on the prairie, galloping on horses in pursuit of something. Their chairs vibrated, suggesting motion, and they could feel the wind and sun on their faces. They could smell the prairie grass and the sweaty horses. They looked up and there in the "sky" the clouds started to form together into words—The Tipping Point.

"This is a classic," Cecilia whispered to them.

The story took place fifty years earlier. A Midwestern city is facing climate disaster. The heat in the summer makes work impossible, and winter blizzards bury the whole region and stop all movement. Violent storms are an ever-present threat.

Amalia and Bruce are in love and are about to get married. They come from the most prominent families in their city, but conditions are harsh, even for them. Bruce has been organizing the building of a fence around their neighborhood and the delivery of a large quantity of food to last them through the winter. But the local rabble tries to thwart him at every turn. They steal the food and other necessities that he's managed to acquire.

Finally, thugs grab Amalia. Bruce organizes a group of men who fight a pitched battle with the kidnappers and manage to rescue her. Amalia and Bruce go to their church to celebrate her deliverance. They get married and then, with their families around them, Bruce gives a stirring speech, saying that it's time for their people to leave the dying city and create a place of their own. The priest blesses them and the movie ends with a sunrise over the first Haven.

When they walked out into the mall, Jack felt a shiver of disappointment and homesickness. At home, walking out of the movie theatre meant feeling the cool outside air that smelled like the ocean. Here the air was dead. "Air conditioned" was the word they used, implying air that had been processed and de-natured. That's what it was like.

The girls were giggling about something. Gabe looked bored. "Let's go get a drink," Cecilia said. They walked down to an underground level and turned into a corridor that was dimly lit with red bulbs. To their right was a door that pulsated; it seemed like a living thing. As Cecilia approached it, it swung open. The girls went through, but when Gabe moved toward it, it closed quickly.

"What the hell!" he said.

A moment later the door opened but not by itself. A large man wearing a black suit said to them, "The ladies said you were with them. Come in."

They all sat down at a shiny black plastic table and Jack was impressed. Plastic was rare. "What just happened?" Jack asked.

"Oh, it's not a big deal. The door's retinal scanner recognized us but not you, of course," Cecilia said.

"Why did it recognize you? Do you come here often?" Gabe asked.

"No, we've never been here before. We're all on the Data Base," she said.

"What do you mean 'all?'" Gabe asked.

"Well you know, all the Owners." She was a little embarrassed.

"We're going to be on the Data Base," Gabe said.

Jack looked at him and said, "Yeah, and we're going to be cowboys too." They all laughed. The girls ordered drinks for all of them and in a few minutes everything seemed hilarious.

Jack got up to go to the toilet and saw that there were many people sitting at the bar. Some of them were talking to heads resting on the bar in front of them, others were looking at nude dancers, one foot tall, gyrating around their drinks; holographic images. Someone was talking to the bartender. A man with blonde hair wearing a flannel shirt glanced at Jack as he walked by. Jack felt a flash of something he couldn't identify. It was the oddest feeling; his mind was organizing itself in a new way; he felt clearer and sharper than ever before. Patterns were now obvious to him. *That man is an officer in the Corps,* Jack thought, *and he is often in San Francisco. He can help us.*

Nils had been looking at the group of young people sitting at a nearby table. The girls were typical Owners. He normally wouldn't have given them a second glance, but it was an unusual scene—they were sitting with boys who were clearly not of the same caste. And the boys weren't Corps either. Owner men sometimes brought Outsider women who caught their fancy to this bar. But Owner women usually entertained the lower orders privately, yet here they were. And there was something familiar about these boys. The one who looked at him as he walked to the toilet seemed to know him. Now you're getting paranoid, Nils told himself. He had ducked into the bar on a whim, at the last minute. Unless I'm being followed. But no, that doesn't make sense.

When the first boy returned to the table, the other one, a bit younger, got up and as he passed the bar, he looked directly at Nils and smiled broadly.

"Hello," Nils said, "join me for a drink?" He wanted to talk to someone, anyone, and he was curious about this scene. This boy was probably attracted to him—that was to be expected—but Nils knew how to let his admirers down softly, so they barely noticed they were being rejected.

"Okay, on my way back," Gabe said. A few minutes later he pulled over a stool and sat next to Nils.

"Are you from Denver?" Nils asked, sure that he wasn't.

"No. We're not," Gabe said.

"Did you do anything fun tonight?"

"We saw a movie called *The Tipping Point*," Gabe said.

"Oh, god, that old propaganda film!" Nils laughed. "Did you like it?"

"It was okay. But at the end they only talked about Owners and how great they were."

"Yeah, well that's how they think about themselves," Nils said.

"And what was that thing about a True Church? I never heard of it."

Just then the music turned to something frantic, like chase music. Suddenly a chicken raced down the bar, followed by a fox, which was followed by a dog. Gabe jumped up and said, "What the hell is that?"

Nils laughed and said, "They're just holograms. It's a bar game. I think it's stupid, but it wakes people up. It used to interfere with people's individual holograms and it was really annoying, but this new system allows them all to show at the same time. By the way, my name is Nils." They shook hands.

"I'm Gabe. Are you from here?"

"No, I'm in the Corps."

"Wow! You're the first person I ever met in the Corps. Where's your uniform? What's it like?"

Nils laughed. "I don't have to wear the uniform when I'm not on duty. It's great to be in the Corps. I get to travel all the time." Nils smiled. "That's what they say in the City don't they?"

"Yeah. What do you mean?"

"You're from San Francisco, aren't you?"

"How did you guess?"

"I've seen you and your friend on Union Street. You were playing the blues for coins."

When he saw Gabe's reaction, Nils immediately regretted saying that. Gabe got up and said, "I need to talk to my brother."

Jack had been looking at Gabe and the stranger. It wasn't hard to talk to the girls and watch the rest of the bar—they didn't require a lot of attention. He could see that something had happened. Gabe suddenly jumped up from his bar stool and walked away from the Corpsman. Jack had no idea how he knew what the man was, but he had no doubt.

When Gabe sat down next to him the girls were deeply engaged in some conversation with each other that seemed to have to do with perfume.

"He knows we're from the City. He's seen us there, on the street."

"What's he like?" Jack asked.

"He doesn't seem like a bad guy, but he's in the Corps," Gabe said. "What can I tell him?"

"Just don't tell him about the governor; remember what Cruz said; let him think we're going to join the Corps. But we should talk to him; maybe he knows something. This could be our break. Do you like him?"

"Sure. He's a major hunk. But he's not interested in me."

Jack sensed something was wrong. There was a vibration he couldn't hear but he felt it distinctly as a kind of tingling. Just after he became aware of it, the man who had let them in the club came up to the girls and said something to them quietly. They shrugged and turned back to continue their conversation with each other.

"You men are going to have to leave," the tall man said to them.

"Why? We haven't done anything," Jack said.

"We've had a few complaints about you. This is an Owners' place," the man said, obviously expecting them to understand.

Jack felt a flush of anger. He decided he wouldn't move; they'd have to throw him out. Then the man from the bar came to their table.

"What's the problem?" Nils asked the tall man.

"They're Outsiders, sir, and a few people here are nervous about them. They have to leave."

"Didn't they tell you? They're cadets from the Corps academy. Tell your Owners not to worry; we've got it all under control," Nils said.

"But they weren't on the Data Base, sir," the man said.

"They're new. Don't they teach you anything?" Nils' voice was stern, authoritative.

"Sorry, sir, I'll pass the word on. Sorry, gentlemen." The man left.

"Thanks," Jack said, "I kind of thought we'd be outnumbered."

"Why don't you both come over to the bar? Bring your drinks," Nils said.

"Bye, girls, see you around," Gabe said.

At the bar, Nils and Jack shook hands and introduced themselves.

"Thanks. I don't know why you did that, but thanks anyway," Jack said.

"I'm not sure either," Nils said. "For some reason I had to. But now that we're alright here, let's go somewhere more fun." Jack got it—Nils was in some kind of trouble. The understandings were coming so fast to Jack and he didn't know why. It was like he was a mind reader.

Nils was shocked by his own lack of caution. Throwing the mantle of the Corps over people he didn't know because he was bored would certainly open him to criticism, if he was found out. It wasn't done.

They left the mall and started walking north, away from downtown. The streets were dark, and there were few people on foot. Police cruisers glided by.

"You boys are doing right to tell people you're Outsiders. They won't understand if you tell them you're city dwellers from San Francisco. How many days are you giving yourselves in Denver before you join the Corps?"

"As long as our money holds out," Jack said quickly, before Gabe could say anything. He was trying to think of a way to ask Nils if he knew anything about what was happening in the Central Valley, but it seemed impossible. Then he decided to just do it.

"Uh, Nils, I've heard something's going on in the Valley. The Corps is doing something there. I wonder what it is. Do you know?" He paused for a moment and then said, "I was just thinking that maybe when we join they'd send us there and it wouldn't be too far from home." He was not a convincing liar, though, and his words dropped with a clang.

They were walking briskly and Nils stopped suddenly and turned to Jack. He was speechless for a moment. "Who the hell are you?" he asked.

Now it was Jack's turn to be dumb. He sensed—he understood—that Nils's trouble involved the place he had just asked about. He grabbed Nils's sleeve and looked directly into the older man's eyes. "Hey, we're just two dudes from San Francisco and we're in this weird new city and we don't know much about anything." That was all too true.

"How do you know about the Central Valley?"

Jack drew a blank. He couldn't think of anything but the truth, and he sensed that it wouldn't hurt them to tell this man. "Governor Cruz told us about it. He wants to know."

Nils felt the fear that had seized him with such ferocity retreat back into the shadows. He laughed briefly and said, "Yeah, well Cruz sure picked some low-rent spies! That's not much of a surprise. Maybe you better go back to wherever you're staying. I'm not sure I want to hang out with Ray Cruz's friends." Nils laughed again.

Jack was feeling a little humiliated, but leaving now would make it worse, so he said, "Look, I'm sorry if I put you on the spot. Just forget I asked anything. We really want you to take us to the new place."

Nils looked at the two boys. They were naïve, sure, but it wasn't possible to think they were malicious. Their story made sense—there was no love lost between Cruz and the Corps and plenty of reason for him to be suspicious of something going on in his backyard. No risk, really, and Nils didn't want to be alone that night. "I have no idea what's happening in the Central Valley," Nils lied easily. "But I have a pretty good idea of what's going on at Betty's Place."

After a few minutes, he found the address he had been looking for. Nils had heard about it for years, but there had never been a chance to go; he was always too busy when he was in Denver. They walked up the wooden steps of a very large old house. The upstairs windows were dark but they could see through the downstairs windows lights deep in the interior. A substantial woman dressed in a yellow muumuu opened the door.

They paid her the small cover charge, and as they went in, Nils said to them, "No retinal scans here. All she cares about is the money."

The rooms were illuminated by candles, and there were at least a hundred people milling around, drinking, talking, and laughing. Loud rhythms throbbed and couples and threesomes were dancing. Jack had never seen such a mixture of people: Owners, slim and glittering in their high-tech clothes; Denver citizens, mostly fatter than the Owners and much more drab; and Outsiders, colorful in cowboy hats, chain mail, and leather skirts. This was a place where conventional hierarchy was overruled by the implacable logic of sexual attraction.

Jack was temporarily deafened. His head was filled with noise, most of it gibberish. Gabe looked around in wonder. He had a huge smile on his face. "This is awesome."

Nils smiled, "Let's get a drink. On me, boys."

Soon, Nils and Gabe were deep in conversation with a couple of indeterminate sex, and Jack decided to wander off by himself. Each room looked different, but the energy was the same. Everyone trying hard to have fun, to forget, and each one had a different thing he wanted to forget. Jack's deeper perception was intermittent; he caught thoughts and lost them and he didn't know what to make of it. At first, when he entered the place, he just wanted to have fun, but now he felt deeply unsettled, knowing too much about people he didn't know.

He saw a girl standing by herself in a corner, his age, maybe younger, long black hair and olive skin. She wore a simple sky-blue dress that matched her eyes and a thick silver and turquoise necklace. He was sure he had seen her somewhere before, although he knew that could not be true. There were people near her but she seemed to be standing alone on a mountaintop. She looked at him and smiled. Jack was next to her in a flash, with no recollection of how he got there.

Hi, Jack, she said, *you don't know me. But I know you.*

Jack suddenly realized with a shock that she hadn't said a word. He looked at her again.

"I'm Jill," she said out loud. "Jack and Jill." He hadn't told her his name.

She reached out and touched his neck. He put his arm around her waist. *Let's go outside. I know a place in the garden.* There was no need to think. He no longer felt distant from his surroundings—reflection and perception merged and he felt whole. And she was at the center of it all.

It was very dark but they found a bench to sit on. He turned toward her and she said, "Whoa, slow down, take a deep breath. Let's just sit here for a minute."

"You can see inside my head, can't you? Why, how?"

"You're a special man, Jack, but you don't know that yet."

"You're so beautiful, you're a wildflower." He took her hand and looked into her eyes. "I didn't know I was looking for you."

"Do you think it's an accident that we met here? Nothing's an accident."

"How old are you? You look twenty but you talk like someone much older."

"I was born a year after you, but you know girls mature faster." She laughed.

Jack felt his moorings loosen. He hadn't told her when he was born.

"You are remarkable; it's true what they told me," she said. "But you're a baby—you don't know how to walk yet. But you will, and then I will come to you again."

Urgent questions forced their way into Jack's mind, but he dismissed them rudely. He understood nothing and didn't care. He pulled her toward him and they kissed. He pushed his tongue into her mouth and felt himself dissolve. The urgency of his flesh faded and they were no longer different beings struggling to fuse into one another. Now, there was no separate Jack and no separate Jill. They had drifted up into the air and were floating and they were one—a cloud of sparking electrons. Below were two bodies, arms wrapped around each other and above there was only ecstasy, no beings separate from each other, no breaking apart by time, a horizon rising endlessly into the light.

And then he heard, somehow in his own head he heard her say, *Jack, I can't stay with you* and he found himself clawed back into his body—oh, sudden grief and loss! She was gone. He heard the uncanny trill of a screech owl, and he was awake and he was Jack again.

Nils left Gabe to go to the bar and noticed all at once that there were no Owners in the room. There had been a few of them when they arrived and now there were none. Just as the bartender was pushing drinks across the bar to him, tequila and mesquite juice, Nils heard loud crunching sounds. Someone screamed. There was a stampede away from the front door. Nils couldn't see Jack, but he saw Gabe, who was looking at him from across the room, puzzled. Then the room was filled with men in gray uniforms. Nils tried to run toward Gabe, who had been thrown to the ground. There was a lot of shouting and screaming and the sound of truncheons hitting flesh. A uniform had grabbed Gabe and smashed handcuffs on him. Just as Nils reached him it all went black.

CHAPTER ELEVEN

When Jack returned to himself the eastern sky was already pale blue. He walked back into a silent house. It was a mess—broken furniture, shattered windows, clothes strewn everywhere. Jack looked in every room and closet and possible hiding place that he could find but no one was there. Gabe was gone.

He felt his way back to the hotel somehow, and the door to their room opened at the touch of his hand. All his things were there, just as he had left them, but Gabe's had disappeared—there was no trace that his brother had ever been there. Jack sat down on his bed, his knees suddenly too weak to hold the weight of his body. He had never felt so alone. Gabe was his whole family; there was no one else except a father he had never seen, who might no longer exist.

Where had they taken him? Who had taken him and why? Was Nils somehow responsible? Jack felt like he had been caught in a net and someone was pulling the strings tight around him. What would happen next? Dread and fear—for Gabe and for himself—were massing in the darkness around his mind. Soon it would overwhelm him.

Jack took two pillows and placed them on the floor. He sat on them, crossing his legs in a lotus position. He folded his hands in his lap, with his thumbs touching, as he had been taught when he was a small child. Keeping his back straight but not tense and concentrating on his breath but not controlling it, he tried to let go of the fear, to loosen his grasp on it. His breath, which had been shallow and quick, returned to normal and he felt a faint touch of calm descend upon him. There were practical things he had to do. Find Gabe. Survive.

He packed his things and went down to the front desk to check out of the hotel. Staying was unbearable, and he knew somehow that Gabe wouldn't be coming back there.

Jack left the hotel and walked into chaos. A violent storm had begun its assault on Denver. The dark sky was crazy with bolts of lightening, and the thunder was deafening. People ran for cover and in a moment the skies opened and water fell in sheets. He ran back to the hotel, relieved just to be inside. The lobby of the old building was large, with wooden pillars and couches and chairs, run-down stuff but still serviceable. It didn't smell. He sat down, his backpack next to him, and looked out the window, trying to pull himself together. Jack sat in the lobby for an hour. He was glad of the storm; it gave him time to think. There was no one in Denver he could turn to. Then he remembered the phone he had been given by the governor. He took it out and dialed the number he had memorized.

"Hello, can I speak to Uncle Ray?"

"He's not here. Do you have a message?"

"Just tell him I'm in Denver at the Hotel Grayson."

"Don't leave. He'll get back to you."

Jack looked around and realized that the desk clerk, a pale man with a thin face, was staring at him. Jack knew he was shocked to see someone he thought was an Outsider with a mobile phone. A middle-aged woman with makeup crudely plastered on her face was looking at him also. She couldn't look away, although she was afraid of him. Jack could feel her fear.

Outside it was clearing up. A car pulled up silently, and a nondescript woman got out and came into the lobby. He looked up as she said to him in a voice that didn't project, "Let's go, Jack. Uncle Ray is waiting."

He followed her to the car and got in the passenger seat. She drove west toward the mountains. Finally, they turned onto a dirt road inside a forest. After about twenty minutes they pulled up in front of a very large A-frame house. She had not said a word and her mind was closed to him.

She took him to a room at the back of the house. It opened onto an enormous deck that looked like a raft floating in a sea of trees. There was an overwhelming smell of wet pine warming in the sun.

Gladys, the woman who had driven them to Sacramento and introduced them to the governor, was sitting at a large table. She got up and went to Jack. "Hello, Jack. Here, sit down and tell me what happened."

"How did you get here?" he blurted, "Why?"

"You mean why me? That's easy. Because I understand you," she said.

"I don't have the information they want."

"I know that."

"I have to find Gabe. Nothing else matters now."

Gladys was looking at him with evident interest. "So what I saw from the beginning is true, isn't it? You can read minds."

"What's happening to me? Does this have anything to do with Jill? Do you know about her?"

"Yes. I talked to Jill this morning."

Jack sat back, stunned. "Where is she? You know where Gabe is, don't you?"

Gladys stood up and turned away from him. "What am I thinking?"

"You know he was taken by the Denver police. You'll try to see that he doesn't come to harm."

Jack moved toward the older woman and looked directly into her face. "How am I supposed to trust you? Who took Gabe's things from our room?"

"We have a lot to talk about," Gladys said. "Why don't you start by telling me about the man who took you to the club."

Jack stood up and walked to the railing. The air was cold but the sun was warm on his face. "His name was Nils and I knew somehow that he was a Corps officer. That's everything I know. Are you going to help me find Gabe? And where's Jill?"

"Did he tell you that he lived in San Francisco?"

"No, but Gabe said that he recognized us from the City. We really didn't have much time to talk to him." He sat down again and for a moment relaxed and felt immense relief, but then he thought of Gabe and his mind went back to high alert.

"Jack, I'm going to tell you something. I'm not sure that you're in shape to hear this, but I don't have any choice. You need to know this now."

"Is it about Gabe?" he asked, jumping up.

"No it's not. Sit down. This is it, short version. What they're building in the Central Valley is a Plantation for poeple from San Francisco."

"That's ridiculous. Who would go there?"

Gladys moved over to a chair next to Jack. She took his hand and looked directly into his face. "The Owners have ordered the Corps to invade San Francisco and force the entire population of the City out so they can take it over for themselves. The San Francisco citizens are to become Guests in the Central Valley."

He pulled away and jumped up. He was carried on a tide of anger, "What the hell is that about? Why would I believe that? I'm tired of being jerked around!"

She looked at him and he saw the vision—tens of thousands of people, his people, being herded by horsemen with whips, crying, begging for food and water, driven from their homes into servitude. His City, his community, his life—obliterated.

He let out a bellow, a vast, crazy noise that should have flattened the trees for miles around. He was shocked, when he opened his eyes, that they were still standing.

Gladys was looking at him with an expression he couldn't read. "Good," she said, "you understand."

Nils woke up in his hotel room with no memory of how he got there. Rayna was sitting in an armchair in the corner watching him.

"You have no idea what a hassle it was to get you to bed. I should get a medal," she said.

Nils was too astonished to say anything. Rayna laughed, "You look like a fish out of water. What a hoot!"

Finally Nils managed, "What happened? I was at Betty's Place and that's all I remember."

"The Denver vice squad raided it. A misunderstanding. Betty paid the wrong person this month and, what's worse, didn't pay the right person. They saw your Corps tattoo, they always check for it, and called us."

"Well, thanks, I guess," Nils said, "I thought you had more important things to do than rescue a Corps officer from a vice squad raid."

"It isn't what I usually do. But they told me it was you and I had to get involved. Colonel Hastings doesn't know that you're back in Denver, and he might wonder why you are."

"Hey, what happened to the other people who were there?"

"The usual. There were a few other Corps officers there we got out, and the Denver citizens were let go with a small fine. The strongest of the Outsiders were sold to the slavers and the rest were deported. The Denver police don't do anything unless they get paid for it, so the slave market has worked out pretty well for them."

"What happened to the boys I took there, the ones from San Francisco?"

"I don't know anything about that."

Nils got up. "If you don't mind, I'm going to the bathroom and I'm going to change clothes. These feel crummy."

"You might as well put on your uniform. You have an appointment in an hour."

"No. I have to go to the Denver police. Colonel Hastings can wait. I have some responsibility to those boys."

Rayna looked at him. "What makes you think the appointment was with Hastings?" Nils noticed her omission of the title and wondered what it meant.

"Who is it with then?"

"General Couseau, the Commandant of the Corps. You better shine your shoes."

An hour later Nils and Rayna were ushered into a spacious room. It was paneled in dark wood and there was a coved ceiling. On a side table was a model of an early nineteenth century sailing ship. There were actual windows looking out toward the east, toward the prairies; you could see the weather coming. Two walls were lined with books. A secretary sat at a desk in a corner, a mature woman with gray hair wearing a navy blue cardigan sweater over a gray silk blouse. She motioned the visitors toward the sitting area, a sofa and two easy chairs surrounding a low table. Nils and Rayna sat next to each other on the sofa.

A few minutes later the door opened and four men in uniform walked in. Nils recognized the oldest—his picture was on the wall in every Corps office. Nils and Rayna stood up. General Couseau came up to them and shook hands, looking closely at Nils. The other three officers took chairs near the secretary. The general didn't introduce them. He sat down at one of the easy chairs facing the sofa.

"Glad to meet you, Radovic."

"Rakovic, general."

"Yes, of course. I've heard quite a bit about you lately. And, you know, I knew your wife when she was a little girl. I haven't seen her for a long time. Lucky you happened to be in Denver this week. I wanted to hear what you think about Project Moses. I want you to speak honestly, from the heart, not just the brain. I ought to warn you that I have a very finely tuned bullshit detector. Don't spare me."

"My expertise is as a psychologist, sir," Nils said.

"I know that. Just tell me what you think."

"I think it's an abomination, sir."

"Yes, go on."

Nils started talking, and everything he had been feeling since he learned of the plan tumbled out. General Couseau listened closely and didn't interrupt. Finally, he said, "Alright, thanks, Major. I get the drift. Now I want you to go somewhere out of the way and finish your report. You don't need to talk to your former supervisor or colleagues. Leave them out of this. You are to leave the recommendation section of your report blank and pass the report on to Colonel Hastings as you were instructed to do—after you send it to me. Rayna will tell you where you're going and explain to you how to contact me. Nice to meet you." He got up and everyone in the room stood up.

"General, can I ask you one favor? There are two young men from San Francisco who disappeared last night and I need to find them."

"Disappeared from the club you took them to?"

Nils was startled for a moment and then caught himself.

"Yes, sir, that's right. I have to make sure they're alright. They could be sold as slaves."

"It's barbaric they've brought that back, isn't it? The economists insisted on it and the Owners love it. Some of them would like all of us to be slaves. But you have to leave Denver right now. A car will take you from here to the airport. I'll have someone look into it. Goodbye, Major Rakovic."

Rayna walked outside with him, and they found a car with his name on the ID strip.

"Where am I going?" he asked.

"You're going to Maine. It's a good place to get lost. I hope you like trees."

"How long will I be there, and what about Philippa?"

"I'll talk to her. I can't tell her where you are, but I'll tell her you're safe. Here are your orders. Check them out; they're marked top secret."

"I can't believe I'm saying this, but I wish you were coming with me," he said.

"That's just shock talking. You'll be alright. You might even like it. A lot of Owners go there in the summer."

"Now let's eat something," Gladys said. Jack had forgotten to eat and now he was starving. They had been sitting silently for an hour or so, working together to calm his mind. Now he could think and talk again.

They went inside, and there was a table spread with crusty, dark bread, cheese and butter, apples and peanuts.

"Does the governor know you're here?" Jack asked.

"In a way. But he isn't one of us, you know."

"What does that mean, 'one of us?'"

"Jack, you and I can hear people's thoughts. And we're not the only ones; there are others. You're still in the awakening stage."

"Who is Jill?" he asked.

Gladys smiled. "She's your guardian angel."

Jack was confused.

"Don't worry, she's real. Yes, I know all about it. What kind of mind reader would I be if I couldn't hear it all from you?"

"Gladys, what am I supposed to do next?"

"One thing is for sure. You can't stay in Denver."

"But I have to find Gabe. I can't leave him here."

"Your whole City is at risk. Gabe is just one person."

"Gabe is my brother; he's all I've got. I have to find him."

Gladys stood up, and Jack noticed that she was far older than he had realized. She moved with the energy of a much younger person, but her hands were old. He had been brought up to respect old people—the influence of his Chinese grandmother.

"It won't mean much when you find him if your home is gone," she said.

"What can I possibly do about that?"

"I don't know. But I think that you might be the one who can stop it from happening," she said.

He jumped up as if he'd been touched by a flame. "Stop it!" he shouted, "I can't take it."

"Yes, you can," she said quietly.

"Send me back to Denver. I have to find Gabe. Now."

"If you wish, I'll send you back to exactly where we found you. It's your choice. But if you let us, we'll help you realize your powers. Think about it—you can go back to square one or you can make yourself into someone big enough to help your City and your brother too."

Jack shrugged free of her and then realized that he was utterly exhausted. He slid into an easy chair and slumped into a deep sleep. He dreamed he was flying. He looked up and down and realized that he could move in any direction, at will. Flying down, he banked to the right and then the left. He was in an airplane, but then he was the plane and his arms were wings.

He woke up and saw Gladys looking out the window. Going back was death. He had to go forward.

"What do you want me to do?" he asked.

CHAPTER TWELVE

It was Sunday, and Hugh did his duty. He went to church, as usual, and was gratified at the homily. The priest talked about how grateful we should be that in these difficult days we all know our place in society, a place set out for us by our birth. When we obey authority, we are heeding the commandments of God, the ultimate Authority. Hugh thought Father Clark was quite intelligent.

Monopoly was the spirit of the times so it was only natural that there should be just one religion in the Havens. The Roman Catholic Church was familiar with this role—after all, it had always considered itself the one true church—and its structure was highly compatible with the Great Companies, of which it was now a member.

He had been going to St. Benedict's his whole life and he only really noticed it if something changed, which was not often. The congregation was a comfortable mix of Owners, who sat in the front in their own pews, and their servants, who sat in the back. Everyone knew everyone else, which did not necessarily mean that everyone spoke to everyone else. There was that fool, Ron Simpson, for example. Hugh thought he was a weak degenerate, a man who refused to support his own kind. And his crazy wife, the no-talent movie star. They invited Helpers and even troits to their parties and treated them as equals.

The parish priest greeted his congregation as they left, Owners first. A very proper order, but also inconvenient, leaving most Owners waiting for their servants. It was annoying, but what was the alternative—Owners waiting in a line behind Helpers to be greeted by the priest? Impossible. Hugh made his driver Henry—not his real name but Hugh called all drivers Henry—sit in the very back and rush out of the church immediately after the mass to bring the car around. Once the family was sitting comfortably in the car, Henry was permitted to go to the priest and get his blessing. Today, Hugh didn't get in the car himself.

Hugh said to his wife, Sylvia, "You go ahead with the kids. I've got some work to do." He couldn't imagine spending a Sunday afternoon with them; it was too boring. In any case, he really did have work to do. He had finally found a project worthy of his energy and dedication, and he threw himself into it with everything he had.

Sylvia said, "Of course, Hugh. Certainly. When will we see you again?"

"I wish you would stop asking me that," he said. "You'll see me when you see me."

"Yes, of course. I'm sorry. Don't work too hard, dear."

He turned away from her and got into a second car that was waiting for him.

A few hours later he was in his apartment on Telegraph Hill. Most of the windows looked out to the west and north. The Golden Gate Bridge. Do we really need it, he wondered. It'll cost a lot of money to fix once we take over the City. I might have other priorities. In some ways, it might be better to demolish it. We wouldn't have to take down the towers; that would be quite a job. We could just take out the spans. That would make both MarinHaven and the City easier to defend. Or would it make them harder to defend? He couldn't figure it out, but then, he thought, no one else could either. Everything was changing so fast, and it seemed that the world was unraveling. Would there even be airplanes in ten years? It was getting harder and harder to find the engineers and technicians who knew how to make and service them. The Rowan mechanics were all old men. And the fuel was hard to get, too.

The Corps might have a better handle on this, but the institution itself could no longer be totally trusted—there was rot at the top. But there were still some good people, and Hugh knew how to use them. Doug Hastings, for example. Hastings was wonderfully dog-like; he'd slash the heart out of whomever he was told to attack and submit with a whimper to blows from his master. Too bad there aren't a lot more like him in the Corps. What did we do wrong? Hugh mused. Well, we'll deal with the Corps in due time.

But now it was time for some relief. Hugh called for Gloria, his assistant. She had worked for him for two years and knew how to satisfy him. She had already changed into a black leather bustier and high boots with six-inch heels. She wore a leather mask and carried a whip.

"Get down on your knees, you piece of shit," she barked at him.

Hugh fell to the floor and cowered in front of her.

"Now lick my fucking boots, asshole."

The sex play went on for about an hour, and then Hugh took a break. "Gloria, you're terrific. I hurt all over. I'm giving you a bonus!"

"Thanks, Mr. Rowan. By the way, don't forget you have a dinner engagement with the mayor this evening."

"Damn. I had forgotten. Thanks for reminding me, Miss Jones."

A few hours later Hugh walked three blocks down the hill to North Beach and entered a small and very elegant restaurant where he was well known. Actually, he owned the place, through a citizen intermediary who was paid for her discretion. Raoul, the maître d', ushered him quickly to a private room in the back—he was the only employee who understood the arrangement. The room was designed to be a discreet meeting place and was never used by anyone else.

Mayor John Johnston had already been there for about half an hour, sitting by himself. Hugh expected that his inferiors would be waiting for him. After all, they were very lucky to be in his presence at all.

Johnston rose when Hugh walked in and they exchanged pleasantries.

"I understand your predecessor told you about our ideas for how to improve San Francisco. I thought we could talk about it here and figure out how to get you interested," Hugh said.

"Yeah, Adams told me about it. Look, Rowan, people don't leave this community; they know what's out there. Give it up."

"Listen, Mayor Johnston, we're just trying to figure out something that makes everyone happy. Face it, how are your people going to survive on their own? Things are only going to get harder here." Hugh motioned for a waitress who had been standing in the corner to pour more wine for both of them. She was one of Hugh's retinue—she went wherever Hugh went and lived in the servants' house. "We're offering the protection of the Corps and the opportunity for a new beginning," Hugh said.

Johnston was a tall, thin man with the light-brown skin that predominated in the City's population. He had just been elected, but not for the first time—he was a man the people kept coming back to in a pinch, the rare politician who could survive changes in political fashion. Hugh thought him an interesting specimen. There was no one like Johnston in the aristocratic world of the Owners or the bureaucracy of the Corps.

The mayor was a product of what they called "democracy," which didn't exist in much of the world anymore. And wouldn't last much longer, Hugh hoped—it was weak, and the world of today demanded strength. A strong leader was one who knew how to impose his will on his subjects, not curry favor from them. Still, Johnston had a lot of influence in the City and could not be ignored.

"Protection, my ass. You people are amazing. You think you have the right to own everything. I came to see you tonight to give you the message—San Francisco belongs to its people and they will not leave it."

"Oh, I think they will, one way or another. It can be easy on them or it can be hard, a lot of that is your choice, mayor."

"Are you threatening me?"

"Of course not. Just the opposite. I want your help, and I want you to know that I would be very indebted to you personally if you would make this process easier. I always pay my debts, you know. You're in a special category, mayor, and you and your family can go where you want. I can give you the money to set up your own estate somewhere Outside."

"How can I get through to you? I'm part of this City—it's my life. And it belongs to its citizens—they'll never abandon it."

"Listen, Johnston, you don't have to answer me right away. Let's have a little fun. We don't have to talk business all the time." Hugh opened the door and motioned to the guard standing outside. In a moment two women entered the room. One was dark-skinned with black hair, and the other was very fair with red hair. They were at most twenty years old, and they were wearing very short, tight skirts, and their breasts bulged out of halter tops. "Take your pick, my treat," Hugh said.

Johnston got up and walked to the door. "If I could, I'd have you frog-marched out of here and deported back to your fucking Haven. And for your information, I'm a married man and I love my wife."

Hugh laughed. "Oh, don't be such a prig. This is just an appetizer. Once you're on board, you'll get this all the time." Hugh couldn't quite get Johnston's expression. Was it fear or just hatred? It was a pity because his help would make the whole project so much easier. If the Council and the Corps leadership believed that there were elements in the City that would acquiesce in the project, no one could seriously oppose it.

Hugh had to admit to himself that he admired the mayor. It would be a shame if we had to eliminate him, Hugh thought. If he can be brought around, maybe we can find a place for him in the Corps. He sent the girls away, telling Raoul to give them some money for their time; he might need them again.

It was always a bit of a disappointment, coming back to the Haven. When he was in the City, he took care to dress like an Outsider. No one knew who he really was, and he liked that. He could see them, but they couldn't see him; it gave him that much more power. People in the street and in those small shops—they had talked to him as if he were anyone or no one. He kept a notebook and wrote down names and events. Payback would be fun, he thought. Everyone who had ever slighted him, or treated him rudely, would be made to suffer. Their expressions would be priceless when they realized who it was that they had treated without respect.

Hugh got home late on Sunday night. He went immediately to his bedroom suite, which was at the opposite side of the grand residence from his wife and children. He needed the quiet, he had told them. Although the house was set in elaborate gardens and surrounded by willow trees (the estate required as much water as a small city), Hugh's room had no windows. He had the most advanced holo technology built into the walls, so he didn't need the "real" outside. This way he could have whatever outside he wanted, depending on his mood. He was tired, though, and went directly to sleep.

The next morning he told Miss Jones to call his staff together. They met at eleven a.m. in what was fancifully called the "Office

Building," a nineteenth-century Maine farm house that had been taken apart and put together on a California hillside. Actually, it was two farmhouses. Those old houses were very drafty, so one had been fitted inside of the other with insulation between the two, preserving the illusion of rustic simplicity outside and inside. His father had delighted in this place, but Hugh didn't really like it. He kept it because it was a reminder of his family's roots and it impressed some of his peers. There were too many windows and it was too simple for Hugh's taste; nothing grand about it. He consoled himself with the thought that his office would be, before too long, on the top of Nob Hill, and it would be a palace.

The Corps officers rose as he walked into the room they used for important meetings. Hugh nodded at the man who was clearly the most senior, and they all took their seats.

"Let's start, Colonel Hastings," Hugh said.

Hastings introduced the four other officers he had brought with him.

"Welcome, gentlemen, I can't wait to hear what you have to tell me." Hugh had tried to keep his tone civil, but it was hard. He expected incompetence from everyone and was annoyed in anticipation. Hastings looked a little nervous, which was appropriate—subordinates should fear their superiors.

"Well, I think it's pretty good news, Mr. Rowan. We've made a lot of progress on the Central Valley Plantation. It should be ready to receive Guests in about nine months."

"No, Hastings, you're wrong there. The troits have to be there in six months at the outside." The officers looked at each other. The word "troits" hung in the air.

Hastings's expression did not change, but Hugh noticed to his satisfaction that a bead of sweat had appeared on the colonel's forehead. "Even if the Plantation is ready, the other side of the equation, the departure issues, are still very, uh, complicated. We don't yet have a time line for that."

Hugh felt a surge of fury. He wanted to murder someone. Like other Owners, he had been taught in childhood to control his temper. Letting it out indiscriminately was shameful and dangerous for someone of his caste. Still, he couldn't help it that his face was turning red and the look in his eye was frightening. Hastings and his men quailed—to an Owner of Hugh's stature they were small objects that he could crush for his amusement. In the ordinary course of things, the Corps might protect them, but this was no ordinary matter.

Finally, Hugh took a breath and said quietly, "And what is the problem with that, Colonel?"

"Internal Security shouldn't do this on our own, sir—we should have more men. General Couseau hasn't authorized any troops at all."

"Have you presented him with a direct request?"

"Yes, sir, as direct as I could be."

"He knows this is coming from me and he still won't help?"

"That's correct, sir."

"Go back to Denver, Hastings, and wait for my orders."

CHAPTER THIRTEEN

Nils's view of the Maine landscape from the sonic window took in vibrant green to the horizon. From the air it looked like the forests Nils's great-grandfather might have seen, had he gone north instead of west in the previous century. But it wasn't the same. Southern climate zones had marched north and doomed the ecosystem that had prevailed for thousands of years. The hemlocks were gone, and there were few sugar maples left at low elevations, their places taken by red and white oak. A more virulent poison ivy proliferated wherever there were clearings in the forest, and there were many, because of the violent storms that raked the region at any time of year, but especially in the late summer and early fall. Even the once-sturdy canopy trees were vulnerable. Their roots were loose from constant flooding, and they easily fell victim to the winds.

Nils was met at the airport by a cheerful female sergeant who drove him to a Corps guesthouse on the coast, about forty miles north of the airport. It was an old stone building on a bluff looking out over the ocean, which broke on the rocks below. French windows opened onto flagstone terraces. His room was large and airy and very old-fashioned. There was a wide desk with a comfortable chair drawn up to it and a fireplace neatly stacked with logs ready to light. A bookcase with glass doors was filled with old books. The ample space of an earlier and more gracious century.

If only Philippa were here with me, he thought as he looked around. She'd love this place. But there wasn't time to think about his personal life—he had a report to write. He rubbed his bracelet first with the palm of his right hand and then the tip of his ring finger and in a few seconds he was surrounded by his virtual computer.

This report was the most difficult he'd ever had to write. Nobody had ever thought before of purposely de-populating a viable city and moving its population en masse to a Plantation, and there was nothing in the literature that was relevant, at least in the twenty-first century. There was an event in Asia a hundred and twenty years earlier, in a country called Cambodia, and before that were some actions in Eastern Europe that might have been similar, but the conditions and technology were so different that it was very hard to extrapolate.

He was deep into the literature when a yellow brick appeared floating in front of him, Rayna's holo call image. He chopped it with his hand, and she appeared in front of him, full-size. She raised a warning hand. "Don't say anything. Hastings is looking for you. Stay off the Net until I contact you again."

"Wait a minute! What am I going to do? You can't just leave me here."

"Trust me, Nils, you're better off there right now. The shit is hitting the fan here. Goodbye." Then her image collapsed into itself.

Nils felt like he had just been dropped out of a plane. He'd been rushing from one thing to another for as long as he could remember but now he'd been shunted off to a remote backwater and left there—for how long? He moved to a window and looked out at the green ocean, the wrong ocean, on the wrong side of the continent.

He walked downstairs to the dark, wood-paneled lobby, where he found the attendant. She was a blowsy old woman, not at all the usual trim Corps type.

"Good afternoon, Major," she said. "Do you want something to eat?"

"Not yet, thanks. I just want to look around a bit, if you don't mind."

"Help yourself. Just don't go too close to the edge of the cliffs, they're muddy and slippery. And don't get off the paths in the woods. We had a lieutenant here last year, young fella, thought he knew everything. He got lost and he's still lost. Maybe one day they'll find his bones, but I don't think so. In the old days a lot of people come up here, but now it's just Corps and not too many of them. And watch out for the poison ivy. Won't kill you, but you'll wish you was dead."

Nils quickly settled into a comfortable routine. The other officers were on vacation, and Nils knew many of them from previous postings. They ate many of their meals together and sat in front of the fireplace at night. They played old-fashioned board games. Nils learned Monopoly and he renewed his interest in chess. He read some of the books from his room.

Occasionally he received updates from Rayna, and he corresponded with Philippa by paper letter. The pilot who flew the most senior people directly to the retreat gave the letters to the old lady, who put them in his room. He wondered how Philippa got his letters, and he thought he'd better be careful what he wrote her.

Sometimes he thought about those boys he had taken to that bar. Was it possible that they were now slaves, trapped underground in the mines?

One day, as Nils was taking his morning walk on a path overlooking the water, he decided to climb down onto the rocks below. He wanted to touch the ocean, as if he could draw strength from it. The water was calm, almost glassy, and above, stratus clouds feathered the sky. He had never been so confused in his life. He wavered between relief at being neatly severed from his work on Project Moses and intense frustration that he was cut off from his home—the home they were plotting to obliterate. His life had run on a smoothly oiled track, but all that was now over—it took a strong act of will to acknowledge the bitter truth—and the future was a blank. He gazed east at the sharply etched horizon of sky and water and ached for Philippa, the anchor of his life.

Jack never knew exactly where the monastery was located. From Denver they drove for about three hours and then found themselves in a valley surrounded by snow-capped peaks in the distance, not close, but still sharp against the blue sky. This is where he would receive his training, Gladys told him.

The following months were arduous, waking at four a.m. eating only two meals a day, some days in profound silence. His meditation instructors were men, but the special training was done by women. Two of them were Buddhist nuns with shaved heads, but the other two were older women, probably around the same age as Gladys, who had come to the monastery just to train him.

They told him that he had been born with telepathic powers but had never learned to use them. Like most others of his kind, Jack had taught himself from an early age to shut them off. Still, he was luckier than many others because he was not brought up to hate and distrust himself. Often people who really were telepathic were so twisted by their early training that they could never learn to harness their powers. Life for them was torment because they heard things but were blocked from understanding them.

The first part of the training was learning how to let go of the fear of what was commonly called the "uncanny." Small children don't have this fear and happily commune with dimensions their elders have forgotten. But, as children grow, they learn from their elders that communication with unseen realms is wrong and they should be ashamed of it. As the poet said, "down they forgot as up they grew." Then the vast universe—which it is the birthright of human beings to perceive, not just with the five senses—becomes the Other, frightening, the uncanny.

When the fear was gone, new worlds opened. "All I have to do is pay attention," Jack said to Nina, one of his teachers. She was a nun, tiny and thin, wearing maroon robes.

She laughed. "That's it! But it's a lot harder than it sounds."

"Can anyone do it?"

"Not everyone can do what you can do, Jack. What's special about you is that you can translate mental images into thought words. Many have the potential to perceive others' thoughts, but not many can process them. It's a mental connection that few people are capable of."

"Can you do it?" They were sitting on meditation cushions on the polished, wooden floor of a bare room, with windows looking out on the mountains.

"Jack, hold my hand for a minute." She took his hand as if to shake it, held it for a minute, and then dropped it. "You never stop thinking about Gabe. He's always in the back of your mind. But you trust that Gladys has people looking for him. Kristin really wasn't for you, was she? And who is Jill, really?"

Jack sat back and let out a low murmur. "Oh, my god. Why did you hold my hand?"

"The physical connection makes it much easier to transmit the thoughts. You can still do it without that, but it takes more time and feels more like fragments. We think that touch completes the circuit and allows the brain to focus."

"Can I try it with you?" Jack asked.

Nina rose and walked to a window, her back to him. She remained there for a moment and then she turned around.

"Jack, I know you've had a hard time—losing Gabe, and before that your mothers dying. But still, you've led a relatively sheltered life. San Francisco is a pleasant little island in a sea of death. You need to complete the rest of the training before you can go into my mind safely."

"No, no. I want to try it. I want to see if I can really hear your thoughts."

"No, we need to be sure you have learned how to listen to someone's mind but not take on their emotions. If you can't do that, you could be seriously traumatized. But don't worry. We're starting that part of your training this evening. You're just going to have to be patient."

Three weeks later, after his morning meditation, Jack walked out of the hall and onto the deck overlooking a meadow that was painted with wild flowers; it was vibrant spring. A young monk came up to him and said, "Sir, I'm to take you to the abbot. He wants to talk to you." Jack started. No one had ever called him sir before.

They walked down several flights of stairs and through many corridors until they came to a doorway. The monk knocked and then opened the door. They stepped into a large room with many windows and a dark wood floor. There were statues and tapestries and paintings everywhere, not an empty space on the walls. Jack bowed to the old man sitting on a cushion in a corner. The man's face creased in a smile and he said, "Welcome, welcome. So, Jack, your preparation has gone well. Please sit down. I have a lot to talk to you about."

Jack felt honored. He had seen the abbot many times, but always before in a group. He went to the corner of the room, took a cushion from a pile, and placed it in front of the abbot. He sat down in the lotus position and waited for the old man to speak.

"Since you came here you've been studying certain skills. You've proven yourself a master of most of them. No, don't say anything. These skills are trivial compared to the wonder of truly waking up. This you've been taught. What is our Practice about, Jack?"

"Master, it is about reaching the Other Shore."

"And how do we reach the Other Shore?"

"By letting go of attachments and learning to truly see."

"And what of these powers that you seem to have in such abundance?"

"Master, those are poor reflections of what is real; they are ephemeral and not to be taken seriously."

"Well said, Jack. What is the way of the Bodhisattva?"

"It is to refuse Nirvana in order to stay in the world and help all sentient beings."

"And why does a Bodhisattva refuse Nirvana?"

"Because he has an overflowing love of the world."

"Jack, you have now known a very small taste of liberation—the tiniest taste!" the monk laughed merrily. "You are on the path and you may remain on it and find your salvation. Or you may choose another even more difficult path."

Jack sat quietly, but his heart leapt.

"There are those of our Order who believe that we should remove ourselves and concern ourselves only with what is true and unchanging. And then there are those who love the transient world. All is change and nothing is permanent. But we may love a person or a place, or the earth itself, and still not leave the Path. And we may devote our energy to helping the impermanent world. Some think we must."

Just then a young monk came into the room quietly and gave the master a slip of paper. The young man bowed and left the room. The master read the message and took a breath.

"Jack we live in heroic times. The earth, our mother, and the sky, our father, have become very angry with our species. There are those who will seize this anger and twist it in unskillful ways to harm and dominate. We believe in non-harming, but that does not mean that we are passive. Everyone has a choice. We are to pursue our salvation with diligence, certainly, but we may at the same time express our love for our fellow beings."

"Master, I am full of questions. Sometimes I think I understand what is deep, but I'm blind to what is in front of me."

"What do you want to do, Jack?" the abbot asked.

"I need to find my brother and help my City. And I want to find my father. But I don't want to leave. I want to stay and learn more. I don't know what I should do."

The old monk sat quietly, looking gently at Jack. "Few people have an individual destiny. But you have been called and you must go. We have done as much here as we can. It is time for you to leave and do what you need to do. But there is something you should know.

The powers that you have and which you have learned to control here are no more than tools, like a hammer or a saw which you can use for skillful purposes. If you use them for harm, even against real enemies, your powers will decay and fall away from you. Remember, Jack, what is real and what is an illusion. Goodbye."

Jack stood up, for an instant utterly confused about what to do next. But when he turned around he saw Gladys waiting for him at the door, smiling and holding out her arms.

"Hello, Jack, go get your things; we don't have a lot of time. There is a Corps train stopping near here in a few hours and we should be on it."

"Are you coming with me?" Jack asked.

"Yes I am. And you're going home," Gladys said.

In three days, he was back in San Francisco. It was July, and the days were cold and foggy. Without Gabe, the apartment was empty, bleak. Jack's childhood, always before so alive, so present, was now just a memory. Being home made it obvious how deeply he had changed. But his senses were open wide and the City was so wonderfully vivid. The salty air off the ocean and the voice of his neighbor singing "L'amour Est un Oiseaux Rebelle" from Carmen delighted him.

He left a note for Kristin, and she came to him quickly. She told him that she was now with a man named Tim, someone Jack had gone to school with. She offered to sleep with him that night, if he wanted, but he didn't. He couldn't stop thinking about Jill—she was the only one he wanted. He wished Kristin the best. She didn't have any interest in where he had gone and what he'd done. It was the same with most of his friends. Gabe would have been the curious one; he would have asked for every detail of what Jack had gone through—if Jack had not taken him to his doom.

Telling Gabe's father Jonah and his family about what happened was one of the hardest things Jack had ever experienced, right up there with finding his mothers. The worst of it was not the blame he felt he had earned, but the girls' simple grief. When they realized that Gabe had disappeared into an incomprehensible world and that there was nothing they could do to find him, they both burst into tears, and Jack felt like his heart was being torn out of his chest. He cried for the first time since he'd left Denver.

The next day, he went to meet Gladys, who was staying at the Palace, the grandest of the few hotels left in the City. Somehow it had managed to keep its nineteenth century glamour, its vast atrium lit by thousands of candles. As he turned from the well-upholstered lobby into a wide corridor, he saw her walking with two distinguished men her age. She was wearing a cloud-gray woolen dress with pink silk trimming around the collar. Wool was the cloth of choice in San Francisco. Cotton was expensive, like anything that required transportation, but sheep grazed everywhere west of Twin Peaks, and most homes had their own spinning wheels.

One of the men she was talking to looked vaguely familiar. He was dark-skinned and wore a dark blue suit and a tie. Gladys and the man shook hands and he walked away toward a dim corridor, followed by two other men, both of whom were trying to talk to him at the same time.

"Well, hello, Jack," she said. "How does it feel to be home?"

"Unfinished. Incomplete. I'm happy to be here but I have to find Gabe."

"Try not to worry—we're looking for him. Listen, I want you to go to the opera with me. I haven't been for years."

They went out the main entrance of the hotel where there was a car with a driver waiting for them.

"Where did you get this?" Jack asked.

"The mayor loaned it to me. We've got it for the duration," she said.

"How long is that?"

"I wish I knew."

They got in, and the car moved carefully up Market Street, dodging pedestrians and horse-drawn streetcars. Jack had rarely been in a car in his native city.

"We could have walked, you know," he said.

"It's always good to have new perspectives on your life."

Jack hadn't been to the opera since his mothers had died, and when he walked into the ornate marble lobby with its gilt-coved ceiling, he felt a flood of memories and a sudden, unexpected grief. For a moment he was lost in time. Gladys grabbed his arm and he felt comforted. They walked into the orchestra section and found their seats near the front. Of course she would have the best seats, he thought.

The opera that night was Gounod's Faust. This was a new production—the music was original but the story had been changed to be more relevant for modern audiences. Faust was a decrepit old man who had seen his city decay and become Outside. Most of its inhabitants had died of starvation. There was nothing left for him and he wanted to die himself. Mephistopheles promised to grant Faust's wish in exchange for his soul. His wish was to be young in the past, when the world was still whole.

His love, Marguerite, was a hippie of the late twentieth century. She raised goats and made cheese from their milk. The skies then were blue and clear, and the weather came on in a regular procession through the year. Enough rain, but not too much. Warm in the summer but not killing heat, and cold in the winter but no deadly blizzards. And he was young and handsome.

Marguerite fell in love with him. But then Faust was corrupted. He killed all her goats and sold them for meat while she was visiting her dying mother. Then he slept with her friends. Her community scorned her and turned her out, blaming her for what Faust had done. By this time Faust was a drunken sot. Marguerite had a baby by him but was so crazed by her suffering that she killed the child. She was banished to the wilderness of Los Angeles, and Faust tried to get her to escape with him to Mendocino, but she wandered away from him, distracted in her grief.

Jack was transported by the singing and for a few hours he thought of nothing else. The opera was a tenuous string that still tied together some parts of the world. The Corps made sure that singers could travel between the few viable cities that still had opera: London, Paris, and Sao Paulo, the cultural hub of the Southern Hemisphere. New York's Metropolitan Opera had left the doomed city long ago, trying in vain to find a permanent home, and finally dispersing. Sydney's great opera house was now half under water, looking like an abandoned ship with sails that would never be reefed.

Gladys had arranged for a table in the loge overlooking the lobby during the second intermission. There were glasses of sparkling wine waiting for them and a plate of honey sweets.

As they sat down she said to him, "I didn't bring you here just for fun, although Gaia knows you need some. We're sitting near someone very important. I wonder what he is thinking?"

Jack glanced over at the next table and quickly took in a man who was obviously an Owner—who else wore so much jewelry? There were two women at his table, one his age and the other much younger. The older one was afraid of the man, Jack got that immediately, and the younger one was bored. The man was enjoying himself. He was amused by his wife's fear of him.

CHAPTER FOURTEEN

Jack knew exactly what would happen next. The man would put his hand on the younger woman's thigh and move it toward her crotch. He would make no effort to conceal what he was doing. Then the older woman would stand up, say to him urgently, sotto voce, "She's your daughter!" and run out to the ladies' room. The man would laugh and take a sip of champagne. The young woman would shift in her seat, looking around, clearly bored. A moment after he saw it, it all happened.

Gladys looked at him with an expression he couldn't read.

"What?" he said.

"I can't read you and that's a good sign. You're progressing nicely. You knew what was going to happen, didn't you?"

"Yeah. It was different this time—usually I get a general idea something is going to happen, but this time I knew it in precise detail."

"Jack, do you see any fuzzy edges around the picture? Because those edges are where you have to put your awareness," she said.

"I know what you mean. That's where the thoughts are. I can see what people are going to do, but if I concentrate on the edges I can hear what they are thinking. Is that what you mean?" he asked.

"Yes, that's right. The trick is to do both at the same time, and to let each field lead you to the other field, or even new areas. Think of it as the exploration of new territories."

To anyone looking at them, Jack and Gladys would have appeared to be a young man taken to the opera by his kindly aunt. They were talking casually, probably about the production, or perhaps he was telling her of his most recent love. Jack turned around just in time to see Kristin.

"Hey, what a surprise. I didn't know you liked opera," he said.

"There are a lot of things you don't know about me," she said. "You remember Tim?"

Jack shook hands with a tall, muscular young man. "Sure. Hey, captain, it's been a long time." Jack and Tim both laughed and Kristin looked puzzled. "Tim's a take-charge kind of guy and we always called him captain," Jack explained. "This is my Aunt Gladys." He introduced them. "She's from Sacramento," he said, to head off their questions.

"Oh, my goodness," said Kristin, "how did you get here?"

"On the governor's boat," she said.

"Oh, is there still a governor? I thought Hernandez was the last one," she said.

"No, there is one. His name is Reynaldo Cruz. You should read the news, my dear," Gladys said.

"I know I should, but I'm so busy. You know it isn't easy to make a living these days."

"I've read about him," Tim said. "He makes his money from the Owners, doesn't he?"

"Would you two like to sit down and join us?" Gladys asked.

"Oh, no, thanks," Kristin said. "You have a good time. Goodbye, Jack."

Jack watched her walk away with her date and kept looking until they disappeared into the crowd. He took a deep breath and said to Gladys, "There goes my last normal relationship."

"Why do you say that?"

"I'm changing. I've changed. I used to not know what she was thinking, which was a good thing! Now it's like I can see inside her head."

"But what if you meet someone different, someone who's more like you?"

"I've already met her, but it isn't what I'd call normal."

"Jill is a very special person. And you're not the only one who knows that."

Jack took a sip of his wine and looked at the next table. The Owner sitting there looked directly at him, obviously noticing him for the first time. A look of displeasure crossed the man's face and his ill feeling was an air pump—the man began to grow, to inflate like a balloon until he took up Jack's entire field of vision. Jack fell off a cliff—down, down—and there was no bottom. He was in a room, no a kind of tomb, hermetically sealed, divorced absolutely from nature. Stick figures, caricatures of human beings, were chattering at each other in stick language. He was flying above a sea of people moving heavily toward their doom. Then he was walking down a street greeting old people, children, his friends, Gabe—they were all his kin and there was only love and compassion. This is how it must be, he thought to himself.

When he opened his eyes he was lying on a narrow bed in a small, white room. Gladys was sitting next to him.

"You certainly know how to call attention to yourself," she said.

"Where are we?"

"In the opera house clinic. It's here for the all the old folks. And you."

"What happened?" he asked.

"You tell me. You fell to the floor and curled into a fetal position. I had no contact with your mind."

"I was somewhere important. Gladys, I saw, I was there…"

"You'll have to tell me about it later and write it all down. I can't enter that door the way you can. Thank goodness! But, you did make us miss the last act!"

"Don't worry. I can see that too. Marguerite is saved," Jack said.

By the time they left, the opera house was empty, except for some ushers who slept there every night, unrolling mattresses in some of the boxes. Jack knew a few of them from school.

"Let's walk. Someone will take the car for us," Gladys said. "The air will do you good."

He was amazed at the older woman's energy; she never seemed to tire. They walked down the quiet streets, and he remembered the old, cozy feeling of safety he had always felt in the dark. It was like a protective blanket.

When they got into Jack's apartment, Gladys sat down and said, "Now let's talk about what you heard and saw at the opera."

"You took me there for a reason, didn't you? Why didn't you tell me?"

"I wasn't sure what would happen. You have to believe I didn't know it would be that powerful for you."

Jack couldn't sit—he got up and started pacing back and forth across the living room. He saw for the millionth time the worn Persian carpet his mother had loved so.

"I'd appreciate it if you'd warn me about your plans," Jack said, surprised at his own anger.

"I'm sorry, Jack, of course, you're right. Tell me about the man at the next table."

"Alright. He's the master of his own universe. It's all in his head. He wants to make it exterior. I'm trying to remember."

"Why did you go through that door? It looked like a seizure."

"It was him! He triggered it. I don't know why or how. Does he have these talents too?"

"I knew it. No, I'm pretty sure he had no idea what was happening. The Owners despise anything that is not meat. Don't laugh, Jack— you know what I mean. If it isn't grossly material they think it doesn't exist. They've declared war on the deepest part of themselves. That's how they're able to do the terrible things they do—they trample on their own humanity and that justifies trampling on everyone else. Maybe it's their religion—they're taught as children to hate themselves and that makes them hate everyone else, too. But the important thing now is that you're connected to him somehow and we need to understand what that means."

Jack got up and went to the wine rack under the sink. He pulled out a zinfandel that his mothers had been saving for a special occasion. It was from a vineyard near old San Jose, where they used to go when he and Gabe were kids. Margaret's uncle owned the place, and that's where the boys had learned to ride horses.

"Let's have some of this before we do any more work," he said. "I need to alter my blood chemistry a little." They sat quietly for a few minutes, savoring the wine and looking out the window at the lights flickering in neighboring apartments. "Tell me more about Jill," he said.

"Sure. She's about your age, and her parents died when she was a baby. She was raised in a Tibetan-American monastery in the Dakota Republic, very remote. Her great-aunt was a nun there. She's passed away now. The monks and nuns were delighted to have her there. I've talked to some of them. She was a gifted medium from an early age, and they nurtured her talents carefully. She was taught to trust in her psychic abilities from the beginning, so she never had to unlearn anything the way you did."

Jack listened but did not respond. For a moment he was distracted—he felt a glow within his heart, warmth where there had been cold. Then he said, "Gabe is alive—I know it. He's not suffering! Hey, what exactly did I have to unlearn?"

"It's the fear of yourself, of the part of yourself that you learned to disown. If we admit who we really are we can't be who we think we are."

Jack laughed and poured her more wine. "I don't know anymore who I think I am. I've forgotten," he said.

He got up and went over to a closet near the apartment's front door. In the back, behind his mothers' coats, which he had not been able to get rid of, was his guitar. He took it out and came over to where Gladys was sitting.

"What would you like to hear?"

"Something hopeful?" she said with a smile.

"That leaves out most of my repertoire. How about something sad but sweet?" And he began to sing an old song of lost love.

After some time, Gladys said, "That was beautiful. It's time for me to go back to the hotel. Tomorrow will be a busy day, and I want you to get a good night's sleep."

When she was gone, Jack walked around the apartment, looking into every room. Never had it felt as alive as it did now, when no one else was there. But they were there—his mothers were alive again, Gabe was present everywhere. Now that he was home he felt the past on his shoulders like a heavy but reassuring weight. He had grown the muscles to carry it and to acknowledge how much it needed him. Like the future, it needed him.

Hugh Rowan enjoyed his wife's outrage. It was really a lot of fun to see people squirm, kind of like when he was a kid incinerating ants with his magnifying glass. But he was annoyed when that boy at the next table had an epileptic fit or whatever it was. Why do they let people like that into the opera, anyway? Well, things were going to be different in a matter of months. The troit will be gainfully employed, squatting in the boiling sun picking strawberries. The image restored his good humor, and he told his daughter to drink another glass of wine.

In truth, the opera bored Hugh, but his attendance had ceremonial importance. There was an elite of city dwellers, and it was important for them to understand that he was there to stay and that the Owners respected at least some of the City's institutions. Those people could make it much easier to clear the City if they chose, or they could stiffen resistance. Later, after the City was subdued, he would deal with them. At the moment they were the elite, but afterward they would be troits just like the rest.

Hugh amused himself with these thoughts while the singers droned on interminably. Finally it was over and he led his wife and daughter out of their box into the lobby. He looked back to urge them to move faster, and when he turned around he nearly bumped into someone.

"Hello, Rowan. What are you doing here?"

Hugh lost his composure for a brief second. "Hello, Simpson. Same thing as you."

"I didn't know you were a music lover."

"It's possible there's a lot you don't know," Hugh said.

Ronnie Simpson turned around and motioned to a beautiful woman who was chatting nearby with a friend. "Come over here, darling."

"Hello, Linda," Hugh said.

"Oh, hello, Hugh." She turned to her husband, "Ronnie, I think it's wonderful that Hugh is exposing himself to culture, don't you? And his family, too. You are so kind to bring them. Hello, Sylvia, come over here, don't be afraid."

Hugh wanted to demolish her, to obliterate her, but she was a peer and he held his tongue. He should have expected the Simpsons to be here; they seemed happiest when they were mingling with scum.

Just then, a man wearing a Corps uniform came up to Linda. "Excuse me, ma'am. I have a message for you." He handed her an envelope with a red wax seal on the flap.

"That's a strange way to communicate," Hugh said.

"Oh, Ronnie, it's from General Couseau. I'm in!"

Simpson laughed. "I hope you're not a lifer. We've got some important parties to go to."

Hugh was confused but tried not to show it.

"Hugh, I'm an officer of the Corps now!" Linda said to him gaily. "It's only for six months, but that's all I need."

"Why would you want to do that?" Hugh asked.

"I want to feel what the Guests in the Plantations feel, see what they see, hear what they hear. In case I make a movie about them. It's called empathy, Hugh," she said.

"You are even stranger than I thought," Hugh said.

Linda took Ronnie's arm. "Let's go somewhere and celebrate," she said, and they turned away with the slightest of goodbyes.

Hugh turned to his wife and ordered her to go home with their daughter. He had business that night in the City, he told her, and for once he was telling the truth. He left the building through the side entrance facing the ruins of the old symphony hall. A car was waiting for him. In a few minutes it deposited him at a small house on the top of Pacific Heights. A door opened into darkness, and he walked in confidently, knowing where he was going.

"Hello, Hugh," she said as she stretched out her hand for his coat.

"Hello, Philippa, how are you?"

"It's a long story, and I'm sure you're not interested. Would you like a drink?"

He asked for scotch with ice and then walked into the living room with the view of the bay and MarinHaven beyond.

When she returned he said, "How is Nils these days?"

"I'm not sure. Where he is, the only way I can communicate with him is by sending a paper letter via a Corps messenger."

"That seems to be the fad," he said. "How is his career going?"

"Why do you ask?"

Hugh could read her moods. When they were children and she was bigger than him, he'd know when she was about to attack. Not that he cared—she could never inflict real pain.

"You were the one who had him transferred, weren't you?" she asked.

"Well, the truth is that I wanted to help you both and I think he's got the expertise for the job. You're my only sister, and even though you chose to marry beneath you, I haven't abandoned you."

"You are so goddamn noble. Did it ever occur to you that you should have asked first? Has anyone told you lately that you aren't God?"

"No, they wouldn't dare. But Father Clark keeps reminding us that there is a pope, even though Rome is gone. Doesn't that count?"

"Hugh, what are you involved in? What is going on?"

"What, you mean Nils hasn't told you? I find that hard to believe."

Philippa reached over to a bottle and filled her glass with red wine. Her face had become blank—aggressively neutral. "I'm starting to hear rumors. They say the Owners want to move into the City. Or at least some of the Owners. There's a lot of opposition to that but some people are saying it might be good for the City, that they would bring in new money. I personally don't know why you'd want to move here. Even with all your money you'd have to put up with a lot of hostility."

Hugh looked at her. "What do you think Nils is working on?"

"Usually he can't tell me until it's over," she said.

"You aren't answering my question," he said.

"Why did you come to visit me tonight?"

"Let's get to the point." He got up and refreshed his drink. "I think you know what is about to happen, Philippa. This rotten city is going to be cleaned up and made a fit place for people like us to live in. But it won't be easy, and the initial phases will be…unpleasant. I think you should come back to the Haven until things are settled here. You can stay in one of the guest cottages if it disturbs your pure-as-driven-snow conscience to be under the same roof as me. Then, when it's over, you can come back here and assume your real status."

"Why this sudden altruism? It isn't like you."

"Let's just say that right now our interests run parallel. It wouldn't do for you to be here during the battle. If the troits find out you're one of us and related to me they might take you hostage or God knows what."

"Don't use that vulgar word in my house! What you're really afraid of is that I might take their side, isn't it?"

"I never thought of you as suicidal and I still don't," he said.

She got up and moved toward the window, looking away from him. "This is the hinge of history, isn't it? We're going to muddle on with some kind of civilization or we'll go into the dark ages. I know what side I'm on."

"Then you're choosing to be a loser. Be realistic. In this world our grandparents and great-grandparents created only the strong can survive. The weak will have to serve us or die. That's just simple fact."

"Oh, no. We have a community here where there are no strong and no weak—we help each other and it makes us all strong. Anyway, you need the Corps to do your dirty work, and they're not Owners. What makes you think they'll do it?"

Hugh was getting bored with this conversation. He didn't think she would accept his offer, and a part of him was hoping she wouldn't. Having her on the estate would be hell.

"You can leave now," she said, but neither of them moved.

Hugh said, "Think about it and call me. You have a week to decide. If you call before the time's up, I'll arrange everything. After that I can't guarantee what will happen."

It was a relief to walk out of Philippa's house. She was one of the very few people in his life that he couldn't control, and he hated that feeling.

CHAPTER FIFTEEN

Nils had never felt so useless—this was the first time in his adult life when he had no responsibilities. He explored the local shoreline and hiked the hills until he had seen every view possible.

All the land around belonged to the Corps, but it wasn't a Plantation, it was a nature preserve, and the forest ecosystems were being studied for their effect on planetary heating. A few of the old mansions had been kept for officers' retreats and relaxation. There were no Guests and no Owners and very little stress. To the north, from Camden to the Canadian border (just a sign post now that there was no Canada—and no United States either, for all practical purposes), the local population had been ejected and the coast turned into a Haven for the Owners.

Having to communicate in letters deepened his sense of being out of time and place. It was a strange experience, writing a message on paper. Nils wrote only in his room, sitting alone and imagining Philippa and her reaction on reading what he'd written. Then he gave the letter to a total stranger, who somehow made sure it got delivered. The reply took days, sometimes a whole week, and then it would come in an envelope he'd have to pry open with a finger or a knife. He'd unfold the pages and smooth them out as he walked back to his room to read in privacy. The letter always felt like a surprise, even when there was nothing really new.

Philippa's latest letter told him about her conversation with her brother. She asked Nils what he thought of her decision to stay in San Francisco. That bastard, he said to himself—is it possible that he's the one behind Project Moses? It was Hugh's kind of idea. He paced back and forth in his large room and looked out all the windows, as if searching for answers. Finally, he got out his hcue and fired it up. Rayna be damned, Hastings be damned. He had to find out what was going on. There were a string of messages from Internal Security, culminating in one directly from Colonel Hastings. He used the word "insubordination"—obliquely, but there it was.

Then he called Philippa. She was at home finishing her yoga when her image appeared in front of him. And here was the cruelty of holography—his eyes accepted her as close enough to touch, but all of his other senses cried out their longing for her.

He told her to go to Denver. "I'll try to set up a meeting for you with General Couseau. He needs to know what you wrote to me."

"No, Nils," she said, "I can't leave now. I've got to help in whatever way I can. Everyone is talking about the possibility of war, but no one's leaving," she said.

"Most of them don't have any place to go. Listen. You know something the general should know and you have to tell him in person."

"What? That Hugh is the motivating force behind this? I'm sure he knows that already."

"But if you tell him, that confirms it."

"Nils, think about it. General Couseau will wonder why I came to him. You have no guarantee he'll trust me. He'll probably think of me as an Owner, a Rowan. Here I can be of some help. Our house could be a kind of sanctuary, if it comes to that. Hugh won't harm me, I'm pretty sure of that. And if I go, I may not be able to come back."

"Phil, please listen to me. The best thing you can do to help the City is to go to Denver."

"Sweetheart," she said, "my love. I just can't leave now; trust me on this."

Nils suddenly felt defeated. As usual, there wasn't anything he could do to make her change her mind.

"Don't you realize that the Corps can't be stopped once the decision is made to take over the City? But they can be stopped before they try. You have to see the commandant."

"Don't underestimate us, Nils. The City is mobilizing and we'll fight. They're going to be very surprised by our reception committee."

"Honey, darling, I'm afraid for you," Nils said, and he stifled the sob that welled up in his throat.

"Find a way to come home, sweetheart. Let's face this together."

When the call ended, loneliness broke over him like a wave. He looked out a dormer window, and he could see in the distance the empty inlet bordered with rocks and, on the other side, more forest. There was a painting in his room of this very inlet in the old days—dozens of small, white sailboats bobbed in its waters. He was overcome with nostalgia for a time he never knew. Once, there had been a whole country of citizens, no Owners or Helpers or Guests or Outsiders. And a sea friendly to little boats.

A yellow brick appeared in front of him and he chopped it with his hand. Rayna's image filled the corner of the room. "Nils, I told you to stay off the Net," she said. Although there was no anger in her voice, there was an edge. She looked like she had just come out of the shower, her hair wet and plastered on her head. "If Hastings finds you, he'll go after you."

"What the hell does that mean?"

"He's decided you're an obstacle to the project. He's under a huge amount of pressure to get this done, and he's gone on a rampage, screaming sabotage. Two officers have already been court-martialed and executed. Internal Security now has its own courts, and you can imagine what goes on there."

"What am I supposed to do?"

"If you get any hint that he knows where you are, you better get as far away from the retreat house as you can. If he gets his hands on you, God knows what he'll do to you. I wish I could help you more, but it's impossible for us right now. Don't try to call me back. General Couseau isn't available."

He shouted at her, "Send me back to San Francisco, now! I'm through with all your insanity!" But she'd already disconnected—he was yelling at a wall.

Nils went downstairs. It was time for lunch, and although he had no desire to eat, he needed to go through the motions or he would go crazy. He took his tray outside and sat alone on a wooden bench on a hillside that looked out over the water. Rayna's words were chilling, but there was no certainty that Hastings could find him. If he had to go, where would he go, anyway? How much time did he have if he did have to leave?

Just as he was standing up, the official Corps logo appeared in front of him, with its motto—*Jure et Dignitate Gladii*, "By the Law and Dignity of the Sword"—emblazoned on a shining globe. This wasn't a call, it was a summons. An officer Nils had never seen before appeared and said, "Nils Rakovic, you are being sent orders to return to Denver. You will board the sonic at zero nine hours tomorrow morning." The officer's failure to address him with his rank of major was chilling.

The image faded quickly. He walked back across the wide lawn to the old mansion. He had seen in the first reception room a kind of kiosk where orders were received by the officers staying there. There was an old-fashioned screen at the top and a slot at the bottom for paper transcriptions. Corps orders were not official unless they were also printed on paper.

Nils looked in the slot and found three sets of papers. One set was addressed to him. The orders were signed "Colonel Douglas Hastings." Nils went up to the old lady, who was part caretaker, part concierge. "I'd like to go for a hike. Do you have a backpack I can borrow?"

"In the closet behind you. You better be careful. People have got lost out there."

"You already told me that. But there are trails, aren't there?"

"Yep. And there are lots a' old roads that are trails now. Problem with folks is they think they know what they're doin' and they don't.

Here's a map. There's Settlements west, in the mountains. Not part of the Corps at all, you know. But don't matter to you—way too far for a day walk, a course." She gave him a sheet of paper that showed only a few trails.

"Is this the best you've got?" he asked.

"Yep," she said. "By the way, saw your orders. You gotta check out tomorrow morning."

It was decided for him. He couldn't stay, and if he went back he'd be going into a trap. *That's easy*, he thought, *now all I have to do is survive on my own in a place I don't know.* He went back to his room and went through a mental checklist. What would he need? He knew he was at the end of a narrow peninsula jutting out into the Atlantic. The map the old lady had given him showed trails leading west, so that was some help. He'd have to head for those Settlements—there was nowhere else to go. He wished once again that he had been educated in the City instead of the Haven. City children learned wilderness skills as seriously as Helpers learned etiquette.

It was the end of July, so he wouldn't have to worry about freezing, and he was far enough north for killer heat waves to be unlikely. Torrential rain storms were always a danger, but he was more worried about what he would eat. And he would have to make sure that he could not be tracked.

Nils looked at his wrist, at the bracelet that had been his since he first became a Corps officer. It was the sign that he was among the privileged of the earth, one who did things and not one to whom things were done. It was his personal identification device and it was his tether to the Corps. Several times it had been his lifeline. He quickly left his room and ran down the stairs and out a back door. He ran for about ten minutes until he came to a cliff. The surf was pounding on the rocks twenty feet below. He ripped the bracelet off and threw it into the ocean. He went back to his room and packed some clothes, leaving some behind, and then went down to the kitchen and took as much food as he dared (all the cupboards were unlocked), and walked out the front door. The old lady wasn't there. He didn't see anyone. He walked into the woods, heading west.

The faux farm house was crowded and nearly everyone was in uniform, the black uniform of Internal Security. Rowan walked into the main conference room and everyone stood up. They should bow to me, he thought. Should it be a shallow bow or a deep one from the waist? He'd have to think about that. At some point it would be nice if everyone kneeled. Well, that kind of thing can wait until after we've taken the City. New etiquette will be required for a new society and perhaps they'll understand when I assume my proper role as Lord—for now. Later, perhaps, King—or Emperor? Anything is possible. Rowan took his seat and everyone else sat. He nodded to the officer at his right, Colonel Hastings.

"Mr. Rowan, gentlemen and ladies," Hastings began, "we're only weeks away from the initial implementation of Project Moses. We're here to report to Mr. Rowan on our progress and readiness. The order of this meeting is set forth in the paper in front of you. We'll go by tasks. Let's start with communications."

The meeting droned on for two hours. Everyone had done everything they were supposed to do and had met every goal that had been set for them. All was in readiness, they said. The operation could begin in about two months, on September 1.

The plan was not complicated. "Keep it simple," Rowan told Hastings from the beginning. Troops would land in three places—in the east, using shallow craft to go up Mission Creek just south of the Bay Bridge; in the north at the old Presidio; and in the west, at the inlet where Baker Beach used to be. A contingent from the third group would seal the populated part of the City off from the Peninsula. They would march inland until they met at City Hall. They would shoot any citizen they saw, in order to demonstrate firmness. When it was secured they would issue a proclamation dissolving the government of San Francisco and putting the city under martial law.

Rowan would use the next week to consolidate his power. The main library would be demolished; it could serve no useful purpose in the new order. All horses and bicycles and cars would be requisitioned. Farms on the outskirts of the City would be cleared and all crops destroyed. All food would be taken to Union Square and burned or otherwise destroyed. The water that had been turned on after Johnston became mayor would be turned off again and no water would be otherwise made available. What was left of Golden Gate Park would be closed off. Finally, the City would be put to the torch and most of it burned to the ground.

There had been quite a bit of debate about whether to let people leave the City in the transitional phase. Many of the Corps officers were in favor of keeping escape routes open and even aiding the citizens to flee. Rowan finally had to confront them. "Don't you understand," he said. "We're not just clearing out the City, we're populating a Plantation." It made the job much harder for them, but the officers finally came around.

They had to time the evacuation just right. It should be when the citizens were desperate and had lost hope but before they were too weak and debilitated to walk eighty miles in the heat. Nils should have been in charge of that, Hugh thought with some bitterness—it would have made his career. Instead he had disappeared like the coward he was.

Hugh had always thought Nils a fool and now he'd confirmed the judgment. Nils should have made Philippa go back to MarinHaven. Family had always been paramount with the Rowans, and they had all lamented her marriage to a Helper and her move to the City. She was a dishonor to the family and a source of embarrassment, but she was still his sister, his blood, and it pained him to think of her on the wrong side of this war.

Well, Philippa would just have to take her chances. What would the City people do if they knew who she really was? If they harm her, they will pay dearly—because she was a Rowan, an Owner. His own sentiments were not a factor—Hugh had taught himself to value people and things by the simple yardstick of whether they furthered his vision of the future or hindered it. Philippa was the exception that proved the rule.

Hugh felt quite optimistic about the plans, but he had one worry—he really should get the approval—or at least the non-opposition—of the other Owners. This meeting had droned on long enough, he decided. "All right, that's enough for now," he said, standing up abruptly. All the officers leapt to their feet and followed him with their eyes as he walked out of the room.

It took another whole day to get a meeting of the Council together. It didn't happen very often and most of its members were annoyed when it did. They had busy lives, some focused on business, others on pleasure, but all filled with activities and meetings. The economy was made up of interlocking monopolies, which this small group owned. Whatever friction between them required problem-solving was generally done by lower-level people.

The Council had short ceremonial meetings three or four times a year. In January they chose a place for the annual Council Ball, a social event that brought together members from all over North America and sometimes even other continents. It was actually a week-long retreat where they could talk informally about any issues that concerned them. Ball Week was also a great time for the young people to get to know each other. The Owners had become an actual caste, and they did not approve of marriage outside of it, so they had to bring people together. These get-togethers had started many years before, in Davos and Jackson Hole and Aspen. Every four years the Council met to choose the president of the United States. It was an exercise in nostalgia but no one wanted to end the tradition.

Emergency meetings of the Council were rare—the last one had been five years ago when ChaseAmericanWells, CAW, the only bank in North America, wanted to re-value its banknotes and had to solicit the Council members' advice on the impact on their businesses.

There were only twenty-three members of the Council, and any member could call a meeting. Hugh had never taken advantage of this privilege before; he had avoided going to these meetings as much as he could get away with it. He hated talking to his peers. They did not recognize who he really was, his greatness. Some of them were his father's age and treated him with obvious condescension. It was intolerable. One day he'd deal with all of them. But for now they were equals.

The Council meeting room was underground, deep inside Mt. Tam. Rowan had been there once, out of curiosity. It was a simple concrete chamber that looked like a storage room when nothing was switched on. No one actually went there physically; they met by hologram and the meeting room was designed for efficiency. Once projected into the room, all of the members not only saw each other, they all saw the same space.

What they saw was decided by the Council's chief secretary, Amanda Black. She had a great sense of occasion and knew how to put them in a place that suited the discussion. Once, when they were discussing the upcoming ball, they saw themselves on a broad lawn, and in the distance was a stone balustrade, and beyond that blue water. Faintly, in the far distance, was the Connecticut shore. They were at a garden party at an early-twentieth-century Long Island estate. Amanda had been reading *The Great Gatsby* and had managed to recreate a scene from the book.

When Rowan told her to arrange the meeting, she asked him what the subject matter was. "Changes in the status of San Francisco," he said.

CHAPTER SIXTEEN

Linda Crowley arrived at West Point late in the afternoon. She could have been inducted anywhere she chose, but she wanted the same experience as other Corps officers, and most of them received their commissions at the Corps Academy.

General Couseau had recommended his tailor, who chose a dressmaker he trusted, to make her uniform quickly. The blue uniform suited her, but then what didn't? Once she had played the part of a slave in a Church-owned silver mine. For a season after that movie, slave-chic was all the rage among Owner women—and many Helpers as well. Clunky silver bracelets that looked like shackles flew off the shelves, and little leather whips hung from many fashionable waists.

Linda loved the Corps. She imbued it with all the romance and adventure that she had never herself experienced. It was the French Foreign Legion, the U.S. Marine Corps, and her Dad, a dashing sailor who had disappeared at sea on his yacht, the *Fury*, when she was fourteen. She was deeply thrilled when she took the oath: "I swear to faithfully protect and defend the Great Companies and the Church upon which the future of the human race depend, and I pledge obedience to the Corps."

It's not a bad world, after all, she thought, that has an institution so dedicated to doing good. Where did she first get the idea of joining, anyway?

The Academy commandant, Colonel Bryce Roberts, hosted a dinner for her after her induction. Department heads were there, but there was also a sprinkling of cadets. He knew she'd appreciate some pretty, young male faces—he did too. After the dessert was served, cherry pie and vanilla ice cream, Roberts rose and lifted his glass of sparkling wine. "I want to offer this toast to our new colleague. I know her tenure will not be long, but it is very important to us and to the entire Corps. She has already shown a lot of courage and determination in coming here, and we know this is just the beginning. Please lift your glasses and join me in saluting Lieutenant Linda Crowley!"

Linda was lifted on a wave of emotion—she was now part of something larger and grander than herself. She stood up and looked around the ornate room that seemed like a cross between an armory and a church.

"Thank you all so much. I can't tell you how moved I am to become a part of this noble institution. I will carry it—and you all—in my heart forever. Thank you." She sat down to thunderous applause.

After, there was a small reception in the commandant's house. As usual, she was surrounded by a group of men. Sometimes she had to break out of the circle around her and corral one or two other women to stand next to her so the men couldn't get too close.

This group was respectful and very curious.

"It's simple," she told a few of them. "I want to go to a Plantation and see what life is like there." Why do they look embarrassed?, she wondered. Colonel Roberts came up to her and the group parted. He whispered something and she nodded. Ten minutes later she said her goodbyes, and a cadet escorted her to Roberts's office. The colonel rose when she walked in.

"Oh, please sit," she said.

"Lieutenant Crowley, I've been told to help you find a Plantation to visit. We'll have to think carefully to get just the right one for you."

"I'm not picky, Colonel. Just assign me to any one that has an opening for a new officer."

"It's not that simple, Lieutenant. We have to guarantee your safety and some of the Plantations are, well, not totally secure."

"You mean weather, I imagine. Well, I'm a lot hardier than I look, Colonel."

"Certainly, weather is a factor. But there's more to it than that. We need to find you a place where the ratio of Corps to Guests is high and where the Guests are not volatile. That's not simple, because the high Corps ratio Plantations tend to be where there's the most trouble."

"Are we limited to North America?" she asked.

"As a practical matter, yes. In South America the Corps is either Spanish or Portuguese speaking. That would be difficult for you, I suppose?"

She smiled and then walked over to the map wall. "Is this a map of all the North American Plantations?"

"Yes it is. But we can't pick one randomly, you know."

"Of course not, Colonel. How about this one?" She pointed to one of the larger circles in the southeast, bordering the Atlantic.

"That's what I mean, Lieutenant. The Guests in that one have been fighting each other for years now. It's not typical."

"I do want a Plantation that is representative—one of those places where we see the Corps and the Guests are working together in harmony." She was puzzled by his expression and then she said, with a slight hesitation in her voice, "There are places like that, aren't there?"

Colonel Roberts was silent for a moment. "Maybe you should work with General Couseau's staff on this. How about if I set up a meeting for you?"

It was a Friday, and he set up the meeting for the following Thursday. Linda was disappointed, but she told herself that hardship was part of the job. So she decided to take the next sonic back to MarinHaven and spend the time at home. Ronnie would be happy for her company, she knew.

San Francisco had never looked more beautiful. It was the perfect perspective to see it all, from the great height of the Bankers' Club at the top of the old Bank of America building. Each member of the Council had a perfect view of Telegraph Hill and beyond it, the blue bay, filled with sailboats, some with pure white sails, others red or orange or blue. The sun was high overhead, and there were wisps of fog curling through the Golden Gate. Cars flowed silently across the bridge.

Now she's gone too far, Hugh thought. We don't need reminders of the City eighty years ago. But there was nothing to be done. Amanda Black had arranged the Council's meetings forever and even he couldn't tell her what to do. Maybe this scene of the past would remind the other Owners of the pleasures of living in the City.

Rowan looked around the room. As soon as he appeared he could see that all of the other Council members were there—at least it looked like they were there. Nowadays it was possible to leave your image in its seat, so to speak, and go off and have a private chat with someone else at the same time, also by hologram. The seated image could be programmed to fidget enough so that it seemed like someone was there. The only way to tell was to ask the image a direct question. A slight delay in the response usually meant that the person was otherwise occupied. If the delay was minimal, it wasn't considered rude.

The chairman of the Council was always the CEO of one of the Great Companies, and the job was rotated every year. The Church, which had a seat on the Council, wanted one of its archbishops to be in the rotation for chairman, but the Great Companies had resisted so far. The brand-new chairman this year was Gray Wainwright, from Edison Atlantic-Pacific. The rotation was always on July 1, the beginning of the fiscal year. Wainwright greeted them all cordially, and Rowan tried his best to be amiable.

There appeared to be twenty-two other men and women sitting around the table. They were dressed in a variety of outfits, from the most formal coats and ascots to jeans and tee shirts. Holo meetings were like that—you went into them as you were, unlike physical gatherings of Owners, where dress codes were expected and obeyed without question.

"Hugh, since you put this item on the agenda, why don't you start the discussion. First, what do you mean by the 'status' of San Francisco?"

"Thanks, Gray. Forgive me if I repeat what you already know, but I think it's important to set the stage carefully. When we got rid of the federal and state governments, San Francisco was one of those few cities that became de facto a city-state of its own. I'm not sure why we let that happen, but the fact is that the City rejected the Great Companies and the Church everywhere it could. It became an economic renegade and it went off into its own religion, or should I say religions. I'm not qualified to talk about that, I admit, but I think the Monsignor here would probably agree that San Francisco has sunk into the worst kind of superstition.

"The more independent the City became, the more arrogant and corrupt it became. At this point, the Great Companies have no commercial interests in the City, except for Nestle Waters. And congratulations for that, Barbara, that was well done." He nodded to a woman near the end of the long table. She gave him a tight smile and a few people clapped. An older man spoke up. He was the representative of UDAT, United Delta American Transportation. "Well, what difference is any of that for us? It's a small city and they can go to hell for all I care."

Another member spoke, Rafe Conner, a youngish man with a shocking head of prematurely gray hair. When they were both no older than twenty, Rowan had gotten into a fistfight with him at an Owners' ball, but now he couldn't remember why. He was from what they still called "Wall Street," although the physical place had been underwater for twenty years. "I'm very busy, as I'm sure everyone is, and I wonder why you called this special meeting, Hugh."

"It's pretty simple," Rowan said. "Most of the country is what we now call 'Outside,' which means it doesn't have any effective government, just whatever security the Outsiders can afford to buy from us by contracting with the Corps. But eventually there will be government and it will be our government. San Francisco is a bad example—it's a danger because it's a model for places that want to be independent of the Great Companies. As long as it exists in its current form it will be an inspiration for rebels and malcontents."

"So what do you want us to do?" Conner asked.

"What I'm asking for is your agreement that the Corps should move into the City and let us turn it into a model for other places," Rowan said.

"What do the San Francisco authorities think of your ideas?" someone asked.

"I've done my best to bring them on board, but they're very stubborn."

The questions came fast.

"How much is this going to cost us?"

"Who is going to be in charge?"

"What will San Francisco look like after this happens?"

"I'm glad you asked that. The way I see it, the City should be ours. Every Council member who wants to build a residence there will be able to. They've kept us out and the result is that San Francisco is nothing but a rabbit warren. What a waste! We can make it into a beautiful place. It is one of the very few cities left that has livable weather. We have our Havens, but we don't have a single city. This could be our capital."

Rowan could almost hear the murmurs of approval. Temperatures south of the forty-fifth parallel could kill in the summer; north of that were winter blizzards that immobilized everything for weeks at a time.

The discussion turned to cost. "This will be a budget item for the Corps," Rowan admitted.

"That means all of us," Conner snapped.

"Yes, but even if there has to be a special assessment, it will be worth it. Think of it like buying something beautiful that is also a great investment. Because that's what it is. San Francisco is a jewel-box of a city. We owe it to ourselves to take care of it."

Wainwright said, "Hugh, you must have some estimate of how much this will cost."

Rowan said, "We're working on the numbers. I'll get back to you on that."

"Why do you think the people in San Francisco will become more tolerant of our presence than they were before?" someone asked.

"I'm glad you asked that. I think this is one of those cases where the facts on the ground will be what counts. Life in San Francisco currently is miserable, and so we're going to offer people there an alternative. The Corps is building a new Plantation in the Central Valley. That will take care of the San Francisco population and give them jobs and lots of new opportunities."

"Is that the new Plantation that we authorized two years ago?" someone asked.

"Yes, it is."

"But I thought that it would recruit from Outsiders all over the West," Wainwright said.

"Well, it could, but I think first we need to take care of the people from San Francisco. If we want the City to be what it can be, we need a clean slate," Rowan said.

The room was silent. Rowan had used the term "clean slate" on purpose, but with a little apprehension.

"Well, it's a bold plan, I give you that," said someone, and there was general laughter.

"I like it," said Troy Cummings of MacyWalWay. "For years we've just reacted to circumstances. I think it is time to be pro-active."

Rowan was elated; he could see heads nodding.

"Mr. Wainwright," a woman from Shlumburton said. "Shouldn't there be someone from the Corps here to brief us?"

"Yes, that's a good idea," Wainwright said. "We'll have Ms. Black contact General Couseau and find out when he's available."

"We could do that," Rowan said, "but it would be faster if I arranged for a briefing with the officer who will be in charge of the operation, Colonel Hastings."

"I don't have any objection to that. Does anyone else?" Wainwright asked. The room was silent. "What's your timetable, Hugh?"

"I'm hoping we can start the operation on September 1."

"That's less than two months from now," Wainwright said. "I'm not sure it's possible. Anyway, we need to see the numbers before we make a final decision."

"I think it's important to stick with the time line. If it gets put off, it'll cost more. I'll get those numbers put together in a week or so."

Linda Crowley, or rather Lieutenant Crowley, was facing a major dilemma. She was about to board the sonic for MarinHaven but she had discovered that her new status earned her a seat near the back of the plane. She was used to sitting in the section reserved for Owners, but she was now a low-ranking Corps officer. She could sit in the front if she changed clothes, but she loved wearing her uniform. Oh, well, she reflected, it's part of the experience. *I might as well get used to hardship right away. Maybe there will be some cute men.* Not that she would ever do more than have a little fling with any of them. She genuinely loved Ronnie and didn't want to be with anyone else, and she knew he didn't mind if she played a little, discreetly. Ronnie was fun and kind and she liked that he was much older. He knew how to take care of her.

When she entered the plane, the attendant waved her to the right and she walked down the narrow aisle. She found her seat and sat down, trying to hold her head high. It was a bit humiliating, and she tried to savor that feeling. *This is what it means to be degraded, cast out,* she thought. Only thirty feet away were people sitting comfortably in large seats, people who were secure in their status. But she was one of the rank and file, doomed to endure life in the raw. How exciting it was! And it was only for two hours, after all.

She sat down, put on her sleep mask, and drifted off. When she woke up the plane was just settling down on the grassy lawn of the MarinHaven airport. *This is interesting,* she thought, having to get off the plane in a public place. Usually she was taken right to the driveway of her estate. The servants would be there lined up, waiting to greet her with big smiles. They were always so happy to see her, and she felt the same. She loved each one of them. Well, almost each one.

As she stepped out of the sonic onto the ground, she became aware once again that no one was looking at her. This is freedom, she thought, for a second. Then she didn't have time to think at all. There was a loud buzzing sound somewhere to her right and shouts from people around her. Everyone started to run, and she found herself carried along with them. She didn't feel like she was running—it felt more like she was lifted up and carried along by an irresistible tide. Then she touched the ground with her feet and was flung down, crushed into the dirt.

CHAPTER SEVENTEEN

Jack sat quietly in his apartment, spreading his consciousness across the City and northward, deep into the Haven. He spent three hours a day in meditation, and when he was done he would immediately dictate his thoughts to a young man whom Gladys had brought to him. Thomas recorded what Jack said and afterwards transcribed it. Jack then read the transcript and discussed it with Gladys. He knew she was showing it to other people, but he didn't ask who.

The first part of the meditation was focused on his breath and was dedicated to all sentient beings. The second part was the transition—

from the general to the specific was what he said to himself, although words couldn't really encompass his actual experience. The last part of his meditation was the opening. His consciousness left the confines of his body and went somewhere else. Each day was different and, as yet, he had very little control, but he was far-seeing, that was clear. He could "see" the landing craft moored off MarinHaven, and he was present at meetings of Corps officers wearing black uniforms, although he couldn't make out what they were saying. The map of San Francisco was like his own body, and it had tender spots—Mission Creek was vulnerable, and Baker Beach too.

He deeply loved the spaciousness of his breath, and he hated to leave it, but he told himself that his resistance to entering the world was just an obstacle that he had to gently remove from his mind. Everyone he loved was in danger and it was his job to protect them. Why he had the gifts, the talents, he didn't know. But he was certain they could not be left unused. Did he have the stamina to continue this? The moment was coming when he would be tested.

One day Gladys said to him, "The mayor wants to meet you—he said it's about time. Is that convenient for you?" She no longer told him what to do, but asked respectfully, and Jack missed her bossy tone.

"What does he want to talk about?"

"Jack, you should know!"

"I haven't focused on the mayor or thought about him. I'm trying to find where we're strong and how we can manifest our strength."

"Of course. I'm sorry. I'm getting nervous just like everyone else."

Jack was surprised. He looked carefully at Gladys for the first time in a while and he saw that she had changed slightly. She had been so sure, so confident in her world and her place in it. He could see tiny tremors in her hands and the slightest twitch around her mouth. Suddenly he was filled with terror; the world turned black.

He opened his eyes and she was wiping his forehead with a cold, wet towel.

"I'm afraid that I passed on my fears to you," she said. "You screamed."

"I did? I'm sorry. I lost control."

"I think my presence holds you back," she said. "It might be better if I keep a certain distance from you for a while."

"No—I can't do this all alone. I need you."

"You need someone, but I'm not enough. I'm starting to get a feeling for my own limitations, watching you grow more powerful. You need someone else."

"Who would that be?"

"Jill is coming."

"Jill! No, I can't do this if she's here. I need to be cool, not passionate. I want to see her too much. How can I do my job? Don't do this to me."

"Jack, you're very deep and you have real powers, but you're not a monk. She is a woman, not an abstract idea."

"What does that mean?" he asked.

"She wants you too."

"How do you know that?"

"She told me yesterday."

"Yesterday! Where is she, how did you talk to her?"

"She's on her way. Actually, she'll be here in a few minutes."

Jack felt a bolt of energy course through his body and a small part of his mind saw it—spiritual and erotic energy woven into a single fabric. He couldn't stop his erection and he turned away from Gladys, who was trying not to laugh.

"I don't know that I'll be able to help the City when I'm so distracted," he managed to say.

"Don't you understand? She's not an ordinary girl—she'll know how to help you. Anyway, you need a woman. You should know that her real name is Grace—Jill is just her public name. Now go take a cold shower and get ready for her. After that we'll go see the mayor."

Mayor Johnston's first act after assuming office had been to cancel the City's contract with Nestle and restart the public water. There were showers again.

A few minutes later, there was a knock on the door. Gladys opened it and Grace walked in. Jack didn't recognize her—her hair was dishwater blonde and she was heavy, her body shapeless. Her face was marked with small patches of acne, her brown eyes unfocussed somehow. She looked at him and burst out laughing. She made her hands into a frame and looked at him through it.

"I'm going to call that picture of you 'Disappointed Boy Losing Hard-On,'" she said.

"No. I am glad to see you," Jack said, taking cover in politeness.

"You haven't seen me and no one else has either, which is more to the point. Gladys, where can I change?"

She went into Jack's room and closed the door. Jack sat down on the sofa in the living room, confused. A few minutes later, Grace emerged, slim and dark with long, brown hair. Her face was clear and her blue eyes startling.

"You think you're deep, but you're just like all men," Grace said as she moved toward Jack. She took his hand and led him back into his room.

An hour later Grace was sleeping and Jack and Gladys walked down the stairs to the street where there was a car waiting for them. A tall, slightly menacing man opened the car door for them and then got in the front seat next to the driver.

"We need a bodyguard now?" Jack said to Gladys.

"You do," she said. "I'm not that important."

"Thank you for bringing Grace here, Gladys. I really mean it. She gets me like no girl ever has. I didn't even know how much I needed her."

"You're welcome. She wanted to come anyway. Jack, keep in mind that Grace has a lot of responsibilities."

"Yeah, don't we all," he said and looked out the window.

Jack didn't like traveling by car. Scenes went by so fast that he couldn't take them in properly. The best pace was on a walking horse; not too fast, not too slow, and the added height allowed him to see much more. Cars were too low to get any perspective. Still, the short drive to City Hall was instructive. People were not going about their usual business, that was for sure. Jack could see his neighbors working together to build barricades. Men with sledgehammers were tearing up the pavement. Stands had been set up where people were distributing food, and he could see kids filling up backpacks with corn meal and vegetables to take back to their families.

"They're preparing for war," Jack said, with wonder.

"Yes. Aren't you?" Gladys asked.

They were driven into an underground garage and escorted to an elevator. Jack walked into it with great curiosity. He had heard about elevators, but had never been in one before. How much power does this draw?, he wondered. He was surprised by how little motion he felt, just the slightest tug on his knees. And then the doors opened and two men in long-tail business suits and starched blue shirts greeted them and took them down the hall to an office at the top of a grand staircase. They were hurried into an inner office where the mayor stood to greet him.

At first Nils cursed himself for not having a compass. But at least he had his watch, his grandfather's pride and joy, an old-fashioned, wind-up number. Nineteenth-century technology, he thought, how appropriate for my new life. Then he remembered a trick his grandfather had taught him: how to find north using his watch. Every time the sun peeked through the clouds, he'd match up the twelve on the watch with it and split the difference between that and the hour hand. That was north. Forty-five degrees to the left of that was west, where there were people, he hoped.

It was surprisingly easy to move. At first he was afraid he'd have to bushwhack but he discovered a path that was once a road—there were still stretches of intact concrete, overgrown on the sides but passable for a single man on foot. The path intersected other paths, other roads, and he had to make decisions about which to follow. Sometimes the path doubled back in the direction he had come from. Once or twice he left it to go through the woods but finally realized that the path would return to its original course and it was faster to just follow it. Sometimes he found what were obviously old road signs, bent over but still recognizable. The numbers meant nothing to him—If only I had a better map, he thought—but he found them somehow reassuring. There used to be a pattern, a system, order and peace.

If I stay on a road, or what used to be a road, at some point I'll come to a Settlement or at least signs of one, he thought. Nils felt the forest around him almost as a sentient being, green and alive, reassuring and terrifying. Life had shrunk to a single goal and a single hope—to survive and to be with Philippa again.

He had taken enough food to last him five days, if he was careful with it. Water was not a problem. All he had to do was listen carefully and every once in a while he'd hear the sound of a stream or brook. If he didn't find people in five days, he'd figure it out then. He wasn't particularly worried that anyone would stalk him. Hastings had much bigger things on his mind and probably would conclude that going into the woods was suicide—by accident or on purpose wouldn't matter much.

Nils had been taught all his life that nature was the enemy. Nature would fry you or drown you or freeze you but it would never nurture you. Life and society should be constructed to keep nature at bay, to make a world utterly dominated by mind. Nature and intuition and spirit—anything that could not be measured or weighed or controlled—must be ordered into non-existence. All pathways into the unknown must be barricaded and their existence willfully forgotten.

But that wasn't the way people in communities like San Francisco thought. They weren't afraid of what was beyond their five senses—they courted the unknown and its strange landscapes.

Some of them even worshiped nature or the earth, calling their goddess Gaia. That's who I should pray to, Nils laughed softly to himself, the Earth Mother. That's who I need help from, that's for sure.

It began to rain gently and he walked on, trying to let go of his thoughts and just live in the moment. He took off his cap and let the rain soak his hair and run down his face. He couldn't ruminate with water pouring into his eyes.

The clouds parted and the sun came out. He started to hear songbirds. There must have been some around the retreat house, but he never noticed them before. At around seven o'clock, by his watch, Nils stopped and considered how he was going to spend the night. He had no tent, but he remembered seeing a picture of a lean-to made of tree branches. He tried to make one but he didn't have anything to hold the branches together, and he didn't have a poncho to keep himself dry.

Then he found a rock that had an overhang large enough for him to shelter under. If it rains hard, he thought, at least I can huddle here. He dug out the damp leaves from the ground below until he found dry ground and then sat down cross-legged. His dinner consisted of several squares of cheddar cheese and an apple. He drank the water from the canteen that he filled at a spring an hour before. He had never tasted anything so delicious.

It was still warm when he went to sleep, his head on his backpack. All night he was awakened by mosquitoes and once a spider crawled into his shirt collar. Finally he fell asleep and slept deeply, no dreams. When he woke it was already daylight. He got up and stretched and ate one of the apples he had brought and noticed that it wasn't very fresh. He needed a shower, he needed to shave. He needed to check all of his messages and write his reports. All that is over, he said to himself. You'll be lucky to be alive next week.

After four hours of walking, the forest seemed to retreat a little. The path began to widen and in the distance he could see some brick buildings. Nils heart leapt but then he thought it was too soon, the Settlements were farther away. As he got closer he saw that the buildings were collapsing, from the top down. Trees were asserting their dominance and taking over the abandoned town. Where did the Corps send the people who used to live here?, he wondered.

Just as Nils began to think that he might find something useful in this place, he saw a store that was much larger than the others. A pile of small boats blocked the doorway. He went toward it and saw that one of the old plate glass windows had fallen out. He stepped inside and looked around. There were hundreds of racks, some thrown down on the floor, some still standing with clothes neatly draped over the hangers clinging to them. The ceiling had collapsed in the middle of the store, and everything under it was melted into a gelatinous, khaki-colored mess.

Outdoor gear of all types hung on the walls—a lot of it looked intact. He went over to the display of backpacks. He found one that was large but light and took it down and dusted it off. Then he went over to the tents. And the sleeping bags. He found a light blanket and a poncho that weighed nothing. He made a pile of the gear and went over to a case that displayed knives. A long, wooden beam of some kind had broken the case open and was blocking it in exactly the place to get inside, and Nils pushed it a few inches.

He heard a loud cracking sound and looked up. The beam had dislodged one of the timbers holding what was left of the roof, and it had come loose and was swinging above him. He ran out just as it came crashing down. In his panic, he had left everything inside. He stood outside the building wondering whether to go back in, and he heard a loud rumble. The whole roof collapsed, and then the walls.

He sat on the ground and put his head in his hands and rocked back and forth for a few minutes, trying to get a hold on himself. He said out loud to the empty town, *I don't want to die.*

Finally it became too hot to sit in the sun, and he got up and started walking around the ruined town. He found another store that had backpacks and tents and sleeping bags. There were also packages of dried fruit and nuts and beef jerky. He gathered everything together and left as quickly as he could.

A few hours later he found a meadow bounded by a flowing stream, and he decided to spend the rest of the afternoon and night there. He needed to rest and he needed to think. He pitched the tent in the nearby woods, as out of sight as he could make it. He had seen no evidence of another human being since he left the retreat house, but he thought he'd better be careful. That night he lay down in his tent, comfortable and thoughtful.

The next morning he woke up refreshed. He walked on westward, noticing the land dipping down slightly ahead of him. At one clearing he could see on his left a large lake and in the far distance, straight ahead, the tops of low-rounded mountains.

He was ruminating about Philippa and noticing the tree roots that were tearing up the path when he realized that there was someone sitting on a tree stump only twenty feet in front of him. For a second Nils froze. He became aware instantly that he had no weapon. But the man on the stump looked at Nils calmly and did not move. He was wearing jeans and a shirt the color of blueberries. He had a thick head of brown hair and a face lined with wrinkles. As Nils approached him, the man smiled and raised both hands, palms outward.

"Hello, Nils," the man said. "Welcome to Maine."

Nils felt his stomach lurch. "How do you know who I am?" he asked.

"I don't know who you are. I just know your name is Nils. We've been expecting you."

CHAPTER EIGHTEEN

Hugh Rowan looked around his office and found nothing in it that pleased him. He had cycled through the possible scenes that would dissolve the walls, and nothing was right. There were the standard ones, the jungles, the tundra, the ocean, and so on. And then there were the scenes that he'd had specially created for himself. These tended toward the heroic, views from a castle high in the Alps, a desert that went on forever. He had commissioned some porno holos, but he only used them with the girls—too distracting when he was trying to work.

Almost every night now he had bad dreams, and most mornings he woke up in a black mood. The worst was that he couldn't quite remember the dreams. For some reason he often thought of the boy he had seen at the opera—that weak creature. These are people who should be used like the sheep they are, he thought. Actually, that's charitable. The old French word said it better, canaille, "mangy dogs." Not every creature that has two arms and two legs should be considered human. Many of his peers were still infected with an irrational regard for the "human race," but the more advanced Owners were starting to see that it wasn't that simple. Why did he keep thinking of that boy? Once in a while, a feeling of dread came over him, and the boy's face came to mind at just those times.

Hugh was burning with anticipation. All his life he had been forced to sit at a desk, go to meetings, speak calmly. Soon there would be action, and there would be blood. And San Francisco was just a beginning, after all.

He did have to get control of himself, though. The headaches that used to come no more than once a year were starting to become more frequent, and they were debilitating. He knew when the lights started flashing at the top of his vision that one was coming on. The worst of it was that when he closed his eyes, he saw that boy again. Why had he gone to the opera? What was the point? He'd have the people he was trying to impress at his mercy soon enough. Certainly, it was the right thing to do—of course he had to be there. It was just too bad that boy was nearby. Accidents do happen, even in the most carefully planned lives.

When he got into this dark mood, he usually turned to one of the women who were available for his pleasure, but he had no sexual feelings now and no other way to dispel the darkness in his mind. And he had a lot to do. He got up from his desk and opened the French doors to the terrace. He stepped outside but then heard a ring at his desk. This kind of intrusion was rare—his calls went to a secretary, who came in once an hour to tell him who wanted to talk to him. Hugh walked back inside, and when he saw who was calling he waved his hand. Philippa appeared in front of him.

"Hello, Hugh, I've been thinking about your offer. There are a lot of details to work out. Can you come to my place so we can talk about it?"

"I don't have time to go to the City. Just tell me now," he said. He imagined she'd plead to bring along some friends and servants. He had already decided to be agreeable, and he congratulated himself on his generosity.

"I think you might want to be here. Mayor Johnston will be at my house tonight and I thought you two would have a lot to talk about," she said.

"Damn. As usual, you win," he said. "What time?"

The trip was a major annoyance. He couldn't draw attention to himself by using his yacht, so he had to take the ferry to Berkeley and from there to the dock on Montgomery Street. He was dressed modestly; no one would guess that he was an Owner. His guards looked like a group of college students. There was a car waiting for him but some confusion about transportation for the guards. Hugh waited with them until another car came to take them to the house on Jackson Street. No one paid any attention to them.

Hugh knocked on the door. What an affectation this is, he thought, to pretend that we're back in the dark ages before retinal scans. Philippa was perverse. She rejected every advantage she had been born to enjoy. She opened the door and gave him a tight smile.

She's nervous, he thought. Maybe she finally understands she'd better change sides.

"Hello, Hugh. Do you mind leaving your guards outside? You might not want to spook the mayor."

"Is he here already?" Hugh asked.

"No, but he's only a few blocks away. He'll be here in a few minutes."

Hugh went into the living room and sat down on the sofa. Philippa went into the kitchen and came out carrying two glasses and a bottle of wine. Her hands shook slightly. She sat down on a chair near him.

"You don't have any servants at all?" he asked. "Don't you think you'll be relieved to come back home and have people wait on you?"

"Listen, Hugh, I love my life here. What I can't figure out is why you're trying to destroy it. You're rich enough to buy what you want, how much more can you consume?"

"Consuming is not the point, dear sister. I can picture the way things should be! It's time we cleaned up this stinking mess of a city and made it fit for our kind to live here. You know as well as I do that the troits don't deserve this place."

"Please don't use that word in my house," she said. "And I'll try to ignore all the rest of the nonsense you're talking."

"C'mon, Philippa, you're one of us, not one of them. Why fight it? We're making a new world and you should be part of it. Our kind of people have to rule—what other choice is there? Anarchy or the mess you have here in the City. We'll bring order and discipline to the mob. Sure, we'll make them work for us, but that's the way it should be. I'm done with the hypocrisy. It's our time now. The lion doesn't lie down with the lamb; the lion eats the lamb. That's reality, that's the future."

"Why did you try to get Nils involved in this? Where is he? What do you know about where he went?"

"Look, Philippa, I'm really busy. Why don't we talk about what you need to come back to the Haven so we can get that out of the way before the mayor gets here. Nils might have had a brilliant career but he threw it away. You never should have married him anyway. He had a chance to be one of us, which was more than anyone in his family could have dreamed, and he threw it away."

"What can I do to get him back?" she asked. "What is your price?"

"I have no idea where he is. All I know is that he left the retreat house and no one knows from there."

Philippa turned away and looked out the window for a moment. Then she turned back to her brother and said, "Hugh, please give this up. I'm begging you."

"Well, that's a first."

"Just leave us alone. What can I do to get through to you?"

"I never thought you were naïve until now. Amazing."

Philippa got up and walked around the sofa to a long table that was placed behind it. She stood behind the table and said, "Hugh, I'm giving you one more chance. Call the invasion off and I'll come and spend some time in the Haven, I'll get reacquainted with your family. I haven't seen your kids since they were babies."

"The answer is no. This is the moment for me to act and I'm not going to let it pass me by. You might as well get used to it because there's nothing you can do to stop it."

She opened a drawer in the table, pulled out an old pistol, and pointed it at him, holding it with both hands. "Oh, yes, I'm going to stop you! I didn't want to do this, but I will, to save my City."

"Put down that antique," he said, "and pull yourself together. We're about to do great things and you will be part of them, if you don't act stupid. We can talk about all this when the mayor is here, if that pleases you."

"The mayor is not coming. You really thought he'd betray the City? You think you're smart, but you're an idiot. I'm never going to be a part of what you're doing. You disgust me. I hate everything you stand for. Goodbye, Hugh. Go to hell!"

Hugh suddenly realized the danger and jumped up just as she fired the gun.

Linda Crowley opened her eyes and sat up to look around her. She felt grit in her mouth and spat out as much as she could. I'm all alone, she thought with wonder. "I need water," she said, but there was no one there to hear her. The sky was clear and blue and it was late in the afternoon, she could see that. Then she remembered, she was on a sonic, she had just gotten off and the memory stopped there. Why was she on the ground? She got up and brushed off her uniform. Her uniform!

She was just outside a low-slung building that looked familiar but not quite. What was it? She walked up to the tall teak doors, but they didn't move by themselves. She pushed one open and walked into the airport lounge. There was no one. She went into the ladies' room and washed her face and hands. She looked in the mirror and was horrified. I look like hell, she thought. Oh my god, I can't let anyone see me like this. For a moment she thought of hiding in a stall, but what then? She didn't have her purse with her phone in it. How could she get home? Where was everyone?

Alright, Miss Polly, she said to herself, using the private name her father had often called her, you are very lucky to be having some really unusual experiences. Remember them! Now what does it feel like to be the only human being in an airport? And to be stranded? Pretend the camera is on you, following every move. Look scared, certainly, but not totally lost. Linda had never played a victim and had no intention of taking on that role. She went back outside to find her purse, but it wasn't on the field where she woke up. She walked back into the building and through it to the front door.

Linda sensed a vibration, a rhythmic pulse that was just below the range of sound. It was pleasant, no, it was really beautiful, and it somehow drew her out of the building and onto the road leading away from it. She followed the road down the hill and around a grove of live oaks. She looked back just in time to see the airport building collapse into itself. How odd, she thought, it's still quiet. There was no fire, no explosion. Is this a dream? But she noticed that she was wearing regulation Corps shoes. I couldn't dream those shoes, she thought, not in my worst nightmare.

She walked on, getting more and more alarmed at not seeing anyone. No cars, how can that be? She turned a corner and saw in the distance a bright yellow band across the road and past it cars and people in uniforms. As she got closer, she saw Ronnie standing just on the other side of the barrier, motioning to her. She could see his mouth open but she couldn't hear him. Then she noticed that some of the others also had their mouths open: they all looked like they were shouting, but there was no sound. The lights on the top of the cars were rotating. She was surrounded by a deep quiet.

Linda was so glad to see Ronnie. He was good to her, a good man. So thoughtful of him to be there, she thought. Why not run to him? She wanted to be in his arms. She got to the barrier just as the ground beneath her crumbled. Two uniformed men pulled her across onto hard pavement and she was carried to a helicopter. Ronnie helped her climb aboard and then they were in each others arms. She still couldn't hear him, but she saw that he had tears in his eyes.

"Why are you crying, darling?" she asked.

When she opened her eyes, Linda was sitting on her terrace overlooking the garden, which was bursting with nasturtiums and bougainvillea. She could hear birds and the rustling of the wind in the trees. In the distance, across the bay, San Francisco sat white and gleaming. At her side was a silver tray, and on it there was a pink porcelain tea pot and a matching sugar bowl and creamer. On the saucer, nestled against the cup, was a small, silver spoon with an interlocking "LC" engraved on the underside. She felt grateful for the warm sun on her arms. Her face was in the shade. She heard footsteps and looked up to see Ronnie come through the French doors.

He asked her how she felt and then said, "Darling, the doctors say you're fine. You have to tell me what you remember of what happened to you."

"I was all alone. It all went silent and then the airport collapsed. Why did that happen?"

"My love, you broke down in the sonic; they carried you out on a stretcher; you've been asleep for the past twenty-four hours."

"But you pulled me to safety, don't you remember, Ronnie?"

He dragged a wrought-iron chair next to her and then sat down and took her hand. "Do you want any more tea, darling?" he asked. She nodded and he poured it into her cup. "How do you feel now? How does the house look to you?"

Linda was astonished. "It looks normal, of course. Why do you ask me that?"

"Darling, don't mind me asking. The ground didn't collapse and I wasn't your hero. You had some kind of seizure in the sonic."

Linda was silent for a moment. "Did the airport collapse?"

"No, darling. It's still there, exactly as before."

"Ronnie, I heard something at the airport."

"What, darling?"

"There was a sound, or maybe just a vibration. It was beautiful. I was so scared but the sound comforted me and I felt like it was teaching me something—I don't know what. It had to be real."

"Real. Why not? A lot of strange things are real these days. Like what Hugh Rowan is plotting."

"Hugh? What does he have to do with the sound I heard?"

"Linda, I probably shouldn't be telling you this in the state you're in, but I can't help it. Hugh's trying to take us into a war with San Francisco."

She giggled and said, "Very funny, Ronnie. That is not the way to cheer me up!"

"No, darling, I'm serious. He wants to conquer San Francisco and send all the people there to a Plantation. That's how he thinks."

She was shocked into silence. She got up, feeling a little unsteady but too agitated to sit. "That is insane. Only the Corps could do it, and General Couseau would never go along with it."

Ronnie sighed and got up and sat down next to her. He put his arms around her. "Darling, I've got some sad news. General Couseau had a heart attack last night. It was a massive one, and he died within a few minutes."

Linda suddenly felt she couldn't breathe. She opened her mouth and took in large gulps of air, feeling like she was drowning. Ronnie drew her gently toward him. She caught her breath finally. "What's happening, Ronnie? Will they revoke my commission? I don't think anyone but Felix Couseau would have done it for me."

"I don't know, darling. I'm afraid the Corps' top brass will be thinking about other things right now."

"The Council won't let Hugh get away with it!"

"I don't know. I've tried to call the people I know on the Council, but our friends are a minority these days. That's probably why

Hugh's doing it now—he's finally got his sort in charge. Anyway, this isn't very important to them—not like planning for Ball Week or something—and they'll probably agree just to keep Hugh from pestering them."

"Those poor people in the City. Is there anything we can do to help, Ronnie?"

"Maybe when I hear back from some people we'll be able to figure something out, but I wouldn't count on it."

CHAPTER NINETEEN

"Good afternoon, Gladys," the mayor said. "And this must be Mr…?"

"Just call me Jack, Mayor."

"Ok, Jack. I'm very glad to meet you. I've heard these stories about you."

"Which you don't believe for a minute, mayor, but you're desperate for any possible help you can get. I don't mean to be disrespectful, sir, but I know you don't have a lot of time."

Johnston looked at Jack and pointed to a chair. "Alright, sit down there please. Gladys, make yourself comfortable." He instructed his assistant to keep everyone out of the office until he told them they could come in.

"Jack, I'll come right to the point. The City is facing some kind of invasion. I don't know who and I don't know why and I don't know what their intentions are."

Jack looked at Gladys and she said, "Go ahead, say what you're thinking."

"You do know who and why and what their intentions are. You are testing me, and anyway, you like to keep your cards close to your chest." Jack had never before heard that metaphor—it was in Johnston's mind.

The mayor sat back in his black leather chair and said, "Who am I thinking of?"

Jack reflected for a moment. "His name is Hugh Rowan." He found the mayor easy to read, he didn't know why. "He's the one you're afraid of. And you know him. You've met with him. No one else knows that."

Johnston stared at Jack. His eyes were actually bulging out of his head, Jack thought; that isn't just a figure of speech. Gladys looked shocked. She turned toward Jack, who suddenly felt a lead blanket of responsibility placed on his shoulders. *I'm really on my own here.*

"Can you look into my heart too?" Johnston asked.

"Well, there isn't really any difference between heart and mind, at least the way I see things. Yes, you are loyal to the City even though Rowan tried to bribe you. You don't know where to turn."

The room was silent for a moment.

"Jack, you're right that I know who and why, but I don't know how. We need to know exactly what they're planning. I've gotten the reports of your, what do you call it?"

"Far seeing," Jack said.

"Yeah, well they've been interesting, but we need more particulars."

"Mayor, do you have anything that Hugh Rowan touched?"

"Like what?"

"Anything. Did he ever give you anything?"

A flash of anger crossed Johnston's face. "No, nothing."

"I didn't mean money. I just need to touch something he touched."

"Well, we shook hands," Johnston said.

"Alright. Mayor, may I hold your hand for a moment?" Jack asked.

Johnston got up from behind his desk and walked over to Jack. He sat down in the chair next to him and gave Jack his right hand to hold. Jack took Johnston's large, soft hand in both of his hands and closed his eyes. Images flew through his mind, some too fast and faint to discern, others full of color. A face appeared to him and it was bright and edged with the fire of Johnston's fear. The face was the man at the opera. Jack gasped—he wanted to drop Johnston's hand, but he held on. He felt himself drawn into a dark place, and he saw images that he couldn't make out. He turned a corner and saw—himself. And he was edged with fire. The man was afraid of him! Now he let go of the mayor's hand and stood up, confused.

"Gladys, I can't do this," he said.

She went to him and put her arm around his shoulder. "Do you want to go now?"

"Yes, but the mayor needs me, doesn't he? Don't I have to do something for him now?"

"What did you see?"

"Gladys, the man at the opera was Hugh Rowan, the Owner who wants to destroy us."

"What, you know him?" Johnston asked.

"In a manner of speaking, yes," Jack said. "We sat at a table next to him at the opera café."

"Oh, well, so did I once," Johnston said.

"Mayor, this was a little different," Gladys said.

Jack burst out with a laugh, but then he saw the alarm on Johnston's face and said, "I'll do whatever I can for you, Mayor. I'm ready to help."

"Jack, can you get me detailed information? Where are they going to land and when? How many troops will there be and what kind of weapons will they have? Can you do that?"

"I'm really not sure what I can do, Mayor, but I'll try my best."

"Also, we need to know more about the Corps. We'd like to understand how it works, its command structure, and so on."

Jack and Gladys stood up; the mayor didn't move. "Alright, Mayor, we'll get back to you as soon as we can," Gladys said.

"Wait a moment," he said. "There is someone here that I would like you to meet. It's a deserter from the Corps who wants to help us. I think. But I'd like you to look into this person, Jack, the way you did with me, and tell me if she's for real. Can you do that?"

"Probably," Jack said and sat down.

Johnston motioned to his assistant, who was sitting in the corner.

He went out the side door and came back in a few minutes with a woman of indeterminate age. Jack understood that she was very carefully dressed and her hair was done in a way that was designed to leave no memories in the minds of the people who saw her. She was in perfect camouflage, the kind that doesn't look like camouflage.

The mayor said to Jack and Gladys, "This is a woman who says she is an officer of the Corps. I won't bother telling you what name she gave us, it's phony." He looked at her and said in a neutral voice, "Please sit down over there," motioning to the chair next to Jack. "Give him your hand, please." She looked at Jack and he could feel her surprise and mistrust.

Jack took the woman's hand, which was surprisingly small and hard. Birdlike, he thought.

"Your name is Rayna Caskey," Jack said

She quickly drew her hand back and Jack jumped up.

"Don't do that!" he said. He felt nauseated.

"I'm not going to stand for this hocus pocus," Rayna said to the mayor. "Do you want my help or don't you?"

"Is that your name?" Johnston asked.

"I already told you my name," she said.

"Answer my question!" Johnston barked at her.

Jack put his head in his hands and rocked back and forth, his eyes wide open. He didn't want to close them. The scene in front of him was unpleasant, but the foul emotions at a deeper level—anger, hatred, fear—were far worse.

"Fuck you. I'm leaving," she said and stood up quickly.

Johnston nodded at his assistant, who opened a door. Two large men ran into the room and grabbed her. One of them put handcuffs on her. For a moment it seemed like she was going to struggle but then she went limp.

"That's not necessary," Jack said. "She'll be helpful. Won't you, Rayna?" he asked her.

She looked at him and Jack felt an odd mixture of compassion and dismay. He inspired terror in her; he didn't need his powers to see that, it was in her eyes. She felt violated.

"Yes. That's my name. Do whatever you're going to do to me. Get it over with." She sat down heavily.

There was silence in the room. Jack realized that Mayor Johnston and Gladys were looking at him. He felt an unaccustomed sense of confidence fill him—he knew better than anyone there exactly how to proceed.

"We're not going to do anything to you, Rayna, we just want to know what you know. I can listen to you from the inside, but I won't understand all of it by myself. We need you to explain."

Jack heard Johnston think—*What is that fool doing telling her he can't understand her information?* And he also heard Gladys—*He's starting to come into his own.*

"Who are you?" Rayna asked, her voice unsteady.

"I'm the future," Jack said, astonished at his own words. Where did that come from?

"The Corps can't be stopped, you know. We're all going to end up in a Plantation—if we're lucky," Rayna said.

"You don't believe that," Jack said. "You still have some hope."

"Why else would I be here?" she asked.

"Maybe so you can tell your Owner friends how the City is preparing?" Johnston snapped.

Jack was again flooded with the mayor's fear and rage. He had been taught at the monastery how to be fully aware of others' emotions without being infected by them, but the emotional levee he constructed was never high enough to stop all the feelings from pouring over him. Now he was in danger of being swept away.

"Look, Mayor, I can't do this with you in the room. You're drowning me in your feelings. Let me talk to Rayna privately, away from City Hall."

Johnston told his men to take Rayna outside to another office. When she was gone, he turned to Jack, furious, "Absolutely not! Are you crazy? You have no idea what you're dealing with! I'm putting her in the City Jail and you can talk to her there."

"I'm sorry, Mayor, but I can't talk to her when she's under duress."

"In spite of all your so-called abilities, she could be a spy. The Owners would love to know how we're going to fight back. We can't take the chance of letting her escape."

"I think she knows a lot that could help us. And she'll close down totally if she's threatened."

"I thought you were a mind reader," Johnston said. "That's what they told me."

"That's a metaphor, Mayor," Jack said. "I'm more like a mind feeler. I get the emotions as well as the thoughts, and they're usually mixed together. She's more afraid of the Corps than she is of us. I don't know why, but I know that's the case."

"No. I can't take the chance. You'll just have to do what you can with her in jail."

"No. I won't do it if she's behind bars," Jack said. "It just won't work."

Johnston looked like he was going to explode, "Look, boy, this is war. You don't have the luxury to pick and choose what you're going to do. If I have to, I'll put you in jail with her."

Jack looked away, but he was really looking deep within himself. Again, he was filled with a sense of utter self-confidence—he knew exactly what to do. He took a deep breath and said, "We're all in this together, Mr. Johnston. We're a community, and that's where we get our strength. We won't defeat fear with fear."

"No, goddamnit. You're a kid. What the hell do you know? I might put you in jail anyway, just so you won't run away if you decide the Owners are a better bet than us."

Jack laughed, and the mayor recoiled as if someone had poured cold water on him. "Mr. Johnston, you don't really need me to answer that." Jack looked at the mayor and smiled warmly.

Johnston's eyes widened, he let out a breath, and his shoulders lowered. He sat far back in his chair and looked at his hands. He looked again at Jack and a current of sunlight seemed to flow between them. The mayor unclenched his fists and said, "You know I didn't mean what I said." He sighed deeply. "Yes, ok. What do you want me to do?"

"Why don't you let us take Rayna to my apartment for a few hours, and then she can stay at the Palace, where Gladys is staying. I'll get back to you in the morning."

"Alright. But you're responsible for her and for what she does. I'll have her delivered there in an hour."

As they were leaving, Gladys turned to Johnston and said, "Have you talked to Governor Cruz?"

"Yes, of course."

"I hope you won't say anything about this woman."

"Why not?" Johnston asked.

"Well, you know Cruz…he's got a lot of irons in the fire. It's probably best to keep it to what he needs to know."

As Gladys and Jack descended the vast, marble staircase that poured down onto the main floor of City Hall, he turned to her and said, "The mayor is a powerful man. Do you think he really trusts me now?"

"Absolutely. He'd better. What about the man from the opera? Do you think you can reach him in your mind?"

"Wouldn't that be convenient? I'll try, but it's not likely. I need a more direct connection with him." When they reached the ground floor Jack stopped for a moment. "How much did you know about him?" Jack asked.

"All I knew was that he was an important Owner and I thought he might know something useful. I had no idea you'd have such a deep connection with him. And I didn't know he'd be the devil."

"He's not a devil. He's a human being who took a wrong turn on his path when he was very young."

"But why did he take that turn?" she asked.

"You mean because he was a rotten son-of-a-bitch?"

They both laughed. Maybe there will be time for that kind of speculation in the future, he thought. Right now they had to work for their survival.

They decided to walk back to Jack's place. They went down the west side of Van Ness Avenue and turned right at Market Street. Just as they got to Valencia Street, Gladys turned to him and said, "How about this. You go back to where you were in your mind when you fell on the floor of the opera café. Maybe you'll find a way of getting to this Hugh Rowan from there."

He felt dread flow through him, a filthy, sluggish stream. "It was horrible, at least most of it. I don't want to go there."

"Jack, something happened to you back in the mayor's office. I saw it. You grew about a foot there. You are much stronger than you were at the opera."

"It helps to have Grace here. I didn't realize how much I needed her. Now if only Gabe were here, I'd feel whole."

Gladys put her hand into Jack's arm and said, "People are looking for him, you know. Have you been able to see him or feel him at all?"

"No, but I keep trying. First thing in the morning and just before I go to bed, every day. I've tried to be methodical about it, but nothing yet. Sometimes I wake up in the middle of the night and try to sense him."

They walked on through the quiet streets. A group of kids raced by, playing some game and laughing.

"Well, one thing I can do is work with that woman, Rayna. I feel sorry for her."

"Don't feel too sorry, Jack. She was an officer in the Corps, after all."

"They're not all bad." Jack thought about the man he and Gabe had met in Denver. He seemed like a decent person, and he was a Corps officer.

A few hours later, there was a knock on the door, and Jack let in Rayna and the policeman guarding her. He told the guard to stay in the living room and asked Rayna to come into the kitchen. Jack put a bottle of white wine, a chardonnay, on the table, and he filled two glasses. She took a glass and looked around for a few minutes. He could hear her thinking that the place looked like her grandmother's, and he felt the relaxation of her defenses. She turned to him and began to talk.

She knew few details of the planned invasion, but she knew about the internal politics of the Corps. She talked about a General Couseau and a Colonel Hastings and Central Command and Internal Security. Jack wrote it all down, but he found it very confusing. Most puzzling was her role. One thing was clear, though. She had deserted because her chief, Couseau, had died. She felt that she was in great danger if she stayed in the Corps. Jack couldn't understand where the danger was coming from; she didn't seem to know herself, but the fear was real.

Rayna was cooperative but very subdued. She was clearly repulsed by Jack. That was strange—he was used to being liked, and he had no experience with someone reacting to him as she did. As she talked, he confirmed without words what she told him. Jack knew that what she was telling him was accurate—at least what she believed was accurate. But was there more that she wasn't telling him? Possibly, but she was hard to read, the opposite of the mayor. Her emotions were complex and her motivations impossible to untangle, even for someone who could see inside her.

By midnight Jack had to admit that he was exhausted. Gladys had been with him all day and was preparing to go back to her hotel.

"Where am I staying?" Rayna asked him. The City policeman was waiting for instructions about where to escort her.

"You're coming to the Palace with me," Gladys said.

"Oh, no, I can't go there! Someone might see me," Rayna said.

"Who are you afraid of?" Gladys asked.

At that instant Jack saw in his mind a slender woman with long, black hair and a man wearing a Corps uniform. He knew the man—it was the Corps officer from Denver, and his name was Nils Rakovic.

CHAPTER TWENTY

They hiked for three days through the forest, skirting lakes and fording small streams. Nick Mason, the man who had greeted Nils, was friendly and talkative—to a point. When Nils asked him how he knew his name, Nick said, "They just told me your name and to find you," and he changed the subject.

They walked on until they came to a river that was too deep to ford. Nick made a simple raft from fallen branches for their backpacks. The men stripped off their clothes, and swam across, pushing the small raft ahead of them. The water was cold but felt delicious to Nils, and when he climbed out on the other side he felt renewed.

Nick began to explain the country they had just entered—the river was its boundary. Many of its citizens had formerly lived to the east and along the coast, in the old state of Maine. They had been expelled by the Corps but had been welcomed by the mountain people, mainly old men and women whose children had left years before. There was land for people who had the ability to cultivate it.

The White Mountain Republic had sufficient clean water, but its people struggled to feed themselves. They were protected from killing heat waves by their elevation, but the soil was rocky and farming was not productive. There was sufficient energy for now—mainly hydro from the many streams running down from the mountains and wood from the forests. But who knew what the future would bring? In some places, the forest was dying, and it was impossible to know what would replace it, what kind of trees, or maybe not even trees but something else. And even the streams might not be reliable. Gigantic storms could dump so much water that the hydroelectric dams themselves might be overwhelmed.

The worst, Nick said, was snow in the winter. Occasionally, storms would stop the entire nation. The only travel was by horse-drawn sleigh, which required the roads to be rolled with logs first, and that wasn't always possible. Everyone was now prepared for those smothering times, storing food and wood for a long, dull wait at home.

The outside world was full of potential threats but also possible allies. To the east there was the Corps Preserve and to the west and south there was Outside, a patchwork of feudalism and anarchy. The flatlands to the north, which had been part of the old province of Quebec, were dotted with Plantations and dominated by the Corps. There was a Haven on the coast that was strictly off-limits. Its presence was rudely announced by the sonic booms of the Owners' planes in the summer months.

When they arrived at the capital, a place called Harding, Nils was not impressed. It wasn't a town, more like a large village, and certainly didn't look like the capital of anything. Nick took him to a farm and introduced him to Joshua Cummings and his wife.

"You'll stay here for a few days, Nils, while we figure out what to do with you," Nick told him.

Charity Cummings took Nils upstairs and showed him the room he would be staying in.

"I expect you'll be comfortable, Major. We're giving you our best room. They told us to."

Nils felt a chill. "How did you know my rank?"

"Oh, we all know a lot about you. You're the first Corps officer to visit us here in the Republic."

"And what do they say about me?"

"Don't know you yet. But I expect people are gonna be watching to see what you are."

"I don't think I'll be here long enough for people to know me," Nils said, hoping it was true. She just shook her head and left him alone.

That night, as he was lying in his bed, Nils took stock of his situation. His gratitude at being rescued was short lived. Now he was burning to get home. The woman said they had been told to give him the best room. So someone in authority knew he was here. That was promising.

Two days passed in slow motion. During the day, Nils was left alone to fend for himself. He walked up and down the only road—he didn't see any cars or other people all day—and then read a book he found in the house, an old novel that took place in Victorian England about two young people hoping to marry, with the odds against them. The author threw so many absurd but amusing obstacles in the way of the lovers that Nils laughed out loud at several passages.

He tried to talk to his hosts, but they were politely taciturn. They talked with each other about farm business and asked him no questions. He tried to find out more about them and their country, but they had an infuriating way of ignoring his questions.

Finally, Nils came downstairs to find Nick Mason in the kitchen.

"Hello, Nils," he said. "How're you doing? They make you comfortable?"

"Sure. Listen, what am I going to do next? I shouldn't stay here much longer."

"I thought me and you could go for a walk."

Nick led him out through the front yard toward the gravel road. They turned to the right, toward the deep woods. The sky was clear—no storms today, most likely, Nils thought.

"You know, Nils, we've had quite a few immigrants, and generally we welcome them, as long as they are willing to work," Nick said.

"I'm not an immigrant. I need to get back home," Nils said.

Nick was quiet for a moment. Then he turned to Nils. "We need you for something."

"When, what?"

"Now. They'll explain the what later." Nils heard a soft crunching sound behind him and turned around to see a small car driving slowly toward them. It stopped, and Nick turned around and waved to the driver.

"But what about my things?" he said.

"You didn't have much! Your things have been packed up; they're in the car. The Cummings understand. I've explained that you had to leave quickly and that you send them your thanks and best regards."

Linda Crowley was confused. She had tried to get through to one of General Couseau's assistants, someone named Rayna Caskey, but with no luck. Linda was still officially a Corps officer and she thought she should report to somebody, but she didn't know who. Ronnie wasn't much help.

"I'm sorry, darling, but I'm no good at bureaucracies," he said, not sounding very apologetic.

She was amazed that there had been no publicity or press interest in what had happened to her at the airport. Nobody had come to talk to her about it, and the few times she had mentioned it to her friends she was met with nervous silence. Several people were missing from her social circle, and there was some talk about them, but the family of each one had an explanation. So and so had decided to stay in an

East Coast Haven for a while longer, another one was in a tropical spa for an extended stay, with her two friends who were also missing. She was even finding it hard to talk about with Ronnie. Perhaps it was better to just forget about it.

The plan for her visit to a Plantation was starting to seem unreal. It was hard enough to cope with the immediate demands of her life—like her new photo shoot. The theme of this one was military. Everyone was buzzing about how San Francisco was preparing to attack MarinHaven, and suddenly uniforms and military trappings were in. Linda had put on her Corps uniform for the first series of shots.

Just before the shoot was to start, her personal assistant, Alice Clavering, hurried up to her and told her that a Corps officer had come to see her. Excited, Linda told Alice to show him in. Finally, someone in the Corps was trying to help her get to a Plantation.

The officer was a tall, handsome young man with slicked-back brown hair. He spoke with a distinctive Quebecois accent. Another Couseau protégé, Linda thought.

"Good afternoon, ma'am, I am Captain Guillaume. I'm with Corps public relations. We want to commend you for your patriotism, and we'd like to talk to you about some possible assignments."

"Thank you, Captain, I can't wait to talk to you, but I'm about to begin a photo shoot. Maybe I can get them to delay it." Linda walked over to where three people, two men and a woman, were huddled together in animated conversation. They all looked up, smiled, and greeted her with kisses.

"Sweeties," Linda said, "I've got some very official business with that man over there from the Corps. Can we put this off for just a few minutes?"

"Of course we can, Linda," said Michael, the director. "But we've got to get the sun at the right angle and I think we better start within half an hour. If you want, we could come back tomorrow, but we can't be sure about the weather."

"Don't worry, honey, this won't take more than fifteen minutes," Linda said. She walked over to the officer and told him to follow her into her study. "Sit down, Captain. What Plantation are you sending me to?"

"Plantation?" he replied, looking slightly confused. "I'm sorry, ma'am, I mean Lieutenant, I don't know anything about a Plantation. I'm here to tell you that the Corps would like you to star in an informational movie we're making. They want it ready to release right after…whatever is going to happen in San Francisco."

Linda just sat there for a moment, not knowing what to say. She thought of calling for Ronnie, but decided no, this was something she needed to do on her own. "You know, Captain, I don't do what you call 'informational movies.' It wouldn't be good for my career. Thanks very much for thinking of me, though."

"I'm sorry. They told me that you had joined because you wanted to be part of what we're going to do in San Francisco. They said you'd do whatever we wanted to help."

"I don't know who you were talking to," Linda said. "General Couseau knew very well that I wanted to visit a Plantation. And I don't know what you're talking about concerning San Francisco. All I know is rumors, and I don't like what I hear. Who took General Couseau's place, anyway?"

"We don't know who the commandant will be—the Council hasn't decided yet. Are you sure I can't make you change your mind?"

Linda felt sorry for the man, but her career had to be her first priority. "I'm sure you can understand. I only do feature films," she said.

The captain stood up and walked to the window that overlooked the garden. He turned toward her, "This is a beautiful place," he said. "Do you want to tell me what happened to you when you got off the sonic?"

Linda froze for a moment. She was back on the road outside of the airport and there was a beautiful sound leading her on. She was filled with joy and she turned toward the handsome officer to tell him about the wonder of it all. Then she realized that he was looking at her with his brow furled and his eyes narrowed. Why, he's afraid of me, she thought. "Did you ask me a question?" she asked.

"Yes, ma'am. Is there anything I can do to get you to change your mind about the film we're making?"

"No. Please go now."

I got distracted for a moment and it's on my mind, that's all, she said to herself. She poured herself a glass of water from a cut-glass pitcher. Then she looked into one of the full-length mirrors in the room and did a double take. Was this really her, Linda Crowley, or was there more to her that couldn't be seen in a mirror? What an odd idea. But she couldn't get it out of her mind. Time to go to work, she said to herself; how do I look? I'll let the make-up people and the hair stylist do one more pass, and that should do it.

The shoot lasted two hours, including changes of costume, and afterward Linda was miserable. She wanted to slink away into a deep cave somewhere and be forgotten. This isn't fun anymore, she told herself. She went into her bedroom and lay down on her chaise longue. She put on her sleep mask, put her head back against the peach-colored satin, and tried to be quiet. But she couldn't stop it from happening.

The worst came at the beginning. She saw a small man with burning red eyes, only about three feet tall, but he was frightening. He came in from the shadows and sat on her chest, and she couldn't breathe. She opened her mouth to scream but knew that she couldn't get any sound out. Then a deep, mechanical noise like a large generator began to hum and whirr. It was overpowering and terrifying. Then, pop, and she was outside of her body, floating free. That part was beautiful and inspiring. It was like the vibration that led her to safety. She could see her body below her and she understood that she had left behind the limited woman trapped in a body. She watched from above as Ronnie came into the room and put a light blanket around her body, thinking she was asleep. He kissed her head, and she was flooded with a sweet feeling that she couldn't label. Then she was back in her body and fell into a deep sleep.

When she awoke it was almost dark outside, and her assistant was working at her desk in a corner of the room. "What time is it, dear?" Linda asked.

"You have time to get ready, Linda."

"Ready for what, Alice?"

"Ronnie is having a few people for dinner. No more than six, I think."

CHAPTER TWENTY-ONE

"Linda, you know Mayor Johnston, I think," Ronnie said as she shook hands with him. She remembered meeting him once at the opera—he wasn't one you'd forget.

"I'd like to introduce my friends," Johnston said. "This is Gladys Yee, Jill Speed, and Jack. I never did get your last name."

Ronnie led them from the reception hall of his house into a room with glass walls, through which could be seen a flower garden spilling down a hillside. A servant came around to offer them drinks. Ronnie's friend, George Harwood, came into the room and was introduced to everyone. George was one of those valuable young men, attractive, cheerful, and often available to round out the table. He had a remarkable ability to blend in with just about any group and seem like he belonged. The stuffiest Owners accepted him as one of their own, but Linda had seen pictures of him working on a farm with hard-scrabble Outsiders. His parents had been cousins of Ronnie's and close friends, and were killed in a sonic crash.

"Mayor, I'm honored that you wanted to join us tonight—I'm sure you're busy these days, and I'm curious about what is going on. We'd like to get your perspective," Ronnie said. "But now dinner is ready, so why don't we go and sit down?" After the soup was served, Ronnie said, "You probably know what they're saying here in the Haven."

"Well, Mr. Simpson, if you mean the stories that we're going to attack you, yes, I've heard about it. I'm sure you know how ridiculous that is. We want peace but we know there are others who don't. I asked to meet with you because I wanted to see if my City had any friends among your people."

Linda wasn't following the conversation. She was looking at the mayor's party—she couldn't keep her eyes off them, the young ones, Jill and Jack. There was a current of energy between those two that was so visible to Linda that she wanted to shout out to Ronnie—

"See that orange flame passing between the boy and girl—isn't it amazing!" Jill turned to Jack and they smiled at each other. Linda was charmed.

"Well, Mayor, you can count me as your friend," George said. "I spent a good part of my childhood in the City and my parents were born there. I don't hold a grudge that we can't own property; it's only fair. Your people were excluded from the Haven long before you restricted us. Don't you agree, Ronnie?"

"Certainly. I'm happy to talk about what we could do for you, Mayor."

After dinner, Mayor Johnston suggested that Jack and Linda should talk privately—Gladys had whispered the idea to him. Linda was surprised, but she wanted to be a good sport and she agreed. When they walked into the library, a large, airy room lined with books on all of the walls, Jack gasped. What kind of place does he live in?, she wondered. But she couldn't summon any kind of mental image.

They sat down on a sofa, and he said to her, "Do you actually own all these books?"

Linda replied, "Oh, yes, many of them were my father's, and some came from Ronnie's family. If you'd like to come back to our house, you could look at them for as long as you want." They had invited people from Berkeley to look at the book collection before, and there had never been any problems.

Linda always found it easy to talk to people, but there was something more with Jack—he really listened to her. He was no more than eight years younger than her, but he was still boyish. It was odd, though, that Mayor Johnston, Ronnie, and George Harwood all seemed to defer to him. She couldn't figure out where his status came from. No one said that he was from an important family or the heir to a fortune. There was nothing extraordinary about him, and he wasn't even handsome. Actually, he was kind of homely, she thought, although in an attractive way. His nose was a bit thick and it made her want to laugh. He was like a little brother.

"So tell me what you'd like us to do," she said. "That's why you're here, isn't it?"

"We need your help. Linda, I'm psychic, and I'm trying to get some information. You might know someone we're interested in, and I think it would help if I could hold your hand for a moment."

"Wait a minute." She laughed. "I'm sure I've heard that one before."

Jack smiled and looked directly into her eyes. Linda felt his warmth and steadiness. *This is someone I can trust.* She held out her hand, and it seemed so innocent, funny, really. He smiled at her, sweetly, she thought, but then his face began to change, to morph into a kaleidoscope of expressions.

"What happened to you at the airport?" he asked, his voice husky, shocked.

Her heart jumped, and when she looked at him she saw her grizzled, broad-shouldered father, who called her sweetheart and made her feel like she could do anything in the wide world that she really wanted. She froze for a moment and then pulled away to the corner of the sofa and buried her face in her hands. She didn't want to open her eyes; she didn't want to lose her father. She struggled to contain her grief.

Jack tried to remain quiet. He wanted to share his calmness with her, when she was ready for it. He had intended to learn more about the Owners, but instead he had seen Linda at a crumbling airport, the dark man who sat on her chest, and her flying free above her body. And more that he couldn't understand or picture at all. And underlying it all was grief and loss.

Jack moved toward her, and she turned. He put his arms around her, and she buried her face in his shoulder. She began to catch her breath and take in his calmness. Finally, she moved away from him, wiped her tears, and took a deep breath.

"I don't know what happened. I'm sorry," she said.

"I know, Linda," he said, "and I feel for you. You've been carrying around so much all by yourself—I don't know how you've been able to do it. No one to talk to!"

"How do you know? I haven't told anyone."

"How could you—who would understand?"

"But then how do I know—how do you know?" Jack could see into her confusion, and he struggled to keep himself free of it.

"Don't try to understand. Just appreciate the fact that you've been able to see more than others and let it go."

"But was it all real?" she asked.

"Sure, it was all real, in a way, and it all hangs together. If you hadn't heard the humming sound at the airport, the vibration, then the dark man wouldn't have come and sat on your chest, and you wouldn't have flown above your body and seen Ronnie come in and kiss you."

Linda jumped up and moved away as if he was radioactive. She put her hand over her mouth and looked at him in horror. "Stop it!" she said in a strangled voice. "How can you know all this about me?"

Jack took a deep breath and looked down. Then he smiled at her. Suddenly the sun came out in Linda's mind, the tide of fear drained out, and there was nothing but love and joy left. She wept again, with relief. She sat down and turned to him. "Tell me about yourself, Jack, I want to know about you and how you can see into me."

They talked for several hours. At one point Ronnie came in and said that Mayor Johnston and the others had left and that a boat would take Jack back to the City any time he wanted.

Linda felt that she had never really talked to anyone so intimately, at least since her father's death. Jack told her about his mothers, about losing Gabe, and about finding Jill/Grace. She told him about her father's death, her affairs, her love of Ronnie, her career. He talked about his powers and their limitations. They were part of him, like his thick, brown hair and almond shaped eyes; no more significant than that.

Jack had made one request, and she would certainly try her best to comply. It would take a lot of thought, but she would do her best to try to get Jack in the same room with Hugh Rowan. He wanted to take Rowan's hand, even if just for a moment.

Jack was almost as surprised by Linda as she was by him. She was as sensitive to the psychic dimensions as he was, but it had not given her any kind of power; she had no control over any of it. He had learned at the monastery to ignore spirits, demons, and strange emanations from other realms of being. None of those creatures had pushed their way into his consciousness as they had with Linda.

She was in danger, that was for sure. What she went through at the airport was a sign that Linda's interior world was rearranging itself. She was connected to the future, and it was undermining her present reality. Only one small man came and sat on her chest at this point. But he could come back with others of his kind and take her away, and if they did, she would return—altered and perhaps insane. Jack didn't know how he knew all this, but he was sure of it. He was the only one who could help her. But he also needed her help. They were now partners.

CHAPTER TWENTY-TWO

The drive lasted less than half an hour. They passed three deserted farm houses, crumbling into the earth. Finally, they came around a bend in the road and could see in the distance a house that was obviously inhabited. It wasn't much different from the Cummings' place except there was a flagpole on the front lawn, the blue and gold flag of the Republic waving in the breeze, and five or six cars parked on the gravel road in front of the house. Nils hadn't seen so many cars in one place since Denver.

"Where are we?" Nils asked.

"This is Jason Harmon's—he's our president, and he wants to see you."

They walked up to a door, and Nick knocked on it. It was opened by a woman who seemed familiar.

"Oh my God, you're the woman from the Corps guest house!" Nils exclaimed.

"Please come in," she said, turning away from him.

A young woman came up to them and said, "Major Rakovic, the president wants to see you. Please follow me."

She led him through several rooms where there were people working at desks. Nils was astonished to see some of them with fully operational hcues, men and women gesticulating in seemingly random arcs, but with that particular rhythm that marks the experienced operator. He would be able to contact Philippa—if they'd let him.

Hillary took him to a door, pushed it open, and said, "Go in here. You'll find him at the end."

Nils walked into a large room that looked like a converted barn. There were tables and desks everywhere and people working alone and in groups. At the far end was a glassed-in office. A tall man in a green work shirt, thick, gray hair and horn-rim eyeglasses, beckoned to Nils from the office door.

Nils went to him and the man said, "Welcome to our capital, Major. I'm President Harmon. Come in."

He followed the president into his office and sat down in a wooden chair next to the desk. "Major…" Harmon began.

"Please call me Nils, Mr. President."

"Alright, and you call me Jason; everyone else does. Nils, tell me, what do you think of our little Republic?"

"I haven't seen much, sir, but I'm impressed that you have hcues. I'm amazed you're connected to the Net."

"Yes, we have holographic computers and we're on the Net. We have an understanding with the Corps, and we cooperate with them pretty well. They don't want our territory, and we're a useful trade intermediary with the Outsiders. That's actually where we make most of our money." Harmon leaned back in his chair and said, "Nils, what do you see as your future?"

"I need to get back to San Francisco. At this point I don't know how to do it. I'd also like to use an hcue, even for just five minutes."

"Sure. Of course. But first I want you to consider something. We'd like you to help us work with the Corps, be a kind of consultant and maybe, if it works out, our ambassador to them."

"But why me? You must have other people who could do this?"

"We don't have anyone who knows the Corps and how it operates. You know how to talk to those people. We know someone there wanted you back in Denver, and you chose to come to us instead. Why did you do that?"

Nils looked around the office and noticed how spare it was: a flag in the corner, a few faded, old-fashioned photographs, two windows with glass that needed washing.

"Mr. President," he began, "I'd like to tell you the Owners' plans for San Francisco."

When he had finished, there was silence. Harmon looked out the window for a few minutes and then turned to Nils.

"I once lived there. My mother was born in Oakland, and she wanted me to see it and experience life there. I went to college in Berkeley for a year and lived in the City, on Russian Hill. Joshua and I went out there together."

They talked for a few more minutes and then Harmon said, "Let's go outside and walk a little. I need some fresh air."

He led Nils out through a back door into a meadow that had recently been mowed. They walked toward the distant woods on a well-worn path. Nils looked back and was surprised that there was no one; no body guards, no assistants. Just the two of them. The day had become overcast, and the air was moist and smelled of cut grass and the rain that had not yet begun to fall.

"Nils, why would the Corps invade a free city? I thought their job was mainly to administer the Plantations, guard the Havens, and run the railroads. What do they have to gain by this?"

"Well, Mr. President…"

"Jason."

"Okay, Jason, I think they're being driven to it by the Owners. But I don't know if it will really happen. The commandant, General Couseau, doesn't like it, I'm sure of that."

Harmon looked sideways at Nils. "Uh oh. Nils there is no way you would know this. General Couseau died last week. We got official notification so we'd be able send someone to his funeral. I'll be going to Montreal in a few days. If you accept our offer, you can go with me. And from there you'd go to Denver."

Nils looked closely at Harmon, trying to read him—was this a lie to manipulate him for some reason? No, that didn't compute. For a moment Nils felt that someone had thrown a rock at him. *This is a whole new world. What happened to Rayna?*

"Jason, how can I go to Denver? At this point the Corps is probably starting to consider me a deserter."

"If you work for us, we'll get a release for you. We make a lot of money for the Corps, and they usually let us do what we want."

"What if I don't accept your offer? What will happen to me then?"

"If you don't accept, you can go back to the Cummings farm and work there, at least for now. But if the Corps finds out you're here and demands your return, we'd have to send you back."

"Why don't you go to Denver yourself?" Nils asked.

"I shouldn't be away that long. There's too much to do here."

They reached the woods and followed the path into a green world, suddenly deeply quiet.

"So what you're saying is that if I don't accept your offer, I could be cut off from my past life forever?"

"I don't know. Maybe. You must have seen that possibility when you left the retreat."

"Yeah, well I wasn't thinking. I was just escaping."

"I'm not sure anyone can escape anymore," Harmon said.

Hugh was furious at his bodyguards—they had overreacted. Philippa wasn't really capable of killing him, Hugh believed, and he was sorry they had shot her. Still, they had been doing what they were trained to do and, even if mistaken, had been trying to protect him. If the troits weren't so stubborn, none of this would be necessary, Hugh said to himself. Her noble blood was clearly on the heads of those animals and they would pay for it.

That would be for later. The immediate issue was the Council and the selection of the next Corps Commandant. When he heard about General Couseau's death, Hugh was at first elated, but then he began to think about what it meant. Now, the Council would be cautious and want to wait until there was a new commandant. And sure enough, he got a message from Amanda Black saying that the next meeting would be entirely focused on the selection process. San Francisco would not be on the agenda at all; there wouldn't be time for it.

If he delayed, there was the danger that the project would fizzle. The troops that were already prepared would have to stand down, and the troops that were getting ready would have to suspend their training. The landing craft would have to be returned to regular Corps command—Hugh couldn't keep them moored in Richardson Bay indefinitely. And, worst of all, the publicity campaign that played up the warlike actions of the San Franciscans would have to be muted. If it went on too long, people in the Havens would start to laugh at it. Building up enthusiasm for the project was one of the hardest things Hugh had ever done, and having to do it all over again was daunting.

No, the best thing was to go ahead and ignore the Council. He'd have to wait for Couseau's funeral, but he would act immediately after that. He'd present it to them as a fait accompli. Maybe it was even better—they might be squeamish about how it was to be carried out, but there would be no point in going into details after it was over. They wouldn't want to know.

If only Hugh could focus on one thing at a time! Now he had to deal with Sylvia and his children. His son, Trevor, was acting out and yelling at his mother and terrorizing his sisters. Hugh's instincts told him to stay away from the situation, but they were all calling him and telling him to come over to their wing of the house. Fuck it, he thought, I'll just have to get it over with. The worst was that he couldn't bring along his assistant, Miss Jones. Sylvia went catatonic when she saw her, and he had agreed not to bring her into the family rooms.

He walked down the wide third-floor hallway until he came to a broad stairway, which he descended slowly. When he got to the first floor he turned left and entered a causeway. On both sides were banks of flowering dogwoods. Nothing could be less native or require more water, Hugh had been told. That was the point—consumption equaled power. He wanted to display not just his wealth but the fact that it was he who made the rules. Weren't they taught that the world was made for man to subdue, to conquer? That was still true, whatever the weaklings might say about living "in harmony" with the earth.

He could hear the yelling long before he got to the pink dining room.

"You fucking don't understand any fucking thing I fucking say." Trevor's voice was pitched too high. The boy's a hysterical pansy, Hugh thought. What did I do to deserve that?

The scene when Hugh entered the room was worse than he had imagined. Sylvia was sitting at the inlaid marble table, the Roman treasure that was "borrowed" from the Getty Museum, her head in her hands, weeping loudly while Trevor strode around the room yelling obscenities. Julia and Honore were hiding under the table. When he saw Hugh, Trevor turned toward him and whined, "All I wanted was to use one of the small boats to go out with my friends, and she said no. I told her we'd only be out for a few hours but she still said no. Why can't I do it, why?"

Hugh felt his blood rise. "Sylvia, why can't he take a boat out? What are you trying to do to this boy, turn him into a girl like you?"

Sylvia looked up and said, "But Hugh, they say it's going to be war and I think it's dangerous on the bay right now. Everyone's keeping their yachts at dock. And who knows what those people from the City are doing now. For all we know they're shooting at our boats."

Hugh laughed at that, and there was a scornful tone in his voice, "Oh, don't worry; we'll go to them before they come to us. Now tell him he can use any one he wants."

Sylvia looked up at Hugh with her cow eyes and then nodded in Trevor's direction. The boy exhaled loudly and ran out of the room.

"Girls, come out from under that table," Sylvia said.

"Let them stay there if they want to," Hugh said. "You've done enough damage today." Hugh turned around and walked out of the room. The boy had a good idea, Hugh thought, I can think out on the water. He took out his phone and made a call.

An hour later Hugh was standing on the midship deck of the *Conqueror,* his motor yacht, crossing behind Angel Island. The island used to be some kind of public park. When the government ran out of money and had to sell all of the public lands, it became the property of a group of Owners, including Hugh, which was fortunate, because it was an excellent staging point for an invasion. The northern side of the island, not visible from the City, was now an arsenal piled high with guns, ammunition, uniforms, helmets, and rations. Alcatraz, by contrast, was useless. There was no way to land on the rock anymore since the ocean rose.

Hugh lifted his binoculars and looked at the City, its white buildings catching the last rays of the setting sun. He sighed at the smallness of his world, and he kept reminding himself that this was only the first. San Francisco was just a small city, but every conqueror had to begin somewhere.

He could make out people on the Presidio beach. They were probably looking at his boat. There hadn't been many yachts out recently—Sylvia was right about that. But he knew—and he was sure the City people knew—that the Owners' patrol boats, small, fast, and armed, still dominated the bay, at least in the daylight. Hugh couldn't help thinking about that boy in his nightmares. Was he watching now? Hugh felt a chill that wasn't from the cool marine air. Put on your armor, he said to himself; stop being a weakling.

CHAPTER TWENTY-THREE

All of San Francisco had heard about General Couseau's death soon after Rayna Caskey told Mayor Johnston, and there were mixed feelings. No one liked the Corps, but Couseau had earned a kind of grudging admiration from the city dwellers. There was the time when the Owners had pushed hard to allow Plantation-grown food, most of it genetically modified, to be sold in the City at absurdly low prices. The mayor and the Board of Supervisors had resisted, and the Owners threatened, but the Corps refused to be drawn into the dispute. The Owners had to drop their plans, and the City's farmers were saved.

And then there was the threat by the Owners to deny equipment to repair the aqueduct that brought water to the City's farms on the peninsula. The Corps quietly ignored the Owners and allowed the City to use its earth-moving machinery. San Franciscans believed that it was General Couseau himself who made those decisions.

But now he was gone and with him the last hope that somehow he would find a way of aborting the invasion. War was coming, no one could deny it. Every neighborhood council was now in constant session, and they were all in contact with the mayor and the City Supervisors, who were coordinating their efforts. Huge barricades were being constructed, Geary and Market streets were blocked almost every ten blocks, and sniper locations were being identified all over the City. Citizens were told to store food and water for a two-week period and those who couldn't fight were instructed to take shelter inside once the sirens went off. Volunteers streamed into the neighborhood councils—everyone wanted to fight the Owners. In a few places there were arguments about who would get a particularly choice sniper position. There were so many excellent marksmen and women in this city that had long taught its children to hunt.

Jack now met with Mayor Johnston every morning. Sometimes Gladys came along and Grace, too. He had told them that he was now close friends with Linda Crowley, but he didn't tell them about her experiences. Grace and Gladys both seemed to understand that he didn't want to open any more doors to those dimensions.

Johnston had introduced Jack to the most prominent people in the City, with instructions to find out as much as he could about their loyalties.

Jack often confirmed the mayor's suspicions. "Sorry to tell you, Mayor, but Pierre and Marie Houghton are meeting with Hugh Rowan's people just about every day and telling them whatever they can think of to help the Owners. They're hoping to become Owners themselves, and they are almost rich enough. They've been told they'll be warned to leave the City just before the invasion, and they'll get a pass to go to MarinHaven. They don't trust Rowan, and they'll probably go to their estate in San Jose, but they are sure the Owners will win."

"Rowan's people are here all the time? This City is a sieve. Well, we've always been open, and we'll just have to do our best to keep our eyes on them. The Houghtons don't surprise me; I always thought they were phonies. But you know I can't put them in jail just on your say so, even though I do believe you," Johnston said.

"Sure. But have them watched. They meet with Rowan's people in the same restaurant back room where you met him."

Johnston winced and Jack resisted the impulse to smile. "Did you know that Rowan owns that place?"

"What? He can't, it's illegal," Johnston said. "I can't know everything."

"Well, he does. I know there isn't much you can do about that kind of thing."

"How do you know?" Johnston asked. "I know you can read minds, but who else but Rowan would know that?"

"Check and see who's the legal owner on the tax record. I've seen him at your dinner parties often and talked to him. You better have that place watched, discreetly."

"I have an idea. Why don't you spend the evening hanging around there, with some undercover cops? They can watch, and you can tell us what it is they're seeing."

"I don't think that's such a good idea. Right now they think you don't know anything and don't suspect them. And the best thing we've got going for us is that no one knows what I'm doing for you."

"Oh, yes," Johnston said, "you're our secret weapon. Listen, I think it's time that you had a title. How about 'Special Assistant to the Mayor for Cultural Affairs?'" Johnston laughed, but Jack knew he was serious.

"What do I have to do?"

"Talk to lots of people. And report to me."

"That's what I'm doing already," Jack said.

"Yeah, well now you'll get paid for it. And I won't have to try to explain why you're with me all the time. They're starting to say you're my boyfriend, and my wife really doesn't like it." They laughed.

"You're lucky, Mayor. I wish Grace minded."

Johnston put his hand on the younger man's shoulder. "Look, you're involved with one of those women who can't be pinned down. She's beautiful, but she could break your heart. Is it worth it? I don't know—only you can decide. But keep a part of your life for yourself, don't give her everything."

"I don't know if that's possible," Jack said. "There's another thing I need to talk to you about. My brother Gabe. I've tried everything I'm able to do, and I can't reach him."

"Oh, yeah. I know that's been weighing on your mind. You know who might be helpful? Governor Cruz. He has contacts everywhere."

"But I thought we weren't in touch with him."

"What kind of mind reader are you? Damn, I've totally lost confidence in your so-called powers," Johnston said with a smile.

Jack looked into the mayor's eyes and saw—layers. One set of scenarios below another set below another. For a moment he was lost in admiration of the sheer complexity of the man's mind. Then he felt deep compassion. So much of Johnston's being was occupied with illusions. What a master of it he was, creating them, selling them, shooting down others. And that's what most people call "power," Jack suddenly understood.

"We have a secure line to Sacramento. It hasn't been used much in recent years, but it's been kept operational. He told me that he feels like he owes you—I don't know why. Look, I'm going to talk to him in the morning. Why don't you come to my office at ten a.m. and you can talk to him too. By the way, one of the perks of your new job is that you get your own car and driver."

"Who said I'd accept your offer?"

"I read your mind," the mayor said.

"Jack, good to hear from you again!" Governor Cruz's voice boomed through the old-fashioned telephone landline, the one few people knew existed. "The mayor tells me you've been a big help there in San Francisco. Doesn't surprise me. I said when I first laid eyes on you that you had the makings of someone important."

"Well, thanks, governor. Listen, you know what happened to my brother and me in Denver, right?"

"Yes, I heard something about it."

"You know my brother Gabe disappeared?"

"Yes. We've been looking for him ever since."

"You have? Thank goodness, but do you have any leads?"

"Maybe. But nothing I can say right now."

Johnston broke in, "Listen Ray, I think you should have a talk with Jack in person. Not just about his brother. I'd like him to fill you in with what we're doing here, and maybe there's something you can do to help us."

"Sure, I'm happy to meet whoever you send. But how are we going to get him up here?"

"We've got a boat that can take him to you. He can leave in a couple of hours."

There was a pause for a moment. "Alright. Send him up and we'll talk."

"Ray, can I ask you a favor?" Johnston asked. "I can't go to Couseau's funeral, obviously, but we really need to send someone. Since he's going to be with you anyway, why don't you take Jack with you to Montreal and he can represent the City?"

Another pause. "You're pushing it, John, but I guess I owe you from that last time. Alright."

After he hung up, Jack turned to Johnston. "What was that about? All this is totally new to me. I didn't see it coming."

"I didn't make the decision until after Cruz picked up the phone. But this is still your job. Figuring out who's really on our side."

Jack looked at the mayor. "Oh. But is this a time for me to be leaving?"

"Nothing's going to happen until after the funeral. Couseau was more important than most people realize, and the Owners are going to be distracted for a few weeks anyway."

"But shouldn't someone more, well, high-ranking, go?"

"I can't spare anyone. And it's going to be the best place to pick up some useful information."

"Oh, I see what you're doing. I'll be your spy."

"That's a harsh word. Let's just say you're the City's eyes and ears. You know, everyone who's anyone will be at Couseau's funeral."

"So—you want me to hold hands with the enemy?"

"Yes, Jack, that's exactly it."

An hour later, Jack was in bed with Grace, a place he never wanted to leave when she was there. "I still want to call you Jill," Jack said to her after he told her he was going away for a while.

"Of course you do. And I still want to call you Jack," she teased, kissing his neck.

"But I *am* Jack; I'm the same."

"No, you're not the same. You're a flowing stream; you're never the same."

"Okay, Jill. You love to drive me crazy, don't you?"

"That's the idea." She nuzzled against him and kissed his neck and chest.

He pulled her toward him, aware of how little time they had. Then there was no more thought of time. They were both nude, she was ready, and he entered her easily—nothing in the world was more natural. He wanted to stay inside her forever, to never be apart. She came with a shudder, he came with a shout but he wouldn't pull out. They lay there panting, entwined, until he got hard again and began pounding again, pulling her toward him, wanting to melt into her.

After, they lay in bed looking up at the ceiling, spent. Jack said, "How come I can't read your mind?"

"Oh, that would never work in this kind of relationship," she said. "I know how to shield it; most people don't."

"Why wouldn't it work? I'm not saying it has to be one way. We could be really close if we read each other's minds."

Grace laughed and said, "Do you have any idea how crazy it would make you if you knew what I was thinking all the time? Think about it—do you really want me to know what you're thinking about me?"

"Yes, I do. I want you to know how much I love you."

"I don't have to read your mind for that. What you're talking about is that you want to know my feelings for you. Right?"

"Alright. Have it your way. You always do anyway."

"Look, Jack, you're still really young. Of course I love you; who wouldn't? In this precious moment. But who knows what's coming in the future? I know you get glimmers of that, but they can be as misleading as they are true. There is no certainty in our world, and you have to understand what that means."

"No. I'm certain about you. That will never change," he said. Grace kissed him on his forehead, got out of bed, and went into the bathroom. In a minute he could hear the shower running.

When she came back into the bedroom, her head sheathed in a blue towel, Jack said, "I want you to go to Sacramento with me and then to Montreal. I need you there."

"No, you don't. I've got plenty to do right here."

"I'm serious about this. I'll need all the help I can get, and you're stronger than anyone I know." Grace unrolled the towel, went over to the dressing table that used to belong to his mothers, sat down in front of the mirror, and started to brush out her hair.

"I think this is something you need to do without me. You're getting too dependent, and I don't like it."

"And you're getting too selfish," he said.

"Self-ish," she said, drawing out the word. "But all we've got is our self, ultimately. And that self has to grow. If it doesn't, it begins to rot and everyone can smell it, you know what I mean."

Jack came over to her, fell down on his knees in front of her, and buried his head in her crotch. Her thighs were warm against his ears and she smelled fresh and clean. Grace put her brush down and ran her hands through his thick, brown hair. She pulled him up to her and kissed him. He got up and walked to the window. The setting sun made the white stucco building across the street golden.

"You're right. I need to do this on my own," he said.

The City boat was waiting for him at China Basin. It was an ancient Chris Craft yacht, comfortable and elegant in a faded way. Jack sat on the starboard deck watching the shore of the east bay go by, and then he moved to look at the fishing village on the port side as they entered the Carquinez Straits on their way into the Delta. The boat skirted the islands and train trestles that had been such an obstacle only a year before. Jack suddenly felt a stab of excitement. Gabe was close. He had to be near.

Jack went to the bow of the boat and sat down there; he wanted to watch as they entered the Sacramento River. There used to be a deep-water shipping channel aimed like an arrow at Sacramento, but that had been abandoned long ago, and now they had to follow the meandering course of the river.

He had tried to get Gladys to come with him but she said the mayor wanted her to stay, so he was left alone with his thoughts and moods, and they were hard to control. It had been less than a year since he had traveled this way with Gabe but he felt decades older. His social status had been elevated beyond his imagining—or wish—but it felt like meager payment for the loss of his brother and his freedom. Life had not been easy but he had never been a worrier. The sense of impending doom that he woke up with most days was new.

A car was waiting at the dock in Sacramento. The driver was the governor's niece, Harmony Cruz.

"Gaia, what are you doing here?" he asked.

"Hey, I'm the one that should be saying that!" she said.

"Oh, you're right. Anyway, nice to see you." He didn't know what of the multitude of things he could say that he should say. They drove in silence to the governor's mansion, and when they got there she said, "Well, here you are. If you want to see me you know where I am." She put his bags on the front steps, went back to the car, and drove off.

The front door opened and a maid beckoned him in and took his bags. Another maid took him to the governor's study. There was no one there, so Jack found a comfortable chair and sat down to wait. After a few minutes he got up and tried to look at the books lining the walls, but found it hard to concentrate. He was feeling a rising sense of excitement—something was about to happen.

Someone was running across the polished, wood floors in heavy shoes. A voice shouted, "Jack, Jack!" He felt the hair on his neck rise and looked around just in time to see Gabe burst through the doorway.

CHAPTER TWENTY-FOUR

The brothers flew into each other's arms, pulled close, and then pushed away to look at each other. Jack felt something brittle lodged deep inside him break open—raw emotion coiled out. Dismay—why didn't I see this coming? Then he was blinded with anger.

"Man, where the fuck did you go?" The instant Jack said it, the feeling evaporated and he was overcome with relief. "I'm sorry, Gabe, I'm so sorry. I've been worried sick for the last six months."

"Hey, I'm here now. Man, am I glad to see you!"

"What happened to you?"

"It's a long story, bro, and I'll tell you everything, but not right now." He held himself close to Jack and put his head down into his brother's shoulder. They both wept with relief. After a few moments, Gabe pulled himself together and said, "Tell me about you. Last time

I saw you, you were hunting down that girl in the club. Did you make it with her?"

"She's my girlfriend now. She's in the City."

"Have you been with her since then?"

"Oh, no. Just for the past month. A lot has happened since I saw you."

"Yeah. No shit." Gabe walked over to a window seat and sat down. "I know what's going on with the Owners. The governor's assistant filled me in. They gave me a briefing and told me I had to know a lot of things before I saw you. Seems like you're some kind of important person now."

Gabe laughed and Jack said, "Don't believe everything you're told."

Jack took Gabe's hand and led him to a couch where they sat down and looked at each other. Jack held on to Gabe's hand.

"I can't read your mind," Jack said.

"They said you had powers. Hey, I always knew you were different, you know, those trances you used to go into."

"There's something different about you," Jack said, and he noticed as he said it that he was not feeling the slight distance he felt with everyone else these days. He was close to Gabe and that was not in spite of not being able to read his mind; it was because he couldn't read his mind. "Usually when I hold someone's hand I can look deep into them, but not with you. It feels so good not to be in your mind."

"Hey, my mind's not so bad, bro. But it's a lot more grown up than the last time you saw me. You still want to go to Maine?"

"Maine? Oh, yeah, that's what I wanted. Was that a hundred years ago? Funny thing is I'm going close to there. I'm going to Montreal. And yeah, I want to go to Maine. I want to find my father. But there are more important things right now."

"Yeah, I know; they told me. I can't wait to get back to the City and get ready to fight."

"Grace is staying in the apartment. I can get word to her that you're coming; I don't think you'll mind sharing the apartment with her. Your room is exactly how you left it. I wish I could see your sisters' faces when they see you."

"Oh yeah. But I have to do something first, before I go home."

"What do you mean?"

"I'm going to Montreal with you, you dolt. The governor told me I had to keep an eye on you."

"Yes, I did and for good reason." Cruz had entered the room and put his big hands on their shoulders. "You're both going with me and officially you will be my military attachés."

"What the hell is that?" Jack exclaimed.

"I'm inducting you into the California Guard. Used to be called the National Guard, but that doesn't exist anymore."

"But I'm supposed to represent San Francisco," Jack said.

"You will, don't worry. The City doesn't have official status but the state of California does. There's a tailor waiting to measure you for your uniforms right now. Better get moving. We're leaving tomorrow."

"Governor, I'm going to have to say no," Jack said. "I can't wear a military uniform."

"It's just a formality. Believe me, it will up your prestige value a lot. And the girls love it."

"Sorry, governor. I can't do it," Jack said. "Gabe, you do what you want."

"I don't need it. I'm with you, bro."

Jack was not smiling, and the governor said, "Alright. I'll leave it up to you. But believe me, the Owners respect anything military, even if it isn't theirs."

"Thanks, governor, I appreciate your intentions, but my best weapon is being underestimated."

Jack saw Cruz react when he said that and went deeper into the governor's mind than he had intended. *Better be careful with this one.*

"Do what you think is right, Jack," Cruz said, with the slightest tone of contempt in his voice. "We're going to leave tomorrow morning, so we'll have a chance to talk this afternoon."

"How are we traveling?" Gabe asked.

"We're going by sonic," Cruz said, "from MarinHaven. I guess you'd call it enemy territory," Cruz said with a light laugh.

The sun was still high over the western hills when the governor's boat docked at the yacht harbor of San Quentin, the water gate of

MarinHaven. Like the governor, Jack and Gabe were traveling on diplomatic passports and passed through the border checkpoint easily. There was a huge car and a driver waiting for them. The driver took their bags from the boat and put them into the car's trunk. He was about the same age as Gabe, maybe twenty, with olive skin and black hair.

"Our sonic leaves around noon tomorrow, so we'll spend the night here," Cruz told Jack and Gabe. "Drive slowly, driver," Cruz said. "We want to see as much as we can."

"Yes, sir. Do you want me to take the Helpers' lanes? They're much slower."

"Oh, we're entitled to the Owners' lanes?" Cruz asked.

"Yes, sir. They gave you an Owners' car because you came with a diplomatic passport."

"What the hell does all this mean?" Gabe asked the governor.

"There are special roads for Owners and others for Helpers. Obviously, there isn't much traffic on the Owners' roads. But you want to see something of the Haven, don't you?"

"Sure, thanks governor," Gabe said.

Jack had gone to Linda's house by boat from the City, but they got off at her private dock, and he hadn't seen anything else of the Haven. Now, he saw how green it was. There were lawns everywhere. He had never seen any kind of lawn until he went to Sacramento, and there they were just scrawny affairs, tufts of grass among the dirt. But here the lawns were thick, luxurious, deep green. How much water does it take to keep these going?, he wondered.

Just as he was musing on that, the governor said, "Most of the water from the Sierras now comes here. It used to go to the Central Valley and Southern California, but now the Owners have first priority. So instead of growing fruit and vegetables, most of it just grows grass."

They had been driving near a high wall for a few miles. and then they came to a place where the wall gave way to an equally high fence made of some kind of glass strands. They could see rows and rows of townhouses and a glimmer of a business district. A road led to a gatehouse. A line of cars was waiting to go into the gate and another line was waiting to go out. "What's that?" Gabe asked.

"That's where the Helpers live," Cruz said.

"What exactly are the Helpers?"

Cruz began to explain—the Helpers were the workers who kept the Havens functioning. Some of them were unskilled laborers, but others were engineers and accountants, doctors and lawyers. They lived in closed communities called Villas. The fences weren't there to keep people out—they were there to keep the Helpers in. They were supposed to be out only for work. The Villas had all the amenities of a city, Cruz said, supermarkets, hospitals, even movie theatres and parks.

The Owners were thinking beyond the current caste structures, toward a future that made more sense to them. The introduction of slavery in Denver was still an experiment, but a promising one. It made sense that most people who weren't Owners would eventually be their slaves.

But the ultimate goal was even more ambitious. The Owners would select the children to be born into their caste through careful genetic engineering and evolve swiftly into a superior race. The remainder of humanity—well, there was a step below slavery, and some of the more advanced economists said that it was even more cost effective. The Church was queasy on the subject of genetic engineering but otherwise understanding about the Owners' dreams for the future.

Governor Cruz was sitting in the backseat with Jack, and Gabe was sitting in the front with the driver. For a moment Jack was overwhelmed with the driver's thoughts and feelings. He caught a thought that surprised him: *the Corps won't allow any of that shit.*

"But not all the Owners are on board with those plans. Nothing's cast in concrete yet and it's all still up in the air," Cruz told them.

"Isn't all this supposed to be a secret?" Gabe asked.

"Oh, no," Cruz replied, "these ideas have been talked about on the Net and proclaimed pretty openly by some of the Owners. They think there's nothing anyone else can do to stop them. The Corps works for them, after all."

There was silence in the car for a moment. Gabe and the driver looked at each other and smiled.

They drove up to a collection of low buildings surrounded by parking lots. There were no signs except for the Corps logo next to a door that seemed to be the main entrance.

"What's this?" Jack asked.

"This is our hotel. It belongs to the Corps, and it's where their officers stay when they visit the Haven. And anyone else who visits here. Except, of course, for Owner visitors. They stay in the clubhouse," Cruz said.

Jack and Gabe looked at each other and broke up.

"What are you laughing about," Cruz said, irritably.

"It's just the idea of staying in a Corps building, surrounded by Corps officers. I never thought in my wildest dreams that I'd be doing that."

"Get used to it. Some of them aren't so bad."

"Yeah, I know," Gabe said, and Jack suddenly remembered that man they had met at the Owners' bar in Denver, the one Rayna knew. Better keep that to just the two of us, Jack thought, and he wondered why that seemed like a good idea.

After they checked in, Cruz told them that he was going to see some old friends, and they had the evening to themselves. There was a restaurant in the hotel and they could charge everything to their room.

Jack said to Gabe, "I guess this gives us a chance to catch up. I want to tell you about Grace and also about Linda Crowley."

"Hey, bro, I'm going to see Oliver. But you can come too."

"What? Who the hell is Oliver?"

"You know. The driver."

"Wow, you sure work fast. I'm not staying here by myself. Where are we going?"

Oliver picked them up in his own car. It was barely big enough for the three of them, and inside it was all hard surfaces. The seats were a bit less comfortable than the back of a horse. But what was lacking in comfort was more than made up for in enthusiasm. Oliver seemed wildly excited.

"I can't believe you cats are from San Francisco! We've never met anyone from outside the Haven before, except for some of the old rich people who come here once in a while."

"Haven't you ever been anyplace else, even Oakland?" Jack asked him.

"Oh, no. If we leave the Haven, we have to have a special pass to get back in and you need a purpose, like a dying grandma or something. But we get to visit the other Villas. There's one near Santa Rosa, and I know some cats there. Anyway, it's safe in the Haven and we're lucky to be here."

"Where are we going now?" Jack asked.

"My boy Eric's place. His Dad's gone and his Mom's out for the night so we can party."

They got through the Villa's checkpoint with no problems. When he saw Jack's and Gabe's passports, the guard looked at them and said, "Be careful, gentlemen, and play safe."

"That bastard," Oliver said as they pulled away. "He thinks everyone here is a whore. And you know the funny thing? He is, in his spare time. I know 'cause my Pa had him not long ago."

They pulled up in front of a row of identical townhouses. There were no lawns here, just small, gravel plots fronting the buildings' blank faces. Oliver knocked on a door, which opened instantly, as if someone had been watching for them, and they walked into a room that was lit only by a small, red diode in the ceiling. The noise was deafening, synthetic music with a rough, insistent beat. Oliver went to the sound system and shut it down. Then he yelled into the silence, "Hey, Collective, this here's Jack and Gabe from the City of San Francisco! Jack digs chicks and Gabe digs cats. But I get first dibs on Gabe. Make 'em welcome." Then he turned the music back on.

Jack and Gabe were instantly surrounded by a group of curious people. They all wanted to talk, but Jack could barely hear their voices. But he heard them on another level. There was so much going on—all he could get were snatches of thoughts, *I'm not having fun tonight; Better take some more happy pills; Fuck it, I have to go to work tomorrow; Why are these City Cats here, are they slumming?; Wonder if I can make it with the taller one.* Jack couldn't make out who was thinking what; it was all too intense.

A short, heavy man came up to them, looking angry, and said with a strangled voice, "Hey, troits, what you doing here? Why don't you stay where you belong, in Troitville." Oliver moved over to him, grabbed his right arm, and put him into a half-nelson; the man screamed in pain.

"Shuttup, asshole. And don't ever use that word again with my friends here."

Jack looked at Gabe and said, "What the hell? What's a troit?"

Gabe laughed and said, "Where have you been? Must have been very polite company." He held out his pinky finger. "That's what they call us city dwellers. It's short for Detroit, the first depopulated city. They can't think of anything worse to call us."

A young woman wearing a skimpy halter top and a skirt that just barely covered her buttocks, hugging them tightly, said to Jack, "I'm sorry for that animal. Don't pay any attention to him. He's a jerk." Jack looked into her eyes and suddenly realized that she was looking into him. *Don't say anything here.* He looked back at her with a question, *Who are you?* She replied, *A friend of Gladys and Grace.* Jack could barely contain himself. The only person outside of the monastery who could communicate like that was Grace, and once or twice Gladys.

She put her arms around him and moved against him. She said in a voice loud enough for everyone around to hear, "Hi, honey, my name's Carmen. I don't care where you came from; I just care what you got." Jack put his arms around her and nuzzled his face against hers. He whispered in her ear.

Gabe looked at them and said, "Hey, bro, I thought you said you were in love. That didn't last very long."

"Yeah, well, shit happens," Jack mumbled as he let the woman lead him into a bedroom. She pulled him down onto the bed and whispered in his ear, "Lay close to me and don't speak. We'll dialogue directly. It's safer."

—The last time I left my brother at a party I lost him. I have to take care of him.—

—Don't worry. That was different. He's safe here.—

—What is going on?—

—I'm with the Sisters. Gladys is one of our mothers. We need to make sure you're safe on your trip. Don't trust Governor Cruz. Watch him and

don't tell him any more than you have to. Try not to let him know that you don't trust him.—
—*What about Mayor Johnston?—*
—*He's solid, on our side.—*
—*Why are you here and not with us?—*
—*These are my people and they know the Owners better than anyone.—*
—*Are you in touch with Grace?—*
—*Yes. She's with us now.—*

Jack shivered with a combination of lust and the thrill of the uncanny. He was overwhelmed by this woman's hot body and at the same time he felt Grace's presence.

Jack; I'm here with you. You can have her; it will be me too. Grace was in his mind, sharing him. Jack was hard with desire but he felt rushed, out of control. He'd been slammed onto a bobsled and he couldn't stop. Carmen/Grace opened herself and he thrust in and filled her up. Afterwards, Jack lay quietly with her and they listened together to the thoughts of the people in the party. Grace was gone.

The mental landscape of these people was different from anything Jack had known. They were subservient, but also rebellious; nothing about them was straightforward. They were in awe of the Owners, but they despised them. They resented the daily humiliations that came with their second-class status in the Haven but they were proud to be living there. Their biggest fear was of being sent away, Outside or to a Plantation. Their only hope was to have fun on Saturday night.

"Hey, we better get back to the party," Carmen said after a few minutes. They got dressed and opened the door to the blaring music. Jack had a moment of disorientation but recovered when he saw Gabe, who was dancing with Oliver.

When Gabe saw Jack he stopped dancing and pulled Oliver with him. The boys came up to Jack and Gabe said, "Hey, cat, that took you long enough. Now it's our turn." He pulled Oliver into the bedroom and shut the door.

Jack laughed and turned to Carmen. A tall, shirtless man with big muscles and hairy shoulders had his arms around her. He looked at Jack with icy blue eyes.

CHAPTER TWENTY-FIVE

The trees were black against the gray sky of early morning and rain beat against the window panes. Nils woke up too early but he couldn't get back to sleep. He loved the room he had been given in Harmon's house. It was on the second floor, on a corner, and there was an old sugar maple tree outside his window. He wished he could lie there, under the covers, just listening to the rain drop onto the leaves.

He got up and began to pack his things. He would need a variety of clothes, all of which had been given to him by Harmon's assistant. Most of them were made of linen or wool, just as in San Francisco. Thank goodness I still have my cotton underwear, he thought. That's what our class distinctions have finally come down to—who has to endure scratchy boxers. There was a knock on his door and someone said, "We're leaving in half an hour." A few minutes later he put his new suitcases into the car's trunk and then climbed into the front seat. Harmon got into the driver's seat and greeted him.

"I like to drive," the president said, "and anyway, it isn't that far. We're picking up the Corps train at St. Johnsbury."

Two men got in the backseat. Nils had never seen them before, but he knew they were soldiers. "These boys are coming with us to the train. We won't be allowed to take them any farther. The Corps will be responsible for our security." They turned into the gravel road and headed north.

"You came at a good time for the weather," Harmon said. "It's been cold and rainy since last Thanksgiving but finally we're getting a break."

Nils said, "What do you mean by Thanksgiving?"

"Don't you know the holiday; at the end of November?"

"Oh, yeah, that's right; some people in San Francisco do it. I've heard of it. But not in the Havens or in the Corps. We're not big on holidays. They're considered a waste of time."

"That's too bad. They give the year a kind of rhythm, you know. Thanksgiving is my favorite. Give thanks for what you've got." They crested a hill and descended into a wide valley; in the distance were low mountains, smoothed at the top by eons of weathering. The sky was still gray, massive over the mountain tops. "We need some kind of pattern to our lives, something regular, and the seasons used to give that to us. They were so dependable, and people here in this country regulated their lives by them. We need that rhythm and so we keep the old holidays to remind us."

Nils wondered if he had been fooling himself. Was he actually facing mounting waves of circumstances that would eventually overwhelm him? He was quiet for a few minutes and then he said, "We're lost, we're really lost."

"Hey, Nils, don't give up hope," Harmon said. "The Owners would like you to despair—if you think nothing can be done then you'll settle for the world they're preparing for you. The powers-that-be have always tried to scare people and make them feel helpless. Optimism is our best weapon."

"Jason, what are we going to be doing in Montreal, and why do you want me to go to Denver?"

"We need friends, Nils, what they used to call alliances. And we want to be friends with anyone who wants to be friends with us. You know more about the world outside our little country than anyone else we have, so I want you to help me figure out who we can trust and who can help us. We are way too dependent on the Corps now and we've got to figure out how we get what we need from other sources."

As they drove north, the road began to deteriorate. The hardtop gave way to gravel and the gravel to dirt. "We're not far from the train now," Harmon said. "You can tell when we've left the Republic, because of the roads. We keep them up, but the locals here don't do a good job of it. Not their fault, I suppose, because there aren't very many of them."

"What happened to them?" Nils asked.

"Most of them couldn't make it here, so some of them drifted to Montreal and others went to work on the Plantations to the north."

Harmon stopped the car at a crossroads where there were a few stores and a very old church. "Let's see if we can get some coffee or at least something hot to drink," Harmon said.

They walked over to a building that had a hand-painted sign hanging on it that said EAT and walked in the door. A gray-haired woman was behind the counter. She was rail thin and tall. She looked at Nils and Jason with what seemed like disdain and said, "We don't have much. What do you want?"

"We stopped to see if you had any coffee."

"Coffee! Haven't had that in years."

"Can we have hot tea then?" She didn't answer but instead turned around and reached for an earthenware teapot. Then she went over to the wood stove, put the teapot down, and picked up a kettle that was heavy with boiling water. She poured some into the teapot and swirled it around to heat the pot. She poured out the water in the sink and then put some leaves in the pot and filled it with the boiling water. She set the pot down on the counter and reached back to get two thick white mugs.

"Do you have sugar?" Nils asked her. She looked at him with disgust and put a pot of honey and a spoon in front of him. "That'll be an extra dollar."

"Do you want anything else?" This was addressed to Harmon.

"Sure. I'd like to find out how things are going here," he said.

"Why? Are you going to do anything about it?"

Harmon looked at her and shook his head. "If I could I would. But I think it's up to your community."

"We don't have no community. We're Outside and you know it. I know who you are with your fuel cell car and your bodyguards, and you don't do nothing for us. Every time we get a good crop or build something, someone comes and takes it. If it's not the wild people it's the Corps, and if it's not them it's the GC's people. They all squeeze us dry, and what do you do about it? Not a goddamn thing."

"Ma'am, you are not in the Republic, and we can't defend you. But you're free to move there, remember that."

"Yeah, well, my people's had this land for a hundred years, and I'm not leaving it to go do chores for someone else. I'll starve here first."

They finished their tea in silence, and Harmon left a few extra dollars on the table before they walked out. They got back to the car and drove slowly west over the rough road. Jason began asking questions about Outside, and Nils found himself holding forth, explaining the world as he knew it in great detail.

"Yeah, I've heard a lot of this," Harmon said. "We've read a lot on the Net, but you never know what to believe. I've spent most of my adult life helping to keep my farm going and organizing the Republic, and I really haven't seen that much of the world since college. So Outside, they don't have technology?"

"No, and that's why I was so surprised to see that you have hcues. They don't even have them in San Francisco; they have very old-fashioned computers with physical screens. They've been recycling them for years."

"What's the state of technology in the Havens?" Harmon asked. "Are they really much different from us?"

Nils looked at him and smiled. "Yes, it's different. I don't think I can describe just how different; you have to see for yourself."

"What I'm trying to get at is this—are we Indians facing Columbus; do we have a chance?"

"Well, they've got internal weaknesses, their own fault lines, and their attention's more on those fights than on anyone who isn't part of their world."

Harmon slapped Nils on the knee and said, "You are telling me just what I suspected! And that's why we're so happy to have you with us. You'll be our guide to the fault lines."

Nils wondered where this could lead. His life was with Philippa; he had to find a way of getting back to her. He admired the Republic, yes, but his life was with her.

They were descending a hill and could see some buildings in the distance. The road abruptly turned into smooth blacktop. "We're in St. Johnsbury," Harmon said. "We'll go right to the train station."

The houses looked freshly painted and well kept up. The whole town looked like it was carefully tended, and then Nils remembered. "This is a Corps town, isn't it?" he asked.

"Yes, it's considered a Corps field station. You have to work for the Corps in one capacity or another to live here." They descended a small hill and drove toward an old, red brick building with dozens of windows capped by limestone lintels. "Here's the station; we'd better hurry. The train should be here in fifteen minutes."

Harmon parked the car next to the station platform, and they all got out, and the soldiers started to pull their suitcases from the trunk. A man in a Corps uniform hurried over to them.

"President Harmon, we've been expecting you," he said.

"Hello, Lieutenant," Harmon said.

"I'm sorry to tell you that the train is not going to stop here today."

"What? Why?"

"The Corps has put in place extra security precautions, and the trains aren't stopping at stations in Outside."

"You mean to tell me that we have to go to a Haven to get on a train?"

"Yes, sir. That's what you'll have to do. They're also stopping at the Plantations, but I don't suppose you'll be able to go there."

Just then there was a rumble coming from the south. In a few seconds the train slid by, slowing down enough so they could read the Corps logo on the side. As soon as it passed through the station, it picked up speed and was gone in a flash.

"How's the road between here and Montreal?"

"Oh, I wouldn't try that, sir. Some of the auto bridges are gone, and I don't think there are car ferries anymore."

"We have to get to Montreal in time for General Couseau's funeral, and it's the Corps' responsibility to see we do that. I need to talk to someone who can help us."

The officer looked down at the ground and then up at Harmon. "Alright, sir. I'll do what I can. Don't you recognize me, Jason?"

Harmon looked in the captain's face. "Oh, my god, Noah Townsend! I didn't recognize you in that uniform. Your parents will be happy to know you're so close to home. I saw them just last week; they're fine."

"Thanks, I've been in touch with them. It wasn't easy to get this posting; the Corps wanted to send me to a Plantation in Florida, but

I pulled every string I could think of, and now, here I am, almost home."

"Well, Noah, I'm glad for you. But now we've got a big problem. Maybe you can pull some strings for us?" A cold, light rain had begun to fall, and they all went inside the old-fashioned railway station, a relic of a much earlier time. The soldiers sat down on the smooth, wooden benches, and Townsend ushered Harmon and Nils into the station manager's office.

Before they sat down, Harmon said to Nils, "Nils, this is Lieutenant Townsend. Noah, this is Nils Rakovic." Townsend looked at Nils and seemed to have a flash of recognition. The old saying came back to Nils: Corps knows Corps.

CHAPTER TWENTY-SIX

The board room was decorated with military images—there were swords, lances, and pictures of artillery pieces from wars spanning two hundred years. There was a whole wall of photographs of great military leaders, generals, and field marshals who had sworn to defend to the death countries whose names were now forgotten.

In the center there was a large, oval table made of one giant piece of driftwood, as if a whole tree had been cast into the ocean and burnished by saltwater.

Why does she do this? Hugh Rowan fumed quietly, how did she even think of a driftwood table? One day I'll put Amanda Black out to pasture and put someone more regular in her place. And at those meetings, I'll be at the head of the table.

Hugh was early, the first member of the Council to appear. But soon the seats were filled. It was a virtual room, and the members simply materialized in their appointed seats, but somehow that didn't detract from the illusion of a real room with real books and a real table. "Who cares what's real and what's not," Hugh had often told one or another of his mistresses. Among all the candidates for real, we choose the one that we want, the one that benefits us most. And then we force the people around us to accept it. That's what "real" is, he said, and no one dared to contradict him.

"Let's get started." Gray Wainwright, the chairman of the board, took a few moments to get their attention. "The purpose of our special meeting today is to get the report from the search committee on the new commandant of the Corps and to talk about the alternatives. So I'll turn the meeting over to Hugh Rowan, who is chairman of the committee."

"Ladies and gentlemen," Hugh began, "thanks for attending today. It's most unusual to have two Council meetings in less than thirty days, but General Couseau's death has made it necessary. The committee has been working as fast as we could, and we've looked at ten possible candidates for commandant. Of those, we narrowed it down to three who we would recommend. Here they are." Three officers materialized in miniature in front of each Council member. After a moment the images collapsed and then rematerialized life-sized at the front of the room, standing at attention.

Hugh briefly summarized the biographies of each man (he had vetoed the idea of a female commandant), and the Council members began a general discussion. Hugh was bored to death by all their talk, and he had to force himself not to shout.

The conversation finally turned in a direction that caught his attention—what kind of person are we looking for?

Hugh jumped in quickly. "We need someone who is in tune with what our times demand. Which means someone who is looking to the future, not the past, and who is not afraid of new ways of doing things." There was no disagreement, and Hugh went on. "We've been very modest in promoting our interests for a few generations now, but we owe it to ourselves and our children to be more aggressive."

"Well, sure, Hugh," someone said, "but what has that got to do with choosing the Corps Commandant?"

Other comments were in the same vein: "Seems to me that we need someone who knows how to stick to a budget," the man from ChaseAmericanWells said.

"This time we should have someone who will come to our meetings," someone said.

These people just do not get it, Hugh thought, they have no imagination and they need to be led just as much as the troits do.

The Council decided to put off the final decision for another six months, leaving the acting commandant in charge. General Bast was a careful man who had no enemies.

Hugh considered bringing up San Francisco, but decided no, better not. Now's not the time for something new, they'd all say; better wait until there's a permanent commandant in place. But who knew what the next leader of the Corps, if it wasn't Hastings, would think of the plan? Bast would be easier to get around than a new permanent commandant. All the more reason for getting it done as soon as possible.

When the meeting switched off, Hugh found himself in his study. It was always a bit of a shock, returning from a virtual meeting and being in your own skin again. The advantage of a holo meeting was that the sense of sight was so dominant that you forgot the other senses. Returning to a real place meant smell and touch and unexpected sounds; it meant random sensory input that couldn't be controlled; and even worse were the images inside his head, the pictures that seeped through from dreams and somewhere else, too.

Hugh had been dreaming about the boy from the opera. In a recurrent dream, the boy would walk toward him, and the closer he got, the bigger he became. By the time he was a few feet away he towered over Hugh, who realized just then that the boy wasn't becoming bigger—instead, he, Hugh, was shrinking and was overcome with shame as he became small.

In another dream Hugh was riding a horse and he saw the boy, who was standing in a field looking directly at him, an incomprehensible smile on his face. Hugh decided to run him down, exulting in the prospect of the horse's hooves smashing the boy's body. But at the very moment the boy was to be trampled, he turned into a wisp of fog and drifted away. Sometimes Hugh woke up gasping with frustration.

But the worst dream was the one where the boy came into Hugh's bedroom. Hugh would be in bed, paralyzed, and watching with horror as the boy leaned over, a knife in his hand, and calmly, with a charming smile, cut his heart out.

There was a knock on the door. "Come," Hugh said.

A maid walked in and said, "Will you have lunch downstairs, sir, or would you rather we bring it to you?"

He had to think for a minute. Why was he having a hard time making a decision? He decided he didn't want to be alone just now. "I'll be down in five minutes," he said.

The family meal was predictably boring but it cheered him a little to see his family around him and everyone watching carefully to see what his mood was. He felt generous and told Sylvia and the children to spend the afternoon shopping on him. Buy some new clothes or whatever. He returned to his study refreshed and resolved to deal with his fear. He summoned the chief of his private security team, Armand Riley, and also Colonel Hastings. He met with Riley first, on the south terrace.

"I was at the opera some months ago," Hugh began. "It was a production of Gounod's Faust, and at the intermission there was a boy sitting next to us at the café. He had some kind of epileptic fit, and I think they took him to the opera clinic. We have to find him because I have information that he's been plotting with the war mongers in San Francisco and that he's leading the group that wants to blow up the Villa's daycare facilities. They've made it their goal to murder as many Helper children as they can. We've got to stop them."

Riley appeared suitably impressed. "Yes, sir, we'll certainly get on this right away. Can you describe him? Do you have any specific instructions?"

"He's in his early twenties, I think, and rather slight, not tall. I think he has brown hair and light brown skin. Typical San Francisco type. You can probably find out who he is from the opera house records. Use my San Francisco contacts to get you in there. Miss Jones will give you some names to start with. When you find out his name and how you can get to him, contact me and tell me the details. But remember, this boy is the ringleader. He may look innocent to you, but take it from me: he's very dangerous, so you better make sure you have enough men with you to handle him. By the way, you are to do whatever is necessary and not worry about the expense, within reason. This is the highest priority."

"And what are we to do with the boy, when we find him?"

"Get rid of him and then send me a picture so I can confirm you got the right one. Kill the boy and you'll stop this whole operation and save your people a whole lot of grief."

Hugh went back into his study, a grand, windowless room with a twenty-foot ceiling, and called for Hastings. Hugh sat behind his vast desk and motioned for the colonel to sit in a chair facing him.

"Hastings, it's time. As soon as Couseau's funeral is over, I will place a holo call to you. You will not accept it but you will send the troops in as soon as you see the symbol in front of you. Then you will take off your Corps bracelet and hide it somewhere. You are not to send or receive communications from anyone on the Council or Corps Command until I contact you or see you. Do you understand?"

For a moment, Hastings looked like he had swallowed something unpleasant but then he said, "Yes, sir. Which symbol will you send?"

"The order to invade will be this." Hugh took a small gold case from a drawer and twisted the numbers on edge. An image appeared in front of Hastings. It was a silver sword against a blue sky and under it a white city. "After I send you the signal, I don't want to hear from you again until you've secured the City. Send someone to my house to tell me, and I will meet you there soon after that. I expect you to finish cleaning the City of the troits within twenty-one days of the landing. That should be plenty of time."

"Yes, sir. Are we getting the extra troops from Central Command?"

"No. This is going to be an Internal Security operation from top to bottom. No one in Central Command is to know about it until we've secured San Francisco."

"Yes, sir. If we need more troops..."

"You can contact them once you're in the City and in control. They won't refuse to help at that point, I'm sure."

"Sir, we haven't completed the facilities for the non-working population."

"That again. You figure it out. I don't care what you do with them, just get them out so we can start the demolition. Or leave them in place and get rid of them at the same time you get rid of the old buildings."

"I don't think the troits will leave them when they go, sir."

"It doesn't matter! Just make sure we can take the old city down to the ground within three weeks of when I give you the order. We've got to be ready to start building our houses as soon as possible." Hugh wanted to go to the next Council meeting prepared to sell large plots of clear San Francisco land to any Council member who wanted it.

Hugh hated having to go to the funeral in Montreal. Most of the Council would be there in person, and he'd have to pretend he was sorry that Couseau was dead. There would be interminable speeches and endless dithering about issues of no consequence.

He was ill with frustration—it was time for action. But the delay would not be long while his absence would be resented by the people who mattered—it would be a notable breach of protocol. Still, it wouldn't be long now. As soon as Couseau was put in the ground, the sword hanging over San Francisco would smash down.

Jack was sitting on a fake leather sofa surrounded by couples in various stages of love-making, and he had never felt more alone. The hairy muscle man had taken Carmen out of the house, and she hadn't even said goodbye. No one was talking to Jack, and he was doing his best not to hear their thoughts. Finally, he was learning how to turn off the outside noise.

The bedroom door opened. Gabe was in front and Oliver behind, his arms tightly around the smaller boy and his face nuzzled into Gabe's neck. Jack jumped up and walked over to them. "Let's go, Gabe. We have a big day tomorrow."

"Okay. I'll drive you back to the hotel," Oliver said.

When they arrived at the hotel, a bellman told Jack that someone was waiting to see him. He walked into the lobby and a small young woman came up to him and said, "Hi, I'm Alice Clavering, Linda Crowley's assistant. Miss Crowley has invited you to go to Montreal with her, on her sonic. Someone will come to pick you up at noon tomorrow."

Jack was surprised. He hadn't heard from Linda in a few weeks and didn't even know that she was going to the funeral.

"That sounds great, but what about Governor Cruz? He's expecting us to go with him."

"Miss Crowley has invited the governor too."

The boys went back to their room, a simple space: two chairs, two beds, and a table. Jack sat down on a chair and said, "Alright, what happened to you after Denver? You've been avoiding this."

Gabe threw himself down on his bed, rumpled the pillows so he could sit up, and sighed. "All right, bro, I'll tell you all about it. You went off with that girl and I was dancing with some boy I just met. And the dude we met, you know, the dude from the Corps, he went to the bar to get us drinks. Suddenly I heard a crashing sound and everyone began to scream. I started to run for the door with everyone else and then, blank. I know I got hit because when I woke up there was a big lump on my head. I woke up in a cell with a bunch of other cats they had taken from the club."

"Cats?" They both laughed.

"Yeah, dudes, whatever. Anyway, it smelled horrible; there was vomit all over the floor. The police marched us out of there before noon, and we all had to go for inspection. It was pretty humiliating, I have to say. After that there were three lines and they told you which one to go to. The big strong looking guys went to the right, the older ones straight ahead, and I was sent to the left. I kept trying to talk to someone to tell them that I didn't belong there, but no one would talk to me.

"They sent me to a Corps brothel just outside Denver. It was actually not too bad and some of the girls were really friendly. There was only one other cat there, and he was a real bitch. There were hot showers, so that was good, but the food was that processed factory stuff and it was nasty, but I got used to it, and they gave me some nice clothes.

"Not many customers chose me. Delores, the madam, said I wasn't the right type—she said I was too rough around the edges to be the boyish type—I liked that!—but too skinny to be a jock, even a runner. See, I told you I should eat more! But she told me not to worry about it; they'd take care of me anyway. Delores said it was lucky for me to be sent there because I never would have survived the Church silver mines.

I met a few interesting men, and I learned a lot about the Corps. We thought it was a single big thing, but it's more like a lot of little things. Everyone seems jealous of everyone else, and they really don't like the Owners even though they work for them.

"I was worried about you, Jack, but I figured since I didn't see you in jail you escaped somehow. That chick you were going for, I only saw her for a minute, but she looked strange—you couldn't forget her. When I thought about it, I wondered if she knew about the raid and was trying to protect you. I wish I had had someone like that! That Corps dude, his name was Nils, seemed like he was ok, but I don't know. He wasn't in jail with me either, but I'm sure he was right there when the police raided the place."

"He brought us there," Jack said. "Do you think he was trying to trap us?"

"No, I don't think he intended for us to get busted."

"I know who he is, kind of. It's too much to explain, but he's connected to some important people. But go on, tell me more of what happened to you."

"After I had been there for a while, Delores told me that one of the few customers who liked me wanted to hire me to work on his ranch and was I willing to do it. If not, I'd have to find some other place to go."

"Why didn't you try to get back to the City?"

"You know, if you're in Denver without a job and without money they can pick you up, and you're going to end up in the mines, so I was afraid to leave the house without another job. Anyway, I decided to go with the dude, his name was Harris, and he took me to his ranch in Wyoming, a beautiful place in a valley surrounded by mountains. I had to sleep with him, but it was ok; he was pretty good to me. Only thing was the weather; it was so wild—sometimes on a sunny, calm day the wind would come up with no warning and you couldn't even stand up. It didn't rain very often, but sometimes when it did it would come down so hard you felt like you were underwater, and god help you if you were in the path of a flash flood.

"He raised sheep and llamas there, and somehow they managed to survive. The llamas guarded the sheep—can you believe that?

"You know I love to ride, and I got to be on a horse all the time. He gave me a rifle because the place is Outside, and you can't go anywhere without a gun that you're prepared to shoot. Mostly the people who come by are not tough; they're just starving and looking for some way to survive. Harris shot a few of them, and I told him that he had to stop, that it was wrong. If someone's threatening to attack, that's one thing, but just helpless pitiful people; no, you can't shoot them. He listened to me. We had a pretty good understanding at that point, but he probably does it again now that I'm not there. I think some of them are escaped slaves."

"How did you get out of there?"

"Oh, that's a story. One day a small plane, not a sonic, landed in front of the ranch house and a man in uniform came out. He asked for me by name, Gabe, and he told me that I was going back to California.

"Harris was shocked and said no, but then two soldiers came out of the plane and stood next to him. No protest from me! I ran for the plane but, you know, the only sad thing was when I looked out the window and Harris was crying. It really shocked me. In a few minutes we were in the air. They took me to Denver and then put me on the Corps train to Sacramento. When I got there I didn't know what to do, so I went to Governor Cruz's house. Was he surprised to see me! But he took me in and a few days later told me you were coming."

"So where was the plane from?"

"It was Corps. And the soldiers were Corps."

"I wonder if that guy Nils sent it. Who else could it have been? But he couldn't have taken your clothes from our hotel room. What was that about?"

"Hey, Jack, you're supposed to be the psychic. Anyway, I still miss my yellow sweatshirt."

CHAPTER TWENTY-SEVEN

The next morning they met Governor Cruz at the hotel restaurant. A waitress came up to their table and asked for their breakfast orders. Jack wasn't hungry but he made himself order scrambled eggs and toast. He needed all the energy he could get. Cruz's thoughts were a jumble of emotion and calculation, and Jack couldn't make much sense of them, except for one thing. The governor was puzzled about why he had been invited to go on Linda's sonic and was not particularly pleased. Cruz didn't want to be compromised by associating with her—she was considered a bit of a rebel by the more conservative Owners.

"I'm sure we'll spend time with you in Montreal and go to events with you," Jack said. Instantly he realized it was the wrong thing to say. Cruz would know he was reading his mind.

"Of course you will. So you heard about Linda Crowley's invitation? I thanked her and told her it would be simpler for us to take the public sonic."

"Governor, I think I'd like to go with her. She's my friend," Jack said.

"I heard you were psychic, but I didn't know you were crazy," Cruz said. "You think someone of her caste is your friend?" Cruz let out a harsh laugh.

They sat there quietly until the food came and ate in silence. Jack considered the alternatives. Carmen's warning flashed in his mind. What's important, he finally decided, was to go with the person he trusted.

Finally, Jack said, "Governor, I don't think we promised anything in particular about this trip. We're going with Linda. Thanks for all your help." The brothers stood up.

"I brought you here, you little bastard; I made you what you are now! You'd be singing for change on Mission Street or dead in some Church mine if it hadn't been for me. I brought your brother back to you! Mayor Johnston expects you to go with me. I'm warning you. There will be consequences if you don't go with me."

Jack leaned over the table and said in a quiet voice, "Governor Cruz, in the beginning, why did you trust us to go to Denver and get information for you? You didn't know us or anything about us."

"You're the mind reader; you should know that. It all turned out just great for you, didn't it?"

"Governor, did you even need to know what the purpose of the new Plantation was? Or did you already know?"

"Why would I ask you to find out if I already knew?" Cruz asked.

Jack paused for a moment and then looked directly at Governor Cruz, into his eyes. "We were your bait, weren't we? It was your way of helping the Owners figure out who in the Corps wasn't loyal to them."

A dark cloud passed over the governor's face, followed by a smile that was much more frightening than a scowl. "Well, alright, boys, you go and have a great time with your movie star. Don't call on me again; from now on I don't know you." He stood up heavily and walked away from them.

Jack said, "I guess we just burned our bridge with him. Was that a smart thing for me to do?"

"I personally found him kinda creepy and now we're free of him. Isn't that a good thing?" Gabe didn't seem at all concerned.

"Yeah, but I tipped our hand."

"I think it just confirmed what he already suspected," Gabe said.

"Now we don't have his protection and we're in a goddamn Haven!"

Just then a bellboy came up to Jack and told him there was a call for him in the lobby. "It's Linda."

Jack came back to the restaurant after about half an hour, and he found Gabe talking and laughing with one of the busboys.

When he saw Jack, he suddenly became serious.

"What's the matter, bro?" he asked.

"It's all set. Also, I called Gladys, and she and the mayor and Grace are going to Linda's now to meet with us. But you know what, Gabe? I think it's best if you don't go with me."

"What the hell? I thought you needed me with you there."

"What I need the most is to know you're safe. I already lost you once. Linda suggested that you stay here in the Haven while we're gone. She invited you to stay at her house. We'll be gone a few days at the most."

"Jack, why even go at all? Is it that important? Why don't we just go back to the City? We can be home in a few hours."

"I keep forgetting that you haven't been there in more than a year. I should have made you go home instead of coming with me."

"That's not it. I'm not going home by myself—I want to go with you."

"Well, then, why don't you stay at Linda's? It's a beautiful place, like no place you've ever been to, and then when I get back we'll go home together."

"But what about you in Montreal? Cruz told me I had to go, that you really needed me there."

"That does it. If he told you to go, you better stay here."

"We have to be in Montreal by tomorrow night at the latest," Harmon said "What are the possibilities, Noah?"

"Well, sir, you could drive south to BerkshireHaven, the road's not bad. It would take a few days to get there, that's the closest. DowneastHaven is farther."

"There's no time for that," Harmon said.

"Lieutenant, you get us a plane right now. Call Division Headquarters and tell them President Harmon is here and needs to get to the general's funeral. Jump!" Nils realized a moment too late there was a touch of hysteria in his voice.

Townsend looked at Harmon, who said, "Yes, Noah, that's a good idea. I was just about to suggest it myself. Can you do it?"

"Alright, Jason, if you will excuse me a minute I'll see what I can do."

Night had fallen, and it was raining softly. The train station was brightly lit—no shortage of power in the Corps. Nils and Harmon went back out to the waiting room and sat down on one of the smooth benches.

"You're very direct," Harmon said.

"I know a bureaucrat when I see one. His instinct is to do the least work possible, but if you push him, he'll do what you want just to get you off his back."

Jason frowned and said, "Oh, Noah's a good boy; he's not lazy. Funny, not many of our young men have joined the Corps, and I don't think anyone from the Republic is working for the GC. That boy's parents are hard-working people."

"Jason, what do you hope to accomplish in Montreal?"

"Almost all our trade involves the Corps, and we've got to diversify. We shouldn't be so dependent on one partner. We need the Corps, of course, because the trains are the only way to move things, but we have to trade more directly with other republics and cities. Everyone who's anyone in North America is going to be there to pay respects to General Couseau, so it's a great opportunity to meet our counterparts."

"What level in the Corps have you been dealing with?"

"What level? You mean Central Command? That's who we talk to. They have a small countries division. That's who we get our hcues from, by the way."

Lieutenant Townsend came out of the station manager's office and walked up to them. "They tell me they'll try to get a plane here for you tomorrow morning but they're not sure. We won't know until about six in the morning. Tonight you can stay in the officers' guest house. It's not far; I'll take you there."

"Let's go, boys," Harmon said to his guards.

"I'm sorry, Jason, I'm afraid they won't be able to stay there. It's only for rank."

"Well, where will they spend the night?" Harmon asked.

"We actually don't have any place for them."

"Lieutenant, you take them to your own quarters, and you give them your bed, if you have to. You can sleep on the floor," Nils said. Where did that tone come from, Nils wondered; I'm not myself.

Townsend looked down and replied, "Yes, sir."

Harmon glanced at Nils and then put his arm around the lieutenant's shoulder and said, "Thanks, son, for your help. When I get back home I'll call your parents and tell them I saw you. Would you like them to come and visit you here if they can? I'll let them use one of my cars."

"Thanks, Jason, I'd really appreciate that. I don't know the next time I'll have leave to visit them."

They settled for the night into the officers' quarters, a large, old clapboard house that hadn't changed much since it was built more than two hundred years earlier. The housekeeper gave them dinner in a dining room with rose-colored wall paper. They ate quietly; Harmon seemed to have no interest in talking.

Nils went to his room and lay down on the bed still dressed, his mind racing. What was Philippa doing at this very moment? General Couseau's death had surely made the situation more dangerous for her. All the rigmarole about his report and trying to rationalize the invasion would probably be thrown out the window. The only delay now would be for Couseau's funeral. There was no time to even flirt with Harmon's offer—Nils had to get back to his wife as soon as possible.

Nils was starting to think that maybe he had been rash in throwing away his Corps bracelet. He went over in his mind the events that had led him to this very moment, in this remote town, and he tried to understand his own motives and thoughts. He left the Corps rest house in a panic, that was for sure, but was it justified? Would it have been better to go back to Denver and face Colonel Hastings directly? What is the worst that could have happened? That he'd be court-martialed? That he'd be forced to help destroy the City that was his home? There was more than one worst.

But whether it happened or didn't happen was not up to him— he had no control over it. And if it was going to happen anyway, was it smart to give up his career? What kind of future could he have outside the Corps? Nils looked around the room. It was old-fashioned. There were several lamps with flounced shades, and a curved wall, old furniture, and a dresser crafted by someone who had died before electricity was tamed. In the dark, the rain was punishing the trees standing guard near the house.

Is it going to be possible to live outside of a Haven? The weather was still changing, and there was no telling when or even if it would finally stabilize. Right now, the White Mountain people had managed to feed themselves, barely, but how long would that be true? They've been able to live through long droughts and long stretches of heavy rain and snow, but what if those become measured not in years but in decades—or centuries? And what will eventually replace the fatally disrupted forest ecosystem?

Perhaps it was true, what the Owners believed—the ship of human civilization was sinking, and there were only enough lifeboats for First Class and their servants. Philippa and he were among the privileged, and he had thrown that away.

Could it be that the price of physical survival would be moral death? But then wouldn't he be able to do some good just by being there? Until now, Nils had always been able to justify his actions. Even in the worst of the Plantations, he had found a way of making things a little better. The Guests might still be whipped if they didn't work as fast as required, but he could recommend that they get an extra ration of protein every day. He had managed to stop the growing practice of keeping Guest children in pens like animals by showing that it decreased the productivity of their parents—that was one of his proudest achievements. But without Nils, would that last? Daycare cost money, and the Owners were always criticizing the Corps for being wasteful. Wouldn't he be able to do more good by being in the Corps?

But how could he get back in, if he decided that's what he wanted? If he could get access to a hcue he could try to find Rayna and see if she could help him. If that didn't work and he was truly desperate, he could play his trump card; he could call Philippa and tell her to ask Hugh for help. The last person he wanted to ask for a favor, but the one person who could definitely help him.

Harmon must be having doubts about me, Nils thought, but what can he do? He took the gamble of taking me with him. If I leave him when we get to Montreal it won't really harm him; he'll be back to where he was before I showed up, that's all.

In the morning, Nils went downstairs for breakfast. Harmon was already seated at the table. He smiled at Nils and they wished each other good morning. A maid poured them coffee and set out a silver service with cream and sugar.

"Nils, I want to talk to you about this trip," Harmon began.

"Sure. Did you want to talk about the logistics when we get to Montreal?"

"Actually, now I'm thinking it might be better for you to stay in the Republic. And I can get along alright without you in Montreal. So why don't you go back in the car with the boys? The Cummings will take you back, for a while anyway."

Nils' felt like his heart had stopped for a moment; then, involuntarily, he laughed.

"Don't worry about it, Jason," Nils said. "I think you're right. I kind of came to the same conclusion myself—you don't really need me. But I don't want to go back. I want to go to Montreal too."

Jason sat back in his chair and stared at Nils for a moment. "You know that when we get there we'll have to go our separate ways, right? I'm afraid it would be better if I wasn't seen with you. I've got to be on good terms with everyone, especially with the Corps."

"No problem. I've been there before and I know my way around."

"But what are you going to do when you get there? I'll give you a little money because I brought you here on expectations that didn't work out, but it will only last for a few days."

"Hey, Jason, I have to move forward—I've got to find a way of getting home."

CHAPTER TWENTY-EIGHT

Linda was surprised at how excited Captain Guillaume was when she told him that she was going to star in a short documentary about the general's funeral. It was to be called Homage. She was sure that Felix Couseau was a good, kind man, a fine man, although she actually hadn't known him very well, and those things she had heard about him and his hideaway in Telluride were surprising. But who could believe what Rhoda Baxter said anyway; she was probably lying, and it was only right that she, Linda, should feel his loss keenly. It made her so sad to think that he was gone; how wonderful that she could make this short tribute to him and lend herself to burnishing his legend. It would be simple and perfect. Homage.

Ronnie, as usual, was very supportive. As long as he didn't have to go, he'd do whatever he could to help. He told her he was glad that Jack was going too because he had seen the boy's calming influence on her. She knew the rest of the crew well; they had worked with her on many projects. Still, on the day before the flight she was a nervous wreck. She couldn't stop thinking about coming back from West Point.

Linda sent a car to pick up Jack and his brother at the Corps hotel, but when they arrived at the house she was too busy to greet them personally. Linda had to consult with her wardrobe person, Harry Hudson, and make the final decisions about what she was going to wear. Funerals were tough: you had to be conservative and respectful, but at the same time chic and just a little sexy. It was so hard to not be cliché and still not be inappropriately unconventional.

And this one was especially complicated, since it was a military funeral and Linda was, in some sense, in the military herself. Harry suggested, for the day of the funeral at the church, a kind of black, uniform-like dress, not a uniform because it would clearly be unique, but yet military, something that would show that she and the general were cut from the same cloth, so to speak. She was sorry not to greet

Jack personally but she consoled herself with the thought that she was doing her duty.

A large, pink car with dark blue windows pulled up in front of the Corps hotel. It looked as out of place in that semi-military setting as an orchid in a barracks, and Jack knew it was there to take them to Linda's. In less than an hour, the car crossed a small bridge and went through a set of tall gates that looked like they were made of glass—they were almost, but not quite, invisible. The car climbed a hill and drew up in front of a large veranda. Linda's assistant, Miss Clavering, was waiting for them. She greeted them and invited them to explore the house and gardens while they waited for Linda.

Jack had become very thoughtful as soon as they got there. "I hate to leave you, Gabe. I feel like I just found you. I don't know if I want you to stay here."

"Why? Looks like a beautiful place to me."

"Yeah, of course. But it's not home. I don't think I understand this place. You know, Gabe, the world is a lot deeper than we ever realize at any particular moment. We only get a glimpse of it in reflection."

"Sure, bro, whatever. So what do you want me to do? I don't get it."

"Never mind. I'm just a little nervous. Grace is coming. No, I'm glad we're here."

Linda's house was on a cliff overlooking the bay. Jack and Gabe went down to the dock to wait for the others to arrive from the City. Jack felt a surge of confusion when he saw Ronnie's yacht pulling into view, around the point just south of where they were standing. He felt Grace's presence like a hint of perfume. Who was she, really?

The hugs and kisses and introductions of Gabe were done quickly and they walked up the long flight of stairs clinging to the hillside and crossed the wide lawn to the house. Grace was between Jack and Gabe. She said to Gabe, "I've heard so much about you. I'm so glad to finally meet you."

"Hey, I have a question for you," Gabe said to her. "Did you know there was going to be a raid that night in Denver?"

"Let's keep that for later, if we have time," Jack said. "We have a lot to talk about right now."

They climbed wide, stone steps leading to a terrace and walked through French doors into the library. Johnston sat down on a blue brocade wingback chair, and Jack sat on the matching sofa next to him.

"How is it you're going to Montreal with Linda Crowley instead of the governor?" Johnston asked.

"She invited me and I realized I trusted her more than Cruz. It's that simple."

"How for Gaia's sake did you come to that conclusion?"

"Someone warned me about him. Did you know about him, mayor?" Jack asked.

"What are you talking about?" Johnston asked.

"Yesterday I was told by a woman to be careful with Governor Cruz. She told me, well, it wasn't in words exactly, but it was real, that we couldn't trust him. And then this morning I talked to him." Jack reported his conversation with Cruz.

"Jack's right," Gladys said. "I thought it was important that you didn't know this until now. Ray would have detected any mistrust on your part and it was important that we get Jack this far with Ray's help."

Johnston looked around the room at each of them and said, "Who are you people? You're driving me crazy. First you tell me we have to work with him and now you're saying he's not on our side. What do you know about him anyway?"

"I've known him since he was a child. His mother and my mother were good friends," Gladys said. "He's a slippery character."

The room fell silent for a moment. Grace turned to Jack, who was sitting next to her on the brown leather sofa, and said, "You do know I was with you last night, right?"

"Yes, I heard you loud and clear. Otherwise how could I have trusted that woman, Carmen?"

"What are you all talking about?" Johnston asked, irritation in his voice.

"Sorry, Mayor, last night is when I was warned about Governor Cruz by a woman at a party."

"A woman at a party! What the hell—you throw over our most powerful ally because some woman whispered something to you! That's ridiculous," Johnston said.

"It's not ridiculous," Gladys said. "The Cruz brothers own farms that feed MarinHaven—the Owners are his best customers. My guess is that he's trying to get the Owners to allow him to operate the new Plantation instead of the Corps and that means he's got to suck up to them."

"So what do we do now?" Jack asked.

"That's the point of our meeting now, to advise you about what to do next. But you have to make the decisions yourself," Gladys replied.

"Me? I make the decisions? Gaia help us all!" Jack said, and everyone laughed, except Mayor Johnston, who looked like he had a bad headache. "Alright; so what's your advice?"

Johnston said, "You're going to Montreal, and you're going to try to meet Hugh Rowan and hold his hand. Then you'll tell us what you've learned—when the invasion will start, where they're going to land, as specific as you can get. There's nothing more important to us now, and I don't see any reason to change any of that. Governor Cruz was supposed to be your entrée, but Linda Crowley will do just as well, maybe better."

"Mayor, you're going to have to talk to Cruz about Jack," Gladys said. "And we need to all know what you're going to say, especially Jack, since he will probably run into the governor in Montreal."

"I guess the simplest story is the best," Johnston said. "Jack is crazy about Linda Crowley and that's why he's going with her. Jack is in despair because nothing has happened between them but he's still got hopes. He'd jump at any chance to be with her."

"You know that isn't true," Jack said to Grace.

She smiled and kissed him on the lips. "I wouldn't care if it was, honey—you love me, I know that."

Jack turned away from her and looked out the window.

"The question is," Johnston said, "if you're right that Governor Cruz is not our friend, is he our enemy? I just can't believe he'd help them destroy the City."

"He doesn't have to help them; he just has to let it happen," Gladys said.

"But what I don't understand is why he wanted me to go with him in the first place," Jack said.

"Because he trusts your powers; he really wanted you to help him deal with the Owners," Johnston said.

"Oh, shit, then I should have stayed with him. I could have learned a lot."

"It's too late now. We'll have to see what happens. Maybe you can make up with him when you're in Montreal," Johnston said.

Just then Linda Crowley walked into the room and said, "Come into the garden, everyone! We've got a little light supper for you."

"Thanks, Linda, you all go ahead. Grace and I will stay here for a minute," Jack said.

When they left, he locked the door and sat down in a chair next to the sofa. "I didn't think I'd see you before I went to Montreal. Last night was so strange and a little creepy. Who is that woman Carmen?"

"She was born in the Villas, and her foster parents are loyal Helpers. But she spent a good part of her life at the same monastery you were at, believe it or not. The muscle man who took her away is her husband."

"How did you know about that?"

"We talk all the time. She felt very bad when she saw your expression at the end, when you saw him hugging her."

"Why did I have to have sex with her?" Jack asked. "All I needed was the information."

"There's more to it, my sweet Jack, and it will happen again with other women, so try not to fight it."

"Why are you doing this? I love you. I don't want to be with anyone else."

Grace took his hand and put it to her forehead and then kissed it. "That era is gone, my dear heart," she said. "We can't live just for each other; there's no place to run to, there's no private garden for us. We have to make a future that belongs to us and not to the Owners, and we need more of our kind who have powers. There are many women with powers, but you're the only man we've run across. Jack, we need your seed, we need as many of your children as possible. You need to reproduce with women like Carmen, who have powers also, and there are dozens of them on this continent."

Jack smiled at her, expecting a laugh, but she looked back at him, her face earnest. There was a moment of uncertainty and then he realized that she wasn't kidding. Instantly, he felt like he was zapped by a lightening bolt, and he jumped up.

"You're insane! I'm not a prize bull! I tell you I love you and it doesn't mean anything to you. What am I to you? Just a piece of meat? I should never have left San Francisco in the first place. I wish I'd never met you."

"Don't say that. There's a reason we met, and it's bigger than either of us. Jack, I do love you, of course I do. But we don't live in a time when that's all that counts. We don't have a choice; we have to fight any way we can. The Owners are stronger than us, and we have to use any advantage we've got."

"No, no, no. Of course we have to fight, but as a community, in the daylight. Don't you see that when we sacrifice the deepest, best part of ourselves for something we think is more important, we've betrayed ourselves—and our cause?"

"Listen, Jack, we don't have a lot of choices. The Owners will keep expanding their power until nothing is free."

"Who's free now? You want to make me into your stud puppet on the off chance there'll be more telepathic children in the world? So what? There's a war coming right now, and if we don't win it, it won't matter how many little people like me are running around."

"Jack, I know it's hard, but you've been chosen and it isn't by any of us. For some reason it's your destiny to be the forerunner. Believe me, Gladys and I were surprised that it was you; we expected someone older and, I know it sounds silly, bigger. More manly."

Jack smiled. He moved to the sofa and put his arms around her.

"But I'll tell you this—you're as much a man as I'll ever want," she said.

They sat quietly for a few minutes and then pulled apart, and Jack stood up. "You know, I wanted to feel that there were no barriers; you and me would kind of merge and be like one person. Now I understand—it's not going to happen. And I don't want it, not anymore. There's a lot I have to do, and you can't do it with me. You've got good intentions, I know that, but I'm not going to be anyone's pawn, not even yours."

CHAPTER TWENTY-NINE

Nils was happy to be in Montreal—it was a step closer to his old life. He parted amicably with Jason, who had given him enough money to last maybe a week, and checked into a cheap hotel on Rue Ontario. There he spent a sleepless night lying in bed in the dark going over all the possible scenarios. Staying in Montreal for more than a few weeks was impossible, even if he were able to get more money—you had to speak French fluently and have a job to get a residence permit. Simply going back to Corps HQ in Denver without preparation was dangerous—he needed protection from Hastings first.

He kept coming back to the two certainties of his life—Philippa and the Corps. The reason he had run, the invasion of San Francisco, now seemed less important. Yes, it was rotten and inexcusable, but he couldn't stop it or even slow it down. But he could help mitigate the worst of it for the people who were being sent to the Central Valley Plantation. Why hadn't he thought of that before? Surely he could bring Philippa around to accept reality. He had worked himself into a panic when he should have been more analytical. Partly, he had caught her hysteria.

Maybe everyone on both sides had been right after all. The marriage of an Owner and a Helper was a bad idea. Can we ever really understand each other? Philippa's class privileges were part of her, like her auburn hair, while Nils had to earn his bread of simple respect, each day. They loved each other, and that had seemed like enough at the time.

But what could he do now? He couldn't just go to the nearest Corps facility and throw himself on their mercy. He'd be ground up by the bureaucracy and probably end up in prison as a deserter. He needed to find a friend, a champion, who would bring him back into the fold. Well, everyone would be in Montreal for the general's funeral, and there must be someone who could help him. If all else failed, he could ask Hugh Rowan. Nils would just have to swallow his pride. But what about Philippa? She disapproved of just about everything about Hugh. How would she react to Nils's asking for his help? Maybe someone else would be there. Maybe it wouldn't have to be him.

At least he had some decent clothes. Jason had let him keep the two woolen suits that had been made for him. They came with broad, cotton waistcoat strips, which even some of the Owners preferred over full cotton shirts. He would look like an ambassador, and that was something.

He shaved carefully with his straight razor, one of the few things he still had from his early years—his father had given it to him—and then he dressed. His blonde hair had been cut just before he had left Jason's house, and he now felt that he could meet anyone. Still, he thought, it would be good to wear the uniform again.

It was about a twenty-minute walk to the Waditon Hotel on the Rue Sherbrooke, where most of the dignitaries were staying. First, he would try to use a hotel hcue and get in touch with Philippa and Rayna. After that, he'd play it by ear.

Corps soldiers in dress uniforms were outside of the hotel keeping people from coming close. Bystanders were gathered in little clumps, talking cheerfully. A large car drove up, an old-fashioned limousine. It was going very slowly, and when it stopped Nils noticed cameras trained on it. A beautiful young woman emerged, dressed in a kind of black uniform and carrying a bouquet of flowers. She looked somber, as if she had been crying, but calm and proud. On the sidewalk waiting for her was a dignified, white-haired lady and two middle-aged men in dark suits, evidently her sons. The younger woman went over to the older and gave her the flowers. The old lady gave the bouquet to one of the men and then she embraced the younger woman. They kissed on both cheeks and drew back from each other.

It was Linda Crowley, no mistaking it. Nils moved closer, wondering if she would remember him, although clearly now was not the time. As the small crowd started to move, Nils accidentally jostled a slender young man who had been standing quietly watching the scene. The man turned and looked up into Nils's face.

Jack had been absorbed by Linda's spectacle and was slightly annoyed when a man bumped into him. Then he looked up and blurted out, "Oh, my god, you're the guy from Denver; you took us to that bar where Gabe got busted. You're Nils." He was instantly alert, and everything he had learned from Rayna came flooding back into his mind. Without thinking, he grabbed Nils's hand and went deeply into his mind.

Nils said, "Wow, this is a surprise. What are you doing here?"

"Same reason you're here, why everyone's here. The general's funeral."

"But how did you get here?"

Jack laughed and said, "Am I so improbable? I came with Linda, on her sonic."

"You know Linda Crowley? How can that be? Hey, what happened to you and the other guy, wasn't it your brother? I felt bad about that, you know, but General Couseau told me he'd have someone try to find him."

"Oh—so that's how he got rescued! Yeah, I didn't see him for almost six months." Jack saw that the man he was talking to was confused and desperate, and he couldn't help feeling pity.

Nils was astonished at the change in Jack. There was nothing left of the tentative, almost shy boy. He was a man in control of the situation.

"I'm sorry to hear that. Is he okay now?"

"Oh, yeah, he's fine. So you've had some adventures too?" Jack asked.

"Why do you say that?"

"Well, you just kind of look like that," Jack said.

"Well, it's nice seeing you, but I think I'd better go inside. I have some things to do."

By this time, Linda had gone into the hotel and Mrs. Couseau and her sons had left. The crowd was drifting away.

Jack said, "Hey, why don't you come in and join us for lunch?"

Nils had just enough money to last him until he could figure out his next move. Lunch at this hotel would take most of it.

Jack smiled at him and said, "This is on us, of course."

Nils was embarrassed and slightly annoyed—it felt like this boy was reading his mind, but he couldn't resist the offer. "Alright, thanks, that sounds nice."

Linda was pleased to see Nils; she remembered talking to him. She didn't understand why he wasn't in uniform.

It was a large group at lunch, her entire film crew, and it hadn't been possible to talk, so Linda invited Jack and Nils to her suite for coffee afterward. She took it for granted that Jack and Nils knew each other—in her world everyone knew everyone else. She sat down on a large sofa and motioned for Nils to sit down next to her. He was wearing an odd suit that slightly put her off, but under it she could see the outlines of his muscular torso. Jack sat in an armchair nearby.

"How well did you know General Couseau?" Linda asked Nils.

"Actually, I only met him once, but it was important and I remember it well. What about you?"

"Oh, I knew him for years. His son went to school with my favorite uncle. Did you know that I joined the Corps? General Couseau arranged it for me."

"What? Why did you do that?"

"So I could go to a Plantation. It was your idea, don't you remember?"

Nils laughed and visibly relaxed. "Sure. But it was a joke. I didn't think you'd take it seriously."

Jack just watched quietly and listened to their thoughts. *This is really not polite*, he thought, *he has no idea I can hear what he's thinking.* He would have preferred not to hear Linda—she was his friend and she trusted him, but he had to listen to Nils. From the time he stepped out of the sonic in Montreal, Jack knew that he had to be sharper, deeper, and more present than at any other time in his life. So much depended on what he did here.

He could feel Nils's pleasure in being near Linda but also something calculating. He was trying to get back into the Corps and he needed help. He was wondering how much he could tell her. Linda was pleased by Nils. She thought he was sexy, and she was also intrigued by something unusual about him. It's his time spent wandering in the woods and being at that place, the White Mountain Republic—"That air of the woods hangs on him still," Jack wanted to tell her, "but it won't last for long." Jack closed his eyes and went deeper into Nils's mind. He saw Nils's panic and before that, Nils with a woman, obviously his wife. Behind her stood a man Nils was afraid of, someone who was oddly familiar to Jack. Then he saw Rayna. Oh yes, it was clearly her, but around her was only confusion. Nils was struggling for his life and didn't know where to turn.

Once again, Jack was frustrated by his own powers. He was able to perceive much more than he could understand. He could hear words and see images from people's minds and along with those were often emotions he could decipher, but he couldn't get causal relationships. Who was the man standing behind Nils's wife and why was he there and not somewhere else? What did any of the clutter in Nils's mind have to do with what Jack needed to know? And yet the feeling was growing on Jack—Nils is essential. *I need to have him with me.* Jack's precognition wasn't developed, and he didn't rely on it. Yet his intuition was insistent.

Jack sensed Linda's boredom a moment before she did, and he wasn't surprised when she dismissed Nils. "It's so nice seeing you and I hope we'll get together again soon," she said.

"Nice seeing you too, of course. But I was wondering... I'm looking for someone who was on the general's staff, a woman named Rayna Caskey. I wonder if somehow you could help me find her. Or even someone else who was on his personal staff. I need to talk to them."

"Oh, gosh, I don't know any of those people. But I'll keep an eye out for you!" she said brightly as she got up.

They all stood up and Jack said, "I'll walk Nils out."

Jack returned to Linda's suite after a few minutes and sat down on the sofa while she walked around the room, looking idly around her. "I invited him to come to the church with us," Jack told her.

"Oh. Why did you do that?"

"I don't know exactly. But I have the feeling he'll be helpful in some way."

Linda laughed. "I didn't know you liked to pick up strays."

"Aren't we all strays?" he asked, smiling.

"Oh, yes, I guess you're right. Jack, I have something really important to talk to you about. It's been so busy since we left home I haven't had a minute alone with you."

"Ok, sure," Jack said, trying to sound surprised.

"What did you think of my arrival dress? Was it too I'm-trying-hard-to-connect-with-the-locals?"

Jack tried to keep a serious face. "I thought it was very appropriate, and the scene of you embracing Mrs. Couseau will make people cry."

"Really? You think so? She's an amazing woman, although those sons of hers are not very appealing. Would you mind looking at the rest of my wardrobe with me? I'm nervous about it. Harry Hudson is always so sure, but I don't know."

"Sure I will, but I don't know anything about clothes. I don't see how I can help you."

"I don't care about that. You know about me and that's what counts."

Nils was surprised and pleased that Jack had invited him to go to the church with them. It was by invitation only, and there was no way he could have gone otherwise. Jason will be surprised to see me there, Nils thought with some satisfaction. And there will surely be people from the Corps who could help me.

Now, finally, he had a moment to contact Philippa. He went to the concierge and asked to use a hotel hcue. At first the young woman refused, saying it was only available for hotel guests, but Nils managed to convince her that it was Corps business. She seemed doubtful but finally gave in and told Nils to look into the verification mirror. He was relieved that his Data Base profile still worked, but he realized that, from this moment on, someone would be trying to find him. When he saw his reflection in the mirror, he began to feel more confident. I don't look too bad, he thought to himself. The hotel was filled with people of all types from all over North America, and Nils felt like he was actually one of the better-dressed among them.

He felt his heart thumping in his chest as he entered the Net Booth. Please God, she's alright, he said to himself, and doesn't feel that I've abandoned her. Please let her understand that I had to disappear for a while. He slid his hand over the soft surface of the cube. The hotel device was covered in sky blue satin, which made it look like a large pin cushion. It was attached to the table by a yellow velvet cord. Within a few seconds he was surrounded by the computer's controls. He went right to Philippa's Net address.

No response at all was odd. Philippa always left a video message for callers. He wasn't sure if he should try to reach the neighbors or some friends of theirs, so he decided to call his old secretary, Cathy. If she was surprised to hear from him, she didn't let on; it was like they had been talking every day. He asked her to try to track down Philippa and let her know that he would try to call again soon. "Tell her I'm well and can't wait to see her." He then tried to reach Rayna, and he had to leave a message. Finally, he tried his own mailbox. It was still there, and there were hundreds of messages. They would have to wait. Right now he had to find a way back to his life.

CHAPTER THIRTY

Nils emerged from the booth frustrated and unsure about what he should do next. Then he spotted Jack and walked over to him.

"Let's sit down here and talk," Jack said, motioning to a small sofa that was placed in a corner behind a pillar. They could look out but would be largely hidden from the view of people walking by.

"Tell me about Maine, in as much detail as you can. I want to be able to picture it," Jack said. "And what happened to you when you left the retreat house?"

"I never told you about the retreat house. How did you know about it?" Nils asked, alarmed. Was this some kind of set-up?

"Nils, I am telepathic," Jack said. "I can read your mind. Actually it's more like looking at pictures than reading, and I can't always understand everything I see."

Nils looked at him searchingly but found no trace of humor. "Well then, why do you want to talk to me? You should know everything already."

"No, that's not how it works. Nothing's real until it is said out loud or written down. Real means that it exists in the world and has consequences. Thoughts are like clouds; they look big but there's no weight."

Yeah, Nils thought, real means something you can base a case of desertion on. But then he was surprised to find that he trusted Jack. He could tell the young man just about anything and now he felt the need to tell him everything. Still, he thought the part about being telepathic was a joke, an indirect way of saying that Jack was very intuitive.

"I left the retreat house so I wouldn't have to go back to Denver to work on the invasion. It's that simple."

"I need to know everything you know about the invasion plans. But first why don't you tell me about Maine? Where did you go, who did you meet, that kind of thing. What does it look like?"

Jack was fascinated by the stories of Maine and the White Mountains. He could almost see the eastern ocean breaking on the rocks, the dense forest, a dying ecosystem echoing the planet's brutal transformation, the hard life of the farmers—these images moved him. Weren't these people fighting a losing battle? The word for this feeling came to Jack—pathos.

While he was listening to Nils talk, he couldn't hear his thoughts—he had to wait until Nils paused and then he would pick up a thought, an image. This happened when Nils was trying hard not to mention someone. It was the woman Jack had seen in Rayna's mind—Nils's wife, it had to be, and the man, the Owner behind her—it was Hugh Rowan! Jack blurted out, "Is Hugh Rowan your wife's brother?"

Nils nodded, feeling the flash of resentment that had been a leitmotif of his life since he first met his brother-in-law. "How did you know that? Have you heard of him?"

"I saw him once, at the opera. He and I intersect somehow that I don't understand. I'd like to know more about him."

"Why don't you ask him? He might even be here in Montreal, I don't know."

"I'm sure he'll be here, and I'm going to meet him. I wish you'd tell me everything you know about him."

Just at that moment, a tall, slender man walked up to them and said, "Well, hello, Nils, you're looking good. Glad to see you here. How are you getting on?"

Nils stood up and shook the man's hand and then introduced him. "Jason, this is my friend Jack—what is your last name, anyway? Jack's from San Francisco. Jack, Jason Harmon."

"Carey, Jack Carey. Pleased to meet you Jason." Jack noticed a reaction from Jason when he told him his last name, and his mind was flooded with images, too many to sort out.

"Carey? I knew someone by that name when I was there years ago. Margaret Carey. Are you any relation?"

"That was my mother," Jack said.

"Really? How is she? Send her my best regards."

"She died a year ago."

For an instant Jason looked confused, then visibly pulled himself together and said, "I'm so sorry to hear that. Well, I've got to go now. Good seeing you, Nils. Nice meeting you, Jack." He walked away and within seconds was talking to a group of people in another corner of the lobby.

"That's the great Jason Harmon, president of the world's smallest country. Well, maybe there are smaller ones these days, who knows," Nils said. "Too bad you didn't have more of a chance to talk to him. He's actually an interesting guy."

Jack looked after him, overcome for a moment with wonder. *That's my father.* He wanted to run after him, grab him by the arms, and look into his eyes, but he told himself that it was better to just let things unfold.

"I'll see him again," Jack said, knowing for certain that he wouldn't leave Montreal without talking to Jason. "Why don't you tell me more about him?" he asked Nils.

"I actually don't know that much about him personally. He lives in a big old farmhouse that is also the official capital of his little country. It's very old-fashioned but they have good power and even hcues. He has his own car, but he doesn't seem to want very much. He's not at all pretentious, kind of the opposite of what the Owners are like."

"Nils, can I hold your hand for a moment? If you don't want to, I understand, but it would give me more direct access to your mind."

Nils laughed and said, "I don't care, just as long as it doesn't hurt." He held out his hand.

Jack was everywhere at once; with Rayna in an underground conference room; with Philippa in a large bed with blue sheets; walking hopelessly through dense green woods; watching with horror as a building collapses. He brought his focus carefully onto the tall, thin man who wore a green flannel shirt, and he tried to filter out all of the competing images. He perceived that Jason was not the simple man that he tried to make others believe he was. He was subject to fits of despair that he overcame by throwing himself into his work. He had to be busy every waking moment, and that's why he took on the responsibilities that other people shunned. His wife had left him, and he was intensely lonely. *Nils sees all this but he doesn't know it*, Jack realized.

He let go of Nils's hand and settled back into the deep armchair. The transmission had taken only a minute or two but it felt like hours.

Keep your focus; it has to be the invasion, Jack reminded himself, but he couldn't stop thinking about Jason Harmon. *My father*. But how to get together with him, how to arrange it? And who would he tell? The one person in the world he wanted to share this with was Gabe, but not yet, not until after he talked to Jason. And then there was Nils. He had to keep him close. Although it was too early to know exactly why, it was clear that he had to be helped and could not be abandoned.

He must not forget that he was here to meet Hugh Rowan and do whatever he could to stop the invasion. Jack sat back and let his emotions pour over him. When he felt that he was being ripped away from his moorings he took a breath and tried to let the feeling go, fly away from him, and it always did. *I wish there was someone* here who could help me, Jack thought. But no, there wasn't; it was all on him.

The lobby was now filled with people, some walking purposefully right through but most in small groups, clumped together briefly only to break up and reform in other groups. There were Owners, obvious in their jewelry and their silks and furs, as well as many people in Corps uniforms and Outsiders in various garb, some in buckskin, but others in woolen suits like the one Nils wore. The funeral would be tomorrow and the official events not until after that. Jack felt his inexperience keenly. What was happening now?, he wondered. He came out of his reverie and noticed Nils looking at him curiously.

"Are you alright, Jack?"

"Yeah, I guess. Nils, what's going on here?"

"They're making deals. They're going to be doing that all night, and there are as many agendas here as there are people."

"Look, Nils, I really need your help. I don't know this world and can't navigate it on my own. Will you stay with me and advise me on how to handle it?" It was only a moment ago that he had been thinking about how he had to help Nils.

Nils laughed. "That's why I'm here, but it was supposed to be to help Jason Harmon. Listen, I have to find someone who can help me."

"I'll help you," Jack said.

"You? How can you? I don't want to be rude, Jack, but the fact is you're just a city dweller. You're only here because you're friends with Linda Crowley, and I don't think that's going to do much for me. Look, I'm fighting for my life now."

There was a momentary lull in the chatter from the lobby, one of those curious silences that only the most oblivious dares to break. Jack looked into Nils's eyes, and what he saw made him shudder.

"I need you," he said, "and I'm willing to pay for your services. What do you want?"

"Alright," Nils said. "Get me a room here, in this hotel, and enough to live on until you leave. Give me some money to get back to California in case I don't manage to get back into the Corps. Oh, and I want to see Linda again. Can you do that?"

"Sure. From now on we're working together." They shook hands.

CHAPTER THIRTY-ONE

The suite was too small and it faced north to the dull bulk of Mont Royal instead of the scenic river to the south. Incompetence is ubiquitous, Hugh Rowan fumed, and stupidity universal. Wherever you go, there it is. Lop off a few heads and watch them smarten up—that's the answer.

The canaille had been allowed to wallow in their laziness but that era is coming to an end. Self indulgence will be replaced by discipline and order, the Owners will be Lords and those who want to survive will learn to serve us. How else could civilization survive on a ravaged planet? Hugh didn't allow himself to linger very long on those pleasant thoughts. There were too many practical steps to be taken first.

The most important was the choice of General Couseau's successor as Corps Commandant. Hastings would be optimum, if he could be shoe-horned in, but there were several more popular men. The meeting of the search committee was scheduled for Hugh's first evening in Montreal. They would discuss the final three candidates over dinner in Hugh's suite. If they could come to a unanimous recommendation, it would be highly likely that the Council would go along.

Hugh was hoping he could convince the others, but it wouldn't be easy. There were some nasty rumors going around about Hastings and the overly harsh punishment of cadets—several deaths, apparently, and Hugh would have to somehow finesse that. Hastings had nothing to do with it, he would tell the other committee members.

Before the meeting there was one ceremonial duty that he had to perform. The daily schedule that Miss Jones gave him included a visit to Couseau's widow. He was acquainted with the woman and slightly awed by her. She was a lady of the old school, an Owner and a friend of Hugh's mother. It was his marriage to her that made Felix Couseau's advancement possible in spite of his modest birth.

The well-known story of the Couseaus had given the Rowans some consolation when Philippa married Nils Rakovic.

Hugh was admitted to Madame Couseau's suite by a maid who ushered him into a parlor exactly like the one in his suite. In a minute he was joined by a lady in her late sixties, perhaps a little older, dressed in a dove-gray silk dress. Her white hair was short and straight and framed an angular face with high cheekbones.

"Hello, Hugh, so nice to see you," she said as she offered her hand.

"Hello, Anna Claire. I wanted to come and offer my condolences. Felix was a great man."

"Yes, he was. Sit down, Hugh. Let's chat for a few minutes. I know you don't have a lot of time, but I did want to talk to you." They sat at opposite ends of a sofa and turned toward each other. "I heard about your sister," she said, "and I'm so sorry. How did it happen?"

"We're not sure, but we think it was a hate crime. Someone found out that she was an Owner and she became a target. We've pushed the San Francisco authorities to investigate, but you know what they are. So I've sent my own people in there."

"She was a fine woman and an interesting one. And what about her husband? Felix thought he was a promising young man."

"I actually don't know where Nils is right now."

Madame Couseau picked up a little silver bell from the table and rang it. A maid came in with a tea tray and poured for both of them.

"Hugh, Felix was a great organizer and leader. The Corps was his creation. He took something that wasn't much more than a private security firm fifty years ago and made it into a great institution. Now it's the glue that holds everything together. I want his legacy to continue, and I was hoping you would help me."

"Certainly, Anna Claire, we all want to honor his legacy."

"Felix was an idealist, and he believed that class distinctions have become too extreme. What counts is individual merit, he always said, and you find just as much of that among city dwellers and Helpers and even Guests as you do among Owners. Hugh, I want the Council to pick for his successor someone who will carry on his vision."

Hugh cleared his throat and looked around the room, wishing he could be anywhere else. "This process has been going on for several weeks, ever since the general died. We've narrowed the search down and already presented the finalists to the Council. I understand your concern, but I don't know that there's anything I can do for you."

"You know, there's no rush. General Bast is a good man, and he'll keep things humming until a replacement is chosen."

"You certainly know what's going on," Hugh said with a tight smile.

"I might as well tell you that I have been nominated to join the Council, at the next meeting. Some people said that I should be the chair of the search committee instead of you, but I told them no, I'm sure Hugh is doing a fine job. Just put me on it to help him, that's all."

Hugh paused for a moment and then said, "Well, that's wonderful, Anna Claire, I am grateful for your help, although I'm a little surprised that no one told me. We're going to have a dinner meeting tonight. Would you like to join us?"

"Thank you so much, but as you can imagine, I am booked for tonight and the rest of the week, in fact. Why don't we just delay the meeting for a few weeks? We can all get together next month."

"I don't think we can do that. The other two search committee members are going to be in my suite in a little more than an hour."

"Oh, don't worry about that. I've already told them it won't be necessary; they've gone by Corps plane to see the Laurentian garrison. See, I've freed you up, aren't you grateful?" She laughed lightly.

Hugh sat back, speechless. For an instant he was standing in front of his father, his head down, ashamed and powerless. Then fury. Who was this bitch to derail his plans?

"I don't know why you think you can take over this process, Anna Claire, but I can assure you that I will be in charge."

"Oh, Hugh, I'm so sorry you feel that way. Of course you're in charge, that's why I declined the chairmanship of your committee. Would you like more tea?"

The next few minutes were excruciating for Hugh. He felt waves of rage course through him that he had to conceal. How she would have enjoyed his discomfort! Finally he stood up, said goodbye with as little warmth as possible, and walked quickly out of the room.

He took the elevator up five floors and let himself into his suite. He went into his bedroom and closed the door. Then he took out what looked like a pen from his pocket and twisted it clockwise twice, and counterclockwise once. He was surrounded by his hcue and in a moment Armand Riley appeared in front of him.

"What have you found so far?" Hugh barked.

"Well, sir, we've found out who he is."

"What's the boy's name?"

"His name is Jack, sir."

"They do have family names, don't they?'

"Yes, sir. But there seems to be a little confusion about him. We think he is called Carey and we know that was his mother's name, but we got a birth certificate where his last name is listed as Harmon."

"Oh, it doesn't matter as long as you know what he looks like. Have you gotten close to him yet?"

"That's the problem, sir. We think he's not in San Francisco right now."

"Where in the hell is he then?"

"We think he's in Montreal, sir."

Hugh was stunned. Then he said, "Do you think he's stalking me?"

"We don't know, sir. He might be."

"Well then get over here, you idiot. Why didn't you tell me this earlier?"

"You gave instructions not to be disturbed, sir."

"Come to Montreal immediately with three of your best men."

"Yes, sir. But…"

"But what, Riley?"

"Sir, we aren't permitted to board a public sonic since we're only Helpers. Do you want us to come by train?"

"No, I don't want you to take two days on the train, stupid. I'll send a sonic for you. Go to the landing field and wait for it. Come directly to my hotel when you get here and ask for me no matter what else is happening. You should be able to get here by early tomorrow morning. The funeral is at eleven a.m., and I want you here before I go to the church. And one more thing—do you have any pictures of him?"

"We do, sir, from the public library security cams. He spent a lot of time there."

"Send me the pictures now. I'll see you in the morning." Hugh made a vertical cutting motion with his right hand, his left thumb out at chest level, and severed the contact and at the same time collapsed the hcue and he was alone in his room. He went out into the parlor and sat down on a sofa. The blinds were drawn and the room was very dark. He waved both hands and all the lights came on. The room was suddenly too bright. He wanted that.

A few minutes later, after he had instructed Miss Jones to call the pilots, he was looking at the two-dimensional pictures. He recognized the face only in one or two of them. The boy looked so ordinary! Light brown skin, almond eyes, curly brown hair, slender and not tall, he could have been any Helper trimming a hedge or mopping the deck of the *Conqueror*. Hugh looked as carefully as he could but he could feel no fear or sense of dread from the pictures. Is this really the boy who's been coming into my dreams? Perhaps I'm mistaken. Well, better be safe than sorry, and it's not like the world needs more troits.

The enemy now was much closer and much bigger, Anna Claire Couseau, with all her bullshit talk of individual merit. He knew what she was trying to do. The world to come required a master, and she wanted it to be the Corps, with her as the power behind the throne.

The immediate problem was what to do with his free evening. He asked Miss Jones to show him the invitations he'd received for various events that she had already declined for him.

"There's the Ellison family dinner on their yacht, sir, or the Great Companies benefit for the Supreme Court. Everyone says that one's a lot of fun. The justices sing and dance for the Owners. And then there's the Ken Lay Commemorative Dinner honoring the martyrs of the Enron persecution. There's a Corps screening of a retrospective of General Couseau's career, and there's also the Vigil at the Couseau's house followed by a VIP supper. Linda Crowley is the featured guest at a reception to benefit General Couseau's favorite charity."

"And what is that, Miss Jones?"

"It's something to do with educating Plantation Guests, I think."

"What a strange idea. I wonder why anyone would want to do that? Isn't it typical that Linda Crowley would be involved! Anything else?"

"There's an Outsiders' Trade Fair. A Small Countries Forum on Adaptation to Climate Change. Oh, and a private dinner at the Hotel de Ville for Council members who aren't going to any other event."

"I'll go to that. It might be useful."

It took only ten minutes to drive to city hall, but it was an experience. The rain was coming down in torrents and the driver could barely see; Hugh felt like he was underwater. It brought back his childhood, when his mother took him to New York, which was even then struggling with the deadly combination of giant storms and rising ocean levels. Still, he had some good memories: the Central Park Zoo; Wollman Rink in the winter; cozy dinners in his family's apartment on Fifth Avenue, overlooking the park; a fire blazing in the large fireplace. But by his late teens, when the subways and the underground infrastructures flooded for good, it was over. The power died, and New York died.

And then came the struggle over New York's treasures. The contemporary world was shaped in part by the fight over what would happen to the contents of the Metropolitan Museum. The treasures couldn't stay in the dead building on Fifth Avenue—they would rot there or be stolen. But where would they go? Once there would have been lawsuits, but the courts no longer functioned—starved of tax revenue, government was dying.

Finally, the Corps sent in its soldiers, took possession, and auctioned off as much as it could. For several years, dividing up the treasures was the Owners' preoccupation. Optimists called it a win-win—the art work got saved by being taken into Owners' houses and the Corps used the money to help build the railroads that tied its empire together.

That became the model. The Corps took over all of the other museums in New York and then all of the museums in Washington, D.C., much of which was now below sea level. Only the Corps could save the treasures of a world that was slipping away.

Where is it all going? Hugh wondered, giving way to rumination. How do I make my peers understand that if we don't step forward and take control of this decaying world now, not twenty years from now, the human race will descend into anarchy and we'll lose everything our forefathers struggled so hard to build?

The car pulled under the Hotel de Ville's ornate portico, and a servant opened the door. Hugh got out, and as he was walking up the broad stairs he heard a familiar voice behind him.

"Hugh, wait a moment, I'm almost up to you."

He turned around and said, "Why, Amanda Black. What are you doing here?" She was a large woman, taller than Hugh, and wide. She was swathed in a black cashmere cloak.

"Oh, you never know when the Council will need me, and most of them are here. Plus I was related to General Couseau. Did you know that? Actually, to his wife. Anna Claire is my cousin's wife's sister."

"Really. How interesting."

"Yes, I always had the greatest admiration for the general. And Anna Claire is wonderful. A force of nature. He can't be replaced, you know."

"What do you mean by that?" Hugh asked.

"There's no one like him. He got along with everyone and yet he always got the job done. That's a rare combination."

"Maybe now we need someone different. Someone who isn't afraid to knock heads together if he needs to."

Amanda laughed. "Maybe it should be you, Hugh! You've liked to knock heads together since you were a little boy. I remember how bossy you were with your playmates. Your mother used to worry that you'd get into serious trouble, but look at you now, on the Council and everything."

"You know the commandant has to be a career officer," Hugh said.

"I'm just kidding! I'm sure the Council will find the right person, and it looks like you're the one to tell them who it will be."

"Thanks, Amanda. But Anna Claire has some ideas too. I heard she was going to be on the Search Committee. How did that happen? Who nominated her to the Council and the committee?"

"It was all comme il faut. The Nomination Committee sent her name to the Council."

"But how is it that I didn't know?"

"It just happened in the past few days, Hugh. You know this wasn't controversial. It just seemed like the right thing to do."

Hugh was not above using flattery. "You know the inner workings of the Council. We all know that you're the one running this show. That's why it's done so well—you do a brilliant job, Amanda".

"You make me blush, Hugh! I just do my job."

"This couldn't have happened unless someone very important was pushing it. Who was it, Amanda?"

"Oh, I think it was Ronnie Simpson and his wife, Linda Crowley, who wanted her. Weren't you at the party at their house? Most of the Council was there. You know how Linda is. A lot of them love her."

CHAPTER THIRTY-TWO

Hugh found the Council dinner heavy going. He was charming to some and deferential to others. He flirted with a few and flattered many. This wasn't the time to talk about serious matters, but it opened up channels of communication for more private conversations. He did get some useful information. Anna Claire Couseau was not well liked and was distrusted even by some who had agreed to her membership on the Council. They felt that it was safer to have her in the fold than outside. Her supporters were a minority, but they were among the richest and most powerful of the Owners. Linda Crowley's name came up several times.

By the time he left, the rain had almost stopped; a cold drizzle fell from the black sky. He relaxed into the soft cushions of the car's backseat and closed his eyes for the short trip back to the hotel. He climbed out of the car under the hotel's portico and walked into the lobby. There was an area cordoned off and a line of well-dressed people waiting to be admitted through the velvet ropes. He went over to take a look and saw a receiving line and people being escorted through to shake hands with Linda Crowley and several others. She looked up, saw Hugh, and smiled and pointed to a place where an attendant was poised to admit any Owner who wanted to enter. Whatever he thought about her politics, he, like most men, was drawn to her. So he went up to her and shook her hand and they exchanged pleasantries. Her beauty was disarming.

Jack had told Linda what he needed and she was prepared. She thought it all so much fun and, after all, harmless. She held on to Hugh's wrist with her left hand and turned and motioned with her right hand. Jack came forward. "Hugh, I want you to meet a friend of mine. This is Jack Carey. Jack, this is Hugh Rowan."

It happened so fast that Hugh didn't have time to think about it. He held out his hand automatically and Jack took it. For an instant, their minds merged. Jack saw the world as a chessboard and people merely pieces to be moved or countered according to their status. He felt the cold isolation of someone who was obsessed with the delusion of power and domination, and he was flooded with compassion for this lost man.

Hugh saw the world in the round, with colors and scents, and he remembered his early childhood. For an instant he was lost in delight but then he became aware of Jack, who was looking at him with an odd expression. The boy was feeling sorry for him, for Hugh Rowan! Suddenly, Hugh was flooded with anger. He tried to pull his hand away, but Jack held on to it and put his left hand on top of the joined hands and held them fast together. Hugh felt his mind pried open against his will, helpless as an oyster. Then, in a moment, it was over and Jack let go. Hugh slapped him hard across the face, and when Jack returned a goofy smile, he slapped him again. Then Hugh walked away quickly.

"My goodness, are you all right?" Linda asked. "Why did he hit you?" She looked really distressed.

"It doesn't matter; I got what I came here for."

"But you're still going to the funeral aren't you? I need you with me."

"Sure, if you need me, I'll go, but we'll go back home right after that, won't we?"

"We'll go right from the church to the airport. I'll tell everyone to pack tonight."

"I have to go," Jack said, "and do some writing."

Jack went to his room and made sure the door was double locked. Now there was so much to do; he had to write down what he had just learned before it all became a jumble.

The invasion could be the morning after tomorrow! And then there was so much else—the Corps, the Council, whatever that was, and then there was the other stuff very prominent in Hugh's mind, his sister Philippa—and suddenly Jack understood who she was. Gaia, Jack thought, Nils's wife is dead. But even that receded next to the key fact—the invasion would begin within forty-eight hours. But I might not make it back, Jack realized—Rowan's people are coming in the morning to kill me.

Jack was instantly sure of his next steps. I have a lot to do between now and the funeral. He wasn't fatalistic—he would try to save himself, but there were many things to do first.

He picked up the hotel phone and called San Francisco. He had to tell Mayor Johnston, Gladys, and Grace everything he knew right now, at once. It took a few minutes to get everyone on the same line.

Johnston thanked Jack for the information. "I'll make sure we put our defenses in those three places. Baker Beach? I wouldn't have thought they'd go in there. The Presidio is not a surprise—that'll be hard to defend right on the beach—if they're able to land. Mission Creek is where the main action will be, I'd be willing to bet. The neighborhood councils are on high alert, they never adjourn now, and just about the entire adult population has volunteered. We'll be ready for them. And so what you're telling us is that the invasion could be as early as tomorrow evening? I don't know how you'll be able to get home if that's true."

"I don't know either. To tell the truth, I'm having a hard time thinking clearly. I found out that Rowan has ordered his thugs to kill me."

There was a moment of babble on the phone; everyone was talking at the same time. Then Mayor Johnston said, "Why didn't you tell us that at the beginning? What precautions are you taking?"

"I don't know what to do. I'm in my hotel room. I know his people are not here yet, but they're on their way, they'll be here by the morning."

"You have to clear out before then. Get on the next train going anywhere, but not California. Don't tell Linda Crowley about this. She'll go right to Rowan and tell him to stop and he'll know you know," Johnston said.

"No, he should stay where he is. Rowan's people won't dare do anything while he's with Linda Crowley, and if Jack disappears, he'll know anyway," Grace said.

"I think Grace's right," Gladys said. "But you shouldn't be alone for a moment. Go to Linda and tell her you need to stay in her suite."

"So should I tell her?" Jack asked.

"No, no. That won't work. They'll be looking for the one moment when he's not with her; Montreal is too dangerous for him now. He's got to get out immediately," the mayor insisted.

"What do you want to do, Jack?" Grace asked.

"All I want to do right now is sleep, but I know I can't. I have to write down everything I've learned—I want you to have every last detail of the invasion that was in Rowan's mind. I can't leave right now; I've gotta do this. I'll send it all to you when I'm done, sometime before I go to sleep. Thanks for the advice, but I'll have to make my own decisions, and I'll try to let you know."

Next Jack called Gabe, who said, "Hey, bro, good to hear from you. I wish you were here! Me and Oliver went sailing in one of Ronnie's little boats. It was a lot of fun. Ronnie said he could stay with me until you get back. We're helping in one of the gardens. Did you know that they grow all their own fruit and vegetables here?"

"You call him Ronnie? You sure have gotten chummy," Jack said.

"Yeah, he's really nice. Hey, they also have sheep and cows here. Ronnie says that the stuff from the Cruz farms is second-rate. By the way, have you seen Governor Cruz there in Montreal?"

"No, I haven't, though he's probably staying at our hotel."

"How's it going there? Do you wish I was with you?"

"It's okay. I did what I came for and I'm glad you're not with me—at least I don't have to worry about you. Listen, Gabe, I want you to know that I love you and you mean more to me than anyone in the world."

There was silence for a moment. "What the hell is going on, bro?" Gabe asked.

"I can't talk about it too much right now; I've got a lot to do tonight. There's another thing. I saw my father today."

"What? How, what are you talking about?"

"Yeah, and I also saw Nils, you remember the guy from the bar in Denver?"

"Wow. What's wrong, bro, what are you not telling me?"

"Nothing, it's just that everything seems so uncertain now. You should know my father is named Jason Harmon and he's the president of some small country called the White Mountain Republic."

"What's he like? Is he hot?"

"Very funny," Jack said. He was overcome with gratitude for Gabe. Who else could make him laugh no matter what was going on?

"So are you going to stay with him for a while? I'm kind of getting ready to go home and Oliver is going with me, but I've been waiting for you."

"Oliver is going with you to the City?"

"Yeah, we're together now and I'm not about to become a Helper, so he's going to come back home with me. Do you think he'll like our apartment?"

"Listen, Gabe, there's going to be a war. You're safe where you are."

"I know, bro. But if there is a war, I want to be with my own people. That's more important than just being safe. I know how to shoot a rifle better than anyone you know."

"I know you do. Remember that Grace is there. That's good, she can help you."

"So come back home. You can always visit this Harmon dude some other time. Or he can come see you."

"It's not that simple. I'll come home as soon as I can; I promise you. Listen carefully to me, Gabe. War could come even before I get back to you. I'd rather you stay at Linda's house, but if you really want to go home, go right now, as soon as you can. Don't wait a day. Ronnie Simpson will help you, if you ask him; I'm sure of it."

When he hung up the phone, Jack felt a stab of homesickness so vivid it made him feel ill. When will I see my home? Will I ever see it again? And then he pulled himself together. The future was unknowable, except sometimes there were flashes—a sudden beam of light that collapsed just at the moment when he was about to understand what he was looking at. None of that mattered now. Decisions had to be made; there was immediate business to attend to. He couldn't wait for daylight. He picked up the phone and told the hotel operator who he wanted to speak to.

"I've been waiting for you to come to me," Jason said quietly. His room was much smaller than Linda's suite, just a bed, a table, and two easy chairs. It was on a low floor and the view was of the parking lot. Jack's mind was on overdrive—he registered every detail of his surroundings, even though he was overwhelmed with a stew of emotions so complex he couldn't name any single one of them.

At first they had been awkward with each other. They looked in a mirror together and remarked on the resemblance; Jack's nose and mouth were similar to Jason's and their bodies were the same shape: broad shoulders, slim hips, although Jason was much taller. Jason's skin was white while Jack had his mother's brown skin.

Jack wanted to hear every detail about how Jason and his mother met, how long they were together, what their feelings were for each other, and why Jason left her.

"I didn't know she was pregnant with you when I left and she never told me. I wanted her to go back to Maine with me, but she wouldn't leave San Francisco."

"Were you in touch with her later?"

"Not much. I tried, but she almost never answered my messages. I told her when I got married and she told me when she married Jean. But she never told me about you."

"She left me a note with your address on it," Jack said.

"That wouldn't have done you much good. The Corps took over Camden, the whole coast of Maine, and threw us out. I made my way west and found the White Mountain Republic."

Jack stood up. "Jason, I wish I could talk to you all night, but I have to go now."

"We just started. I want to let this sink in; I have a son."

"And I have a father. But, Jason, my life is in danger. Hugh Rowan has ordered me killed and his men will be here in a few hours. I have to do something."

Jason smiled, "Isn't that a little melodramatic, Jack? And who is Hugh Rowan, anyway? There must be some misunderstanding."

Jack looked away for a moment and then turned toward Jason and said, "Give me your hand. I'm going to try something I've never done before. Only because you're my father."

Jason said mildly, "Jack, are you alright? Maybe you haven't had enough sleep since you got to Montreal."

"Trust me and try to relax and open your mind. Listen to the sound of your breath for a few moments. Give me your hand."

Jason smiled and closed his eyes as he put his hand in Jack's. Within a few seconds his body tensed and he broke out in a light sweat. Jack withdrew his hand and Jason opened his eyes. He looked at Jack and this time he wasn't smiling. "How do you do that?" he asked.

"I don't know. But usually the transmission goes the other way. This time I wanted you to know what I know."

"This is going to take me a while. But now I understand what you were trying to tell me. He hates you! But why?"

"He's afraid of me. He has nightmares about me."

"What, you? How could that be; there's nothing scary about you."

"To you. But Rowan and I are connected. We're matter and antimatter. He's afraid I'm going to annihilate him."

"I have no idea what you're talking about, but I do believe you're in danger. What can you do?"

"I don't know."

"Say, maybe we should get Nils in here. He might be able to come up with some ideas. Do you know where he is staying?"

"Nils? Yes, I need to talk to him."

Do I have to be the one to tell Nils? Jack's thoughts were moving fast; his mind had never been more focused. He concluded swiftly that he couldn't conceal the shattering truth. Nils needed to know.

In a few minutes Jason opened the door and Nils walked in. He wasn't surprised that Hugh Rowan wanted to kill Jack. Hugh wanted to kill everybody, Nils told them. He didn't react when Jack told him that Jason was his father. Jack couldn't even be sure he had heard it.

"How about going to Denver? That's the last place they'd look for you. Or the White Mountain Republic. No one could sneak up on you there," Nils said.

"He can go to my house," Jason said.

Jack was watching them both closely. He said, "I don't think you have to work this out. I've decided I'm not going anywhere. I'm going to the funeral in the morning and then back home on Linda's sonic. I'm not running away."

"Alright," Nils said. "You look so young, but you seem to know what you're doing. Now I've got to go and try to make some calls."

"Nils," Jack said, "I learned some terrible things from Hugh Rowan that I have to tell you." Nils sat down on the bed and Jack sat near him on one of the chairs. Jack leaned forward and took Nils's large hands in his. But this was not a time for mind to mind contact; this had to be told with words. He looked into Nils's eyes and told him as gently as he could about Philippa and how she died.

Nils pulled away from Jack and said. "Why are you doing this? I don't believe a word of it. You hold that asshole's hand and think you know about my life? Look, I can't help liking you, I don't know why, but you're still a kid. Maybe you believe all your mumbo jumbo but I don't. Philippa is alive and she'll be there when I get back home. I have to think that or I'll go crazy."

"Okay," Jack said. "All I know is what is in Hugh Rowan's mind, and maybe he's wrong."

Nils said, "He lies about everything. I'm sure you're wrong. Anyway, Philippa's a lot tougher than he is. Now if there's nothing else, I'd like to go and get some sleep. We have to be up early for the funeral."

When he left, there was silence in the room for a moment and then Jason said, "He's in full denial. What's he going to do when he finally accepts it?"

CHAPTER THIRTY-THREE

Hugh had a busy day ahead—two meetings in the morning, the funeral, and the flight back to MarinHaven. But what really mattered would happen later. When he got home he would give the order and the invaders would begin to move on San Francisco. Hugh would go out on his yacht and watch the action. Soon, very soon, he would go ashore in San Francisco—not as a visitor but as its master.

No doubt there would be dismay among some in the Haven, the Linda Crowley and Ronnie Simpson set, but the buzzing amongst themselves wouldn't change anything. The operation's success would silence them.

"Riley is here to see you, Mr. Rowan." Miss Jones was the only person Hugh could tolerate first thing in the morning, and she came into his room without knocking on his bedroom door. She had seen everything, and sometimes that was part of the fun.

It was barely light outside but Hugh got up, put on his bathrobe, and went into the parlor where there was a tray waiting for him. He sat down on a brown leather armchair and poured himself some coffee. He liked roughing it once in a while. Miss Jones opened the door and Armand Riley and two of his assistants came in and stood in front of Hugh, waiting for him to speak.

"Alright, what's your plan?"

"Well, sir, we'll try to find him asap and get him at the first possible moment."

"You will not *try* to find him. You will find him or you will be in a world of trouble. I now have evidence that he wants to harm me personally. And he's staying here, in this same hotel. I saw him myself last night." Riley shrank a little from Hugh's gaze. "Do you understand me? No delays."

"Yes sir. We'll take care of him right away."

As soon as they left, Hugh told Miss Jones to put through a call. Colonel Hastings appeared in front of him, wiping sleep from his eyes. "I'm sorry, Mr. Rowan. It's the middle of the night here."

"Oh, no, I'm sorry, Colonel Hastings. I was under the apparently mistaken impression you were leading an important military operation. Perhaps you are finding it too difficult?"

"No, sir. I'm ready. I apologize for not being in uniform."

"Never mind. I'm checking to see if you're ready."

"Everything is in place. The men will be boarding the landing craft at sundown, and as soon as you give the order, they'll move in according to plan. I wish we had more troops, though. I'm using everything I've got, but Internal Security was not designed for this kind of operation."

"They'll just have to be tougher, Hastings, and not coddle the troits. Give them a good scare and they'll run like sheep."

"Certainly, sir."

Hugh cut off the call and savored a moment of something he thought of as happiness. *It's close now, I can almost taste it.*

A large awning of black canvas had been set up in front of the basilica of Notre Dame de Montreal. The covering extended all the way to the three pointed arches framing the narthex. As it turned out, the precautions were unnecessary—it was a bright, sunny day, and the awning, instead of being a comfort, lent an aura of menace to the event.

Well, it's supposed to be somber, Linda thought. She was glad that Jack had decided to come after all. She wouldn't be able to sit with him up front with the other Owners, naturally, but she could ride with him and be with him afterwards. She felt comforted by him—as long as Jack was around, she wouldn't be prey to those terrible things she couldn't understand.

She turned to him as they arrived and pressed his hand. "I'm getting out. Jack, would you mind waiting until the car pulls around the corner and then get out? They're going to be taking pictures here."

Jack said, "Of course. I don't want to ruin your reputation!"

Her life was so complicated and demanding, a rococo of details, all of which were inordinately weighted with importance—what to wear, who to talk to, what to say, what to think, even. Poor Linda was bound hand and foot by requirements whose purpose she only dimly understood. But underneath her burnished public image she was a kindly soul and she wanted to do good. He knew how she felt about him, and he was happy to be the little brother; it was a novel experience. Her presence comforted him, and her beauty lightened the darkness that sometimes surrounded him. Jack was deeply grateful for her presence this morning in particular.

The driver left him off on the Rue de Bresoles, just east of the church. As he walked down the short block toward the entrance he heard, but not with his ears, two men communicating about him. There was a man watching him from the secluded doorway of a closed shop. The men were intensely frustrated because Jack was walking in the midst of a crowd of people.

Jack quickly joined Nils and Jason, who were waiting for him at the corner. They went in together, and Jack was relieved. They can't get me in here, he reasoned, and I'll have time to figure out how to make sure I'm not alone for a moment until I get on Linda's sonic.

The usher, a Corps lieutenant in full dress uniform, examined their tickets and said, "You'll have to go in the side door. There should be seats for you in the overflow room in the basement. You'll be able to see the funeral on monitors."

Nils tensed visibly and the lieutenant glanced up at the three men. Jack smiled and said, "Sam, you're looking very official these days." The officer looked at him, recognition dawning slowly.

"No, it can't be. Jack, is it Jack Carey? You sure grew up! What the hell are you doing here?"

"I could ask the same thing! It's a long story. I saw your parents in Oakland last year and heard you joined the Corps."

"Listen, I can't talk now, but meet me later, over there." He pointed to the far corner of the Place des Armes.

"Sam, can't you get us better seats?" Jack asked.

"Yes, I believe I can hook you gentlemen up. Follow me." He took them into the church and seated them next to the center isle, about forty rows back from the presbytery.

Sam then seated two somewhat shabby old men in the row in front of them and whispered to Jack, "That's the president of the United States and the prime minister of Canada. The Corps brings them to special events. I'm not sure why because nobody ever talks to them." Four pews in front of them was Ray Cruz. He had walked by them without saying a word, but Jack knew that the governor had seen him. Most of the mourners were seated according to caste or official status. The most important Owners and Corps leadership were at the front with the family

Jack had never been in a Christian church before, and he was excited by the beauty of this one. The altar was gold, surrounded by gold statutes, and the windows above it were blue. Filigreed skylights illuminated the mammoth organ in the back and the choir in the front. He was fascinated by the crucifix that dominated the church. He had been raised to worship Gaia, the earth, as Mother, and to understand Her as a metaphor—the Great Spirit lives everywhere and in everything. The monastery was Buddhist, and he had seen many images of the Buddha, who was depicted in joyful repose. Here, there was a man in torment, nailed to a cross; that's what they worshipped.

He could hear the faint sound of the doors being closed and then the procession began. Men in black and violet robes and boys in white moved slowly down the nave. When they reached the alter, the priest began the mass. Bells rang, the crowd knelt, then stood, then sat, and Jack followed along.

The priest went to the pulpit and began a reading of the Gospel and concluded with, "Keep awake therefore, for you know neither the day nor the hour." He crossed himself and went on, "We know neither the day nor the hour of our death. But though we don't know when, we do know it will come. We must have our lives in order and our preparations made. And what preparations does the Lord expect of us?

"The Lord has created an orderly world. Obey those whom the Lord has put in authority over you, for only in obedience shall you find salvation. And for you great ones, you who are called by the vulgar "Owners," I say to you, you are responsible not just for yourselves, but for all those who follow you. For you too there is a guide—the Holy Mother Church. Obey it faithfully and you will be ready; you will know heaven.

"Do not be led into error by those who say safety can be found by huddling together in what they call 'communities.' There is no community outside the Church and the established order—it is anarchy in disguise! There is no safety outside the Church; there is only the sin of him, whose rejection of the Lord led to eternal torment."

Jack tried to listen carefully to these strange ideas, but he was distracted by the feelings of the people around him. When the priest spoke, he could feel fear rising in the church like a kind of flood. But as the mass went on, the people were comforted by the calm beauty of the ceremony. There were more bells, and the priest held up a chalice and people started to line up down the middle aisle.

The Owners sat in their places and a priest went to them to offer communion. Eating the wafer confirmed for Hugh the order of his world and his place in it. He hated complacency, but he did allow himself this one moment of satisfaction.

After all of those who wanted communion had it, the priest once again took the pulpit and said, "We are here to celebrate Christ's resurrection, and to say farewell, but it is also fitting that we remember a great son of the Church and leader in this world. Here to speak is Etienne Couseau, the son of the deceased."

After he spoke, the chairman of the Council spoke, and then General Bast. Then the priest came back to the pulpit and asked for a silent prayer. There was a song of farewell, sung by the choir, and the priest announced the procession and invited everyone to participate and to come to the cemetery of Notre Dame des Neiges, Our Lady of the Snows. Pallbearers lifted the coffin and moved it forward down the nave. The priests came after it and then the Couseau family and numerous others, mainly in Corps uniforms. Hugh joined the other Owners walking behind the priests and the family. He was reassured by the ceremony and felt, as he walked, the certainty of his place in the world. The Owners walked up the aisle in twos. On Hugh's right was an aged lady who had been his father's mistress many years before.

Nils registered very little of the ceremony. He had gone directly to the hotel audio phone and called San Francisco, feeling angry and anxious, but not hopeless. He finally got through to a neighbor who hesitantly confirmed the nightmare. Philippa's body had been found lying in a pool of blood in their living room—a week earlier. Nils spent the rest of the night by himself in his hotel room, rocking back and forth on a hard chair, too stricken to weep. When dawn came, he dressed and left his room, numb. By the time he was seated in the church pew, he felt like he was wrapped from head to toe in thick cotton batting. Nothing penetrated. The bells, the incense, the priest's words were images seen through the wrong end of a telescope.

When the recessional began, he looked around and suddenly felt the reality of where he was. General Couseau's coffin was moving slowly up the aisle, and Nils saw his life illuminated as if from the inside. *I should be in the coffin.* Nils felt the energy draining out of him—but then he saw Hugh Rowan moving slowly up the nave, surrounded by other Owners.

Hugh had been his enemy since the first moment Nils met Philippa. He was the first one in her family to oppose their marriage and the last one to grudgingly accept it. He had murdered his own sister. Hugh was responsible for everything that had turned Nils's pleasant life into hell. The sorrow and apathy that were lapping at Nils's mind were instantly displaced by rage.

As Rowan passed close to him, Nils pushed his way to the aisle and jumped on him, throwing him onto the floor. He had one large hand around Hugh's throat and his other arm pulled back, ready to smash the man's face, when he saw the resemblance. Philippa's flesh and blood. The thought cut through him and he released Rowan and sat back on his heels, his face now wet with tears.

Hugh struggled quickly to his feet and looked down on Nils. His breath came in gulps and he hissed the words, "You coward, you dog, you pathetic troit."

Nils jumped up and moved toward Rowan, who stepped back, tripped, and fell hard, hitting his head a glancing blow on the sharp edge of a pew. From there he fell onto the marble floor. Blood erupted from his head.

Guards rushed toward them but were slowed down by the crowds, the pews, the coffin. All the Owners in the procession had fled from

Nils, and the priests looked on in horror, from a safe distance. Jack saw it all happening in slow motion and when he tried to stand up, he felt encased in some thick viscous substance. But he struggled to his feet and forced himself to move toward Nils. The thickness around him evaporated and suddenly he was moving at lightning speed. He put his arms around Nils's shoulders and tried to pull him back toward the pew where they had been sitting. His back was turned to Rowan. Suddenly Jack felt a hard sharp blow on his right ear, and he staggered and fell. As he started to get up, he heard the sharp crack of gunfire.

Linda was still near the alter when she heard the screams from somewhere in the middle of the nave. She saw people running and shouting, but she became oddly calm. *Jack is here,* she thought to herself, *and he'll come to me and explain this.* She sat down quietly in the pew and waited. An old nun came to her and said, "I'm such a fan of yours! Can you give me your autograph?" Linda looked at her, astonished, and said, "Of course. What just happened?" Then she turned around and Jack was next to her, saying something. But she couldn't hear him, his voice was coming from somewhere far away. Then he faded and she was alone in the pew. The nun was looking at her curiously, "Are you alright, Miss Crowley?"

"What is happening?" She was almost alone in one of the front pews and she could hear shouting, but all she could see were the uniformed backs of Corps police between her and the others. She got up and walked toward the back of the church. Jack and another man were being taken out, half pushed, half carried, their hands behind their backs in handcuffs.

The next hour was a blur in Hugh's mind. When he first managed to think consecutively, he understood he was in a place called the Royal Vic Hospital. His head wound was not serious, they said, but had required many stitches. He should rest for a few hours before going back to his hotel. Miss Jones came into his room and told him that his security people were waiting to talk to him.

"They can wait. I'm not sure what good they are anyway. Gloria, what happened? I can't remember it all."

"I'm sorry, sir, I wasn't close enough to see. Your security people shot the man who was near you, that's all I know. I think he's dead."

"Who did they shoot—the tall man or the smaller one?"

"I'm sorry, sir, I don't know. I actually didn't see anything myself."

Hugh asked for Armand Riley to come into his room, and he got out of the hospital bed and sat down on an easy chair to receive him. Riley stood in front of him, clearly uncomfortable. "I'm so sorry, Mr. Rowan, that we weren't able to stop Rakovic from attacking you. The Corps police assured us the church was secure, so we kept to the sides and the back."

"I'm not interested in your excuses, Riley. Did you get rid of the boy, as I told you to?"

"Well, sir, we weren't intending to do it in the church, of course, but then when that man attacked you we thought that was the right moment. But we never got a clear shot at the boy. We tried at the only time we thought we could do it, but we missed him."

"Did you kill Major Rakovic instead?"

"I'm afraid so, Mr. Rowan."

Hugh rubbed his eyes and became aware that his head hurt. He felt a pang of regret and was surprised. So that's the end of Philippa's story. She's gone and the only person she ever cared about is gone now, too. Both cut down trying to harm me, and all I ever did was try to help them.

"The Corps wanted to question me right away," Riley went on, "but I told them I had to talk to you, and they said I have to go to their headquarters right after I see you."

"So you didn't kill the boy. Where is he now?"

"He's in Corps custody now. When Rakovic was shot, he fell on the boy, but I don't think he's injured."

"How the hell did he get into the church in the first place? What's his connection with Rakovic? And with Linda Crowley? There's more to him than I thought—he's not just any troit. Go to the Corps headquarters and tell them to put the boy on my sonic. If they're not cooperating, tell them to contact Colonel Hastings, the chief of Internal Security. He'll order them to give us the boy. Keep him in handcuffs and make sure you don't touch his hands—that's very important. You guard him personally and if he escapes, you're going to a Plantation. Miss Jones, please go and get some clean clothes from my hotel room. And get us ready to go. I want to be in the air in three hours at the most."

CHAPTER THIRTY-FOUR

They put Jack in a small, white room with no windows. There were two hard chairs and between them a table. Overhead lights made the room uncomfortably bright.

He'd been in there for only a few minutes when a soldier came in and said, "Someone important, I don't know who, wants you."

Linda must have arranged this, Jack thought. Thank Gaia, I'll be able to get back to the City before the invasion. The soldier removed his handcuffs and escorted him through a succession of corridors until they got to a stairway. They descended two flights of stairs and went out through a double set of glass doors. The soldier put Jack into the back seat of a Corps car and closed the door. Jack turned to look into a familiar face.

"Man, you sure stepped into deep shit," Sam Ward said. "I'd say you're pretty lucky to get out of here so easily."

"Nils Rakovic is dead, isn't he?"

"Yes. Bullet tore into his heart."

"I'm really sorry. But I don't think he wanted to live."

"Jack, how did you get here, how do you know all these people?"

"It's a long story, Sam. Come back home and we'll sit in your mother's kitchen and I'll tell it to you."

"She'd like that, wouldn't she?" Sam said.

"Wouldn't you? Wouldn't I? Where are we going now?"

"To the airport. Linda Crowley, the movie star, she knows you too? She told my superiors that she'd take you home with her, and I think they're really glad to get you out of their jurisdiction. They don't know what to do with you. Nobody can peg you, so they don't even know whether to treat you as low caste or high caste."

"Hey, where we come from, Sam, there aren't any castes."

"Yeah, but this world is going the other way. Anyway, I'm glad I got to take you to the airport myself. Hey, why'd that guy attack the Owner?"

"It's a long story. He was kind of out of his mind 'cause he just found out that his wife had been murdered by the Owner's guards. Where is the other guy I was with?"

"Oh, you mean President Harmon? I've seen him before, a few times. I think they're talking to him now, our security people. I guess they want to know how he happened to be sitting next to Rakovic. He'll be alright. He's pretty well known in the Corps in this part of the world. How do you know him?"

"He's my father."

"No shit!"

"Yeah, I know, it's really strange, but I found him here, in Montreal."

"Did you come here looking for him?"

"No, I stopped looking for him and that's when I found him. Listen, Sam, there's some terrible stuff about to happen back home." Jack told him about the impending invasion.

"Hey, we're almost at the airport," Sam said. "So if they take San Francisco, how long will it be before they go after Oakland?"

"Who knows? Anyway, can Oakland survive without selling stuff to the City?"

"Wouldn't be easy."

"And it won't be easy for them to take San Francisco. We're going to fight and I've got to get there tonight to help."

Their car drove right onto the airport tarmac. Not far away were a line of sonics being prepared for take off. Sam opened the car door, and they got out into the warm muggy air. The driver stayed inside.

"I sure hope one of Linda Crowley's people comes out here," Sam said, "'cause I have no idea which plane is hers."

Two more cars drove onto the tarmac and stopped close to them. Four men got out and walked over to Jack and Sam.

"Mr. Carey, we'd like you to come with us."

"Are you with Miss Crowley?" Sam asked.

"No, they're not. They're Hugh Rowan's thugs," Jack said.

"This man is under Corps jurisdiction; he's not going anywhere with you," Sam said.

All four men pulled out guns and pointed them at Jack and Sam. "Let's go, now!" their leader said in a low voice. They pushed Jack into their car, and it drove down the row of sonics to the last one, the largest, marked with the Rowan logo in black and yellow. They hustled Jack up the stairs and into a seat near the back, fastened him in, and put his hands in velvet-lined handcuffs.

Jack sat there trying to regain the calm he had discovered in himself in the car with Sam. His guards' minds were open to him, but they were sewers of fear, and he had to work at not getting infected by them. They were afraid of a lot of things, but chiefly of Hugh Rowan. They were desperate to please him and they knew that giving Jack to him was the best way to do that. They would treat Jack with the gentle care of a pastry chef presenting a cake at a banquet, knowing that it would end up a sodden mess at the end of the evening. There was no point in talking to them, and Jack let himself fall asleep, the deep sleep that he needed so badly.

He woke to a youngish woman washing his face, almost tenderly. The warm water felt so good on his forehead and cheeks. She looked at him with evident pleasure and said, "Good evening, Mr. Carey. I'm going to prepare you." He understood she meant he would be talking to Hugh Rowan shortly. They were in the air now, and he could see through the small window the curve of the earth and the sun rising in the west as they rushed toward it. When she was finished, one of the men who had taken him from Sam came to his seat. "Please get up, Mr. Carey, and follow me." Jack stood up, still handcuffed, and walked to the front of the sonic. He was told to sit down in a large, leather seat. On the other side of a table was Hugh Rowan.

"I'm curious about whether you knew Nils was going to attack me in the church."

"No, I didn't. He didn't know himself. But I do know why."

"She was my sister too, and I regret losing her. But she tried to kill me, so what else could they do?" Rowan looked out the window. "We don't have a lot of time before we land, so let's make the most of it. Why did you follow me to Montreal, for starters?"

"I didn't follow you to Montreal."

"Why did you go, then?"

"Same as you. To go to General Couseau's funeral."

Rowan frowned. "Don't play games with me. You know I can do whatever I want with you. In my world, you're less valuable than a dog or a cat. You're just an object that I can dispose of as I wish."

"It makes you feel more powerful to say things like that, doesn't it, Hugh?" Jack said.

Rowan flushed and opened his mouth, then thought better of it. "I'm Mr. Rowan to you."

"Alright, then you can call me Mr. Carey."

"I could have you taken out to the Farallon Islands and thrown to the great whites."

"Yes, and I could tell you that one day you will die. The difference is, you're talking about a possibility and I'm talking about a certainty."

"Oh, no. The difference is that I can do something to you but you can't do anything to me."

Jack laughed. This was easier than he thought it would be. "Oh, we're all doing it to each other. Don't you see that we're not separate? That's the myth, that we're different and apart from each other. Especially you and me. You can kill me, but you can't take me out of your dreams. It's the opposite—if you kill me you'll never get me out of your dreams."

Hugh blurted out before he could stop himself, "How do you know I dream about you?"

"But what I do there comes from your own mind. I don't cut people's hearts out."

Rowan shuddered and turned away. He said to Riley, who was sitting nearby. "Take the boy back to his seat." And to Miss Jones, "Get me a drink. Whiskey. Now."

Hugh was at a loss. This boy contrived somehow to rise above what anyone could see was a hopeless situation. He wasn't afraid! He should be; it wasn't reasonable for him to be so cool. What if there were others in his city like him? Was it possible that Hugh had underestimated the troits? He considered the problem for a few minutes, and then ordered Jack brought back to him.

"Why do you think you know what's in my dreams?"

"I can read minds—I'm telepathic."

"What am I thinking about now?"

"Mostly, you're obsessed with the invasion of San Francisco. You're going to order it to begin as soon as we arrive. You don't know what to do with me."

"You could have deduced all that—you didn't have to read my mind to figure it out."

"I don't care if you believe me or not. I was just answering your question."

"How am I going to order the invasion, exactly?"

Jack paused for a minute. "You are going to take the small gold case you have in your vest pocket and twist some numbers. Colonel Hastings will see a holo image of a silver sword against a blue sky. Under it will be a white city. That's his signal to invade. He will confirm the order with you and then break off communications with the outside until he's taken the City. You're going to be on your yacht watching the invasion. You'll be in communication with some officers under Hastings, but he doesn't know that."

Hugh was shocked—and thrilled. What power this was, to know someone's mind! He felt his sonic's engines change vibration and knew they were beginning their descent and would be on the ground soon.

"Jack, I believe you are exactly what you say you are. And since you've been completely honest with me, I'll be honest with you. Anyway, you'd know if I wasn't. I only see two possibilities. One is that I have you killed as soon as we get back. Mr. Riley over there will take you to some remote spot and shoot you in the head. You can read his mind all you want. When I order him to do something, he'll do it.

"The other possibility, and I'd like you to think about this carefully before you answer, is for you to work with me and be my partner in what we're about to do. I know you think it's all bad, but it's inevitable—the weak always give way to the strong. And you're strong, Jack, you belong on my side."

Jack sat back, stunned. Why hadn't he seen this in Rowan's mind? Jack looked at the older man and found he no longer needed the hand contact to see deeply into him.

"Think about this. If you work with me instead of trying to fight me, you can have power in the world, real power."

"I don't want power. I just want to help my people," Jack said.

"That's how you can help your people, by having power. This is what I'm offering—and this is just the beginning. When the troits—the city dwellers—are moved to the Central Valley Plantation, you can make sure they're treated as you think they should be. Ray Cruz is hoping he's going to run the Central Valley, but I never really promised it to him. You will become an Owner—I can make that happen—and you'll outrank Cruz anyway. Look into my mind—you'll see that I'm sincere about this offer."

Hugh was not lying. He saw Jack as a kind of super-weapon, but there was also a need for an ally and partner, someone who wasn't afraid of him, someone who could one day inherit the world he would build—an inheritance which his own weak son didn't deserve. There was in Hugh's mind a nascent desire for an heir and the beginnings of a suspicion that it could be Jack.

"You aren't really a troit, Jack. I don't know how it could be, but you're more like an Owner than most of the ones I know. Listen to me, we're the same, aren't we? The two of us together can change the world."

Jack flinched as if he'd been slapped across the face. "We're not the same, we're opposites! What you want, what you care about, means nothing to me. I don't want to order people around and make them afraid of me. That's you, not me. I want to live in harmony with the earth and my community. I don't need to conquer anything except maybe myself."

"Wake up, Jack! The world won't let you live like that anymore. This planet has become hell for the human race, and anyone who dreams that they won't have to fight and claw for survival is going to be swept away. Shall I make the decision easier for you? I have an idea of what to do with the non-working population of San Francisco. We've got dozens of these rusting ships from the old government's navy. We'll pack them full with old people and babies and the cripples and tow them out to sea and sink them. Problem solved. But if you're working with me, you can figure out something else to do with them. Or you can choose to die and they'll die too."

Jack looked at Hugh closely and saw that the Owner was sincere about everything he was saying; he wasn't holding anything back. Then Jack said, "Why am I so important to you?"

"Because you're the future," Hugh said.

Once again, Jack was astonished. That's exactly what he had said to that woman from the Corps, the deserter, Rayna Caskey, not understanding what it meant.

"I need to think. Have them take me back to my seat."

"Too late for that. We're landing. We'll talk after we arrive. Mr. Riley will escort you. You can think in the car. But I need your answer today."

"What if I can't answer you right away?"

"I'll be very sorry, but I'll just have to take that as a no. But don't worry—I don't consider you a real troit, and your death will be quick and painless. Riley will make sure your body is buried and no one will ever know what happened to you. We can't have any more delays."

Linda saw the resemblance at once. This man, Jason Harmon, claimed to be Jack's father and it wasn't hard to believe him. They were standing outside the basilica in the Place d'Armes, where Linda was waiting for her car.

"They let me go almost immediately, but they took Jack somewhere, I don't know where," he said.

"Is he hurt? We've got to get him. He's going home on my sonic and I know he wanted to leave right away. I do too." She was feeling queasy and she needed something familiar. "How can we find him?"

"I think I know the person to talk to. He's one of the top Corps officers in this region," Jason said.

"Here's my phone." She rummaged in her purse.

"I have my own," he said, to her surprise. He pulled it out of his pocket and said a name into it. He turned away and put his hand over his free ear, talking urgently into the phone. In five minutes he turned back to her. "They're going to send Jack directly to the airport. We can pick him up there."

"Will you come back to California with us?" Linda asked. "I think we need some extra support. You can use my sonic to go wherever you want after that."

"Yes, of course. But all my things are in my hotel room."

"I'll send someone to collect them for you."

"I do need to be in Denver in a few days," he said.

"Sure. A few days."

Her car nosed its way through the crowd and pulled up to where they were standing. She got in and Jason climbed in after her.

They got to the airport just in time to see Jack being hurried up the steps of the Rowan sonic. Before Linda could say anything, the sonic's door closed and it began to roll away slowly. A young Corps officer came up to them and introduced himself.

"I'm really sorry. They took him at gunpoint and I couldn't stop them," Sam Ward said. "But I've called the tower and told them to hold that sonic on the ground as long as they can."

Linda barely heard him. She ordered the driver to take them the short distance to her sonic and then hurried up the steps. She said to the pilot, "I'm going to call my house. Let's take off as soon as I'm done."

"Linda, darling, what's happened? Are you alright? I just heard there was a riot at the church." Ronnie's voice comforted her; she wanted to be with him right at that moment.

"It wasn't a riot. Someone attacked Hugh Rowan, but he's alright. I'm alright too. I can't talk long now, darling, we've got to get in the air. Hugh has Jack, and I don't know what he's going to do with him. I'm afraid to go home without him. You know what happened last time. Well, yes, that was a public sonic. Okay, I'll try to be brave.

Jack's father is coming with me, and you'll meet him when we get home. Why don't you send Jack's brother—what's his name?—to the airport to meet us? See you in a few hours, darling."

CHAPTER THIRTY-FIVE

Hugh now had in his possession the most powerful weapon he'd ever known. A troit boy—who would have imagined such a thing? Combining Jack's powers with Hugh's will and intelligence would create a force that nothing could withstand. The conquest of San Francisco would be just the opening move in a game that Hugh couldn't lose. With Jack's help, Hugh would bend the Council to his will and dominate the entire Corps.

But Jack could be as dangerous an opponent as he would be a valuable ally. It would be a terrible shame to kill him, but Hugh would have to hold to his resolve, if necessary. The invasion of the City would begin within hours, and if Jack wasn't on Hugh's side by then he'd have to go. Jack was brave, and Hugh decided he would have him executed with the dignity of a soldier, standing and blindfolded. Perhaps he would even put up a gravestone for Jack. But let's not be pessimistic, Hugh told himself. After all, what I'm offering Jack is a prize anyone would betray his mother for.

When they landed, Hugh told the others to wait onboard for a few minutes, and he left first. He wanted to be far from Jack—he didn't want his mind invaded. Jack would be a tricky partner, knowing Hugh's thoughts. They'd have to be physically as far apart as possible most of the time. Well, that's what holos are for, Hugh said to himself. He got into the car that was waiting for him on the tarmac and told the driver where to take him.

Linda was tense the whole two-and-a-half-hour duration of the flight, afraid of what she'd find when they arrived. But when she stepped out of the sonic the airport looked as normal as it ever had. In the distance she saw another sonic setting down softly. "I bet that's Hugh's plane," she said to Jason. "Let's go over there and find out if he's got Jack."

"Do you have any security people, Linda?" Jason asked.

"No, certainly not. Why should I?" Linda asked.

"I don't think they'll just give Jack over to you."

She heard someone yelling her name and turned around to see a young man running toward them. He was wiry and blonde, not tall. When he was near he burst out, "Linda, hi! It's me, Gabe, Jack's brother. Thanks for letting me stay at your house. Where's Jack?"

"Yes, hello, Gabe, of course I remember you. Gabe this is Jason—what's your last name again?—Harmon, Jason Harmon. He's Jack's father, aren't you, Jason?"

"Gaia! You're the reason this all started. We went to find you and now here you are. So where's Jack?"

"I'm afraid he's on that sonic over there," Jason pointed to Hugh's plane.

"Well, let's go get him, then," Gabe said.

"I don't think it's going to be that easy," Jason said. "He's Hugh Rowan's prisoner."

Gabe looked around wildly for a moment and then turned to Linda. "I have an idea! There's just one road out of this airport, isn't there?" Gabe asked.

"Yes. I know it well." She remembered walking down that road as it collapsed behind her. The isolation and the silence; how could she ever forget that?

"Ronnie sent three cars and four guys with me. Let's find a narrow place in the exit road and when we see Hugh's car coming, we'll block the road and demand they give us Jack."

"What if they refuse?" Jason asked.

"We don't move until they do. Best thing would be if more people are trying to leave the airport and are blocked by all of us."

"I don't know, Gabe. People will never stop talking if we do this."

Gabe looked like he was going to explode. "This could be a matter of life or death! Look, you can say that Jack and I made you do it—you know how the dirty, violent troits are."

"I don't think that's fair, Gabe," Linda said, in the mildest tone she could muster.

"I don't think it's going to work," Jason said. "You think they'll give up Jack because they're stuck in a traffic jam?"

"Can you think of anything else?" Gabe said.

Ever since his last conversation with Hugh, Jack had noticed a difference in the way he was being treated. He was still handcuffed, but his guards had become subtly deferential. When he spoke to them, they would drop whatever else they were doing and bend toward him. Their minds were buzzing with the thought—This boy could be our master, better be careful. Through their minds he saw vistas of power that he had never before imagined. Of course, he should reject Hugh's offer. But if he took it, he could ease the blow for his community—and he could immediately save the most vulnerable. And he could protect Grace. They would think he was a traitor, but he would know that he'd sacrificed himself to help them.

He had to keep in mind his one sovereign advantage over Hugh—he could read his enemy's mind but his enemy couldn't read his mind. Wasn't that it, after all? Hugh was his enemy, there was no ambiguity about that. Hugh was the enemy of everything Jack believed in and loved. How could he ever be his partner? But—maybe it was precisely by being his partner that he could change Hugh and lead him out of his world of delusion. Would Jack ever see Grace again? How, except by agreeing to Hugh's terms?

A few minutes after Hugh left the sonic, Armand Riley and the other guards escorted Jack down the stairs and into a large car that was waiting for them. They drove around the airport building and onto the narrow road leading down the hill. When they got to a place where the road descended through a narrow defile, slopes heavy with eucalyptus trees rising on both sides, one of the guards exclaimed, "What the hell is that?"

"Pull over," Riley said. The guards got out and walked up to the cars blocking the road. Their guns were in holsters under their jackets. They left Jack in the car by himself, strapped in, handcuffs on. But he could see clearly, and he opened his mind to hear thoughts. He knew immediately that Gabe was there, and he felt intense annoyance—better to face this alone and not have to take care of his brother. Then he heard shouting. In a moment, the guards came back, with Gabe. They put him in the car, in handcuffs, next to Jack. The cars blocking the road turned around and moved forward down the hill and their car drove on.

"Sorry, bro. I guess I wasn't thinking very clearly."

"Damn, Gabe, the whole purpose of leaving you at Linda's was to keep you safe."

"I was just trying to help you."

"Yeah, I know. We're in it together now, little brother."

It was now night, and Jack couldn't tell what direction they were heading. The guards didn't know either and the driver was thinking of the trouble he was having with his girlfriend. They crested a hill and drove down into a marina. Jack and Gabe were hustled out of the car and onto a large motor yacht. The moment they boarded, the gangplank was pulled back and the boat began to ease away from the dock. They stood by the rail and watched the lights of MarinHaven recede. In the direction they were heading there was total darkness.

"The City is blacked out. I wonder if the invasion has started yet," Jack murmured to Gabe.

"You told the mayor all the details, didn't you? Bro, I'm so glad to be with you, no matter what happens."

Gabe's words ripped into Jack. A young woman in a blue uniform with white piping came up to them and said, "Mr. Carey, Mr. Rowan want to see you now. Please follow me. He wants your brother there as well."

She led them through a doorway and down a passageway. As they approached, a man in the same uniform opened a door, and they walked into a large salon furnished with easy chairs and sofas. Hugh Rowan said, "Welcome, Jack. Why don't you sit here, near me? Gabe, you can sit over there." He motioned to a chair on the other side of the cabin. "We have so much to talk about, Jack. I actually think it's good that your brother is here. He might as well know right away what you're going to do."

"I haven't decided what I'm doing yet."

"I've got a surprise for you. I was going to order the invasion in the morning, but I think you should give Hastings the order to invade. It will give you a taste of power."

"You're insane, Hugh."

"You know when we talked on my sonic my hand wasn't quite as flush as it is now. Your brother here is my extra ace. Let's try this—either you give the order to invade or I throw Gabe overboard."

Four guards had appeared, two next to Jack and two next to Gabe.

"But—if we're partners, you can start thinking about where you'd like your estate. You can go back to San Francisco, our new San Francisco, and build a house right where you used to live, and if you want, Gabe can live there with you. You really need to be there—it's going to be a capital someday, and you and I will be the most important people there."

"What the fuck is going on here?" Gabe exclaimed.

"Riley, put tape over his mouth and tie him up," Rowan ordered.

Jack jumped up, "Don't do that!"

"Alright, have it your way. Never mind, Riley. See, Jack, I'm treating you like a partner already."

Jack opened himself to the others' thoughts. The guards' minds were exploding in little bursts like popcorn. They were hoping Rowan would order them to throw Gabe overboard, and Jack too, excited by the prospect of the boys' screams, their bodies slapping onto the dark water. Hugh was troubled. He badly wanted Jack to work with him but he was afraid of Jack's powers, and he wasn't used to being afraid.

The Owner's fear gave Jack a surge of self-confidence. "You think you know what power is, but it's a mirage, an illusion. You make people afraid of you and you think that's power. But when even one person shows he's not afraid of you, you doubt yourself, and that makes you weak. We're all connected in a web of cause and effect, and whatever harm you do injures you too. The law of karma is strict and you can't escape it. In your religion it's called, I think, heaven and hell."

"You think I'm a villain," Hugh said, "but I'm not doing this out of vanity or anger. I have a vision of the future! The earth is a hostile place and yes, I know my ancestors were responsible for it, but that's history, we can't change it now. You'll thank me one day for forcing this on you, I'm sure of it. I have nothing against Gabe—he's got lots of spirit and I like that. But this is no time for personal sentiment—we're at war. I don't want to kill him but I'm helping you make the decision I know is hard for you."

Hugh got up and moved over to the sofa and sat down next to Jack. "Here's the device." He pulled out of his vest a small golden case. "You take it and I'll tell you the numbers to twist to give the order. Oh, I guess you don't need me to tell you! After you do it, you and Gabe will be my guests and you can help the city dwellers, if you like. We'll tell the officers I'll be in touch with to find whoever you want and make sure they're safe. Do you have a girl or a boy there? We'll bring them here for you. Friends too—I think you could bring up to six back to the Haven, until the City is ready to live in again. You'll have a lot to do in the next few days, figuring out how to save the non-working population. I know you want to do that. I'm offering you this special courtesy, to order the invasion, but remember that if you don't do it, I will—the invasion will proceed but if I do it, Gabe will have to die."

Jack looked at Gabe, who said, "Don't do it, bro! He's tricking you!"

"No, Gabe, I'm in earnest. Your brother can see into my mind, he knows I'm telling him the truth. I will kill you if I have to."

Jack put his head back against the sofa's cushions and closed his eyes. He let his consciousness move out and away. Grace was there somewhere, and he had never before felt such a need for her presence, her strength.

"What's he doing?" Hugh asked Gabe.

"I guess he's going into one of his trances. Sometimes he stays that way for a day or two. Nothing you can do about it."

"That's ridiculous! Riley, shake him, wake him up." Hugh ordered.

The guard grabbed him by the shoulders and shook him hard but Jack was completely limp, his eyes closed. They took him out to the deck and poured cold water on his head, but there was no reaction.

Jack was open to the night sky; his mind skimmed across the bay and spread over the City. Its people were his people, and he felt the heat of their fear and determination. It was a clean feeling—their simple courage washed away his confusion. The City was now an armed camp. It was bristling with guns aimed outward against the darkness. Free citizens with hunting rifles had once before on this continent defeated men with imperial visions, and the people of San Francisco knew that.

Grace was working with her neighbors building another barrier on Market Street, but she stopped and looked up. Then she sat down on the sidewalk and cradled her head in her hands, feeling him close. They spoke in the silence of their minds.

—Jack Jack I'm with you!—
—I need your help, Grace, I don't know what to do.—
—Yes you do, Jack, you have the answer to every question inside yourself. Go deep and you'll find the answers.—
—Are you prepared for them? They're coming.—
—We're ready Jack, we'll never be more ready.—
—Stay with me, Grace, stay in my mind.—

Jack felt her draw close and he let her in. Their minds merged and she saw through his eyes the yacht and Hugh and Gabe and the overhanging threat. And he saw it all through her eyes as well as his own, and he tasted the flavor of victory.

—Do it, Jack, Make them start now, the sooner the better. We're coming for you.—

Jack snapped back into his body.

"Let me see the device, Hugh. You're right—I need to give the order."

"I knew it! Good for you, Jack. You made the right decision." He took the small gold case out of his pocket and gave it to Jack.

As soon as Jack gave the device back to Hugh, the Owner told the guards to remove the handcuffs. He shook their hands and said, "If you'll excuse me, gentlemen, I've got some business to attend to. Give me an hour or two and I'll be back with you, and we can talk about our schedules for the next few days. We're going to be very busy."

When Hugh walked out of the cabin, Jack turned to Gabe and smiled.

"What the fuck?" Gabe said. "What did you just do?"

"Someone once told me that the best way to reach your goal is to walk away from it," Jack said. "I think she also said that patience is a virtue, but maybe I just learned that from being around you all my life."

"Hey, I never said I had a lot of virtues," Gabe said.

"Oh, yes you do, but just not patience. You better work on it now."

The door opened and two servants wheeled in a table covered with silver bowls and salvers. They put it in front of Jack and ceremoniously removed the lids—a lavish display of Owners' cuisine.

Gabe said, "I'm not sure I have an appetite right now."

"We should eat. We don't know when we'll have a chance again, and we need our strength. Come on, Gabe. Trust me."

Two hours later Hugh returned, and they all went out on the deck. The *Conqueror* had drawn close enough to the shore so they could hear gunfire, but the night was black and they couldn't see anything. The boat, which had been brightly illuminated at the dock, was now dark, every porthole covered.

"It will be light soon and we'll be able to see what's happening." Hugh was exultant. "I hope you liked the supper I sent you." He could not have heard the faint sounds of oars moving in oarlocks muffled with thick cloth, but Jack heard the rowers' minds, and he worked hard to stifle the excitement that coursed through him.

Hugh was gripping the rail, and then he jumped back as if stung. "What the hell is that?" A large hook clasped the rail and from it descended a rope. There was another clang and similar hooks jumped over the railing down the length of the yacht toward the stern. A head appeared at the rail and a man jumped on board. Others followed, and within seconds the citizens were in control of the main deck and fighting their way upward, toward the bridge.

Hugh turned toward Jack, but it wasn't a man he saw, it was a tunnel, a black emptiness that extinguished all light. Utter negation. Every certainty of his life, his power, status, will, physical strength, revealed itself to him in a flash as so much tinsel. Weak. None of it could protect him from annihilation.

Jack was awestruck by Hugh's abject terror, the sudden collapse of his enemy. Helplessly compassionate, he moved toward the Owner, his hands out to him.

But Hugh saw only a ravening beast, ringed all around with fire, and he backed away from Jack, whimpering piteously. Jack took a step toward the bigger man and Hugh recoiled violently. Insanely frantic to get away, he jumped up on the rail, and threw himself overboard into the roiling waters of the Bay. The current drew him away from the boat, beyond help, out through the Golden Gate into the endless ocean.

Eighteen Years Later

The dawn of the twenty-second century was marked in San Francisco with a torch-light parade that snaked north on Montgomery Street and then over Columbus Avenue and down to Carey Basin. When the parade ended, the sky over the bay erupted in fireworks.

Earlier there had been a concert in Golden Gate Park that was well attended despite the rain. A sea of people sheltering under large umbrellas clapped and danced to the best of the City's bands.

The New Year's Day ceremony in the rotunda of City Hall was no different than every other new year—the main event was the reading of the Annals recounting the Battle of Mission Creek. Each year a high-school student was chosen to read from the official text. This year's reader was a sixteen-year-old girl, slender, with long, black hair and glowing, olive skin.

"They came in long boats up from the bay and fired on us with everything they had. The invaders aimed for three places on our shoreline, but we were ready for them. Our Jack had warned us in advance and told us exactly where they would land. Jack tricked them into beginning their invasion on an ebb tide, when the waters of the bay were our allies. He made them begin in the dark of a new moon, when we knew every inch of the land and they were blind. In the west and the north we defeated them while they were still trying to land their boats, and they fled in confusion. In the east, at Mission Creek, we were ready. A great battle was fought, and though there were more of the invaders than us, we vanquished them and they never came back."

The recitation went on for a full hour, every important detail was recounted, and the names of the fallen spoken, so that the citizens would never forget.

Every year Jack and Grace sat on the dais, but today they sat among their fellow citizens. He wanted to see their daughter's face as she read the text. Gabe loved to sit up there. It was his moment of the year to be a celebrity, and he always held Oliver's hand through the whole reading. On this special day there was another person there. Next to Gabe sat the new Corps Commandant, General Sam Ward. Portraits of Gladys Yee and former Mayor John Johnston were on easels flanking them. Though it was the middle of winter, the dais was brightened every year by the flowers Linda Crowley sent from her hothouse.

The reading's conclusion always gave Jack a thrill.

"When it was clear that the invasion had failed utterly, the Corps abandoned the Owners' cause and became the City's friend, and the friend of our fellow communities. And Jack Carey and his brother Gabe came back to live among us as our fellow citizens."

She glanced at her uncle and then looked up and smiled as the audience applauded and Jack's neighbors slapped him on the back and shook his hand.